THE LEGEND OF THE DEAD GIRL

BY DAVID CAY

Lightner Publications

The Legend of the Dead Girl
Copyright © 2022 by David Cay
Illustration Copyright © 2022 by Priscilla Kim - priscillakim.com

ISBN (paperback) 978-1-7379493-0-5
ISBN (ebook) 978-1-7379493-1-2

Interior design by Aaxel Author Services

Printed in the United States of America

Have you heard the one about the girl who came back from the dead? Maybe you heard a story, a rumor that became a legend: *la leyenda de la chica muerta*, the legend of the dead girl. I can tell you that story. I probably know more of it than any other human being.

And it's a story I want to tell. It's time to start telling it.

Maybe you know the place where it all started. Or maybe you think you do. I will just call it La Ciudad, the City. I want it to be more of a mythical place, more of an anyplace or a no place. Maybe I want to do it this way because, even though the events I am going to describe are real, they are so extraordinary that a place with a real name would never seem like a place that could sustain them. Or maybe I feel the need to conceal the actual location to give myself that last little bit of protection…just in case.

So, La Ciudad will be a sketch of a city, an outline, a suggestion. Imagine a Mexican city in the northern desert, right up there near the border. So far from God, so close to the United States, as the old saying goes. But in some ways, the United States *is* God, the Unmoved Mover, who governs almost everything about La Ciudad. It moves us toward it in the form of clandestine immigration. Or it moves its jobs toward us in the form of those atrocious factories called maquiladoras. It moves its citizens toward us, tourists, usually looking for various sorts of trouble, minor or major. And it moves peril toward us in the form of the dance of supply and demand that is the drug trade.

Narco traffic. It overshadows everything; it rules La Ciudad. It makes it a dystopia of endless violence, extreme violence, both violence that has a purpose and violence that has no purpose. Killing over the drug trade: that has a point. But there is a lot of killing that has no point, unless the purity and perfection of brutality itself is the point. Take, for example, the murders of hundreds of women over the years, their bodies mutilated and cast away in the desert.

That's where this story really begins, I'm sure.

I'm not an honest man, but I intend to tell you the truth, even some drab and unpleasant truths about myself.

My parents were somewhat well off and considered themselves educated people. They named me Cervantes—Cervantes Castillo Cruz. I can thank them because they made sure I became what could be called an educated person. And I can also thank them because they left me a small house in a quieter part of La Ciudad. Other than that, I barely got by, although on the surface my existence resembled a dignified life.

I'm not sure how much I should dwell on myself, on how I was when it all started. Perhaps if anyone ever reads this, they will have some curiosity about me that I should satisfy. But I wasn't a person who enjoyed his own company all that much, so it's not a subject I want to spend much time on.

I was fifty-five, bearded and fat. People said I reminded them of Orson Welles in his later years. My trademarks were white suits, usually rumpled and a bit dirty, and a white fedora, to conceal the fact that I was balding.

My official profession was reporter. But I didn't report as much as I concealed and lied. I was on the payroll of one of La Ciudad's newspapers, and I drew a small salary. But in reality, I worked for the narcos, shaping information about certain events the way they wanted them shaped. They paid me a small salary. They also paid me by letting me live. That was not a privilege granted to all reporters in that city, especially the ones who wanted to tell a little too much truth.

My life hadn't always been that way. In my younger days, I had taken pleasure in the weirdness of the world. I scraped by, writing freelance articles about UFOs and strange creatures and weird cults for anybody who would pay. A lot of editors liked to have a good UFO story up their sleeve in case it was a slow news day…or if they needed a distraction from something they weren't supposed to say too much about.

So, there I was, always ready with some chupacabra or little gray man—or at least a decent saucer sighting out in the desert.

Unfortunately, that made me a bit of a clown to some. But to others it also made me a perfect candidate for the job of crime reporter. My predecessor had gone too far with the facts about a shooting that had accidentally killed a kid…and he ended up being accidentally killed himself. The narcos wanted what they considered a better man for the job. So, an acquaintance of mine passed along a suggestion that I apply for the job. It was also suggested to the management of the paper that I be hired. With that kind of reference, who would question my qualifications? I was hired over the phone.

Basically, my job consisted of this: X was shot. I went to ask Y or Z for a comment. They told me what I needed to know, what not to mention, what message had to be sent. I wrote it up for the paper. I got paid. Sometimes Y or Z insisted I have a drink with them. Sometimes they told me what was really going on. I hated when they did that because it didn't enhance my chances of survival. It didn't do somebody like me any good to know the truth, to know what was going on in La Ciudad.

Yeah, knowledge was a burden, and I carried a heavy load of that shit. But now, this one time, I have a story I want to tell and I'm going to lay that shit down hard.

Would it surprise you to know I drank a lot? Mescal, mostly. I liked a brand with a scorpion in the bottle instead of a worm. Maybe I felt too much kinship with the worm. I frequented the more subdued bars. I didn't mind sitting by myself; I didn't mind if someone joined me. I knew a lot of people. I listened to their stories because they distracted me from my own.

That was how I first heard the story I want to tell you, the story of the vengeful fist of God concealed in the hand of a teenage girl. A girl who was dead.

At night the desert talks to itself. It whispers to itself in its winds. It whispers to itself about death. And that night it would have a lot to whisper about. But at first it would be talking to itself, because the three men out there in nowhere's middle weren't listening. They were dealing with shit, too. One was getting it kicked out of him. The other two— they were doing the kicking.

It was a ritual far from uncommon: an account settled, a score evened. The desert at night, out beyond La Ciudad, was the frequent arena for that sort of event. And the script was almost always the same. Somebody got cheated. Or somebody felt cheated, shortchanged on a dirty deal in one way or some way. Then somebody else might want revenge on the person who had gotten their payback. The details all blur together in a rush as the bodies go into the ground.

I was never a violent man. In fact, I tried to avoid violence to such an extent that I would have to accept being called a coward. Truth is truth: the label would have been accurate. So, I had no understanding of the lust to inflict brutalities, which lived so intensely in the hearts of many of my fellow citizens. But I did have a fascination, perhaps a coward's fascination, with violence. That was one reason why people talked to me in those bars, usually late at night. They knew I would listen as much as they knew I would keep quiet. Maybe I could even have been viewed as a confessor.

And the story, for me, began the night that Martin and José caught Enrique interfering with the free flow of their capital. So, Enrique got snatched and driven out into the desert for a little talk with some boots. And those boots were screaming Martin's rage. The steel tips ruptured organs and broke ribs with a joy that some would call inhuman, but that I would have to call human.

Even José stepped back from his share of the kicking, a bit in awe of his compadre. The headlights of an elderly jeep spotlighted the stage as José passed from actor to audience. Inside that jeep was Pedro, a young man who was learning the business. Driving and watching, that was part of his instructions. He turned away and then forced himself to look and then turned away again. You know the scenario, somebody who wants to be a big shot but isn't quite prepared for the real deal. But if things had gone the way they usually went, Pedro would have ended up getting accustomed to things, would have become first a reluctant participant and then a willing and eager one.

The usual, though—that was not going to be happening.

A woman…a girl…perhaps a teenager. She was standing there, watching. José hadn't seen her arrive and it startled him to see her there. He jumped back a bit, enough to draw Pedro's attention. He looked and saw her too, revealed clearly in the headlights. She was completely naked. But the first thing he noticed was a huge and horrid scar that traversed her throat. Then a pretty face framed by long black hair. Then a body that was frail and slender, almost anorexic compared with the typical build of Mexicanas. But her skin tone was the native brown, not pale, not white. Her face was a mask of impassivity, of indifference to the spectacle in front of her. Pedro suddenly had the thought that perhaps she'd just escaped some kind of captivity. Maybe some freak had been holding her hostage out in the desert. Maybe she'd escaped from one of those psychos who had been killing women and leaving the bodies. Or maybe she'd just been left to live or die by someone who was done with her, who didn't care anymore.

Martin stopped kicking and Enrique didn't move, just lay there in a beaten heap. Maybe there was some life left in him, maybe there wasn't. Martin spat on the body and took some deep breaths to recover from the emotion and the exertion. Then he looked up and finally saw the girl, the last person he would ever see.

"What the fuck! What the fuck is this?" The first reaction was one of anger at an intruder. But when he realized what he was seeing, his expression of fury passed into a sinister smile. "What do we have here?" Martin was grinning as he bounded to the girl and grabbed her by the arm, trying to yank her toward him.

Pedro was watching intently, again captivated and appalled by what he thought was about to happen. But he didn't see what he expected. He didn't clearly see what the girl did. All he saw was that Martin was suddenly about ten feet away from the girl, back flat in the dirt.

Everything was still for a few moments. None of them moved; the scene was frozen. Only those whispers of the desert could be heard, and the engine of the jeep, still running. The girl smiled, looked at her hands, looked at Martin—who let out a moan—looked at her hands again. Then she took an ungainly step toward Martin…and another…with the smile growing on her face. She crouched down beside him and started to extend her hand, reaching for his face. All at once, Martin grabbed her wrist, yelling something. Pedro couldn't understand the words. For just a second, the girl had a look of fear. Then she became angry. With her free hand, she seized Martin's throat and, with a snap and the splatter of blood, crushed it instantly. Again smiling, delighted with her work, she stood up as Martin's dead hand dropped to the ground.

Then she looked toward José. He had been slow to react. The girl's intrusion had been bizarre, but it had seemed harmless. Then, all at once, there was a dead partner on the ground. So, when the girl did turn toward José, she found herself facing his vintage .44 Magnum. José loved Dirty Harry.

The girl hesitated. José didn't. He took the head shot. I suppose you could give him credit for how quickly he realized the fatal danger of that weird, fragile-looking thing, who at first had seemed to be nothing more than another victim. Others wouldn't catch on as fast in the future. Not that the results wouldn't be the same.

José was a great shot. The bullet hit her right in the forehead, and the power of the impact took her backward and down. The action froze again…just for a second…as the night swept away the gun smoke. José began to lower the weapon.

Then the girl sat up.

She touched the point of impact. She realized she was unharmed. There wasn't even a dent, just a black mark. In that same moment, José also realized she was unharmed. He took another shot, but now there was panic and he missed the mark. The girl was getting up. The third shot laid her back down in a rigid and awkward way because she was trying to resist the force that time, but the loose soil was not giving her anything to work with. She sat up again. A fourth shot put her back down. Then up again and down again. Did anyone hear Clint Eastwood's voice asking the famous question about being a punk and feeling lucky?

José had only one more bullet to delay his fate. If he'd chosen a weapon that used a clip, he would have had a few more. But the revolver had looked cool. That said, it wouldn't have mattered. He didn't take the last shot. Maybe he was finally stunned by the impossibility of the situation. Maybe he was trying to figure out an option. Either way, he missed out. She was on him in an instant, grabbing the gun and twisting it out of his hand, half tearing off the trigger finger. The shock made him fall to his knees. He began to moan something, but the girl grabbed the top of his head with a slender hand and crushed it, making a very messy noise. She shook some of the remnants off her hand as the body slumped facedown into the sand.

Pedro hadn't reacted. He was held motionless by abject fear. No flight, no fight. He just sat there in the jeep, with the lights illuminating the scene. It probably saved his life. He could have floored it and slammed the vehicle into the girl head-on. Or he could have done the opposite, tried to escape. But I can tell you, from future experience, that neither of those things would have worked.

So, he just watched as the girl stripped some of the clothing from José's corpse and put on a shirt to cover her nudity. Her legs and feet would still be bare, but at least a sense of modesty could be protected. Then he just watched as she casually walked over to the jeep and got in on the passenger side.

The river of Pedro's short life rushed like rapids through his mind because he was sure that he was about to be very dead, just like his two mentors lying in the sand. Instead, the girl just made a sign for him to drive. Then she looked out the window, staring into that desert night, waiting for him to obey.

He did.

Silently they drove through that night, the girl keeping her gaze directed out over the road or at the terrain passing by.

Not knowing exactly what to do, Pedro headed back toward La Ciudad. He found himself feeling oddly calm. Unlike his late associates, he hadn't done anything to the girl or even tried to do anything. So, he was beginning to convince himself that she was going to skip off and leave him to live as happily ever after as he could manage.

Reentering the oppressive outskirts of the city, he looked to the girl for some indication of where he should go. She gave no direction. At one point, he even took a chance and pulled over and stopped, hoping she would get out and go away. Without even looking at him, she motioned for him to keep going. For a moment Pedro considered getting out himself. Perhaps he considered it for even two or three moments. But really, why even think about trying to escape something that bullets couldn't make bleed. The girl wasn't a shuffling, mindless zombie. She could easily catch him and crush his little life out of him, leaving just another corpse on the streets of La Ciudad.

Best to keep driving.

Pedro tried to pick random roads and streets where there wasn't much traffic because he was afraid of being seen or being drawn into some other confrontation. And what if the wrong somebody saw him driving this chica around, without José or Martin, when he was supposed to be working? How the hell would he explain that? There was already going to be a lot that would have to be explained, and he was nowhere near ready to explain it.

It even started to get boring after a while…like a bad date when you couldn't get the girl to talk, and you could tell she just wanted the whole thing to be over with so she could go home. Too bad he didn't know where she lived.

Time was passing deeper into the night. The gas was getting lower. Pedro was getting tired as the monotony began to wear away the shock. It started to feel like it had never happened, that all he was doing was giving some chica a ride.

But he knew that wasn't true.

Finally, he took a chance and turned on the radio. No corridos please, Pedro liked American rap. The girl didn't seem to mind, so at least the weird shit he was in had a soundtrack. He wished that he hadn't been the one to make sure the tank was full, the one who wanted to show Martin and José that he was on top of the details. If he could have already run that fucking jeep out of gas, the girl would have had to give up and leave him stranded.

Or kill him.

A combination of desperation and fatigue finally made him drive toward the heart of the city's nightlife, the frolic and fun zone, the 24/7. It was the place where gringos came to play, the narcos to unwind, the maquiladora workers to blow their cash.

He ran the risk of getting into some kind of trouble there, but maybe something would entice Supergirl to get out of the vehicle and forget about him.

Gritty neon and cheap streets. The crap. La Ciudad.

He never would have admitted it to his mentors, but the whores always made Pedro feel sad. Way too many and way too young, with as much flesh as possible exposed to the buyer or the renter. It bothered him. He had sisters. He wanted to earn a good living so they would never even have to consider that kind of life. Not that his choice of career was pure, but at least it might get him some willing women. And the thought of trying to get up into El Norte just to clean up after white people didn't suit his dreams either. Did any of it matter anymore? By morning, would he still be around to have to worry about earning money?

There was a sudden move, making him jump in his seat. The girl had grabbed his arm, and she gave him a signal to stop. Slamming of brakes, honking of horns, pulling over. Her grip hadn't been meant to cause harm, but there would still be damage…at least a huge bruise.

They were right next to a row of hookers. The girl rolled down the window and stared at them. Some started their approach but hesitated when they saw that dirty and blood-splattered female face that studied them from the jeep.

Right away, there was going to be a problem. Seeing that something was agitating the merchandise, a pony-tailed guy in a leather jacket popped out of the shadows to check out the situation for himself. Deciding he didn't like what he was seeing, Ponytail strutted over to the vehicle and came up to the open window on the girl's side.

"This is asking you nice, the first time. Keep moving," he said, directing his words at Pedro.

And before Pedro could even react, the girl reached out and seized Ponytail by the throat. Snap, pop, and crack. She let go and he fell to the sidewalk.

Then the girl actually got out of the jeep and began to search the body. The hookers scattered in different directions as three goons who must have been Ponytail's backup rushed forward. The girl already had her victim's wallet as she turned to face the men.

Pure reflex. Pedro hit the gas and shot down the street, swerved around three cars, ran two lights, just missed getting hit—and was gone.

I'm an insomniac. I hardly ever sleep at night. My eyes usually won't close until the sun comes up. So, I would sit at my desk in the newspaper office with my mescal and my cigars, staring at my computer and hoping for some glimmer of inspiration. I wanted to write something true; I didn't want to have to conceal, hide, or lie. Sometimes, with the mescal crawling through my brain, I would get idealistic like that.

One night my phone rang. I answered. It was a sort-of friend of mine who worked for La Ciudad's sort-of police force.

"Yo, Cervantes. Want a story, tio?"

"Got one?"

"Pimp and three of his compadres got killed."

"And?"

"A girl killed them."

"Hmm. That could have potential. How'd she do it?"

"You won't believe it, but all the witnesses say the same thing. She tore 'em down with her bare hands."

The first thing I thought was that it was most likely a hefty load of goat shit. But if it was a story that people were telling, there was no reason I couldn't tell it too.

Left the mescal, took the cigar, and started off toward the scene of the crime…or whatever the hell it was. It was close enough that I could walk, but far enough that I considered driving my old Beetle. I opted for the walk. No hurry. Clear the brain a little in the night air.

A few blocks of fading nightlife later, I found a couple of cops I sort of knew still hanging around pretending to be busy. The bodies were gone, but I saw some blood. Of course, it could have been blood left over from the night before…or the blood from some other night before.

One of the cops greeted me with a half-hearted nod.

"Is anybody left who saw whatever it was they think they saw?" I asked.

He nodded again, this time to indicate a halfway attractive and way too young puta sitting on the curb and staring at nothing in particular.

"Everybody else told the same story as her. Nobody thinks it was a narco thing, so you got some people willing to jabber. They fuckin' all agree, too. But go talk to that girl…hear this shit for yourself."

I slowly approached her, expecting her to be frightened and in shock, trying to get her wits back and gathered after seeing whatever it was that she had seen. Instead, she looked up at me with the smile of a saint. There was no fear in her eyes. More like joy.

"I'm waiting for her to come back," she said, just as I was about to introduce myself.

"Who is she?"

"She must be Death herself, the Santa Muerte in human form."

"Damn," I thought, "this is going to be a good story." Then out loud: "What happened? Could you tell me?"

Ponytail went down. Three goons came at the girl as she searched the body. They were so used to having absolute power over their young ladies that it didn't seem to register that they might be the ones asking for trouble. Ponytail had fallen for some trick, gotten taken by surprise. It happened. But now it was time for business as usual.

First guy tried to grab her. The girl braced herself and shoved him with such force he slammed back twenty feet straight into a wall and collapsed to the ground. That was where he would be body bagged. The other two froze. It registered. Too late. The girl took a swing that was clumsy, but the second man still went down with the lower part of his face smashed. The third turned to run, but another awkward punch broke his back. He was starting to crawl, but she put a foot to the back of his neck and finished it.

Then the girl went back to Ponytail's corpse, found a wad of cash, took it—and then leaped forty feet straight up to the top of the nearest building and was gone.

"The Holy Death has come to visit us in this hell we have made," concluded my witness. I wrote it all down and left her to her meditations.

Went back to the cops. "That's really the story?"

My informant just nodded.

That was really the story.

I loitered for a bit, trying to figure out what to do next, where to go next, who to talk to next.

I'd already talked to a witness and had the cops confirm that story, as much as they could. And if there really was some girl who could kill pimps and enforcers with her bare hands running around loose…well, I was sure that she would probably be making her presence known again.

Then something across the street began nagging the corner of my eye for attention. A tourist, probably from up north, was apparently watching some footage on his camcorder. He wore a baffled expression.

I realized there was a chance he'd managed to take some video of the incident while documenting his night out on the town. If he did, I wanted to be at the premiere of that movie. I wanted front row seats. But if some authority noticed and got there before me…

So, I tried to make my stride nonchalant, like I was randomly crossing the street and departing the scene. If I was casual enough, maybe there was a chance that I could talk to the guy without anybody else noticing.

Yeah, there was a chance.

As I closed in, he suddenly became aware of me and looked up, seeming to sense my intentions.

"Hey, mate, are you a reporter?" he asked bluntly, speaking English, as I'd suspected. But the accent wasn't from El Norte. Instead, it sounded like Australian or maybe Irish. I wasn't sure. I spoke that language adequately but wasn't expert enough to recognize all the regional variations.

"In my own way," I replied, using his language.

He laughed, taking my bitter irony as a joke. "Want to see something really strange?" His tone became more polite, almost formal, even though up close he seemed a little drunk.

"Is it the girl?" I asked, trying to conceal my eagerness.

He nodded. "Come over here, mate, it's more private." He led me to a dark doorway. "Yes, the girl. I saw it start to happen and even thought to film it."

"Did you?"

"Oh yes, oh yes!"

"May I see it?"

"Well, that's the thing, mate…" The words seemed to get caught somewhere between his brain and his tongue. Was he going to ask for money? That would complicate things.

"What?" I tried to be neutral. I sure as hell wasn't going to suggest payment.

"Christ, just see for yourself. You tell me…tell me how this could happen. It makes no bloody sense, none at all!"

He held it so I could peer at the tiny video screen.

Remember that classic film of the Sasquatch, the one where the camera bounces all over the place before stabilizing on the creature as it strides away? What I saw played out like that. That guy must have struggled and fumbled to hold his device steady because I saw street, walls, random people, night sky, and streetlights flying all over the place before the footage fixed itself on the action.

I saw Ponytail's corpse.

I saw a pickup truck fleeing the scene.

I saw the first guy sail into that wall.

I saw the second man fall, his jaw a total gory wreck.

I saw the third man drop like a broken puppet, crawl away desperately, then suddenly stop moving.

But I didn't clearly see what caused all of that. There was just a blurry form, a hazy bipedal shape doing all that damage. Everything else was crystal clear. Every human and every object…all the scenery, all the backdrop. The only thing that was horribly out of focus was the girl. It was like some weird special effect, like a cloaking device in a sci-fi movie.

He let me watch it a second time, with the same result.

"But you saw her, you saw the girl doing all of that with your own eyes, right?"

"Clear as day, mate…clear as I'm seeing you right now. Nothing strange about her, other than the fact that she was tossing those men around like toys."

I looked around to see if we were being watched, but I saw nothing that looked suspicious. Then I considered what to do next. I quickly decided to err on the side of caution, for me and for that tourist.

"If you want my advice, you'd better just get out of here. Leave La Ciudad. Leave this country. Don't show that tape to anybody else, don't even mention that you have it. Things are going to get even more dangerous in this town. Just go, amigo, go."

He didn't hesitate. "I think I agree, mate, I think I agree!"

And with that, we parted.

That was the way it would always be.

If you saw the girl with your naked eye, or just viewed her through glass, such as the lens of a telescope or binoculars, you would see her just like you would see any ordinary person. But if you tried to take her picture, or record her on film, or view her through any electronic device, you would get that severe blurring effect. It was similar to what they do on the news when they obscure someone's features to protect their privacy.

And I'll tell you now, all these years later, that I never found the explanation for that odd effect. I would learn many strange things as time went by, experience many amazing events, but I never learned why her image refused to manifest itself for modern technology.

By the time I got home, it felt like my ass was dragging me. Usually I don't sleep well, but once I found my way back to my little house, I was pulled down into my recliner and yanked away from wakefulness.

And I dreamed long, and I dreamed intensely. I was wandering in a strange white desert for what seemed like hours. The scene was so bright, so vivid, I could feel the sands beneath my feet. Then something or someone stood before me, taking me by surprise. A skeletal girl…she was laughing at me…mocking me. The dream kept going and she kept laughing at me. I finally wanted to scream at her to stop. But I couldn't. Then she threw something at me: a severed head that landed at my feet, the eyes wide open and filled with shock. The thud seemed so real that it woke me up.

At first, I was aware only that I was still fully dressed, and so sweaty that I felt like I'd bathed in soup.

For a moment I panicked, as if the skeletal girl and her trophy were in the room with me. Then there was a feeling down in my gut…this strong feeling that the story of the girl dealing out easy death had to be true…had to be real. Maybe it was really a hope for redemption… for my own redemption. Maybe it was a hope that a lifetime of half believing that there is more to this world than the usual shit could really lead somewhere…that my desultory quests for something alien and supernatural would finally find their dark grail.

Maybe it was my moment to know secret things.

I had to find that girl.

Dreams.

Dreams are important in this story.

Sometimes they are even waking dreams, trances, visions.

Sometimes they are even more than that.

For years, for most of my life, there had been no dreams to cause even the slightest ripples in the black waters of my sleep. But then, just before that girl who is Death made her appearance, I suddenly began to dream.

I dreamed of Flor, my one and only true love in this life, and maybe in any other.

At first, it was always the same. For days it was the same.

She would be sitting at a table, darkness all around her, playing with her tarot cards.

Unable to approach her, I would call out to her. But she wouldn't hear me. Or else she was ignoring me.

Yeah, at first it was always like that.

But the white desert and that skeletal girl would be a signal that things were beginning to change.

Not really rested but refreshed enough not to want to be home when something big was trying to go down, I dragged myself back to the office as dawn was rising up.

They told me somebody was waiting to see me.

Pedro.

He was the nephew of this guy I knew. So, he knew who I was, and he wanted to tell me his story because he didn't have anybody else to tell it to, and because he knew I sought out this kind of story. At first, I was impatient. I didn't know he was going to tell me more of the story I wanted to hear. But I'm courteous, so I listened. He probably didn't think that even I would believe him, but he didn't hesitate to relate his tale. He was still freaked out, rushing and stumbling over his words. When I realized what he was telling me, I clung to every word.

When Pedro finished, he waited for me to respond.

"It didn't end there, where you left it," I said.

"What do you mean?"

"Just that." And I told him what the young hooker had said and what the cops had confirmed.

"Shit."

"Any chance Enrique is still alive?"

"I don't know."

"Can you take me there, to where you first saw her?"

He was silent for a moment. "Yes. But after that I'm leaving this fucking loco town and I ain't coming back."

The desert sun was whipping me, punishing me for some forgotten offense. I could feel the sweat coming back and invading my clothing, a territory it had already conquered during my short and troubled sleep. I had not bothered to change. I hoped Pedro couldn't smell me as I drove him out into the desert. I kept a cigar lit the whole way just to screen out the embarrassment. Even I usually wasn't that much of a slob.

Of course, Pedro had other things on his mind.

Three bodies. Enrique hadn't survived, either. I almost felt sorry for him because his death was banal in comparison with the deaths of the other two.

Nothing to my eyes automatically proved the reality of a girl who had dealt those other two deaths. But there was nothing that clearly disproved her existence either.

"What direction did she come from?" I asked as I tossed away a cigar. We were finally out of the car, and I was sick of smoking.

"That way, I think." He pointed farther out into the desert.

I shrugged and we started walking in that direction. It wasn't like I really wanted to walk more out there, but I had to hope I would find more than just heat and dust. The three dead guys supported Pedro's story, but the fact of their deaths was nowhere near enough.

There was a small hill ahead of us, in the direction that Pedro had indicated. "Let's go up there and see if there's a way to take my car farther out." I was already wiping my forehead every minute with an old handkerchief that wasn't holding up very well.

Pedro just started walking. He had his own problems, but he was younger, smaller, and faster than me. So why wait for an older, fatter man who had to constantly take off his hat and wipe his brow? I had to ride my willpower to the top of that hill to find him staring down the other side.

"Something weird down there," he said in a monotone as he pointed stiffly.

My eyes followed the direction of his finger. At the base of the other side of that hill, I could make out three pits...or craters...or holes of some sort. Three in a row. Not natural.

I started down ahead of Pedro, taking a risk on a dose of heatstroke.

Three pits in a row. I could already tell there was a body in two of them. The middle seemed empty. We drew closer. The naked, semi-mummified bodies of two young women...or at least that was my impression...that they were—had been—young women. Their lips were shriveled to reveal hideous rictus grins. There were huge and gaping gashes where their throats had been. The work of a scavenger? Or of a killer? Probably the latter.

I wanted to be sure the middle pit was vacant. It was.

For years, La Ciudad had been haunted by an especially sinister and grim murder trend. Scores of women and girls savagely killed...their remains often left in the desert, like the ones we had found. Hundreds of other women were missing, vanished. Some may have merely fled bad situations. But most were presumed dead. Suspects were arrested, locked up pending trials that never came. And the murders never stopped. Rumors-of-rumors of various weird and tangled conspiracies filled the void of real information. Were we a vacation destination for the world's serial killers? Were corporations behind it, seeking to keep their mostly female workforce living in fear and easily exploited in the maquiladoras? Were the narcos doing it out of spite or for sport? There was even talk of man-eating chupacabra, devil dogs, and little gray aliens. As I mentioned, I'd fed at that trough a few times in my own articles. But this was the first time that I'd come up against the real deal.

My eyes kept fixing on that empty pit.

For a few moments, it hit me. For a few moments, there was no doubt. The girl I sought had been a corpse in that vacant hole. She had been just another pathetic victim. Then something had happened. Something had brought her back and raised her up, like Lazarus or even Jesus.

Yeah, for those moments I had a vision of an insane savior for an insane world. A savior that performed miracles but not miracles of healing. No, these were miracles of mayhem and vengeance.

Of course, you can't really believe something like that for very long before the skepticism begins to set in. Almost all faith casts its shadow of doubt.

"I want to get the fuck out of here now," said Pedro.

"So do I. I'll take you back to town and then—"

"Then I'm gone."

With deliberate slowness, I headed back to the car. I wasn't in a hurry like Pedro, and I was still sweating like a beast.

And I couldn't help but keep glancing back at the empty, shallow wound that had been left in the desert.

After a very silent drive back to La Ciudad, I wished Pedro the best. As a goodbye, it was awkward, but the handshake at least felt sincere. I didn't expect to ever see him again.

I headed back to the office, where I had some mescal in my desk drawer. It was never too early for me to pour a shot. I sat at my desk, thinking about those bodies in the desert. There were five of them out there. I had to decide if I should tell somebody.

I decided not to.

I called some of my connections, put out feelers, tried to find out if there had been any more encounters with the girl. Nothing. So, I sat back in my chair, planted my feet on my desk, and began a heavy session of wall staring.

My doubts grew stronger. No way could it be real. It would turn out to be a mistake or a misinterpretation. It wasn't that women couldn't be killers. Some were. The narcos were using that trick more and more for assassinations of all sorts. But those chicas used guns, not their bare hands. Could be that people just weren't seeing something. It was night. There could have been some kind of weapon involved. As the day kept crawling along, the whole thing got more and more improbable.

And the phone wasn't ringing. At least not with reports of a girl who was tearing people apart and crushing their flesh and bones with her hands and fingers.

I still planned to type up the story. Like I already told you, it didn't matter if what I wrote was true. But in the end, all that I accomplished was falling asleep in front of the keyboard—and dreaming that undead things were laughing at me.

Nobody would bother to wake me up. I was probably the only employee who could get away with snoozing in the office for a couple of hours. Everybody knew what my deal was and why I had been hired. If they didn't need me to slant the news in a particular direction on a particular day, then I could do whatever I wanted: sleep, drink, play solitaire—or dabble in other news. I did actually sometimes make an effort to help out with local interest or entertainment news. That way, the people who had to really work wouldn't think I was a complete piece of shit.

While I slept, things happened.

The girl walked into a bar and killed a few guys, even though it seemed like she was after only one of them. The rest of the damage was, as they say, collateral.

Lucio Valdez was a neighborhood moneylender, a low-level company man who had his little operation in one of La Ciudad's many shantytowns. These were the places where the maquiladora workers and their families tried to put together a life, the same way they put together their impromptu homes.

The bar that Lucio used as his headquarters had also been thrown together out of haphazard materials. Need a little money? Come on in, have a drink on the house, leave with a little extra cash to make ends meet or get that something extra. Just a loan between friends. Can't pay it back as soon as you promised? That's okay, but there will be some more interest. Have another drink on the house. I'm not a monster, after all. Payment going to be late again? Well, now we might have a little bit of trouble. No free drink this time, and you might have to take a couple of punches just so you remember I'm not in this business just to feel good about myself. Still late? Well, the interest is going up and you might get the beatdown. There might be some fractures involved.

That day, though, Lucio would pay back what he owed. And he owed a lot of people.

I didn't get the calls until it was all over, but my little network of contacts didn't waste any time letting me know and they all gave me good directions. I quickly arrived on the scene, even before all the bodies had been identified, tagged, or bagged.

Lucio's boys had all sported the same basic look: heavy muscle, tattoos, shaved head and goatee, sunglasses, and a tight black shirt to show off the goods. Unidentified body #1 could have been the prototype. Seeing the girl heading straight for his boss, he casually blocked the way, most likely intending to tell her she needed to wait for her invitation, not seeing her as a threat. When she didn't stop her advance, he pushed his hand into her chest. She took that hand and twisted it. And everyone heard the bone snap. Then she tossed him aside before he could collapse from shock.

There was nobody between her and Lucio. He froze for a moment, the situation still not registering completely. Then the girl was right up on him. He was sitting at a table, counting money, doing accounts, drinking cheap beer. He looked the girl in the face and an expression of recognition seemed to dawn on his features. Then confusion. Then anger.

Three more goons began to move in on her, shaking off their surprise, knowing that the girl was somehow a danger. They were too late. With one hand, she had flipped the table out of the way, sending it spinning through a flimsy wall. Lucio tried to get up. His expression was one of terror. The girl seized him with both her hands, taking him by the throat, forcing him back down into his chair as he gasped and choked. She wasn't killing him quickly like the others. She seemed to want him to suffer.

Lucio's three would-be saviors closed in. The girl tensed up, but she didn't relax her grip on her victim. Unidentified body #2 gave her a swift and brutal kick to the back of the knee, right in the joint. That should have taken out her leg. Instead, it must have been like kicking a tree because the leg didn't give, forcing the attacker to suffer the force of the impact. He managed not to fall as he let out a curse and stumbled backward.

Unidentified bodies #3 and #4 each grabbed one of the girl's arms, intent on forcing her to release their boss. Full strength, pulling in opposite directions…and they couldn't do it. The two goons strained and groaned, their eyes astonished and fearful, watching as a smile grew on the girl's face, listening to Lucio choke as she increased the pressure just a little bit.

Then unidentified body #2 suddenly popped back up in the spotlight, holding a shotgun. He stood behind Lucio, aiming the weapon directly over the head of his boss, placing both barrels point-blank in the girl's face. Her eyes widened. The other two let go of her as they jumped away.

Boom!

The girl was blown back, but she didn't let go of Lucio. He went with her, getting yanked out of his seat.

For a few moments, there was no movement. Everyone was deafened by the blast. The girl lay on the floor, holding Lucio above her, still by the throat. Her face was blackened but completely unharmed. She began to laugh silently.

Then Lucio's neck snapped.

The girl sprang up and turned her attention to her victim's henchmen. That was when they became unidentified bodies #2, #3, and #4, and not forgetting #1, who was trying to stagger away with his destroyed wrist.

◈

As I arrived, black SUVs were already hauling away the bodies. No insignia, no indication that they were official vehicles.

Interesting.

The witnesses were mainly local suck-ups, an entourage who ran errands for Lucio and fed him the local gossip in exchange for some of his cheap hospitality. I hung out with them for a while. I watched as a police car showed up, but not until after the SUVs had left with the dead men. They were willing to tell me the basic story and their details were in agreement. But they were reluctant to answer any other questions. I could tell they knew more, like maybe who the girl was and why she had come to that place to do what she had done. Whatever they knew, they didn't want to spill it. So, I handed out some business cards and left them to figure out what to do with themselves.

I sat in my VW and watched the cops. They didn't try to talk to anybody. They just poked around the bar for a little bit and then left.

My cell phone buzzed. It was one of my cartel contacts, a guy who represented my true employer. The guy who told me what I could, should, and would write.

"Amigo, Cervantes! Que pasa?"

"All good."

"Listen, my friend, we know that you're down there, snooping around the unfortunate demise of Brother Lucio. And I know that the story of this girl is right up your path, the weird shit you like to fuck around with. But this chica loca is taking out folks who are affiliated with us. And that means the chica is going to belong to us. Not you. Not the public." End of call. Just as well. I might have been tempted to ask how they planned to eliminate somebody who could take a shotgun blast to the face without being harmed. And I doubt that kind of question would have been appreciated.

I just sat in the car for a while, staring into the space before me, deciding what to do next. Probably go back to the office and drink mescal.

The phone buzzed again…caller ID blocked. Could be important… could be crap.

"Speak to me."

A woman's voice. "A year ago, Lucio beat the hell out of a guy who owed too much for too long. Crippled him. The girl that killed Lucio was that guy's daughter. She vanished a month ago. Everyone thought she had either gone to El Norte or had gotten herself killed. Whatever happened to her, it must have been an interesting month. But I have no doubt that this was revenge for the father." End of call. I hadn't recognized the voice. And I hadn't talked to any women about the killings…all the witnesses I'd seen had been men. Somebody else was paying attention. I guess that made the game more interesting.

Lucio had been a little fish. He ran his little operation and gave his cut, a price he was supposed to pay for connections and protection, to a bigger fish. He hadn't gotten what he'd paid for. So, if for no reason other than street cred, the death of Lucio would have to be avenged.

I needed in on this action. I needed to find the girl, to finally see if there really was something inexplicable in this world. I wanted to find her first just in case the cartel did figure out how to kill her…again. And if they did kill her again, would she stay that way?

I would have to lie a little lower, take a little time with things, not be so obvious. If I was extra careful about sticking my nose in a few places…if I listened to a story here and there…nobody would really care. Not as long as I didn't publish anything.

Deciding to drive home and stay out of sight for the rest of the day seemed like the best idea. I'd sleep and then hit the streets at night. If the girl didn't show up to release some more havoc on some other sorry asshole, there might still be a couple of quiet leads I could follow.

Being fairly well known as a semiofficial employee of the cartel can give you a certain immunity. I could generally move around on the streets without fear of the misfortunes that could befall other residents of La Ciudad. People would die in the night, but I wouldn't be one of them. Pimps would nod as I passed by, and some of their girls would call my name. Narco juniors would slap me on the back and offer me a toke. There would be gunshots in the distance. I'd sit in a few bars and talk to a few people. I'd get offered a couple of free cigars.

The sun would rise.

And I would go home to my fever dreams without hearing anything more about the girl. Nobody had even been talking about her. Nobody even spoke about things I already knew. Maybe the cartel wanted to handle it with as little attention as possible. All the leads were dead.

At home, I stared at my reflection in the bathroom mirror. That was something I usually avoided, but once in a while I couldn't help but check out the damage that time was doing to my aging and tired face, the gray taking over the hair, the wrinkles taking over the skin, the fat taking over the chin that I concealed with the beard.

I laughed at myself. A middle-aged man, perhaps even a bit beyond the middle, in pursuit of a young woman. I'd never really had the lust to chase after young women, even when I was young. I didn't care about that shit. I'd developed a contempt for the players, the guys that were always on the make, and I had the same contempt for the boring married life.

That was why I lived alone, I guess.

It was hard to believe that once upon a time I had felt differently, that in a prehistoric past that I sometimes barely remembered and sometimes didn't want to remember, I had what I would call a true love. Her face would sometimes appear in my memory when I least expected it…often in a mescal haze…bringing with it my biggest regrets. That was Flor. I've already told you I'd been dreaming about her.

I'll tell you more about her later.

But now I had a new love, after all those years, all those decades, of decay. A love who could tear down the shit shack we were all squatting in.

Those were my thoughts as I went over to sleep in my recliner, a deeper and better sleep than I was usually blessed with.

Did the girl kill again? That was the question. There were no witnesses, at least none that stuck around to answer questions. A body stuck around, though, stuck up in a tree. And how do you get a corpse up in a tree without equipment—or superhuman strength? He'd been all wedged into some branches and his throat had been crushed, just like Lucio's.

Damn, all the way at the top of the tree.

It was still there when I hit the scene.

The cops were trying to figure out how to get it down. Some law enforcer had managed to climb up there and was yelling the details down to others.

An unmarked SUV sat a little ways down the road, its windows a smoky black.

My cell beeped.

"Talk to me."

"Don't write about this one either, Cervantes." A quick hang-up. My cartel connection.

They were thinking the same as I was, that it was probably the work of the girl. Did they believe in her? I still wasn't sure that I did, even though I wanted to. But if it was some kind of trick, I sure the hell couldn't figure out how it was being pulled off. Maybe it would have been a good idea to look up some sleight-of-hand guy, or better yet a stage magician, and ask him if there was any explanation that didn't require…what? God or Satan?

I sat on a rock, fanned myself with my hat, took off my jacket, and lit a cigar. I had nothing better to do than watch the dark comedy of people trying to figure out how to pull human remains from a treetop with a little dignity. If I'd had someone to wager with, I would have bet it would end up undignified.

The place smelled of feces and garbage and piss, nothing unusual for those poor-beyond-poor shanty neighborhoods. Because that was where I was again. In fact, it wasn't very far at all from the Lucio slaughter, another reason to suspect the new killing was connected to the girl.

A crowd gathered. Locals. The mood was hushed and nervous. It was certain that word had gotten around about Lucio, and these people knew that some deep, weird shit was going down. So maybe…maybe with a little luck I could get somebody to talk to me. If my mystery caller knew who the girl was, then it was likely that a lot of the people in that barrio would know, too.

It was just a question of fear. How afraid would they be to talk?

My cell beeped again.

"Speak to me."

"The dead guy in the tree? He raped her sister and smashed her up pretty bad." Another call that ended before I could respond.

But I recognized the voice. That woman, the same one who had called to tell me Lucio had crippled the girl's father. Now it was revenge again, for the sister. It made sense. If you rise from the dead with supernatural strength, you might as well deal with all your serious grievances.

My caller had a nice voice, cultured, not necessarily of the middle class, but probably with some education. It wouldn't have been hard to get my number. I was always handing out my cards to potential sources. No way to know what she looked like. We all know that a nice voice can come from a person who isn't all that nice to look at. So, there was nothing unique about her, except for the fact that she was the only one interested in telling me anything. And she wasn't even asking me for money for her info. Most people in her position would have definitely tried to get a few bills for what she'd already told me for free. I even considered the possibility that she was the girl herself, but that didn't feel right. I didn't think that was the answer. Whoever she was, she must have some angle, and I couldn't help but think I would be hearing from her again.

The police officer in the tree finally lost patience and just dropped the rapist's corpse out of the tree, letting it thud to the ground. Then it was quickly removed. It wasn't one of those *CSI* shows.

I left too. With so many eyes and ears around the place, nobody was about to talk to me. Later, maybe, I would be back to see if somebody might have a tongue loosened by booze, stress, or solitude.

"God gave me a second chance. On the Virgin, on Santa Muerte herself, I swear I'm going to make good on that second chance. I never realized what a fucking asshole I'd been. It's this shitty town, Cervantes. Its filth soaks into you and changes you. I'm getting the hell out of here… tomorrow. But first I'm going to tell you my story."

It was night again, and I was in one of my regular bars with my usual mescal and my usual cigar. I was sitting at a tiny table, listening to Felipe Montoya, one of my many acquaintances on the streets of La Ciudad. Felipe was a local cop with the usual amount of dirt on his hands. A little payoff here and a little cut of the action there…a belly that had grown too big and a sense of honor that had grown too small. And he wasn't lying. He had been an asshole, a guy who went out of his way to fuck with people when there was no point to it, when it wasn't just business. Of course, by that standard, there were a lot of assholes in La Ciudad.

"I was in the squad car with Vincente. He was driving. I ain't gonna lie, Cervantes, I was in a bad, bad mood. The ol' lady was naggin' on me, and our brats she gave birth to were wailing the whole time I was getting' ready for work, and I had a motherfucker of a headache. And boy, was I ready for work, that was for damn sure. When I get in that mood, I'm always ready for work because I know I can take that shit out on some fool. When I got in the car with Vincente, the pills had mostly killed the headache, but I was still in that bad, bad mood. Yeah, I needed something to take it out on…something that wouldn't get me in trouble…something that didn't have no connections or protection."

He took a shot. I nodded encouragement. I could tell that this was going to be a very good story.

"So, here's this mangy girl in a dirty shirt and baggy pants walking all by herself on a street she shouldn't of been on anyway. And I didn't know how far I wanted to take it, but I knew I wanted to take it a little ways. She was on my side of the car, so I told Vincente to roll up on her. Through the open window I said something crusty and dirty to her… don't remember exactly what. And that girl, she didn't even look at me.

She just lifted up her arm and gave me the big, fat middle finger, even though it was really a skinny bone of a finger because she seemed kinda anorexic or some shit like that. And she just kept walking, kept on not looking at me, kept that finger up…and I was getting even more pissed off."

Took a shot. Poured himself another. I nodded again.

"Vincente knew the script and kept rollin' slow alongside, matching the girl's walking speed. 'Dumb bitch, huh, Felipe?' he said and snickered. But it wasn't funny to me. I'd lost my shit. I told him to stop, and I tossed myself out of the car, stumbling, then storming up to the girl. Yeah, we'd heard that they were looking for some strange girl that had somehow killed a few shitbags…but who the hell would've thought it was this girl?"

We repeated the ceremony of the drink and the nod. I already knew what the real question was. Why did she let him live? Why was he sitting with me that night, still able to share shots and tell his tale?

"I grabbed her wrist. I was in a rage. I really think I was after that finger that she still had raised. I wanted to bend it back and snap it. And then I'd have her on her knees, in pain and begging. Who knows what I might have done, what I might have made her do?"

The answer was easy to guess, but there was no point in interrupting the story.

"But before I could do anything, she yanked herself out of my grip, even though I was holding her so hard that she should've already been beggin'. And to make it even more of an insult, she just kept walking, kept on not looking at me, kept that finger flipped up. I was confused for a second, not sure how the hell she'd gotten free so easy. Then the anger drove me harder, and this time I bulldozed her straight on into a wall. I was gonna twist that arm with that finger up behind her back. I was gonna cause some serious pain. But it was fuckin' weird. Her body didn't have any give. It was like pushing a mannequin or a dummy. And her arm wouldn't give way either. I couldn't pull it down…it was like trying to bend a metal rod. And she didn't make a sound. No groan, no gasp of pain, no scream of fear. I was just pushing this statue face-first into a wall, trying to break an arm that wouldn't budge."

Another shot and he let out a sigh.

"You ain't gonna believe it, Cervantes."

"I'll believe you. I've already heard some stories about this girl. You're here to tell your story, so it must be one with a happy ending."

Felipe seemed to shudder and then continued.

"Vincente was like, 'What the hell, Felipe?' He probably thought I was fucking around somehow, I guess. I was gonna answer him when suddenly the girl did something and we both flew up into the air. I lost my grip and landed on my ass hard on the sidewalk. The girl went over me and either landed on her feet or was back up on them with a quickness. And I was fuckin' ready to kill her. She was embarrassing the fuck out of me. Plus, my back hurt like hell. But even hurting like hell, I forced myself up because that bitch wasn't going to get away. I pulled my baton, swearing under my heavy breathing, swearing that I wasn't going to be fooled by any more of her damn karate tricks or whatever the hell she was doing.

"She wasn't even trying to get away. She was just standing near the rear of our squad car. She was lookin' at me…watching me…waiting with this bitchy little smile on her face. Vincente just seemed confused. I was ready to finish it. I raised my baton and charged at the chica. I thought I was ready for anything…anything but what happened. She bent down and reached under the bumper. With that one hand, she lifted the back of the car off the ground until the tires were level with her head. Vincente yelled something and I stopped dead in my steps. The girl was laughing, but silently. Then she followed through with her lift and flung the car up and over to crash it upside down.

"The girl clapped and looked like she'd gotten a damn birthday present that she'd always wanted. Then she looked at me again and her face went flat, and she started to advance on me. I backed up without even thinking about it and fell on my ass again. I let go of my baton by accident. I managed to pull my gun on purpose.

"She stood there looking down at me as I aimed up at her head, trying to get control of my shaking hands. 'Now what? Now what's up?' I shouted. But she didn't seem scared. She just had an expression of disgust, like she'd stepped on a big bug or something. And that's when I got it, knew it, felt it. I could shoot her, and it wouldn't make one fuckin' bit of difference. She would crush me like I was a big bug. I knew it, knew that my only chance to live was to do nothing—to lower the gun and wait for her mercy, if she was going to have any. She stopped and waited, like she could tell that I knew. So, I put the gun down.

"And you know what she did? Do you fuckin' know what she did? She just turned and started walkin' the way she had been going in the first place…like it had never happened…without looking back again.

"I lay on the cement, breathin' hard, panting like a dog, staring up into the night for however long it took before I could finally get up and check on Vincente. He was alive, but unconscious. I called in to get him an ambulance. Then I noticed there were people around. They'd been watching, quiet and from a distance. When they saw that I was noticing them, they began to disperse and go off in different directions. Not how onlookers usually behave, but I didn't really care at that point.

"The medics came. Vincente would be okay. I went and found a church, fell to my knees on the stairs, and cried like a baby, beggin' Jesus and the Virgin for all the forgiveness they were willing to load me up with for every shitty thing I had ever done. Then I came here and you found me, and I guess I wanted to confess to you. But I'm telling you, Cervantes, that girl ain't natural. She has to belong to heaven." He squinted. "Maybe hell."

"Or to La Ciudad," I thought, as Felipe finished his last shot.

In the name of honesty, I have to admit I wasn't happy about the God talk, the religious overtones. First the little hooker and then Felipe. That irritated me. I didn't want the mystery girl to be associated with our old beliefs. I wanted her to be something new, something different.

A man should at least know, if not admit, his prejudices, and I will admit mine. I was not a fan of the deep, tainted roots that religion had sunk into my country—but not because I was an atheist. I believed there were unknown, magical things in the world. I already believed in the girl…or at least in the possibility of the girl. But it was the mystery that counted, that made things exciting. All those people who were so sure they knew the answers, even though they had no way to know if their answers were correct, they just took it on faith. Too many people believed in too much shit. That was why I tried to look for things that you could see. That was why I spent so many years chasing UFOs and strange creatures. Sure, the trail always went dead. But that wasn't the point. The point was that if there ever was something at the end of those trails, it would be something real in a real world.

That had been my quest, back when things mattered more to me.

Sometimes I liked to think that maybe a man's life was a book you couldn't read until it was finished, until he was dead. Then you could look stuff up in the index to see what had happened here, there, or elsewhere. Or maybe there were answers in the back of the book, solutions to the tough questions his life had posed, the problems he was supposed to solve. Maybe there were answers after his life was snuffed out. That was a mystery to which I would eventually learn the answer because a life was a trail that always had an end. But so far, I hadn't found many answers in my life.

Maybe the girl would have some of them.

Taking the first steps to seek those answers didn't entail a lot of effort, just checking around to see what girls had gone missing approximately a month earlier. Anyone with the least bit of awareness knew about the dead girls, the missing girls of La Ciudad. Books had been written. Documentaries had been filmed. And that meant infrastructure existed for me to do my research. I got on the computer at the office.

I was excited. I had a chance to find her first, to find out who she was. The unknown woman who had called me had given me clues no one else seemed to have.

A few young women in the right age range had disappeared around the time in question. And some of those matched the general description my friendly witnesses had given to me. Some of those missing girls had probably run off with boyfriends or headed to El Norte. Some had probably been killed. Two of those were probably in those pits I'd found out in the desert. And one of them had somehow been transformed into a high-powered assault weapon.

I was starting to feel really bad about those other two bodies that I'd just left out there. Somewhere there were people still holding onto the hope that maybe they had just taken off, that they were still living and healthy and happy. But I wasn't sure what I wanted to do about it. Maybe I would use a pay phone and give an anonymous tip. Maybe I could take away that hope and replace it with a horrid certainty. Maybe I wouldn't do anything and just let somebody else find them…eventually. I would either decide or let it ride after I found the one girl I needed to find.

My list got razored down to five girls. I printed out their pictures and thought about who I could show those pictures to. I called Felipe. No answer. Left a message: "Call me as soon as you can." Pedro was long gone. There was no sure way to find the witnesses at Lucio's bar…even if they would still be willing to talk to me. That left only the little hooker who had been enthralled by the street scene massacre. I didn't want to just wait for Felipe to call me back, so I decided to head back down and look for that wacky little witness. If she was willing and if she could give me an ID on the girl, I could always confirm it with the cop later. He would be more reliable, anyway.

But I couldn't find the prostitute. She'd also vanished like the dust. I found folks that knew who I was talking about. They'd been calling her Santa Loca because all she did was talk about the "holy girl." Her managers had started to get annoyed with her, and the quality of her work had deteriorated.

Then she was gone.

Nobody knew why. Nobody knew where.

Shit.

I was dead-ending.

There was one place I could go and ask questions, one place where no one would care if I asked those questions. It was even a place where those questions might get an answer. It was a place where the narcos never went, a place they didn't give a shit about.

It was a place that repelled most people.

But sometimes it was a place where I could actually find a bit of peace, a bit of comfort.

And I even had friends there.

It was an atypical day. I was up before noon and not as hungover as usual. So, I got in my Beetle and sputtered out into the desert, out into the other direction, not the way the girl had come from.

Hit the highway out of La Ciudad, leave the city behind, and travel for not that many miles. Then, if you know where to turn, you turn. There's no sign, you just have to know. It's a dirt road that you'd never even notice if you weren't looking for it. You'll end up heading toward some stubby mountains, but you won't have to go that far. The end of your journey, the end of my journey, as well as the end of that road, will be a collection of irregular hills and gullies. It's an area that perhaps you would think was deserted. But you would be wrong.

That place, for those who knew it existed, was called Los Locos.

It was a place for those with broken spirits and broken minds, a place for those whose souls had been broken by La Ciudad.

As I got closer to the end of the road, to the point where I would have to halt, I knew that the signs of habitation would become visible. There were dwellings. Tents, sloppy plywood shacks, boxes covered in tarps and old blankets…those were the kinds of things I was going to see, that I did see.

Some of the inhabitants sat and watched me, others tried to hide from my sight, and others ran away. A few who knew me, or at least had seen me before, even gave a wave or nod as I got out of my car.

I tipped my hat to them as I lit up a cigar.

Most of them, to be honest, looked like people who had been camping in the desert for a long time. But that was the reason they were there. It was a relatively safe place for those folks, a place that had arisen on its own.

It was an ad-libbed outdoor psychiatric facility.

Except in this case, there were no doctors, nurses, or orderlies. But there was an administration…sort of, anyway.

I honked my horn five times. That was my usual signal. Then I leaned against my car and waited. Nobody showed up right away, so I kept puffing on my cigar and pulled my hat down more to shield my face from the sun. It was the kind of day where I didn't really mind having to wait.

My vision was fixed on a path where my friend usually made his appearance. And I was just sort of daydreaming and musing about the girl who is Death. So, I wasn't really paying a whole lot of attention to what was happening behind me.

Until a noise startled me, a quiet, tittering laugh that someone was trying to stifle.

I quickly spun around, surprising myself with the quickness of my reflexes.

A woman was approaching me from the other side of my vehicle.

The clothing she wore had been fashionable at one time but had now become dirty and worn…yet still far from being just rags. Her long hair covered half her face. She wasn't young, but she didn't look old. She wasn't beautiful, but she was far from ugly. And to be completely honest, my first thought was that if she cleaned up just a little, a lot of guys might find her desirable.

What was my second thought?

Too bad she was a resident of Los Locos. Her strange, fixed smile, along with the glassy stare of her one visible eye, told me she probably didn't care what I thought about her looks.

She continued to shuffle toward me, coming around the car. But I wasn't that worried. Few of the residents of that place were ever dangerous. Perhaps surprised in her own turn by my lack of concern, she stopped and stared at me with that one eye and her frozen grin.

"Hello," I said, and gave her a nod.

Her smile suddenly vanished. Then she shook her head slowly, as if answering no to a question I had never asked. With one of her hands, she swept her hair back and revealed that the other half of her face had been horribly burned, leaving nothing but scar tissue. Before I could react, she put that hand over her mouth, letting her hair fall back over her disfigurement, and giggled like a schoolgirl.

After that, she turned her back on me and began to stiffly walk away.

Not feeling obligated to do anything else, I kept smoking my cigar. That was just how things went when you were in Los Locos.

"Señor Cervantes!" a voice called to me from another direction, from the path I had been watching before the woman had interrupted me. A boy, probably around twelve, was running toward me.

"Señor Gustavo!" I replied.

He skipped and skidded to a stop in front of me, seeming to be delighted by my feigned formality. He quickly took one of my hands and eagerly started to pull me, to lead me, down that trail. "Señor Eduardo is busy, but he told me that if a friend came, someone that I already knew, that I could take you to him."

"Just take it easy on me, Gustavo. I'm too old to be running, I'm too old!"

He laughed. "Why can't old people run?"

"Some can, but I can't…most of us can't. It's because…well, it's because we're old!"

The boy laughed again. "Then I don't want to get old! I like to run!"

"Be careful what you wish for."

"I know, Señor Cervantes. I'm always careful about what I wish for."

"And don't get fat either, not if you like to run!"

When he was younger, Gustavo had come to Los Locos with his mother. I'd never known what had driven that woman to the place, but in such a place, people like me didn't ask. You were told…or you weren't. After her death, Eduardo had, for all intents and all purposes, adopted the boy. It wasn't a legal adoption, but nobody had ever shown up wanting to claim custody of Gustavo.

Eduardo was my friend. We'd grown up together, we'd gone to school together, and we'd always stayed in touch. At one time, we'd both wanted to make the world, or at least La Cuidad, a better place. But he was the one who had been successful. He was the one that fate had led to Los Locos when he began working for the Church. He was the one who had volunteered to watch over the place, to try to take care of those poor people that ended up there. He even lived there, with Gustavo as his assistant. He had never become a priest, but a lot of folks treated him like one. And a lot of people responded to his dedication and charm, donating food and supplies that he needed to help his "patients."

Yeah, my old friend Eduardo had become almost a saint.

All I had done was become a reporter...sort of.

Gustavo continued to lead me down the path as it wound its way around rocks and through gullies, past more tents and propped-up shelters. I recognized some of the residents, and some of them recognized me with various types of acknowledgment. Others hid, just like earlier, and most remained indifferent or only slightly curious as we passed by. Some were talking, but not to me and not to Gustavo. Who were they talking to? Well, that was an open question.

Eventually we arrived at a cabin, a structure that had been put together with care, with the intention of being permanent. There was even an outhouse in back. Gustavo knocked elaborately on the door. I knew there was a code the boy used to let my friend know what was going on before Eduardo opened that door, but it was too complicated for me to figure out.

"Cervantes!" I heard Eduardo's voice from inside.

The code worked as well as ever.

"Cervantes!" The door flew open and my friend popped out, ready for a hearty handshake and a hug. He was quite a bit shorter than me, a whole lot thinner, and noticeably much happier with his life. He knew that I was a mess, that I had been for a long time, but he was usually nice enough not to make it obvious.

Eduardo's drink was whiskey. So, if you were an honored guest, you were obligated to have a glass with him. But only one glass because he wasn't a man who liked to get drunk. That worked for me...whiskey wasn't my drink.

And if you were an honored guest, you were expected to sit and chat for a while as you sipped that whiskey...to shoot the shit, catch up, or talk about the old days. And that was exactly what we did, for a long time.

At one point, I told him that I'd dreamed of Flor.

It was the only thing I'd said that make him visibly unhappy.

"That girl is long out of your life, hermano. You need to forget about her!"

"A dream, Eduardo. It was a dream. I can't control my dreams."

"Didn't you once tell me that some people can control their dreams?"

"Yeah, some people. Not me."

Then we changed the subject, doing a few more rounds of reminiscence before it was time for me to get to the point. I hesitated a little, because if Eduardo still hadn't heard about the girl, he might doubt my sanity.

He could sense that reluctance. "Go ahead, hermano, spit it out!"

"Well, Eduardo, it's like this. There are a lot of people who'll talk to me who won't talk to anybody else, and they've been telling me some stuff. And there are a lot of people that you talk to that nobody else talks to, that even I don't talk to…so I want to ask you…have you heard anything about a strange girl, a girl with…power?"

Then I waited to see if he knew…or if he would just think that age and mescal were starting to rot my brain.

But my friend laughed and slapped me on the shoulder. "You mean the one they call the 'the girl who is Death'? The girl that they cannot kill but that kills others at will. You mean that girl?"

"Yeah, that's the one!"

"Never heard of her." He laughed again and I joined him. Then he immediately became more serious, quieter, leaning in even though no one was around to hear us. Even Gustavo had scampered away.

"Yes, Cervantes, I've heard of that girl. My mad ones and my sad ones, the ones who come and go from this place…the ones who try to live on the streets and then come here when things get too rough…they've seen that girl. She's saved the lives of some of them, they say. And some of the people call her the holy girl. At first, I couldn't believe something like that. But so many spoke of her that I began to believe it, began to believe that something unique was happening in La Ciudad. Yet I think I only half believed it until now, until you came and asked me about her." He finally finished the whiskey he had been nursing all that time. "But I don't know anything about her, who she is, or what she really is…or where she came from…or if she'll leave. I should have known that you'd be on her trail, though. Maybe she'll even finally catch a chupacabra for you!"

Then he chuckled and allowed his mood to lighten again.

After that, we just shot some more shit as night began to fall.

When I got home, I was in a much better mood. And because I'd had only that one glass of whiskey, my head was much clearer than usual.

Then I realized I was being a total moron. There was still one factor that I could consider.

Location.

I knew the general area where the girl who is Death had come from, assuming the woman who had called me knew the truth and was telling it to me. It was the neighborhood where Luis had done his business, crippled the girl's father, and paid the price. That was the neighborhood where the girl and her family had lived and suffered.

Were any of my suspects from that neighborhood?

One. There was one.

Her name was Guadalupe Castaneda.

Reported missing thirty-three days earlier, Lupe C. was eighteen…not much education, a maquiladora worker. Probably a good girl, trying to help out her family, going to church with Mom, taking care of the father who couldn't walk anymore. No mention of a boyfriend. But yeah, she did like to go out and dance once in a while, party, stay out late with her friends on a Saturday night.

And that was when she vanished…on a Saturday night…last seen by and with her friends in one of La Ciudad's many clubs. Somehow, they'd lost track of her. Somehow, she was gone.

I looked at the picture of Lupe C. She was pretty but not ravishing. Long black hair that had a little bit of a curl. She was taller and thinner than her peer group. She fit the description. No reason she couldn't be the girl who is Death. But no reason that she should be either, except those few facts about her that seemed to match up with what I already knew.

I had to decide if I wanted to try to find the Castaneda family, which might not be that easy in Shantyville, a place without real street names or addresses. And I would have to do it quietly, making sure I was the only one to figure it out. Because if the cartel boys had already been tipped off, that route to the girl would be on shutdown, and that family would be in the deep shit, shit that would make all the shit they'd lived through before seem like heaven on earth.

Felipe called me back. He agreed to meet me briefly at the bar again. Only briefly. Only one shot of mescal…and no cigar. He was truly on his way out, out of La Ciudad and out of his own life, just like Pedro before him. I wondered if he was taking the wife and kids with him, but I decided not to ask.

I showed him the picture.

"Yep," was all he said.

He didn't even want to know who she was.

We shook hands at the door and then he was gone.

I didn't expect to see him again.

After that I went and did a walkabout, talked to some people, listened to some people, tossed out a discreet question, gave a slight nod to a whispered answer. And yes, the cartel was looking for the girl. But she was just "the girl." There was nothing floating in the background air that was saying anything about any Guadalupe Castaneda. Amazingly, that was still my little secret. Nobody who knew her in Lucio's bar, including my unknown caller, had given up the marrow. For once, just that one time, the people had something that scared them more than the cartel. The narcos were who they were, but the narcos still existed in the world as it always had been, and they were creatures of that world.

That girl, though…she wasn't part of that world anymore. With her, the normal rules no longer applied.

When I got home, something foul crawled up from my gut, and I had a savage attack of the pukes. Bad food or bad sickness, I couldn't tell you which. After finishing the first round, I tossed a cushion on the bathroom floor so I could lose consciousness more comfortably next to the toilet, because I was sure there was going to be a second round.

Passing out more than falling asleep, I was tormented by visions and dreams.

A sky of blood above a desert…a hum of insects…three pits, each of which contains a body. The corpse in the middle pit jerks up…a grotesque and mummified thing pulled to its feet by some invisible puppeteer. Then it stands still as desiccated flesh and dead, dried skin begin to fill with life again. And in an instant, Guadalupe Castaneda is standing…as if she has replaced the corpse…standing among the living again, but in some state that is beyond death and life. The only damage that remains is the brutal scar that shows her throat has been cut.

Can she see me watching her? She seems to, even though it is only in the eye of my mind…the eye of my soul that is having that vision. She seems to…as if her regenerated sight can see things that normal mortals cannot see.

She is naked. Her nudity makes me wonder if I should be aroused… even just a little bit…even though I don't feel like I'm in that mess that is my physical body. There is just this little twinge, more a memory of desires that I probably once had. As if aware of my feelings, Guadalupe smiles oddly, shakes her head in dismissal, and begins to walk away. I try to follow her, but that eye of my mind, that eye of my soul, is frozen in place. I can only watch as she walks up a hill. But I know that hill, and I know what is going to happen on the other side.

I came back to myself on the bathroom floor, barely able to rise and vomit into the toilet. After that, I lost awareness again.

There were no more dreams, no visions.

In the middle of the next night, I was finally able to drag my ragged old ass up and serve myself a sip of mescal, hoping that would finish killing off whatever had burrowed into my stomach, even if the cost was another quick wave of nausea.

Then I braced myself to get into the shower. I was in there for a long time, but bit by bit I started to feel better.

I toweled off and checked my messages.

While I had been out of action, Lupe C. had returned to the stage for another act in her eldritch play.

Salvatore was a fat, drunken slob, one of La Ciudad's many losers. His wife had managed to get a job in a maquiladora and was naturally supporting him and his alcohol consumption. You know the type. Everyone knows the type. Some people even thought that I was one of those guys. But I could pay for my own booze, and I didn't have a wife.

And, of course, he was abusive.

Then that day, perhaps because of the job, the wife had sprouted some self-esteem and left the house. Salvatore, after getting a few drinks in himself, worked up enough raging motivation to go out searching for her. It wasn't a very good game of hide-and-seek, and he quickly found her at the home of one of her relatives. There was some sort of violent moment that ended up with the wife in an armlock, being forced to head home and begging for mercy.

According to the witnesses, the girl followed them down the street for a while, silently and calmly. Nobody could say for certain where she'd come from because at first, Salvatore's antics were drawing everyone's attention.

The wife stumbled, which made Salvatore even more angry. He twisted her arm harder, making her cry out. That was when Lupe closed the gap that she had been maintaining, dashed forward, reached down, grabbed Salvatore by an ankle…and lifted his leg up off the ground and up over her own head. Caught by complete surprise, he let the wife go. Then the girl let Salvatore go and he plopped to the ground.

His dignity ruffled, he struggled to get up. Lupe just stood there, waiting. When he saw who his attacker was, Salvatore got in her face, screaming incoherently. The girl just watched him impassively for several uncomfortable seconds. Then she picked him up, this time lifting his whole body over her head. He must have had three times her weight, but she made it seem like she was raising a big pillow up that high.

Rage turned to terror as Salvatore's addled brain realized that something really, really not right was happening to him.

Then came a shot from a high-powered rifle.

The bullet hit the girl full in the back. It's no surprise that it didn't penetrate the skin, didn't spill even one tiny drop of blood, but that impact drove her off her feet and the weight of her hostage caused them both to topple to the ground.

Salvatore's head hit concrete, knocking him out, and his part of the story was finished. The wife took off. And Lupe quickly jumped up, only to catch another shot in the chest, which lifted her up and landed her on her ass.

One of the cartel's sicarios had finally found his target.

The shooter was firing from the back of a pickup truck a couple of blocks away. The driver kept the engine running, waiting for the signal to take off. They'd been on the streets, they'd been looking for her, and they wanted her dead. They probably didn't know that she'd already been dead. They sure didn't know that they couldn't kill her a second time.

What did the man with the rifle think when he saw that chica hop back up again? He was most likely a professional, knowing that he'd taken two mortal shots and still seeing the target unharmed. Something must have been going through that homicidal mind, something to make him hesitate. Because he didn't fire again. Not right away.

Lupe didn't do anything either. Not right away. She just stood still, looking at the pickup and waiting. Time lingered for almost a minute. Then the gunman gave in to temptation and took a head shot. With the scope he had, with the target that close and standing still, he most likely got her right between the eyes. The impact took her back down again, but she held herself rigid, so that her body was like a metal post falling over.

In less than a second, she was back up.

Then she rushed the truck, each step turning into a leap that carried her twenty or thirty feet.

In his panic, the shooter began to pop off more shots.

They all missed. And suddenly the girl landed in the back of the truck with him. One hand seized his rifle and the other crushed his throat. Then she hurled his body high into the air. It landed in a ditch. She stayed in the back of the truck, examining the rifle that she'd won in that unequal contest.

After his own moment of hesitation, the driver bailed out and started running away.

Lupe seemed surprised by that move. For some seconds of her own, she just watched him run. Then she raised the rifle and tried to shoot the fugitive. Her aim was awful. Despite her strength, the recoil took her by surprise and threw her severely off balance. She was so light and clumsy with the weapon that it was probably only that demon strength that saved her from the total embarrassment of falling down.

With an expression half pouting and half angry, she hurled the rifle at her target. It converted into a whirling blur and caught the guy on the shoulder. A bone cracked and he gave a sharp yell of pain. He fell. But fear drove him back to his feet, drove him to keep running, his injured arm hanging limp at his side.

He was about to vanish behind some buildings when Lupe sailed out of the back of the truck and began to chase him down with those same bounding leaps. She'd been learning, learning what she was capable of doing.

Both of them were lost to view, so there were no witnesses that saw what actually happened. But the results could have taken an oath. Broken neck, the head twisted around to face backward, with the stomach on the ground.

And no trace of the girl.

My dreams were changing, becoming more coherent. They were showing me other events. Other people, their thoughts, emotions, motivations. They were giving me a peek behind the curtains of secret stages.

He was, like me, fat. Like me, he smoked cigars, but he savored his more slowly because the quality was much better. And, like me, he wore a suit most of the time, but his weren't rumpled or stained. They appeared to be European and custom made.

He owned a lot of fancy clubs and bars, using his favorite as his base of operations. He would usually be up on the second floor, in the part of the club where you would have to get a very, very personal invitation just to set foot in the elevator that would take you up to his lair. And if you did get that invite, you'd be offered the finest tequila or perhaps a vintage wine.

I could clearly see him in his very big and comfortable chair, behind a very big and expensive desk…both also imported…as he drank and smoked and drank some more. I could see him sitting alone, with the lights dimmed…deep in thought…because he had a problem…a problem he couldn't believe was real. But it was a problem he was slowly coming around to believing in. All his sources, a lot of people he trusted, had told him it was true.

He was the guy who ran La Ciudad, the guy in charge of supplying El Norte with all the cocaine it needed to feed its endless appetites. He was the guy who said what stayed and what went away. He was the guy who had climbed to the top of a mountain by climbing over many bodies. He was the guy who knew if you wanted to keep running the city, you'd better be ready for anything and you'd better always be ready to pull the trigger. He was the guy who knew that somebody was always trying to take a little cut that they weren't entitled to, always trying to take some little bit of what belonged to him. And when that happened, he was the guy who made counting the dead a full-time job in our town.

But something was happening. The town that should have been under control was getting loose and weird. Some scrawny little bitch was starting to fuck shit up. Somehow, she was killing people in his food chain and walking away from it, leaving her own body count. And he knew how that would look to his associates…and to his competition. It would look like blood in the water. His blood.

Yeah, I could see him in my mescal-driven dream, sitting by himself as he contemplated the absurdity of the situation. Then I could see him calling in his top enforcers, his most skilled, most ruthless killers. I could see him giving them free rein to find that girl and turn her into a smear.

La Ciudad was about to see some hell it had never seen before.

The next day I didn't have anything better to do, so I went back to Lucio's bar.

Of course, I wanted a shot of info more than I wanted a shot of mescal. I had no other reason to go there. That dump proved that even I had standards.

It was still in operation. Somebody else had taken over. They'd put it back together. The bartender radiated hostility, but at least he served me. He was an ugly little man that I didn't remember seeing on my last visit. He took a bit of time to stare at me coldly before taking payment and turning away. His way of telling me that I wasn't wanted there, but that nobody cared enough to do anything about it. But if I showed up again….well, you never know…maybe somebody would care enough.

Four guys calmly played cards at one table. A couple of other guys were drinking alone. All of them gave me a quick glance up front, then actively ignored me. None of them were familiar. None of them, as far as I could recall, had been witnesses to the death of Lucio.

The card game puzzled me. Dead silent and listless, no drama, no argument, no shit talkin'. They were like extras in a movie.

Then I chuckled and toasted the card players before downing the crappy mescal…because that was when I realized what was going on. It was playacting…a set…a setup. Those guys were all gunmen under orders and placed there in case the girl came back.

No, not the place to be. If they recognized me and thought to mention it to the wrong people, it could cause me grief. Technically, I was following the rules since I wasn't writing anything for the paper, but it probably wasn't a good idea to be dropping my fat, nosy self into the middle of an ambush.

I allowed myself just a tad of self-indulgence…allowed myself to sit calmly for just a moment…then a second moment…but I wasn't going to stay and smoke a cigar. I left as casually as I could, nodding to the bartender on the way out. He made a point of looking down at something as I passed him by.

I didn't leave a tip.

◈

I had wanted to get a lead on the Castaneda family. But it looked like I wasn't going to be following that lead without being followed myself. If I hadn't noticed the undercover operation at Lucio's bar…if I'd mentioned the super girl's real name…it would have been over for that family.

I spotted a bench in a place that didn't smell like sewage and garbage, so I took a seat, still in sight of the bar, and mopped off some sweat, fanned myself with my hat.

None of the guys in the bar seemed to give a crap about what I was doing. But other adults in the vicinity stared at me strangely and went inside when they saw me sit down. Children who were playing outside their hovels were called inside. There was no way I would be gathering any info.

Nobody wanted to share the day with me except for stray animals and scavenger birds that picked at debris and dead things.

About to leave, I heard my cell phone buzz. Caller ID was blocked. But I still knew who it was.

"Talk to me."

"Ah, Cervantes, that bar must've not been welcoming. You weren't there long."

It was my anonymous lady friend.

"Is this a social call, my dear? Or are you willing to tell me something about Guadalupe Castaneda?"

Something deep down had told me to drop that name, had almost forced me to do it.

Silence. Had I given her a shock?

"We've been discussing whether we should talk to you seriously.

You'll be hearing from us very soon."

The call ended abruptly.

We?

Somebody out there, very close by, seemed to know something. Or else they were doing a fine job of pretending to know something. Maybe they were fucking with me. No way to know for sure. But if they had the real info, why tease me with it? The cartel would pay in gold or cocaine for the girl's real name.

But my intuition told me my caller was the real deal. And even though that intuition had often failed me in other ways, it was usually perfect at letting me know a real source from a crap one.

In the end, nothing to do but wait it out; wait until she called back.

My car was right where I'd left it. Not that I had any doubts about that. Nobody was going to mess with a vehicle parked next to a nest of assassins.

I drove home to snatch a nap.

Let me tell you about Samurai Sanchez.

One of the chief enforcers. One who helped keep La Ciudad's graves full and its gravediggers employed. One of our most colorful, volatile, and bloody characters, the kind of narco who would get a lot of attention when the stories of those days came to be written.

Not content with the delightful reputation of the Mexican gangster, he'd taken a fancy to things Japanese, especially the group of folks called the yakuza. He imitated them by getting those elaborate, full-body tattoos they were known for. He claimed that his ink had the same meanings as they did in Japan. "We're in the same business, after all," he would brag. But he wouldn't explain what those meanings were. "Those who know, they know."

Somehow, he had gotten hold of an authentic, high-quality samurai sword, actually made in the Land of the Rising Sun. I would have supposed the real deal was hard to come by, but it wasn't like Sanchez was hurting for cash. I think he bought it after watching those Kill Bill movies, but maybe he had it before. Either way, that sword earned him his nickname. He loved that fucking weapon. Scabbard strapped to his back, it went everywhere with him. Somebody once told me he wouldn't even take it off if he was with a woman. But it wasn't a woman who told me that. And of course, if he took personal charge of an "errand," he completed it with that blade.

So that night I was sitting in one of my bars, with my mescal and my cigars, when Sanchez swaggered in with some of his boys.

Seeing me, a big grin twisted up onto his mouth. Even though he smiled often, his smiles always seemed forced. Shaved head, acne, knife scars, average height for a Mexican man, but a lot of muscle. We got along okay. He liked to shoot the shit with me sometimes. And sometimes he would spill some shit off the record. Everything really interesting and important that happened in that town ended up being off the record.

"Cervantes! You big, fat fuck!" I stood up to greet him and he gave me a bear hug. "Doing your usual throat and liver damage, I see!" Then he let out a laugh and let me go with it. "Bartender, his drinks are on me!" The man just nodded, wanting to draw as little attention from Sanchez as possible as the gangster plopped down at my table.

I made sure I had a smile on my face as I sat back down. "What brings you to this dump, Sanchez? I know you can afford to stink up a classier joint." Then I watched for his reaction. If he seemed amused by a little needling, I would be able to relax. If he scowled, then I'd have to watch my tongue and be very attentive…maybe suddenly have to go take a piss and hope that something else distracted him before I came back.

But he didn't seem to care either way about the shit I said. He seemed to be considering something, following some trails of thought shifting around inside his skull. Then he snapped back, and his eyes focused on me like two lasers.

"I know, Cervantes, I know that you know about that girl."

I took a shot of mescal, swallowed, forced the amiable smile to stick on my face. But there was ice in my spine, a fear that Sanchez was going to ask me what I knew and that he would be able to tell if I was concealing something. Because guys like that were good at telling if you were hiding something from them, and I didn't want to have to give up the girl or her family.

So, I waited for the knife to be drawn, waited for it to be put to my throat, either figuratively or literally.

Then…the reprieve. He wanted to broadcast and not receive.

"I'm gonna get that girl, gonna kill that girl. She must have some fancy quadruple black belt or some shit. She must be catching these slacker ass-draggers off guard with some severe butt-kicking skills. But when I find her, there ain't gonna be any more surprises. Everything will keep running the way it's always run…and she'll be the one who gets run down. And then you know what's gonna happen." He reached back and patted the hilt of his sword.

Yeah, sure, karate explained what Lupe C. was doing. But I just nodded. I wasn't going to contradict the guy. If he found her…or she found him…then she could do the contradicting.

Sanchez leaned in closer. "And you know what, Cervantes? I'll bet that girl isn't even really a girl. I'll bet it's some kind of sick-ass freak transvestite quadruple black belt…all dressing like that for the ambush… the element of surprise…a twist on that hard-core ninja shit."

I feigned that I was impressed by that line of reasoning. "Could be, could be," I said in a quiet and thoughtful way, as if pondering it seriously.

"But woman, man, or monkey, there's gonna be a head on a silver platter being served up to the Boss…and it's gonna be served up by Sanchez the Samurai!"

I nodded, taking the role of silent co-conspirator.

"Oh, I know you can't write anything about all this right now, maybe not ever. But let me tell you, Cervantes, if this story can ever be told, I'm going to tell it to you, and you can tell it to the world."

"If you have a story like that to tell me, Sanchez, if you kill that girl, I'll be here to listen."

He let loose another loud laugh and slapped me way too hard on the shoulder. "Good man, Cervantes, good man!"

Still chuckling, he got up, smoothly uncoiling from the chair. I'd probably be grunting and breaking a sweat trying to get out of mine. Looking at the man, being in his presence, I could almost believe that if anyone could lay Lupe C. back down into that empty hole in the desert, it would be Samurai Sanchez.

He motioned to his men to follow as he left the locale. The meaning wasn't lost on me. Sanchez had come there to talk to me, had actually tracked me down just to tell me what he'd told me. He wanted me to know that he was all in to get the girl. He was declaring war, like he had done in the past with rival gangsters. There had been other smoky nights in dim bars where he had told me who his next trophy was going to be. There had been other blood battles, and each and every time the winner had been Gabriel "Samurai" Sanchez.

A little too much mescal that night, went past my limit. But I found my way back to the office and then to my house. The sun was coming up as my head was going down onto the pillow.

There hadn't been any more news about Guadalupe Castaneda.

I woke with a choking sob because I'd dreamed about a woman; a woman looking down at me as I slept. So vivid, it was as if she had really been there, even though, once fully awake, I realized I was alone.

I had dreamed about Flor. But this time she'd been close to me, standing over me, aware of me.

I guess I should explain now. In the beginning, when I first heard about the girl who is Death, I never would have thought I'd need to talk about Flor, but she ended up being part of this story.

Now, if you were to see me, you would see a rumpled, aging "gordo" whose days of semi-invincible youth had long ago receded into a background of gray memory.

Yet once upon a time my balls weren't full of cigar ash, and my heart wasn't embalmed with mescal. Yeah, there was a time when I wasn't loaded with cholesterol and failure, a time when there was a crack in my soul and a little bit of light was able to enter.

And that little bit of light was named Flor.

There's only one woman in my memory who can make my heart pump a little harder, who can make my aging eyes still spit out a tear or two every so often.

Flor. Other than her, there had been only a few minor romantic misadventures in my younger days, all of them best forgotten. She was the one.

People called her La Gitana, because she was a fortune-teller and because she was a free spirit. She also loved the rumors of weirdness in the world, and she loved to be beside me when I quested after that weirdness. We talked about nothing and everything. I felt like I'd known her forever…and yet I didn't know her at all.

We kissed once but never made love. There didn't seem to be any urgency. I thought she would always be in my life…that there was plenty of time. I never thought to propose because our spirits already seemed to be wedded.

Then one day she was gone…without word or warning. Nobody

knew what had happened. I tried and tried, but I never found a clue or a trace…and I tried for a long time. But as time went by, I had to give up.

After that time—after she was gone and after I had given up searching—that probably would have been a good time for me to die a quicker death. Because after that I felt like I was dying anyway, but slowly…very, very slowly. I began to drink a lot more, smoke a lot more, eat a lot more shitty food. Much of the magic and mystery of the world seemed to become a dreary stagnation of cynicism and mescal.

Flor, did you leave because you saw what I would become?

Ah, there it is. Even now, a tear hits this page as I write these words.

God, how I sometimes hated my fucking city, that foul place of poverty and narcos, of cheap deaths and even cheaper lives. If Guadalupe was real, I wanted her to smash it all!

After that dream of Flor, I still managed to fall back to sleep, a troubled sleep. I was still sleeping around noon. And that was when the girl returned to Lucio's bar, walked right in, just stood there and waited.

That bartender saw her. The pantomime card players saw her. The trap had been sprung.

The bartender's move was smooth. He leaped over the counter fluidly, a shotgun suddenly there in his hand. The girl kept standing there, watching him as if his actions didn't even involve her, watching the gun barrel rise up, aimed point-blank at her chest, watching the trigger get pulled.

Boom.

She rode the blast a few feet up into the air and let it lay her down on her back. Then she sat up, unharmed as always. But the card players weren't slow on the draw either; they knew the girl had her own cards to play. One of those guys was right there with a metal baseball bat, taking a home run swing at Lupe C.'s head. She saw it coming and placed a hand on the ground to brace herself for the blow, so that she wouldn't be so easily moved. There was no give in her body; she was able to hold herself absolutely still and rigid. The bat connected and then bounced back across the floor with a big dent in it, leaving the batter cursing in pain and gripping his hands.

Quickly and almost casually, the girl reached over and got hold of the batter's ankle. The snap was loud, and he fell down as she popped back up onto her feet.

Boom again…the other barrel of the shotgun slammed her in the back. As invulnerable as she was, she still had only the mass of a skinny girl, so with no way to prop herself against the impact, she ended up on another short flight, landing face-first.

She was immediately up again.

The shotgun was empty, but three pistols were raised and unloaded a barrage of bullets that pounded Lupe C. back through the flimsy makeshift wall of the bar.

That coordinated attack meant that all the assassins had to engage in a panic of a reload at the same time. And with that little doorway of opportunity, the girl came rushing back in. There was no grace in the wild swings of her fists, but the shattered bodies weren't going to offer any criticisms of her fighting style.

The bartender was running away. The guy with the destroyed ankle was crawling away. She didn't try to stop either of them; maybe she wanted to leave some witnesses behind who could enhance her reputation.

She was about to leave and then hesitated, moving into a full pause as she looked back at the carnage. An idea lit up her face, and she began picking up the guns and ammo belts. Doubtless seeing that it would be awkward and obvious to be walking around with that much visible weaponry, she found a dirty old backpack behind the bar and stuffed her prizes into it. Still considering the possibilities, she went for the wallets and found many US dollars in large denominations. It was not like they had been the sort of gentlemen who would have had to worry about getting robbed carrying around that much cash.

One last thought. She stripped the blazer and shirt off the smallest body. The T-shirt she had found to wear had been destroyed by the shotgun. The new clothing was too big for her and made a strange fashion statement with the old jeans and bare feet, but you could tell she thought it was better than nothing.

They'd have to find the dead man another jacket for his funeral.

Then the girl did leave Lucio's bar. The streets were deserted, but dozens of eyes peered out from behind ragged curtains as she walked away with her new possessions.

It took me a while to get the story on that incident. I had to hear much of it from the second or the third hand, had to reconstruct it a little bit. I had to dream about it a little bit. And, more and more, I was beginning to trust my dreams.

I shouldn't even have to say it. It's obvious that the local cops are in the pocket of the cartel. Take the cash or take a bullet. So, it was no surprise that the police didn't touch anything on Lupe's most recent battlefield, keeping things waiting for Samurai Sanchez and his posse of enforcers to arrive on the scene. That was what the real authority had told them to do.

Once there, Sanchez prowled around that bar, giving the bodies a once-over. His attitude was a mix of anger and bafflement.

"What the fuck? What the fuck is her trick? When I catch this bitch, she's gonna be telling me how she does this shit, even if I have to take her apart, one chunk at a time!"

Then he started screaming at the corpses, almost like he expected he could make them cringe. "How, how, how could you, all of you worthless cocksuckers, fall for it? Whatever it was that she did?"

You could tell he wanted to kick the crap out of those bodies, but he caught himself…restrained himself…and used his martial skills only to split a table and send a chair flying out the door.

Following the chair outside, he began shouting at the empty street: "And you, all you useless pig shit eaters! I know at least some of you know who she is! I know it! And the time is coming, you donkey fuckers! One of you trash cowards is going to tell me, tell me what you know! You don't have very long! If the right little bird doesn't sing its little song in the right ear real soon, then all the little birdies are gonna get a taste of napalm!"

Then Sanchez jumped in the back of his SUV and told the driver to get moving.

In the middle of the night, an old drunk was shambling near an empty parking lot. He saw a girl messing around with some guns, trying to aim them, trying to figure out how they worked. The old drunk had once been in the army and still knew some of the basics of weaponry. On a whim, he offered to show her how the pistols should be loaded and operated, how the safety worked, how to hold them and aim them. He had enough of his brain working that he could do that. She accepted his help with a silent nod and a silent smile once she realized it wasn't somebody else looking for the kind of trouble that would get him a quick ride on the six-feet-under express.

After a quick, basic, and somewhat incoherent lesson, the girl went on her way, leaving her guns behind, no doubt realizing she could find more whenever she wanted them. The aged alcoholic didn't know what he had done. He didn't know that he'd just shown the main antagonist how she could escalate La Ciudad's weirdest war.

He ended up burying those weapons. He didn't think he could safely sell them, and he didn't want to end up having to explain how he had gotten them.

Later, after he realized who that girl was, he would whisper that story into my ear as we lingered outside a bar. We'd gone to school together back in the long ago. He had to tell his story to someone, but he knew he would tell it only once. I was the person he chose. I guess if there was anything I was good at in this life, it was being that person, the one who got to hear the stories that were told only once.

Flor gazed right into my eyes, and I gazed back into her big brown eyes, full of beauty. She really was La Gitana, all decked out in her fortune-telling garb. We sat at the table facing each other. She was still young and attractive because that was how she was in my memory. Me? I think I was still old, plump, and rumpled, still the creature of now, just as she was the creature of then.

In her hands, the tarot. She kept shuffling and reshuffling and shuffling and reshuffling those cards. I had forgotten that constant, rapid reshuffling, the dexterity that was one of her tricks of trade. It could almost be hypnotic, the way she did it.

But after a while it became monotonous. My eyes wandered downward, and I saw that the table was covered by a huge map of La Ciudad.

Suddenly, with a loud slap, Flor whipped down a card right on that map.

The thirteenth card of the major arcana. Death. A card that could actually mean many things.

I woke with a jolt, as if that loud slapping sound in my dream had been real.

Flor!

I started to sob, crying until I fell back into sleep.

Flor was still sitting there, shuffling her cards and smiling at me.

"You still have to see a couple of things. You can't go yet!"

She threw down another card: the Fool.

"That's you, Cervantes."

I couldn't disagree.

The next card: the World.

"You get to see something interesting now."

Before I could even ask, I fell…or I seemed to fall, to plummet down and into the tarot card…down into the World. Up above me, now a giant, Flor watched my fall, only to vanish as I began to fly through darkness. I was startled, but not afraid.

I trusted Flor.

Everything blurred. I began to descend.

Suddenly it was over.

I was somewhere underground in an installation, a bunker, deep beneath the surface of the earth. I didn't seem to have a body. My spirit was floating in some sort of chamber. The walls were covered by video monitors. They showed scenes from all over the world. Several of them showed that weird and fuzzy footage that took the place of Guadalupe Castaneda on camera.

A chair faced those screens and somebody was sitting in it. I couldn't make out the face, only that it was a male figure in a black suit, a black fedora on his head. The hands were covered with black gloves. Even though I couldn't see the face, I could tell he was very intently and very intensely examining Lupe. And I knew he wasn't happy about what he was seeing, not happy in any way.

Even though I had no body in the place, I still could feel a severe chill in the air. There was a coldness in the place, around that man, that did not seem natural, a freeze in the spirit as well as the flesh.

"Who are you?"

It was a flat, emotionless voice, as frigid as the air that carried it.

And that voice was directing its question to me.

I suddenly felt trapped. I didn't want to answer. But that man, that being, could sense my presence. And I somehow knew he could force me to answer.

I wanted to call out to Flor, to shout for her to get me the hell out of there. But I couldn't find a voice.

The man was about to stand up.

I felt the danger. I felt fear.

Then…a phone rang.

It was an old rotary phone, black, like the kind they had when I was young. I could remember using that same type of phone as a child. It was a total anachronism in that high-tech environment. I think there was even dust on it, even though the rest of the chamber was shiny clean.

"That's not possible," said the monotone voice—or was there just the slightest hint of some agitation?

The phone kept on ringing, demanding the man's attention and distracting it from me. I had the stray thought that maybe Flor was making the call, that she was trying to help me.

A gloved hand finally picked up the receiver…with hesitation.

"Yes, I am here."

The waiting silence seemed to grow even colder.

"I am here," the man repeated, his voice somehow sounding even less human. "There is no need for games. If you are contacting me in this manner, there can be no doubt about who I am; there can be no doubt about where you are from or what you are."

After a brief burst of static, I found that I could make it out, that I could hear it too. A female voice, but it wasn't Flor. Sounding remote and far away, it was still more pleasant at first, more human, than that of the man who answered the phone. There was an accent that I couldn't recognize.

"Hello, agent. I hope you are well?" followed by a laugh that, for some reason, I found disturbing.

"Pointless pleasantries of that nature are not relevant. Which one of you am I speaking with?"

"Such bluntness, agent. It's both admirable and annoying. I don't think I will tell you which one I am. It would just be a pointless pleasantry, after all. My authority will still stand because only those of us with the authority can contact you." Somehow, that woman's voice was beginning to fill me with a sense of dread that I truly could not explain. There was something…not right about it…something off that my spirit could sense, but not articulate.

There was another moment of hesitation before the man said, "Understood."

"Good. Now, a status report please."

"There has been an intrusion. I have been unable to ascertain the source…it is resistant to remote observation. I can only see it has a female form and I know its location. This being has considerable power, yet it seems to pursue only trivial actions. I am about to take my own actions, whatever actions are required to destroy or expel the intrusion. I assume you are contacting me after all this time because of this intrusion. If you have any information that would be useful to my efforts, I am prepared to listen."

The woman's voice chuckled. "I have no information, only new orders."

There was a pause. She seemed to be trying to enhance the drama.

"Yes?" the man finally prodded her.

"Do not interfere with her!"

"What? Are you serious?" A tone of shock broke the monotone. There was true surprise…even frustration. But the tone quickly flattened again. "That order is contrary to my purpose here."

"Nevertheless, do not intervene, not at this time and not until authorized. Understood?"

"Yes, but I must warn you that if a disruption of this magnitude is not eradicated, it may allow further intrusions into this realm."

"Of course, but the risk will be taken. You must obey. There are factors at play that…I am not willing to discuss. And other measures will be taken first. Yet be prepared. You will be held in reserve. Be ready to act only if and when you receive instructions from me…or from one of us."

"Very well." But there was still a hint of doubt in his voice.

"Thank you so much for your service, agent." Was there a touch of sarcasm? It was hard to tell.

"One more thing."

"Yes, agent?"

"A minor consciousness has been monitoring me and may have full awareness of our conversation."

"It is called Cervantes." That strange laugh again. "Yes, it is a minor consciousness, minor to the point of irrelevance. Do not concern yourself. Goodbye."

"Goodbye."

That woman, that being with the voice of a woman, knew who I was. And on a deeply intuitive level, I didn't like that, didn't like that at all.

But there was nothing I could do about it.

The man replaced the receiver with more force than necessary, signaling my own departure. I fell up rapidly into a swirling haze. Was I falling out of Flor's tarot card? For just a moment she was there, waving to me as I flew by, as I flew toward a full awakening.

I was soaked in sweat and my breathing was labored. I needed a shower.

I needed a drink.

I needed two or three drinks.

Had that dream been real?

It would be years before I had the answer.

They were restless, nervous, and agitated this time.

The new killers on duty at Lucio's bar weren't playing cards or even drinking. They just sat there, chain-smoking, barely talking, frequently checking their firearms, and constantly glancing outside. Each one of them was probably asking himself what he had done to deserve that assignment, wondering if he'd somehow pissed off Samurai Sanchez.

Words were being whispered about the girl who is Death, rumors were being passed along, and the stories were being told to others besides me. The legend was going urban.

Those four men had been placed there as an afterthought…just to show a presence…just to show the neighborhood that the narcos were still in charge…just to be macho…just to not back down. But those four men knew what had happened to the ones they had replaced, and that was why they felt no peace or security. They were four men who were going to die just to stake out a crappy, piece-of-shit bar in a crappy, piece-of-shit neighborhood.

Oh well.

The girl came toward them, skipping down the road with her hands behind her back. Each hop carried her thirty or forty feet through the air. She didn't lose her rhythm or her balance; she was much more graceful than she had been in the past. Probably she had been practicing.

The four men watched her approach…frozen…eyes wide with fear and disbelief.

Lupe C. landed solidly at the entrance, coming to a stop.

Only then did those men attempt a defense, trying to aim their pistols, their efforts all sloppy and unprepared. In the end, the only shots fired were hers, the hands she had behind her back hiding the weapons she had acquired at some locale. Her aim was a bit wild, a bit erratic, but she was mentally prepared, she wasn't afraid, and she was shooting at very close range.

Four more bodies seeded their blood in the soil of La Ciudad.

The girl turned around and began skipping down the road…back the way she had come from. She seemed to be the only living human presence in a ramshackle ghost town. And soon she was also lost to sight.

Little Flor. I towered over her.

I think we were in the desert. I think we were in the desert at night. I think we were standing on opposite sides of a pit, the one from which Guadalupe Castaneda had risen from the dead.

Our eyes took their fill of each other.

Nearby…the sounds of explosions…the sounds of gunfire.

"They can't kill her and they can't stop her," said Flor. Her tone was that of someone discussing mild weather.

But in that moment, there was only one issue that I cared about.

"Why did you leave, Flor? I loved you."

Then there was a sudden defiance in those brown eyes. "You never told me you loved me."

That reply made horror pound in my heart, it woke me up out of yet another troubled dream. Hadn't I told her that I loved her back then… back in time…back in that real life? I could swear that I had.

But what if I hadn't?

A cold feeling of panic began creeping around. I couldn't remember for sure…couldn't remember if I had told her. I could no longer distinguish in my memory between "wanting to" and "doing." I thought I had told her.

But what if I hadn't?

I got up to see if the answer was in my mescal bottle. Maybe the scorpion could tell me.

The body had been tortured while the man was alive and desecrated after his demise.

I will spare you the details. If you don't live here, I'm sure you've heard stories about the way they do things down this way. And if you do live here, you don't need to be told these stories. Imagine the worst and you'll be in the right neighborhood.

That body had belonged to some poor sucker that they grabbed, just some sap from the neighborhood around Lucio's bar.

The brutality had been inflicted right there, out in the open. But all the doors and makeshift curtains stayed closed. There were no signs of life coming from any of those habitations. Those folks were getting better and better at pretending nobody was home…that nobody was there to see anything…or hear anything…or know anything.

They left the carcass on the dirt and gravel that passed for a street. And as they got ready to leave, Sanchez put a loudspeaker up to his mouth.

"Oh, this guy…the one we're leaving here…I guess he really didn't have anything to tell us. Too bad…too bad for him…and too bad for me that I chose so poorly…eh, pendejos!? But you know that I know that some of you know what I need to know. And you know that somebody is going to talk, either this way or another way, a little sooner or a little later, but somebody will talk. So why not come talk to us that other way? You know, the way where we're all nice and shit, a way that requires a little gratitude from us instead of our wrath, the way where you don't just walk away, but walk away with a lot of somethin' extra in your wallet. Just a few words, in private, between friends. Is that too much to be askin'?"

Silence was the response…a silence as dead as the man they'd killed. Unless you counted the hum of the flies that had already sensed the corpse.

Sanchez sighed loudly through his amplifier.

"See y'all soon, then."

And they drove away.

How do the police do their job in La Ciudad? They do it by trying to take a little bit of the action for themselves, just a dip into the cartel's barrel of cash. Just a little to look the other way, to stay inside the station or the car. And if you do go walking around, just keep walking past any smuggling, any dealing, or any flesh hustling you see. Go after a jaywalker, maybe a petty thief here and there, maybe a drunk and disorderly. Any amateur who might be willing to pay the fine up front.

And if anybody wanted a bigger dip?

That involved work.

As the sun set that evening, there were eight police officers hanging out in the station closest to Lucio's bar. They were playing cards, smoking, and drinking…because they were on duty. Even though the cells were empty, the heavy metal door sealed the entrance…locked and bolted. The word had come down to those guys…guys that took just the little dip…that the cartel didn't want any law enforcement on the streets in that area. No distractions to worry about when that girl finally got cornered and finished off, when her tricks and gimmicks finally failed her.

They didn't need or want any extra witnesses when that happened… not even witnesses that were on the payroll…not even witnesses who knew their lives would be worth spit if they talked.

Yeah, better to just stay in for the evening shift and collect the cash. And why not unplug the phones or take them off the hook? Why take any calls or complaints? Why give people any false hope that they'd be getting help if there was any sort of problem?

Besides, they had their cell phones in case anybody they cared about…or anybody important…needed to get hold of them.

So, when somebody began desperately pounding on the iron door with some sort of solid object, there was just a quick jolt of surprise and mutual glances of agreement to deliberately return to doing nothing of importance. They'd been given their instructions. You take the money, you'd better take the orders that go with it.

After it became clear that the door was staying shut, the banging stopped, and the ranking sergeant's cell phone let out a loud buzz. He glanced at the caller ID and a look of fear crossed his face as he rushed and fumbled to answer. "Yes! Yes! I'm here!" He listened for a few seconds to a voice yelling back at him and then lunged to release the mechanism of the door, allowing a small man in a very expensive suit to enter. The new arrival was holding the phone he had used to demand the sergeant let him in. He was also holding a revolver that had obviously been fired.

The panic in the man's voice was also obvious: "Shut the door! Shut the fucking door!"

That command was also promptly obeyed.

Once the entrance had been resecured, the man in the suit let out a deep sigh of relief and allowed himself to collapse into the closest chair. By now, everyone in the room had recognized him: Rodrigo Garcia. He was a local "manager" for the cartel, one of the guys who paid the real salaries of those police officers. A short man, pudgy and balding, and also a merciless killer whose normally reptilian eyes were wide with fear.

His suit was very, very nice, complete with flower and handkerchief. He normally sported an Al Capone–type hat to conceal his thinning hair, but he must have lost that touch of vanity in his panic.

He recovered himself and began issuing orders: "Get guns. Get your guns! Not your pistols but the heavy stuff." Then he paused to catch his breath again.

Nobody hesitated or questioned him. A couple of men quickly moved to obey, unlocking another metal door and passing around some heavy rifles, including one to Rodrigo.

"And aim for that bitch's head. She must have some kind of super body armor on."

One of the cops froze. "She?"

And another: "Who? Which she?"

And a third: "You mean…her?"

Fear seemed to suck all the air out of the room. There was sudden confusion and a flurry of glances among the cops.

Rodrigo was about to string some more words together…to try to regain the obedience that he could tell he was about to lose.

Those words never came because the men in that building were stopped cold by a massive impact that shook the foundation of the building and caused a crumple to form in the heavy steel door. Then there was silence. Those men all just stood stiffly and quietly, occupying space. The only noise came from a radio playing a corrido.

Seconds dripped down a black hole. Nobody made a move.

Then, another blow. The door shook and bent inward more. Plaster shook loose from the ceiling. Objects fell from desks and broke.

"That's really her? She's real?" somebody asked, finally breaking the spell and releasing them all to move, to seek cover wherever they could find it, to aim their weapons at the door.

A third blow. The power flickered. More of the ceiling fell in pieces. Some of the concrete was cracking around the doorway. The hinges were starting to fail.

Outside, on the other side of that door, the situation was comical. At least at first glance. The first time the building shook, the girl was punching that big metal barrier with her excessive strength. But because she was so much lighter than her target, the force of her blow had propelled her backward into the street and bounced her across it.

She smiled at the absurdity of the situation as she jumped up and strolled back to the station entrance. For her next two punches, she held onto the outer handle to anchor herself.

After the third impact, panic began to take control of the room, squeezing down on the men inside, those men whose eyes were riveted to that door, those men who managed to keep their fingers on the trigger, even with shaking hands.

"She is real," whispered the sergeant. "What does she want, Rodrigo?"

"Want? She wants to fucking kill me, you dumbass! What else!"

Whap. Without warning, smoothly and suddenly, the sergeant struck Rodrigo on the forehead with the butt of his rifle. Rodrigo collapsed to the ground, dropping the weapon he'd just been given. Another cop bent to pick it up so it would be out of reach. They all knew what decision had just been made, and they all agreed to it.

Rodrigo was floundering and stunned, still partly conscious, but unable to resist as the sergeant grabbed him by the arm and dragged him to the doorway. The latches and locks were already broken; all the sergeant had to do was pull it open.

The girl was standing there, looking just as surprised as the police officer. Rodrigo snapped out of it as the sergeant offered him to the girl. He tried to resist as she took his arm and pulled him to his feet. He tried to yell, but it caught in his throat. The sergeant didn't see what happened next because he shut the door and managed to half rebolt it. Then it was his turn to let out a loud exhalation and fall into a chair. Then he just waited…and waited…and waited…along with his men.

There was only silence. The brief siege was over.

"Back to work, men. If nobody else knows he was here, then nothing happened. Nothing at all."

In the morning, Rodrigo would still be out there. He was lying on his stomach, but his neck had been snapped, and his dead eyes were looking up at the bright-blue dawn of La Ciudad.

With greater frequency, bodies began turning up in strange places…or maybe they really weren't so strange. Alleys, dirty bathrooms, abandoned buildings, vacant lots on the outskirts of town…and always the bodies of men. Each of them seemed to have been killed with extremely excessive force or with some massive blunt instrument, the corpses twisted and posed in impossible positions. It was a macabre yoga. Predators were becoming prey. They were guys who had a reputation of sexual assault and rape, guys who had never been caught, guys who had bribed their way out of jail, guys with connections. But they all ended up getting wrong-placed and wrong-timed by the girl who is Death. She probably played their vile game: let them snatch her and take her to those places like any other victim. Then…no mercy.

And so, there was another whisper on the street that all those rapes, assaults, and robberies were diminishing. Were those predators afraid? Or were they being eliminated?

Civilians were keeping their heads down, with their eyes on the ground. The cartel was on the move. Don't see the evil, don't hear the evil…and especially don't speak about the evil. Nobody wanted to be seen speaking to me…or any other person who could have been described as a reporter…even if they were as domesticated as I was.

If I wanted privacy, I went to very public places, like my favorite bars, a coffee shop, or a restaurant. In any of those places, I would be left totally alone, a pariah, shunned.

Only furtively, in the middle of the here and the there, would people seek me out…in odd places. Or maybe they really weren't that odd. The dark places, the places in between—or just a late-night phone call—because in the end, they wanted to tell somebody their stories.

La Ciudad entered into new realms of absurdity. The population began to see the girl everywhere. Anytime a young woman was seen walking by herself…well, people would act according to their nature.

In blazing daylight, a short and chubby girl strode down the street with a determined look on her face. A girl that didn't resemble Lupe.

"It's her! It's her!" somebody screamed.

Maybe hell didn't break loose, but it definitely strained at its chains.

Among the men…or, at least, a certain type of man…there was a quiet panic. The gentlemen who liked to hang around and leer…the gentlemen who liked to make nasty comments…the fellows who might try to block a lady's way would suddenly excuse themselves to go inside or duck down around a corner.

Guys who were known to maybe, once in a while, give the back of a hand to wife or girlfriend, got a sudden look of fear and stumbled and fumbled to get out of her path and out of her sight before she got closer.

All amusing in its dark way.

The young woman, the non-Guadalupe, kept walking and ignored the bustle and the hustle going on around her. Soon she was the one who was out of sight.

"That wasn't her!" someone else shouted.

"How do you know?"

"I saw her…the real one…leaving Lucio's place!"

Silence.

Then life began to return to normal, at least on that street.

were some things I wouldn't know, wouldn't dream, wouldn't see until much later. But I will weave those events into this narrative…weave them into this story where they belong. One of the most important of these hidden tales, perhaps the most important, would be Lupe's encounter with a man known as Juan El Bautista…and what happened to him afterwards.

Not so far away, the real Lupe was standing on a street corner.

She'd been standing on that corner for quite a while, standing very still, letting the sun move her shadow across the cement. She hadn't bothered with a change of clothing. She was dirty, her hair was tangled. People probably thought she was homeless, but at least she wasn't asking for money. Nobody seemed to recognize her, or if they did…well, they just kept moving.

And she just kept on standing there as the day started to show its signs of ending.

She was using herself as bait, trying to see if anybody would fuck with her.

Nobody did, maybe because the word was already getting around that there was this girl…this girl who wasn't what she seemed…this girl who is Death in disguise.

Yet in the end, there were a few people who weren't with the program, hadn't heard the rumors or didn't believe them.

People who couldn't resist the opportunity to try to conduct business as usual.

A police car pulled up to the curb. Two cops were inside, two of the ones who liked to pick up the extra work, the dirty work.

"Hey, cutie," said the one at the wheel, the younger one. "You're going to have to come down to the station with us. Loitering…that's a crime around here!" He had trouble keeping a straight face as he said it.

Lupe ignored him, looking first at the ground and then looking up in the air, but never at the man who was talking to her.

"She fucked up? Or just stupid?" the driver asked his partner, the older and fatter one, who was chewing gum.

"Don't matter, she's still loitering," replied the second. "Like you said, a crime."

They both snorted.

Then stiffly, with a slight groan, the older cop got out of the squad car, walked around to the other side, and opened up the back door as he spat his wad of gum on the ground with a sloppy splat. "There's the easy way or there's the hard way."

In that moment, the girl chose to meet his gaze as she considered her options. They didn't know it, but for them that was the moment of life or death, their own lives and their own deaths hanging in the balance…a judgment that was now out of their hands.

Lupe clenched her fists and then released them, still just gazing at the man.

The cop was starting to get irritated, starting to get mad, starting to get ready to lay down the heavy hand. "There's some people who want to meet you and they ain't got all day," he said, his tone becoming threatening as his hand began to move toward his baton.

Lupe's own intense expression was suddenly softened by curiosity. These two wanted to move her up the food chain? That caught her interest. With a smile, she strode to the car and hopped into that back seat like a kid going on an excursion instead of someone being arrested. Then she just sat there expectantly, getting comfortable, palms resting on her legs. Her behavior confused the cops for a moment, the older one hesitating for a second before shutting the door on his prisoner.

The younger one snickered. "Too bad all of them aren't so eager!"

They took her down to the station.

But they didn't take her in through the main entrance, they didn't book her, they didn't check for identification. They didn't even ask her name.

Instead, in a furtive way, they took her in through an alley entrance.

Lupe walked with them willingly, not showing any resistance.

The younger cop opened the door to the jail for her. "C'mon, cutie. You're being so nice we didn't even cuff you!"

"She probably wants the free meal," said the older cop with a laugh.

Bypassing anything that seemed official, moving down what looked like secondary hallways, the trio reached the entrance to the cell blocks. A guy at the desk just nodded to the newcomers and buzzed them in. Whatever was going on was definitely off the books…no paperwork, no fingerprints. Most of the prisoners were men, and they just looked away as Lupe was led past them. Then there were empty cells, but those two cops just had Lupe continue to walk…all the way to the back…to the last cell on the left.

The door was open, so Lupe walked in on her own, sat on a bottom bunk, and watched them lock her in.

"See ya, cutie," said the young one as the two men turned to leave. "Your ride will be here soon!"

Lupe just watched them leave, with an air of disappointment. It was probably hard to let them go, but it was the only way to find out what was really going on, the only way to move up the line, the only way to hunt some bigger prey.

Totally alone, she decided to lie down.

There was nothing to do but wait.

Time went by.

It was almost dark.

A young guard made his way down to the end, all the way down to Lupe's cell, constantly looking over his shoulder. He stopped there and stared in at her…and kept staring. But he wasn't gawking as much as he seemed swept up into a turmoil of thoughts.

Lupe ignored him, staring up at the ceiling.

The guard didn't leave, didn't move…he just kept on standing there.

Finally, Lupe turned her head toward him to give him a glance. He was flushed, his uniform was starting to show sweat stains, his hands were trembling slightly. The badge he wore didn't seem to suit him. Nothing about the situation seemed to suit him.

When their eyes met, that young guard made the decision he'd been struggling with.

"I have to get you out of here before they come to take you away."

Lupe appeared puzzled for a second; she wasn't expecting to meet a decent person in that place.

"I have to get you out of here. I need to find the key. I'll get the key and come back to give you dinner. Somehow, I'll have to sneak you out. If I can, it'll be okay because you aren't even arrested, you aren't even here officially. If I can just get you out of the cellblock, you'll have a chance to escape. You have to escape. It's your only hope!"

Lupe shook her head no.

"You don't understand…they're…"

Lupe put a finger to her lips, asking for silence as she rolled off the bunk and onto her feet.

The young man was confused by her reaction and did fall silent. She approached him…they were almost face-to-face. Involuntarily, he took a step back. Lupe grabbed a cell bar firmly in one hand to hold herself steady. Using her other hand, she touched a second bar with her index finger, pushing slightly until the metal creaked and began to bend.

His eyes widened. "You're…her," he whispered in awe.

She put her finger to her lips again.

He nodded.

She motioned for him to leave.

He nodded again and started to comply, but then turned back. "They'll be taking you to Juan El Bautista."

Lupe considered those words for a moment and then just shrugged and smiled.

The young man returned the smile, nodded a third time, and then left her alone again.

Juan El Bautista was also known as El Bautista del Fuego. Nobody knew what his real name was, perhaps not even him. He was another one of the Boss's enforcers. Master of the fiery baptism: that was the name he'd made for himself. It came from his way of torturing and killing his victims. He would truly baptize them, but instead of sprinkling water on their foreheads, Juan preferred gasoline, followed immediately by a match.

Was it a sick joke at first? Perhaps, but as time went by, Juan began to take it seriously. He began saying that his baptism of fire was a ritual, a ritual in the true sense of the word, something sacred. But it wasn't a rite that purified the victim, it wasn't a rite that protected a person from sin; it was only a rite that made Juan's own sins more pure—more unmixed—distilling them down to some vile essence.

And that purity of sin became his obsession.

El Bautista started claiming that it was his sacred mission to discover what he called the absolute sin.

Juan began to talk openly about the strange and dark gods who wanted to gain entry to our realm and to our world. He said he wanted to open the gate, that he wanted to let them in, that it was his personal destiny to do it. But to open the gate, he had to discover and commit that absolute sin. And if he could do it, they would reward him. They would transform him into one of themselves; he would become a god.

He began to preach his new religion.

He started to experiment with more elaborate human sacrifices. He took his inspirations from the times of the Aztecs, which Juan started referring to as the good old days.

I'll spare you what I know of the details.

And at first there seemed to be no reason that he couldn't get away with it because, like I already said, he was one of the Boss's boys, like Sanchez.

Yet even by the loose standards of La Ciudad, he was beginning to scare the people on the street much, much too much. It wasn't just a question anymore of personal style, a signature flair when making a kill. And people were hearing about that weird narco cult outside the city, even in other countries. It was getting press in El Norte.

It was starting to overshadow the Boss, and it was starting to overshadow the operation.

Something had to be done.

But Juan wasn't eliminated. A man like him could still have his uses.

Instead, the Boss sent Juan El Bautista out into the wilderness, bought him a ranch, bought him a lot more land around it, far out from La Ciudad and miles from the main roads. Juan was going to be out in the middle of his own nowhere. Out there, he could do whatever he wanted and with much more privacy. His reputation and the rumors that it generated would keep everyone away, even the few law enforcement types who might not have turned the blind eye. And with all that territory, with Juan to watch over it, the Boss could set up quite a few covert operations that would be hidden by all of that fear and all of that distance.

Out in the wilderness, out in the desert, a fire burned. Other than the stars, it was the only light in all the darkness. That fire was imprisoned in a pit, covered by the metal grates placed over it. There was the sizzle of flesh being carelessly cooked, the pieces too large, burning on the outside and raw on the inside. Even the most casual examination would have revealed that those cuts of meat were human…two legs and two arms… hands and feet still attached.

A metal spike had been set up at one end of the pit, with a human's head stuck on top of it. That head had definitely seen better days. One side still retained the features of a man who might have once been considered handsome, but the other side had been badly smashed up… the jaw and cheekbones crushed and the eye missing, leaving a gaping socket. Ooze dripped from the severed neck, covering the shaft of metal that sustained it three feet above the flames.

On the other side of the pit, facing the head on the spike, a solitary man sat on the ground in Lotus Pose. He wore a cloak with a hood that covered his face, his hands resting in his lap. He seemed to be in deep meditation. After some time passed, he began to chant…a deep and ominous-sounding chant in some unknown language. Or wait, maybe I recognized it…wasn't it Enochian, the so-called language of the angels? I couldn't be completely certain, there was no way I could tell in those moments of vision and dream, but I would have been willing to bet I was right.

With what could have been more of a reflex than an intentional act, his hand shot forward. Wearing a fireproof glove of some sort, he seized one of the roasting arms by its own hand and yanked it off that atrocity of a barbecue. Taking the severed end of the arm in his other, also protected hand, he bit deep into the triceps, tearing away a big chunk of the flesh, a smoking morsel that probably burned the lining of his own mouth. But if there was any pain, he just ignored it as he kept chewing and chewing. It must have been a bit gamy.

Muttering with his mouth still full, but with words I could understand: "Sin, sin, sin, sin…what sin do I have to commit that will please you? What sin do I have to commit to hear you speak to me? What sin do I have to commit to get your blessings? How many sins must I commit?" It sounded like a litany, a prayer that had been repeated many times.

The only immediate response was the crackle of the fire and the sound of continued chewing.

Then…something strange, something beyond strange, began to happen.

The cannibal, lost in his own thoughts and dark prayers, seemed unaware of what was occurring. But that head mounted up on the other side of the fire pit began to twitch…it began to throb and pulsate. The intact eye opened…opened wide…almost as if it were startled…almost as if it were shocked by what it saw. And even though that head appeared to have once belonged to a darker-skinned Mexican, the iris of that eye was a bright green…a green that had its own weird glow…a shade of green that didn't seem to belong to the natural world.

And on the other side of the fire, the man who sat in Lotus Pose swallowed his offering and fell back into his own grim meditations.

The eye in the severed head regarded him for several moments with a glint of amusement. A condescending smile fought to achieve itself against the rictus of those dead lips.

The cannibalistic monk still didn't notice what was happening, and his head was bowed as he began to chant again. He spoke so softly now that most of what he said was unintelligible. Only a few words could be made out: "Sin, sin, sin, sin…what sin…"

The mouth of the severed head opened and shut a couple of times…the tongue protruding…the jaw moving back and forth as if it were a mechanical device someone was trying to operate by trial and error. Then that someone found the right groove and the head began to speak. But even though that head was definitely masculine, the voice that emerged was unmistakably that of a woman. It was a voice that spoke clear and loud, with an odd accent, both pleasant and sinister at the same time. And it was a voice that I recognized.

"What sin do you think you can commit that no one, no other human creature in all of your so-called history, has ever thought of before?"

That question burst out of nowhere in the quiet desert night, taking the meditating man by surprise. He dropped the smoldering arm and was instantly up on his feet, a gun in one of his gloved hands as he looked for the source of that voice. Only when the head laughed at him did he realize the source of his shock…staring with a slack jaw at that one green eye, which was examining him intently. Unable to find words, he gawked at the head as his weapon trembled slightly in his grasp.

"Get yourself together. I thought this was what you wanted: a message from the realms beyond!"

When Juan El Bautista finally managed to get a firm grip on his words as well as his gun, all he could manage to ask was, "Why do you speak like a woman?"

The laugh was harsher, more mocking the second time. "If you would like to take the time to find a head that would be more appropriate for me to speak through, I would be happy to wait for you. But I must admit, I expected more from someone who has begged and prayed for this moment for oh so long!"

In that moment, Juan found his pride again, the mastery of himself, regaining not just his bearings but also his sense of destiny. You could see the moment of realization on his face. You could see the sudden awareness that his destiny had found him, that it was time to embrace it…you could see him taking the words of that voice into his evil heart. He stood up straighter, almost at attention, as he put the gun back in its concealed holster. "No, that will not be necessary. Speak to me from this vessel."

"Gracious of you. Listen up. I don't have time to sweet-talk you, Juan El Bautista. My time in your time is short…this time. But you're going to help me change that. You've wanted this, you've worked for it… for years you've worked for it. Well, you managed to get my attention and now I'm here. So, it's your moment to rise or to fall, to embrace this destiny or to deny it. And if you do refuse me, you can be sure I will find somebody else to do what needs to be done, and you can be sure I will make you pay! If you want to play in the big game, I will tell you what you need to do and you will do it. Agreed?"

There was no hesitation. "Yes."

"Good. First, something is coming to you, coming tonight. It's something that is going to kill you. After that, there will be some things I need you to do, so listen carefully…."

Lupe sat in her isolated cell as night took full command of La Ciudad. She never saw the young guard again, the one who had wanted to help her. But there wasn't really any reason for him to show himself again. He knew she didn't need any help.

Down the corridor she heard the sounds of the shift change.

Another guard soon appeared, the only other one she would see. Smirking, he brought her some food.

She didn't touch it or even go near it. Eating seemed optional for her. She just left it there to get colder and nastier, drawing flies. An astute observer might even have noticed that none of those insects tried to fly near the young woman who continued to sit quietly in her confinement.

What would Samurai Sanchez have thought, what would the whole host of assassins cruising the city looking for her have thought, if they'd known the girl they were hunting was already in custody? What if they'd known she was in that jail, in the hands of cops who would have gladly let them take her?

I can only assume that they would have been pissed off.

I can only assume that they would have rushed to that police station.

And I can only assume that there would have been a massacre.

But they never found out. Nobody suspected that the silent, passive, frail-looking girl was The Girl.

Time passed. Lupe folded her legs up into a Lotus Pose as she unknowingly copied Juan El Bautista, miles away at his sacred fire. Her face became a blank. She wasn't asleep, more like in a trance, her body immobile.

More time passed. Without warning, two brutal types wearing police uniforms were at her door. Whether they were really cops, there was no way to know, but they had the key to that cell.

It opened with a loud slam.

The two men became a bit disconcerted when the girl didn't acknowledge them, when she didn't even react.

"Did they grab us some autistic bitch?" asked one.

The other didn't answer. Maybe he didn't even understand the question. Instead, he just directed his harsh words to the prisoner. "Time to go, puta."

At that, Lupe did look up at the men, deadpan. Without rushing, she unfolded her legs and stood up. Then she just stood and waited.

They handcuffed her.

One laughed. The other grabbed her roughly by an arm and dragged her out into the hallway. Lupe looked down, letting her hair cover her face so they wouldn't see her smile.

They were about to deliver her the head of Juan El Bautista on a silver platter.

◈

And Juan's night was still far from over. To tell the truth, it had barely begun. It wasn't like he had ever been an early-to-bed, early-to-rise kind of guy, anyway. He was far too excited to sleep…and he wasn't sure he would ever need to sleep again.

After all, he was no longer an ordinary human being.

The dark deities, or at least one of them, had granted him a gift.

Juan glanced at the decapitated head. It was once again inert, just dead and sagging flesh. No living green eye peered back at him. Still, he waited patiently, wishing to make sure, wishing to be certain that she was truly gone. He wanted to test what that voice had told him, but his intuition was telling him to wait until he was convinced that her presence had receded from the world, in case she would be offended by anything less than 100 percent trust.

So, he sat back down into Lotus Pose and waited, letting the meat on the fire become blacker and blacker, letting more time pass.

Finally, he took his gloves off and held his hands up so he could gaze at them. A pale nimbus of fire played around the tips of his fingers, coils of tiny, green-tinted flames circled around those digits as he stretched them apart and flexed them, the fire just barely visible but definitely there. His expression became one of rapture.

Only then did he stand up, with one last quick nod to the lifeless head.

He began to half dance, half spin around, swept up in his celebrations, laughing loudly and also weeping.

"This is a holy place," he said.

"This is a holy place!" he shouted.

"I am the grail that has been filled with the blood of the night!"

Suddenly, he plunged to his knees before the bonfire and knocked away the burned and roasted limbs. With his naked hands, he seized the metal grill, yanked it up, and tossed it easily aside. Taking a deep breath, he then plunged those hands deep and deeper into the flames, just holding them there, just holding them there longer.

And he felt no pain and they did not burn.

So, he kept holding them there, a mad grin on his face. And even as his sleeves began to burn, his skin remained intact, undamaged and unharmed in any way.

"Yes, it is true," he whispered to himself, calmed by his own awe. "I have received the true baptism and I will die, just as She has foretold." His voice grew louder, triumphant. "But then I will rise. And it won't fucking take me three days to do it!"

The men led Lupe out the back, into the alley behind the jail, the same way she had been brought in. There were no objections to the removal of the prisoner. In fact, everyone else had simply looked away, ignoring her departure. In the dark, that alley seemed far more dangerous. Dirty and littered with trash, it filled the night air with odors that combined sewage and rot in ways that couldn't really be described. Lupe made a face of revulsion. Apparently, her sense of smell was still human. Her escorts lit up cigarettes, partly just to blunt the reek, as they indicated that she should stop walking, that she should wait there with them.

It wasn't a long wait. An old bus was rattling toward them, so old and beat up that it didn't even seem like it should be running. It stopped right where Lupe and the two cops stood, and the driver opened the door for the trio…and that was the only acknowledgment that grim-looking man gave to his new passengers. He didn't even nod to the cops as they brought Lupe on board.

There were already three other passengers, three men. Like the girl, they were cuffed and they were also shackled to their seats. They all had the aspect of being dangerous men…dangerous men who had gotten on the bad side of somebody even more dangerous. None of them acknowledged the new arrivals, either. They just lowered their faces, more with resignation than fear.

Perhaps because of some slight instinct of propriety, the two cops took Lupe all the way to the back of the bus, far from the other captives.

"Sit."

She obeyed, letting them shackle her without resisting.

One of them stared at her for a few moments, struggling with some evil temptation. If he'd given in to it, events might have taken a different course. Juan's moment of destiny might have been delayed. Maybe it would never have arrived at all.

Instead, the man shook his head, and the two cops quickly filed off the bus.

The driver shut the door. With a jolt, still shaking and still rattling, the vehicle started on its ominous journey.

Lupe gazed out the window, still faintly smiling as La Ciudad passed by.

Juan El Bautista continued to sit near his bonfire, which still blazed. His eyes watched the dead eye of the decapitated head across the flames. It remained inanimate, the green long gone. He wasn't expecting that woman's voice to speak through it again, but he still wasn't quite ready to give up the vigil. He still wanted some time to digest what he'd learned, as well as the flesh he'd chewed. So, he maintained his Lotus Pose, letting his mind be entranced by the blaze for minutes and minutes that flowed toward an hour. Every now and then he would cackle…every now and then a mad grin would take hold of his face.

Then suddenly, the malice returned to his eyes, and he stood up with a strange grace. He glanced at the head one last time and shouted, "I am ready!"

Almost immediately, four disciplined men emerged from a nearby building. They were leading a prisoner, another man, hands bound in front of him, a hood over his head. He walked with them of his own accord, not needing to be pushed or prodded, only requiring a little guidance from his captors. They brought that man directly up to Juan, who was examining his hands again, as if he'd just gotten a new pair.

The prisoner just stood there, awaiting his fate.

The four guards became a bit confused. A usual pattern of events wasn't being followed. Why was their leader more interested in his hands than in the victim they had brought to him?

Juan seemed to remember that something was expected of him. "Kneel," he ordered absentmindedly, still peering at his fingers.

The man stayed on his feet, a muffled but defiant voice emerging from beneath that hood: "Just get it over with, just kill me…or whatever you plan to do!"

"Make him kneel," said Juan, becoming more engaged in the process, now annoyed by the disobedience.

One of the four smiled, then gave the prisoner a very well-placed kick to the back of the leg. The man fell to his knees, trying to keep silent but unable to hold in a grunt of pain.

"Do you want me to get the gasoline, sir?" one of the men asked with a little too much enthusiasm.

"No," replied Juan, his voice becoming more dreamy as he regained his fascination with his fingers. His four men began to show discomfort, not sure what was expected of them. They were expecting Juan to be far more aggressive. So, they just waited for orders, shuffling their feet slightly.

"Take his hood off," Juan finally commanded them.

That was promptly done. The face that was revealed could just as easily have belonged to one of the four…if he'd just chosen a different employer. He had the air of a man who was in that same line of work. He had probably dished out a lot of what he was now being given. His expression was resigned, stoic as he prepared for a brutish death. There was no point in begging for his life. Everybody knew that sort of thing didn't work with Juan El Bautista. It could only make things worse, much worse.

Juan bent down, getting eye to eye with the prisoner, their noses almost touching. The man held himself steady, doing his best not to flinch, trying not to show fear. But El Bautista's breath prompted just a trace of aversion to show on the captive's face.

"You are a very blessed and fortunate son," Juan said so quietly that only the man could make out his words, as if he were trying to keep it a secret from the four who worked for him. "You are going to receive the true and pure baptism of fire."

"Fuck off with that!" the prisoner suddenly yelled right into Juan's face. "Everybody knows about your 'baptism of fire'…you've been doing it for years! Bring it! Where's the gasoline? Or do you just want to shove me facedown into your bonfire?"

Juan stood back up, angry for a moment, and then snickered. "No, my friend, not everybody has heard. Not everyone has heard of this!" His tone had almost become that of a teacher lecturing a student who didn't understand some simple concept. Then he studied his fingers again and saw that the almost invisible halo of mystic fire had returned to play around the tips. The kneeling man didn't see it. The four other men didn't see it. But Juan saw it and was relieved. The gift that had been given by the woman's voice was real.

Tentatively, his hand beginning to shake with the intensity, with the excitement, Juan touched the prisoner right in the middle of his forehead with his index finger…just for a second. Then he took his hand away, his face illuminated by the glee he felt. "I can tell that it will work!" he said, mostly to himself.

The gesture only made the kneeling man more enraged. "What the fuck are you doing? Quit acting like a jackass and finish this shit! Kill me!"

"Done," replied Juan, placing his finger back on the man's forehead, pushing a little, then pushing harder.

That man was about to say something else, but the words got caught in his throat, his eyes widened…and he let out an awful scream, a shriek of agony that made Juan's men step back. And they were men who had heard a lot of screams.

Yet very quickly, the sounds of pain were reduced to a faint gurgling. The prisoner's knees folded under his weight, and he settled onto his butt.

Juan had followed his victim down to the ground. And Juan's face lit up even more, like a delighted child who had received the most wonderful birthday present he could ever have imagined.

A clear fluid began to trickle out of the victim's ears.

A clear fluid began to flow out of the victim's eye-sockets…because his eyes had melted.

Juan finally pulled his finger away. Some of the man's skin came with it, pulled into a long, greasy strand that looked like a string of melted cheese dangling from a slice of hot pizza.

The man was already dead as his face began to bubble and blister and emit steam. The corpse fell face forward.

Juan laughed.

His four men backed away even farther.

Their fear made Juan laugh louder.

"It's just going to get better, amigos!"

Only the headlights of the bus illuminated the rugged road that it traveled on…and not very well. At times, the road seemed more like a trail, but the driver knew the way and he drove faster than most people would have deemed safe. There were many sharp curves and steep ups and downs. Most of the way was so rough that the bus was constantly shaking and bouncing, making the trip very uncomfortable for the prisoners, at least the human ones. The driver fully accepted the challenge, charging from one jolt to another as the three shackled men couldn't stifle their groans. And even that driver would mumble a curse now and again when not all of his wheels were in contact with the ground.

Lupe just sat silently, taking each bounce and lurch without resisting. None of that mattered to her.

All she cared about was the end of that journey.

Juan stepped toward his four men, using his pants to wipe off the goo that was still sticking to his finger. They reflexively stepped back again. But that only amused their boss. He enjoyed their fear as he looked back at the body, a trace of vapor fleeing the holes where the eyes had been.

He turned back toward his men and chuckled. "Stand still or I will kill you with the same holy fire."

Juan stepped forward again, and this time the men forced themselves not to retreat. But they couldn't conceal their nervousness.

"Excellent, you have balls after all! Now listen to me. Tonight is going to be different. Tonight is a very special night for me. They are bringing me a girl, a very special girl. I know that I promised you a girl, but your fun will have to wait. Like I said, this girl is for me. When she arrives, you will immediately bring her to this place. No fun and no games this time. I will owe that to you. Just bring her here to this zone of sacrifice. Do not be rough. In fact, be respectful…just escort her to me. But if the other offerings give you any trouble, do what you want. Then tell the bus driver to wait, that you will be returning, that you will be going back to town with him. I want to be all alone with my guest. Understand?"

The four nodded, mumbling their assent. They looked more relieved than disappointed.

"Good. Go greet the bus. It should be here soon."

All four quickly obeyed.

Juan sat back down by his fire, facing that head that had been so full of esoteric promises, trying to meditate, trying to control his excitement.

From time to time, a bonfire could be seen burning in the distance.

What could still maybe be called a road was taking the bus in that general direction. One headlight of the bus had gone out. The one that remained was barely able to reveal a coyote hustling to get out of the way as a rise of small hills obscured the view of the fire for just awhile.

Lupe kept looking out into the night, immune to the effects of the shocks and jolts and pitches. Then the bus rounded a sharp bend, taking it too fast, and suddenly skidded to a halt.

The bonfire was in sight again, perhaps a hundred yards away, perhaps two hundred.

Four men waited nearby. They had the look of narco men, but their expressions showed a mix of fear and of gratitude for the arrival of the bus.

"You need to wait. We're going to be going back with you after we make the delivery," one of those four said to the driver.

That man behind the wheel nodded, maintaining a sense of neutrality. He was probably the only one of Juan's men who thought things were going along the same way they always did.

All the prisoners, including Lupe, were unshackled from their seats but left in their handcuffs. The man who came for the girl examined her closely for a few moments before unlocking her chains, trying to figure out why El Bautista cared so much. She just kept her head down. He didn't see anything special about her.

"Let's go."

She stood, still avoiding his gaze, still being docile.

He told her to get off the bus with the others. She quickly complied, a perfect model of someone resigned to her fate.

"Have fun, babe," said the driver, smirking, as she stepped out of the vehicle.

Lupe didn't raise her eyes, but she did give him a small nod.

The captives were led toward the roaring fire.

A man sat near those flames. Not so far from him was a severed head that had been mounted on some kind of rod. Various body parts were strewn around that area. The male prisoners didn't falter, not wanting to show anything less than courage, but their faces were very grim. Lupe was last in line, staring intently at the man who stood as they drew nearer. He wore what appeared to be a tattered brown cape with a hood pulled up. The face was concealed by shadow, but the eyes seemed to shine with their own light as he walked around the firepit to meet his guests. Was this Juan El Bautista? she wondered. Or someone else who was about to be collateral damage?

The man patted the decapitated head and took a few more steps toward the group that was being lined up before him as his grin became visible.

"Hello, my friends. Welcome! This is a very special day for me, and it will be for you as well. Come forward, don't be shy!" His tone was jovial, but also filled with the falseness of a man running a booth at a carnival.

There could be no doubt now that this was Juan.

The guards shoved and prodded the male prisoners forward. Fear was beginning to assert itself, beginning to hold the male captives back. Even Juan's men weren't eager to get too close to him. Only the girl stepped closer without encouragement, and El Bautista's eyes immediately focused on her. Was that a tremor in his hands?

He crossed his arms to regain control, now facing the row of prisoners from about ten feet away.

"You may leave us," Juan said quietly to his men.

There was a moment of confusion, but then those men quickly complied, turning and retreating back toward the bus. They knew what they had been told. They knew what they had seen.

The three male captives were baffled. Why was Juan sending his men away? He didn't have a weapon and, even handcuffed, three men could probably take on one man and win. You could see the wheels beginning to turn in their heads. Was this some trick? Or did they have a chance?

Lupe just continued to examine Juan, not feeling any need to save those three men, knowing what they were, and waiting to see what would happen next.

Without warning, Juan eagerly rushed forward and grabbed one of the men by both shoulders. "Are you ready to receive my blessing?"

That first man wasn't prepared to receive anything, but he was prepared to offer something…slamming his forehead directly into Juan's nose. There was a loud crack as El Bautista's head snapped back. The prisoner collapsed onto all fours; he'd stunned even himself.

Juan didn't fall, but he staggered. It took him a few seconds to regain his balance and stand up straight again. The other two men were prepared to continue the attack that their companion had started…until they were frozen in place by what they saw next.

El Bautista's nose had been smashed, yet there was no blood. Instead, plumes of smoke were gushing out of his ruined nostrils, rising into the air, and being absorbed into the starry sky as his laughter filled the night.

Lupe continued to watch intently, unmoving, her own eyes showing surprise.

As one last big puff of smoke escaped his nostrils, Juan reached down and lifted his attacker back up onto his feet. The man tottered, still trying to regain his senses. Juan didn't give him the time. Instead, he seized that man's head with both hands, the strange flames whirling around his fingers now clearly visible. A scream instantly died in the man's throat, replaced by a loud snapping sound and then an even louder whistling noise as a cloud of…something…burst out of his head. The contents of his skull had been vaporized and pressurized, breaking the bone to escape…only to quickly condense back into a slimy drizzle that splattered over Juan, the ground, and the two other men. El Bautista pulled his hands away, along with clotted filaments of melted flesh and wads of smoldering hair. The body tried to fall but ended up being suspended like a giant puppet by those grotesque, thick strings. Juan savagely whipped his hands back, breaking those cords, and then the new corpse fell backward.

Lupe had stepped back just in time to get out of range, avoiding the tiny drops of flying goo as she snapped the chain that linked her arms. Her face showed no fear, just a vivid curiosity. This was no ordinary enemy. Now she knew she was facing something just as unnatural as she was.

The two surviving men tried to run. Juan, with swift skill, kicked the legs of one out from under him, and the captive fell face forward. The other was gaining distance until the master of the property reached behind his back and produced a pistol he'd been concealing. He hit the man in the back with a couple of well-aimed bullets. The victim might have died before he hit the ground, because he didn't move again.

"I don't want to waste a lot of time on you fools," Juan muttered, bending to grab the man he'd tripped by the back his neck. Then he looked at Lupe, smiling, as that cranium nearly exploded…releasing its contents.

Lupe stepped back again to avoid the gruesome shower, absentmindedly snapping the metal rings off her wrists.

Juan stood back up, ecstatic, with his face covered in liquid brain.

The two inhuman antagonists regarded each other for a while, the ruined bodies between them. It was the first time that Juan had a real chance to examine the girl. He seemed to be deciding if he should be annoyed, because she didn't look the part for which she'd been cast. But then, all at once, he smiled again and tossed his pistol aside.

"Hello, hermanita. Welcome. I already know who you are. I already know that a gun means nothing to you." He crossed his arms, waiting to see what she would do…if anything.

Lupe continued to gaze back at Juan, studying him, trying to figure out what she was up against. She looked almost pleased at the thought of fighting something that could actually put up a fight. Her face showed that she was more intrigued than intimidated. She also seemed to be in no hurry, savoring those moments before the inevitable combat.

Finally, Juan held out his arms. "Come forth, mija. You have been foretold to me. Come and accept the baptism of fire…the one and the true baptism of fire that only I can offer!"

Lupe gave a little shrug and stepped over the bodies until she was directly in front of El Bautista. They were almost the same height. She leaned in, almost allowing her nose to touch his. That abrupt and hostile intimacy startled him and he had to resist recoiling.

For a second…two seconds…three seconds they stared each other in the eye. Her eyes contained a darkness, his contained a fire.

Then, gently, Juan took her face between his hands, almost as if he were going to pull her those last inches forward to kiss her. Instead, he held her still as a red halo played around his fingers, swirling up his forearms and Lupe's cheeks and then her entire head…her hair moving as if caught in a breeze.

She smiled.

And nothing happened.

He concentrated harder and his strange fires burned brighter.

And nothing happened.

Then Lupe put her hands on Juan's shoulders, also gently, as if comforting a friend.

Juan suddenly tried to give her head a ruthless twist that would have broken a bull's neck. But Lupe's head didn't budge a millimeter and there was no crack of bone.

"So, it's true," he said with a gasp, more in awe than fear. "So, it's true," he repeated with amazement but not disbelief as the mystic flames of El Bautista formed a vortex around the two of them.

Lupe moved her hands to grip each side of his head and began to twist it. Juan resisted, his flesh and bone giving only a little. Any normal human would have been killed instantly.

"It's true!" he exclaimed joyfully through his exertion.

Lupe began to use more of her strength.

Juan maintained his own grip, a mad smile on his face, as his unnatural fires swept around them, growing brighter.

Lupe twisted harder.

That was the moment when Juan's neck snapped, his head turning completely to face behind him, the dying eyes becoming wide, the man surprised by death's arrival.

El Bautista's flames were instantly extinguished.

She let go and stood still.

Juan's body continued to stand, the hands dropping from Lupe's head. The body teetered, it seemed about to fall…and then it clumsily began to turn until the wobbly head once again faced the girl. Their eyes met one last time. His lips still smiling as those eyes began to close. Then the face went slack, and the body staggered backward and fell into the fire pit.

Lupe watched as that ordinary fire began to engulf the deceased, roasting the flesh, setting the clothing on fire. Her expression had become one of near disappointment, as if she'd hoped for more of a challenge. Then she turned away. She started to walk back toward the bus.

The severed head shuddered. Its one eye opened, again alive, again a brilliant green as it slowly turned on the metal rod with a slight crunching sound to watch Lupe leave. It turned again to look down at Juan with a smile of satisfaction.

Then the eye closed.

The face went dead.

And Juan continued to burn.

Lupe was no longer in a mood to play around.

When she got back to the bus, the motor was still running. The driver was standing behind the bus, zipper down, urinating. He never saw her, never knew he was going to die. She grabbed him by the back of the neck and crushed that neck instantly. He was just another body dropping to the ground.

The back door of the vehicle was unlocked. Lupe hopped up, opened it, and entered.

Juan's men were sitting near the front, quietly waiting to leave, still unnerved by what they had seen…each lost in his own thoughts about the events of that evening. The old engine was so loud, its vibrations so strong, that it masked any sounds of the girl's arrival…not that it would have mattered if they'd had more warning. And when they did see her rushing at them from the back of the bus, it was definitely too late.

In less than a minute, more bodies hit the ground as she tossed them out of the vehicle.

Lupe was about to exit as well, but then on a whim changed her mind, picked up a couple of pistols that had been dropped in the massacre, and sat down in the driver's seat, putting her hands on the wheel. It was quite possible that she had never learned to drive, or even tried to drive any kind of vehicle in her short life…her normal life… let alone a bus, with its complicated clutch. She sat there for a while, contemplating everything, before making the attempt. Yet she did seem to have some idea of how to do it, perhaps from watching the drivers of all the other buses she had ridden in.

Ironic or not, it took her much longer to get that vehicle moving than it had taken to kill all those men who had been expecting to take that ride. With many false starts, engine deaths, jerks and jolts—and with a smile—Lupe eventually managed to begin driving back down the dirt road, back toward La Ciudad.

The flames raged around Juan's body, quickly burning away his clothing. At first, his flesh began to roast just like any meat, but then there was a change. It began to melt and bubble, transforming into something that looked like a reddish, liquefied plastic, which flowed and filled the fire pit and smothered it with a loud *whoosh*. The blaze almost seemed to be absorbed into the mess that had once been El Bautista, causing it to radiate a neon crimson in the darkness that had reconquered that little corner of the night.

For a few minutes, the mass was stilled, steam rising from it, the glow beginning to fade. Then the melting effect began to reverse itself, pulling back together, regaining its shape…or most of it. The outlines of a human form had been restored, but it was still extremely deformed… like a wax figure placed in an oven…a life-size figure.

The corpse, if it was a corpse, continued to lie still. Now the darkness was almost total, except for starlight and a faint red halo that shimmered around that form. Only then did it begin to move, trying to get up. At first the effort was agonized and difficult. Unable to stand, it managed to crawl out of the pit as the joints of the arms and legs began to recreate themselves. Fingers separated themselves, malformed but flexible. And slowly…carefully…it was finally able to stand.

That body began to stumble and bumble around the empty pit,

unable to orient itself, almost falling several times before standing again…realizing there was a problem, trying to figure out what that problem was. Two eyes and a mouth were trying to open, and that was when it became obvious what was wrong. The shapeless head was still facing backward.

Cautiously, as if fearing a critical mistake, this thing that had once been Juan carefully lifted its hands up to that head, tightly pressing both sides, and turning it forward once again, even though there really wasn't a face anymore. The head rotated smoothly, as if its substance still wasn't fully solid. That was when a sort-of face emerged. The eyes opened at last. They could have been human eyes, they could have been Juan's eyes, but the form wasn't exact, and the right eye was a couple of inches lower than the left. There was no brow, there were no eyelids. A hole formed where the nose might have been, releasing more vapor. A mouth tried to open when the creature began to examine itself and saw it had no noticeable genitals, those eyes only then showing shock. His anguish caused his body to shake as cracks and fissures began to show themselves on the surface of his half-formed hands. At first there were only sparks, and then mysterious flames burst out and began to swirl and dance around his fingers, causing him to immediately forget his distress. He was suddenly feeling the power that had been granted to him. That was when the mouth finally opened, into a lipless and toothless expression that could have been a smile…that should have been a smile. He raised those hands over his head in a gesture of triumph, and tiny whirlwinds of that strange fire formed in the palms. He concentrated, and the flames burned brighter and spun faster, becoming more focused and concentrated. When he had taken that process as far as it could go, he swiftly brought his hands down and together, compressing both vortexes into one ball of fire between the two palms. Then he launched his arms forward and released his grip, as if pushing the sphere of energy away from him, sending it flying off into the night until it hit the ground with a muffled explosion.

El Bautista let loose a not-quite-human cackle and began to walk stiffly toward a nearby building. The feet were still ill-formed and the toes were fused together, so he still didn't move as easily or naturally as a human being, but he was no longer slow. The door was thick, solid, and locked, and he obviously didn't have a key. He decided to test his power again, gripping the knob. The metal became red hot, and with a blast, the mechanism was destroyed.

Juan entered and soon came out wearing a hooded sweatshirt and jeans. He hadn't bothered with shoes; those feet were too distorted. He began heading toward where the bus had been, maintaining a normal, even swift, lumbering gait that lacked any grace.

But the vehicle was long gone.

The only thing left behind were the bodies.

The slit of Juan's mouth tried to show his anger as a bit of smoke escaped from the hole that had replaced his nose.

He was about to begin walking, about to follow the road that led back to civilization. But then one of those bodies, the one that had been the driver who had died while pissing, gave a couple of jerks.

Intrigued, Juan approached the corpse. Its dead eyes were open, following its former master's arrival. The mouth of the deceased fell slackly open, and a raspy, whispering voice emerged, as if from the depths of a tunnel.

"We are nothing but dead flesh now. You must help us rise again and feed from the throat of this world. We are nothing but dead flesh for now. But you must help bring us forth into this life that could be more than life for us!"

Juan's eyes showed his rage. "I care only about helping the one who brought me forth!" he said, his own voice rough and guttural. "She told me about your kind, how you would be trying to get in on the action. I don't care about you parasites. If you come through, so be it. I really don't care!"

The eyes of the dead man closed again. The mouth remained open, but the voice had left.

El Bautista bent down and touched the corpse. It burned. He examined the other bodies, but they showed no sign of being anything other than dead, so he turned back to begin his own journey.

Juan walked alone and nothing seemed to share the night with him other than the stars. The only other light was the faint glow coming from beneath his hood and from his bare hands and feet, flaring brighter from time to time.

Yeah, he was sure that he was all alone out there.

So why did he think he heard footsteps coming up behind him?

He turned once to look…silence, nothing to see…kept walking.

Then…that sound of footsteps again.

Again, Juan stopped and turned around and faced…silence. So, he kept on walking.

Then…that sound of footsteps again.

Juan spun around to look for the third time. Everything was quiet, everything was still.

But this time he didn't keep walking. Instead, he crossed his arms and stood defiantly, the eyes blazing from the remnants of his face as his anger flowed from them.

"Show yourself!" An order, not a request.

Slowly, Juan's light began to cast a shadow…even though there was nothing there that could have had a shadow. Yet there it was, barely discernible, just a little darker than the dark night.

And it was no ordinary shadow. It was a shadow that had a third dimension, it was a shadow that stood up.

It might have had the form of a man, but it was impossibly tall, at least twelve feet tall, towering above El Bautista.

Juan stared up at it.

Then an eye opened, the bare outline of one big cyclopean eye, right in the middle of where the shadow's head appeared to be.

Intuitively, Juan raised a hand and launched a fireball at the silhouette. But the figure had no substance, and that rolling flame sailed through it and past it, only to explode harmlessly in the sand and dirt of the desert.

An unpleasant voice, barely audible, faint as an echo, emerged from that shadow thing.

"I am not here yet. I am still far away. But I am getting closer, and I am closer than the others. The one who gave you that fire is very far away. And that fire is from another realm. I see it clearly, it guides me to you. If you are of the wise, you will aid me, because the one who gave you that fire is far away and cannot give you much help."

Juan glared. "Who the fuck are you?"

"I am the master of those you called parasites. But they are more than that, far more. They are my followers, they are my army, and we will be there first. The one that has given you fire has given us a light to guide us now that the way is torn open. Your realm will fall to me… easily. If any others find the way, they will have to take that realm from me, because I will get there first."

Juan laughed contemptuously. "If you're the lord of those parasites she told me about, you're no match for her, for the one who gave me the fire. And I'm already here. I'm the first! So, I don't even give a fuck about you or whatever the fuck you're saying. I don't even care about you or your stupid army. I only want to kill that girl, so if you do come here, stay out of my way!"

"Girl?" Then the voice of that form became a little stronger. "You should serve me because I will be there before the others that seek your world. Serve me—or I shall destroy you when I arrive."

Juan laughed again. "You don't know who you're fucking with. You come here and I will kill you, pendejo!"

The form managed to emit its own laugh. "No, little creature, you will feed me. I will consume your fire and you will be my slave."

"Fuck you and your puta madre!" roared the melted man, spitting a blob of lava at the shadow's feet.

But that eye had closed and the shadow was fading away, leaving behind it nothing except for the ordinary darkness. There were no more words to make threats, there were no more words to reply to Juan's threats.

El Bautista stood there for a few minutes, watching his saliva smoking in the dirt.

Then he turned around and continued his journey.

Sunrise, that same day, and out in the desert there were motorcycles.

Marcial "Barbarossa" Barreno led the way, a big grin on his face. His fantasy had always been to ride with Sonny Barger and the real Hell's Angels up in El Norte. And he was known to fly into drunken rages if somebody pointed out to him that he would probably get himself arrested if he ever stuck a toe across that border. Barbarossa was the nickname of some medieval German boss-king: it meant "red beard." So, to live up to his name, Marcial grew a beard and had it dyed bright red.

Do I need to add that Marcial and his little gang were also cartel enforcers? They were supposed to be out showing their colors and saving face…they were supposed to be on the hunt for that girl who was causing so much drama. But unlike his colleague and sometime drinking buddy, Samurai Sanchez, Barreno didn't take the girl that seriously and wasn't even convinced she was real—more likely an urban legend. Sure, maybe some chica somewhere had managed to kill somebody somehow, but real life was no comic book. And nobody was bulletproof.

If the stories and rumors didn't stop, though, then sooner or later they would just have to grab some dumb girl and blow her brains out and put the legend down. And why not sooner? It wasn't like the lives of those little maquiladora drones were worth that much. They were dying all the time.

But screw all that. Why not take the boys out to patrol the desert. Never know what you might find out there, maybe somebody to fuck with. But at the very least, Marcial probably planned to leave the city and the hunt for the girl far behind for a while, maybe spend the night in the desert and get wasted. Just don't get too close to El Bautista's land. Redbeard had never trusted that crazy mofo.

Farther and farther out from La Ciudad they roared, Barbarossa and five of his best men. The wind was thrashing their hair…because they weren't the guys that would be wearing helmets. Just goggles. Of course, they had the leather jackets and a logo: skulls with red beards. The obvious choice, I suppose.

Rushing down the road…or something similar to a road…trailing clouds of dust…rounding a curve… and Fate dealt a different card… just like when Flor, in my dream, slammed down that tarot card. Death. Because coming right on into the moment…curving around from the other way and heading straight for Marcial's gang…was a creaky old bus. And it didn't even have the good manners to try to slam on its brakes. Instead, it started honking madly as it kept up its velocity and barely avoided tipping over.

The unexpected need to avoid a collision sent cycles skidding in all directions. There were three wipeouts, although Barreno managed to keep his balance as he came within inches of the bus, did some off-roading, and came to a stop with a skid and a spin around. His expression as he watched the bus keep on going must have been something to see. It probably took a few seconds for him to recover from the shock. But then, oh yes, his face twisted itself into a mask of pure rage.

One of his men was not getting up, one was up but wobbly, the third seemed okay. The two who hadn't fallen were checking their weapons. They knew what was about to happen, not that it would have been that hard to predict. Without saying a word, Marcial fired up his bike and took off after that bus. It was taken for granted that those who could follow would follow. So that left "wobbly" behind to…maybe…help "not getting up."

Weapons brandished, the reduced squad launched itself after the bus. It didn't take much effort to catch up to that big, blundering thing. It was like an Olympic sprinter chasing down your humble narrator. Not even a challenge, even though it was swerving around and going at a speed that should have been beyond its capacity.

Barbarossa headed his formation and buzzed right up to about six feet from the left rear wheel of his accidental enemy, an enemy that still didn't show any sign of knowing the danger it was in.

One shot, one accurate shot, shredded that back left tire. The bus became even more erratic, wobbling and skidding, but still managed to stay in the game. So Marcial calmly swung his aim over and tore open the right rear tire with a second shot. Then he signaled his men, and they dropped back as the big vehicle lost the last bit of control, tried to leap a ditch, rose partly into the air, and slammed down on its side.

The motorcycles came to a much more controlled stop on a slight rise overlooking the crash. The eyes of the riders were all intently focused, watching for any sign of movement. A minute or two passed, with nothing moving except for all the dust settling. Maybe some kind of bird passed overhead, riding the wind. Another minute or two and nothing had changed. They still waited, wanting to see if anyone came out before they went in.

Barreno was about to lead a dismount, but then came the loud, unpleasant sound of metal being forced to scrape on other metal as a young woman climbed out with a quickness that seemed more like that of an acrobat than that of a human being just involved in a traffic accident. She stood still on top of the bus as soon as she saw those men watching her. Long and unkempt hair framed a face that could be called pretty, a face that showed no sign of fear, only a slight smile of amusement. Her body was thinner and taller than the norm. She wore a plaid shirt that was a little too big and torn-up jeans. She matched the description.

"Is that her?" asked Barbarossa.

"I think so," answered one of his men.

Then a loud, explosive laugh from the first. "Then fuck my friend Sanchez! Looks like we got her without even trying!" Then he revved the engine and shouted at the girl. "Hey, little niña! Want a head start?"

She just regarded Marcial for a few seconds, then shrugged.

"Better start running…run, run, run!"

Instead, the girl hopped down off the upended bus and started walking toward the three men…no sense of urgency…sauntering.

"The bitch really thinks she can take us?" wondered the first.

"Or else the crash fucked up her head," replied the second.

"Spread out and keep your guns up," ordered Barbarossa. "If any of those stories are true, she must have some kind of tricky shit that she can play. Keep some distance. Watch for some kind of weird weapon or anything. Maybe she's got something we can use."

Lupe stopped her advance and watched passively as Marcial's men followed their instructions, flanking her on the left and right, guns drawn, but keeping about twenty feet away. That left their boss himself standing in direct confrontation with her. Silence fell on the scene as the two of them examined each other.

I find myself wondering if, at that point, Barreno had said to his men, "Let's go," and they'd just left…if she would have let them. After all, she was the one who had almost killed them with her runaway bus. Maybe she would have forgiven him his sudden attack of road rage. Maybe she had been taking her time because she wanted to give them the chance to run.

If that was what she was waiting for, that's not what happened.

"They say you're bulletproof," growled Marcial. The girl continued to put all her attention on him as he spoke. "Not really sure I believe that, not sure at all. But still, I think I'll try something else, something that just might be perfect for a crazy little bitch like you."

Calmly, even slowly, he reached inside his jacket as he smiled coldly at her…and pulled out a big whip, letting it uncoil.

Marcial's smile grew like a rotten weed.

Guadalupe's face suddenly lit up with silent laughter.

Marcial's smile withered a little bit. It wasn't exactly the reaction you expected from a young woman that you were about to flog to death.

"What is with this bitch? She really thinks she's something? Got everybody thinking she's all bulletproof, got everybody thinking she's so hard to kill? Must be the luckiest little bitch in the world—so far. And now she thinks she's got everybody all psyched out!"

He stood and seethed. She just stood. Then Barbarossa suddenly cracked the whip. And she still just stood there, stood and took the hit. All she did was brace herself a bit so she wouldn't get knocked over. There was no flinching, no sign that she felt any pain, just that silent amusement.

Crack. Crack. Crack. Marcial wasn't talking anymore either, but his silence was full of anger as he let loose with a barrage of whiplashes, tearing through her jacket and making more gashes in her pants. The whip brutally caressed her cheeks, making no mark, drawing no blood, and ripped through her hair. And she just took it like she was letting a light rain drizzle on her. Then one last strike and Barreno caused his whip to wrap around the girl's throat. He gave a yank that was enough to snap a bodybuilder's neck. She was sent down hard to the ground without offering any resistance.

"What the fuck? Is she an android robot or some shit like that? If that's what she is, I want that shit! I'll get me some scientist to reprogram her to work for me, like I'm some *Star Wars* boss!"

At that moment, Guadalupe reached out and grabbed the whip about a foot away from where it was wound tightly around her throat. That was it, that was all she did…just held the whip…no other action and no other movement.

A confused frown formed on Marcial's face. He gave the whip a vicious pull, which dragged the girl two or three feet closer to him. She remained inert but didn't release her hold. That grip wasn't going to relax or be broken, not by any force that the narco could muster. But a man like Barbarossa wasn't going to give up, was he? No, of course not. Instead, he gave the whip a series of full-strength yanks, trying to regain the mastery of a situation that he somehow had lost, dragging the girl's motionless body farther over rocks and sand, his weapon still caught in that unrelenting grip.

When he finally stopped, breathing heavily from the exertion, Lupe…still facedown…gave the whip a tug of her own, stripping the handle from Marcial's hand. If he hadn't been wearing gloves, he would have lost some skin along with his weapon.

"Fuck!" he shouted, taken totally by surprise.

Suddenly and fluidly, she was up on her feet, unwinding the whip from her neck and taking mastery of the handle she'd liberated from its owner. All the men stood frozen…spines of ice…watching something they couldn't quite believe. Each one probably felt like a person who found himself or herself being floated into a flying saucer by a gray alien…or who woke up at night in a cabin to see the angry eye of the Sasquatch peering in.

Guadalupe had become the one cracking the whip. And when she cracked it, they said it was like a sonic boom blasting straight at Marcial "Barbarossa" Barreno. He received the impact, which sent him spinning to the ground as a severed forearm went flying into the air.

Their boss had instantly been converted into a groaning, amputated heap in the dirt. And the girl was giving the other two men a clinical, almost indifferent, examination…as if picking her next target. Both of them still had their guns drawn. But neither of them shot. Instead, they seemed to fidget and falter…almost embarrassed. Marcial made some kind of agonized noise: an order or just pain and shock? No way to know. They didn't even want to know.

The girl unbuttoned what was left of her blazer and fully revealed those two pistols that she'd tucked into the waistband of her jeans. Then she stood still and at her ease, like she was waiting to meet a friend who would show up in a couple of minutes.

She was really waiting to see what choice the two men would make. Would they choose to live or to die?

In unison, they chose to live…withdrawing to their cycles and taking as little time as possible to vanish down the road.

The girl looked back at the bus for a moment, then turned away again and started walking…walking back toward La Ciudad. But she took only a few paces before a sudden thought lit up her face, making her retrace her steps back to the remains of her foe.

Later, when the authorities found what was left of him, that forearm lying in the desert was the least damaged piece of Marcial that she had left behind. The motorcycle and the whip were nowhere to be seen.

Flor was standing there watching…watching intently…as two men played chess. The players were Howard Phillips Lovecraft and Aleister Crowley. Both of them had their eyes riveted to their game…neither spoke…each seemed tense. Chess wasn't really my game, but it seemed to me that the two were evenly matched.

My lost love looked up and saw that I was there. Her smile of welcome took away some of the darkness that surrounded us—because that was all that was around us, just darkness.

"There you are!" she exclaimed. "I thought you'd forgotten me!"

In that moment I remembered the music of her voice. I wanted to tell her that I had never forgotten her, not in all those years. But even in that dream, I couldn't find the words. So instead, I gave a nod toward the chess players. "Interesting pair."

"I guess that's true. I think a lot of strange people from the regular world show up in this place…whatever the regular world is…it's hard to remember sometimes when you're out here."

I had a lot of questions, but none of them came out of my mouth. So, I just listened and waited for her to continue.

Flor looked to the side, like she always did when she was taking her time to think about something she was going to say. Then she turned back to me. Her beautiful brown eyes were so vivid in my dream that *they* seemed to be dreaming *me*.

"Well, Cervantes?"

"Well what, Flor? I don't understand."

She kept on meeting my gaze. Those eyes were so distracting.

"Do you want in the game, or do you want to just watch from the sidelines like you usually do?"

"The chess game?"

She laughed. "No, forget about them. I mean your girl, Lupe Castaneda. Do you want in or not?"

No hesitation. "Yes, Flor. I want in."

What was going on?

The bartender was shaking me. "Had enough, Cervantes? You usually don't pass out in here, not this early!"

Damn, I'd fallen asleep at the bar?

When Flor vanished and it became clear that she was going to stay vanished, my life was over. All I was left with was my existence…which I wasn't all that into.

That didn't mean that I planned to swallow a muzzle.

It didn't mean that I was going to down a couple hundred pills with a bottle of mescal and close up shop.

And it didn't mean the death wish deluxe…impulsively stepping in front of a bus or provoking a narco to extract my brains with some high-velocity surgery.

All it meant was that my life would no longer have any real meaning. All it meant was that in some deeper place of reality, I was a failure. All it meant was that it didn't matter anymore what I did with myself. So, I just kept doing what I had been doing, let inertia carry me forward and prop me up with the same old habits. Be a puppet reporter for the narco state? No problem. The magic seemed to be gone from my life too: why keep chasing after the occult and the esoteric? It all seemed to become nothing but a load of shit. I never had found anything real as an investigator even when I had Flor to help me. And I certainly never found anything after she left. But I kept at it for a while. Like I said, inertia. Until I got that job offer to spin the real news.

My life became a sham and a farce in every way, a shell enclosing a sad and hollow meaninglessness. But, as I write this, I have to admit that not every moment was horrible. Even a sham and a farce can be good for a few laughs.

A lot of people have lost loves. After some time, the sharp pain becomes dull. I thought at first that surely I would hear from her again. When I didn't, I settled into my failure, pain, and regret. After some more of that time passed, I even took a certain bitter comfort in it. Once it was clear that I'd somehow screwed up this major thing in my life, I was actually able to relax a little. I was off the hook and out of the game, stranded on the desert island that my life had become. It got to the point that all I needed was a little more mescal and periodic bouts of intense self-pity; then I could keep on gliding. That was my life…a day at a time that became a week at a time…a month at a time…a year after year after year at a time.

Then suddenly, there was Guadalupe Castaneda. I wanted her to somehow be the nemesis of that rotten and corrupt cancer of a city. I wanted her to somehow be the redeemer of my own rotten and corrupt life. I wanted her to truly turn out to be something from beyond the world I had known.

Then suddenly, Flor came back to me in my dreams…those dreams that seemed so shining and real. I didn't even know that I could still have dreams. I thought that the mescal had washed them all away a long, long time ago.

Then suddenly, it seemed like all the nothing was brushing up against…something.

I didn't know how deeply and completely and totally I hated my life until Flor began to rule my dreams. And I didn't remember how deeply and completely and totally I hated my world until someone appeared who could smash it down.

Juan had kept walking and walking. He felt no fatigue. He felt no thirst. He felt no hunger.

So, he'd just kept walking and walking.

He'd walked through the night of his rebirth and entered into the new day.

And he stopped only when he found the crashed bus and the bodies of Barbarossa and his men. At first he was on his guard, looking around, expecting the girl to be there. When nothing happened, he leaped up on the toppled vehicle, peered through the windows, climbed inside, satisfying himself that she wasn't there. Only after that did he approach Marcial's body and gaze down at it, almost with an attitude of respect at first. But then mocking laughter burst out of his throat.

"Good old Redbeard, you asshole. You really thought you could take her? You really thought you could kill her? Idiot! I would burn your puta corpse, but you don't deserve it. I would take one of your stupid motorcycles that you were so proud of, but I don't want any of our former associates thinking I killed your puta ass. It's not like they would recognize me as I am now. Nope, I don't want to have to waste that kind of time. I don't want anything getting in between me and her, not even old friends. The cartel don't matter now. I'm beyond that shit."

The shattered corpse of Barbarossa didn't answer, didn't move, just continued to be dead.

"I guess none of you fucking ghosts have any more to say, either. Good."

And Juan kept walking, walking toward La Ciudad.

Samurai Sanchez slammed a chair down next to mine. I had been so lost in thought that I hadn't even been aware of his approach. So, he scared the shit out of me…making me send my mescal bottle sailing off the little table and shattering on the floor.

Normally, Sanchez would have laughed like a lunatic at something as slapstick as that. But he barely noticed what had happened. He looked stricken. "Get Cervantes something better than that goat piss," he snapped at the bartender. "On the house!"

The man rushed to comply and, after replacing the old drink with a more expensive one, made himself scarce. I poured myself a shot. I would have preferred another bottle of the goat piss, but I wasn't going to say anything about it. I just nodded a thanks to my uninvited guest and waited for him to start talking. It was obvious he wanted to.

"Barbarossa got himself killed," Sanchez finally said in a flat tone and seemed to wait for my reaction.

I made myself as blank as possible. Tabula rasa. No expression… no expression…no expression…being as deadpan as I could. I had to be careful; otherwise, a smile would have leaked out.

The silence dragged, so I finally asked, "Her?"

"Yeah." He stared off into his own space and seemed lost in his own thoughts somewhere out there. No bravado, no self-promotion.

The quiet flowed back in between us, seeming to exclude even the other sounds in the bar. I guess we both had a girl to think about. Mine was Flor. His was Guadalupe. But Lupe was my girl, too. I even knew her name.

Eventually, Sanchez took the replacement bottle of mescal and chugged straight from it…loosening his own tongue.

"You know, Cervantes, that sooner or later I am going to find that girl." It was a statement of fact, made in a low tone.

"No doubt," I answered, reflecting that tone.

"But I need to know…I need to know what her gimmick is. What has she got? A magic touch? Did she get hold of some crazy spy shit… like James Bond crap or something?"

"Don't know."

"C'mon, Cervantes. You're a smart guy and you know all about that weird stuff, conspiracy stuff and all that. What's the game and who's playing it?"

I considered my words. He'd asked about a game. How should I play mine?

"I'll tell you the truth, Sanchez. I have no idea what's going on. But I don't think it has any natural, normal, or Scooby-Doo explanation. And I think, I really think, that if you go up against her, then you are a dead man."

Any other day and any other circumstance, I'm sure that would have blown his temper. Maybe he would have even broken the bottle again—over my head. Maybe he would have yelled at me, slapped me, pushed me down, beaten the shit out of me. And I would have had to take it.

Instead, he just nodded, got up, and calmly left.

If Juan had still been a human being, he would have collapsed out there under the glare and heat of the desert sun. He had been walking rapidly, all day, for hours…the last part of the day was behind him…he was still not resting, still no sign of needing to drink, still no sign of needing to eat.

But it had already been proven beyond doubt that Juan was no longer a human being.

His stride never faltered, even though his gait was still stiff and still clumsy. No sweat appeared on what had once been his flesh, that substance that looked like plastic that had melted and become solid again. There was only one thing that was beginning to have an effect on him.

Boredom.

When he finally reached a real road, a paved road, he was ready to hitch a ride. Or, more accurately, he was ready to force the issue, to make somebody give him a ride, because he knew it wasn't likely that anybody would choose to stop for whatever it was he had become.

It didn't take long for a car to come into view, a generic gray sedan.

Juan's plan was simple. Just keep walking along the side of the road, let the car come close, and then jump in front of it as it was about to pass. The driver would either slam on the brakes in time…or not…it didn't matter. If Juan had to take a hit, he'd take the hit. All that mattered was that the car would stop.

With perfect timing and a flying leap beyond the ability of any athlete, he landed on his feet right in the vehicle's path.

After that, the plan fell apart. The car didn't stop, it didn't even slow down. As it closed the last second of distance, Juan could tell that the man was ignoring him, pretending not to even see him. Juan froze in place, prepared for the impact, already planning how he would punish that driver.

But there was no impact.

The car passed through Juan. Or did Juan pass through the car? Either way, the car continued on its way, unhindered and unharmed.

And Juan was left standing foolishly in the middle of the road. Somehow, he had lost his substance. Somehow, he had become a ghost.

He felt himself sinking into the pavement, not because of his weight or mass…but because of his sudden lack of those two attributes. He was becoming intangible. With disbelief and panic, he held his hands up to his eyes and saw they were becoming transparent. The earth was moving beneath him as he continued to slowly drop into it; he was no longer rotating with it, no longer orbiting with it. The world and Juan were passing each other by. They no longer had a relationship with each other. Would he just slide through and be left in empty space?

Juan screamed.

And then, somehow, the world changed around him.

If I had to pick something that symbolized the shame and embarrassment that I have for this place where I've lived my life, a top contender would be the donkey show. I'm not going to describe it. I'm not going to say what it is. All that matters is that it exists, an emblem of the absolute corruption of La Ciudad.

Just kidding. I couldn't resist that old joke. But some of you thought I was serious, didn't you? At least some of you who live north of the border.

Every year, all the time, we would get these crazy foreigners coming to La Ciudad hoping the find the burro trail, the way to a donkey show. Why anyone would even want to see shit like that…well, I just don't get it. But they always arrive looking for one. Sometimes they'll even be checking in the phone book.

I suppose one reason the story never quite died was because there were always people who found a way to make a little cash off those rumors. Some cab driver or other minor league scammer was always willing to try to find some goofy tourist a show, take him around town to where one might be, as long as he was willing to pay up front for the service, no guarantees. Maybe you even end up somewhere, pay a big cover charge, get a really, really strong drink…on the house, then wake up somewhere else, not even sure if you saw something crazy or not.

Then there was Cristobal, a midlevel operator who ran a place on the outskirts of town. He had turned that con into an art form. He had his own men driving cabs, experts at spotting fools who might be freaks and easy marks.

Charge large for the ride.

Charge large for the admission.

One way or another, make sure they have a friendly drink laced with something extra.

Wait for it to take effect. Maybe throw them off with a dogfight or cockfight.

Or sometimes he'd have a man wearing a plastic donkey head do… things…to a woman in the little arena inside the club just to make sure the addled suckers were even more confused.

Give 'em a hard pat on the back. "Hey, amigo, guess you can't handle the real stuff, huh?" and laugh good-naturedly.

They pass out.

Maybe you get a credit card number or two.

Dump them in some seedy, nasty hotel that will bill them again. Then they wake up with the most awful hangover, not sure what happened, not sure what they actually saw. And even if they realized they'd been conned, would they dare to complain? After all, they were the sick bastards who wanted to see a donkey show. Better just to live and learn, my friend.

Cristobal even called his club El Burro Borroso.

So why am I telling you so much about this particular place?

Because it was Lupe's next target.

It had become night.

Mounted on the stolen Harley, Guadalupe Castaneda came roaring up to the club way too fast. She didn't really know how to operate it… didn't know the subtleties of slowing down and stopping that beast of a machine. So, she used her bare feet to try to brake too suddenly…went out of control…fell over…and both bike and girl slid down the street… stopping only when they slammed into a car. She would have been dead if she hadn't already been there and done that. Instead, she tossed the cycle off herself, sprang to her feet, and stalked boldly toward her target.

Her clothing was now so dusty it was hard to tell what color it had once been. Her jeans were shredded even more. Her hair was a wild, snarled, and tangled mess. Parts of her body were blackened from dirt and dried-up blood that wasn't even hers.

She threw away some goggles that she must have taken off Marcial. A couple of witnesses claimed they saw that strange darkness shining in her eyes. If true, that would certainly have given her a last little touch of the demonic.

The show inside had already started. There wasn't much activity outside…nothing to interfere with her march up to the entrance. Two burly men stood there…smoking…watching her approach with somewhat baffled looks. Maybe they'd seen the crash. Or maybe they just wondered why a messed-up chica was trying to come up to the front door all alone. Either way, Lupe seemed to be planning on ignoring them, focused on going straight in.

One of the dudes grabbed her by the arm. "Performers go in the back, sweetheart," he told her with a chuckle. She grabbed his wrist with her free hand, did a little twist…and there was a loud snap and a sharp groan of pain. Then she kicked his legs out from under him with such force that he spun upside down and hit headfirst like a sack of bricks. Another slight groan, and then no more sound or movement.

Lupe turned toward the other gentleman, whose cig had fallen from his mouth. He raised his hands and stepped back and back and back. Probably had figured out who he was dealing with.

She entered the club without any further opposition. The few people in the doorway, they had seen what had just gone down and were more than happy to quickly get out of her way, including the guy who should have asked her for the cover charge. She was just about to go past him; then she hesitated. That hesitation turned into a full stop as she turned her attention to that man, who was beginning to tremble. She watched him with a small smirk and then held out her hand. The message was clear: give up the cash. And he couldn't wait to cough it up, almost throwing her a big wad of bills, which she stuffed into her pocket.

"What the fuck is going on?" demanded a loud, angry voice, disrupting the transaction.

Lupe and her living ATM machine turned to face another burly security man, who was holding a hatchet.

Hatchet man's eyes widened when he saw the girl. "No way!"

More with reflex than planning, he lunged forward and swung the weapon full-on at her head. There was a heavy, metallic thud along with a yell of pain, the ax flying free as its former wielder grabbed the wrist that had been injured by the shock of the unyielding impact. Lupe was still standing because she had reacted in time by placing her own hand against the wall to keep from getting knocked down. She watched the useless weapon land near her feet after bouncing off that same wall. She stooped and picked it up. Her attacker tried to turn to retreat, tried to run in a panic. But she got him by the back of the shirt and slammed him flat onto the filthy floor. He looked up at her with dazed fear.

Lupe lifted that hatchet as if she were going to bring it down with all of her force…right onto his forehead. Then she just gave him a quick tap on the skull and turned away, leaving him unmoving but alive. She barged through the next doorway and into a crowd that hadn't even noticed her yet.

There they all were, all the distorted creatures in human form who thought they were going to that…event. Who were they? Tourists on a dare, not really knowing what they would see, not really thinking it could be real? The most foul perverts that slip down from El Norte to indulge themselves? Probably some of each, and it wasn't like anyone was going to take a survey. And most of them seemed woozy and heavily inebriated. A few had already passed out.

Lupe tiptoed it, trying to peek over the spectators who encircled the sandy floor, which still had some of the feathers, fur, and blood from the rooster and canine matches that the place was also used for. The spectacle was about to begin, that strange parody that Cristobal had engineered. A young woman in a bikini was slowly approached by a muscular man in a loincloth wearing a ridiculous plastic donkey head. She seemed to be in as much of a stupor as the audience. She staggered, barely keeping her balance. Most likely she had been drugged up, maybe by her own hand, maybe by someone else's.

Over on the other side of that scene, things were a bit more organized. Cristobal and some of his men were hanging out, not even paying much attention to the show. It was routine for them, just business.

Scowling, Lupe stormed into the arena, pushing and shoving people aside. Some of the men tried to resist and found themselves flying or folding like cardboard props, not any impediment to her hopping down into the sandy circle.

The eyes of Cristobal fell on her as the disruption attracted his attention. His face contorted with anger.

"You!" he yelled as he produced a gun. But his hand never pulled the trigger…because the intruder had let fly the hatchet, and suddenly there was nothing left of him except a splattering mess where that snarling visage had been.

By reflex, some of the entourage fumbled for their own weapons. Others still hadn't figured out what was happening. But Lupe had already picked up a pistol that had landed near her feet and had it aimed at them.

For a few seconds, the action froze.

Then Lupe waved the gun, signaling for them all to leave.

Taking that cue, everyone began to exit in an oddly quiet and orderly manner, stumbling audience and frightened employees alike, leaving behind only the dead, the unconscious, those who were too injured to move, and even some who were trying to help them.

It didn't take long. Lupe remained with the female performer and the donkey impersonator in the arena. Something didn't seem right with him, either. He sat down in the sand and rocked back and forth slightly, not even removing his mask. Lupe ignored him. The girl in the bikini just stood there, swaying in an unbalanced way. Lupe tossed the gun away and grabbed her by the shoulders, not to hurt her but to make her turn so that they could face each other.

At first the eyes were blank; then they slowly filled with recognition.

"Lupe?" she mumbled, seeming to lose consciousness, starting to fall.

And Guadalupe Castaneda caught her, easily lifted her up and over her shoulder, and carried her out of that place, once again vanishing into the night of La Ciudad.

Stragglers, still outside and trying to figure out where to go, observed that final act of the drama.

I would gather the story of that latest attack in bits and pieces.

I would sleep fitfully, and I would dream about it.

After that, I would go out again, to gather more of those pieces.

Once I had more details in place, I went to talk to a bottle of mescal. It wasn't like I could do anything else. I was still forbidden from writing anything up. And even if I did it anyway, my paper wouldn't have been allowed to publish it.

My cell phone buzzed. Caller ID blocked.

"Yeah?"

"Hello, Cervantes." Once again, the mystery woman.

"Hey. How's it going."

"The girl in that fake donkey show was a childhood friend, a lifelong friend of Lupe Castaneda's. A fucked-up kid with a fucked-up life. Her stepfather basically sold her to those people. That guy that ran the club fucked her up even more, dragged her further down into the shit. Lupe knew him, too. When she was just normal Lupe, she tried to help her friend get out of there, and he slapped Lupe around before he had her thrown out. So, she hated him, had a grudge. But now she can save her friend, at least from him if not from herself."

"Okay, thanks. Talk to you when you have the next story to tell." I was sincere. I just figured she was going to end the call.

"Wait a second, Cervantes."

"Yeah?"

"You want in?"

I was silent. That was the same thing Flor had asked me in my dream.

"Cervantes?"

I still couldn't speak.

"Cervantes…you there?"

Finally found my voice. "Yes."

"What's wrong?" She actually sounded concerned. "Are you okay?"

"I'm fine. Yeah, I want in."

"Cool. You'll be hearing from me very soon." Then she was gone.

Samurai Sanchez had quickly arrived on the scene at El Burro Borroso and forced people to tell him what had happened, not even letting people be taken to the hospital until he had personally heard what they had to say. He had told the police and medics to stay outside until he was done. And that was what they did.

After the wounded were cleared off, with his permission, Sanchez only became more and more agitated. He stared at the devastated skull of Cristobal as well as the hole in the wall that the hatchet had made as it kept on going. He started wandering back and forth in the sandy circle. His men knew the signs. Their boss was about to explode. So, they gave him plenty of room to pace.

Unfortunately, there was one person who didn't know the level of danger was escalating: the donkey man, still sitting on the ground, still in his mask. Up until that moment, he'd mostly been ignored because he'd been mostly unresponsive to the events around him…and also because his presence was just plain weirding people out.

All at once, Sanchez took notice of him, leaned down, and screamed into that plastic face.

"And you! What the fuck is wrong with you?"

That man, who must have been just as much a victim as the girl Lupe had rescued, let out a braying sound.

Fluid and expert, swift and graceful, Sanchez drew his sword and took the man's head off in a burst of blood. I'm sure that even in Japan, the focus and training for that move would have been worthy of the greatest respect.

Instantly calm again, Sanchez cleaned the blood off his blade but ignored the splatters on his clothing and face. The body fell back on top of its severed head, which was still concealed in the costume.

"Lupe," he said, actually smiling. "The whore called her Lupe. Some of those fools heard her say it. That whore knows who super girl is. So, somebody had better be telling me really quickly who the hell that phony burro bitch is and where she came from!"

After I heard that latest bit, I was afraid. What if Sanchez was getting closer to what I already knew? What if he was about to find out the identity of the girl who is Death?

I ended up at the office, all by myself, waiting for that woman to call me again. It was very late at night…or maybe it was very early in the morning. Same difference to me.

With the first shot of mescal, I started to wonder why I was so worried. Why be afraid? Who was I afraid for? If Sanchez found Lupe Castaneda, it wasn't like she was going to be the one pounded into burger meat. Maybe I should even be the one to tip him off. But no, I didn't want to take that level of risk. Sanchez might figure out that I was trying to set him up. Or the girl could somehow find out I gave her up and get mad at me.

After the second shot, I began to feel sorry for all the people Sanchez could damage or destroy to reach the girl. If he found out who she was, he would do anything he had to do to any friends or family he got his hands on, anyone he could use to track her down or get her to come to him. Those were the people I was afraid for.

After the third shot…and the fourth…I began to sink into an empty drowsiness as the light of the sun began to ooze out through the dying night.

Then my cell phone buzzed me back to reality…or at least drew me back a little more closely to it.

Unknown caller. ID blocked.

"Speak to me."

"Ah yes, Señor Cervantes Castillo-Cruz." The woman's voice seemed more relaxed, less formal in tone. "I suppose it's time we discuss our mutual friend."

"Lupe?"

The unknown woman laughed. "Of course."

I waited silently for a few seconds. I was hoping she would keep

talking, because my brain was no longer operating at peak performance…
even by my standards.

She obliged me. "Anyway, Señor Castillo, my name is Flor—"

"F-Flor!" I stammered, toppling my mescal bottle.

She laughed again. "Yes. Flor. Flor Murakami-Martinez. And if
you want in, we need to arrange a meeting."

Arrangements were made and times were set. After the call ended, my
hands were shaking so badly I couldn't even pick up my mescal bottle.

It's not like Flor was an uncommon name. But to hear that name, to
hear it said to me on my phone after having those dreams? Yeah, it had
an effect on me. And my Flor, in those dreams, had asked me if I wanted
in. And this new Flor, in the real world, had asked me the same thing.

That was too much for me. I still had the shakes. I ended up at the
toilet spewing out all the good drinking I had done, like all the stress was
trying to ride that wave out of me. And maybe it did manage to leave
instead of staying to twist around inside me. Because I did feel at peace,
sort of, as I lay down in the bathroom and passed out.

I dreamed again, dreamed of the first Flor, my Flor, the one I loved.
I was lying in the desert, flat on my back and in the sand. It was night,
starless and moonless. Yet I knew there was some kind of hill or butte
nearby. And I knew that Flor was on top of it and looking down at me.

I couldn't move.

I didn't care.

My Flor was up there, watching over me. It was good to know she
was there. I just wanted to be able to see her more clearly, to see if she
seemed content. Because more than anything, I wanted to know she was
happy with me, with what I was doing, whatever that was.

Instead, my awareness passed on through into that starless and
moonless void, and for a while, I wasn't aware of anything, including
Flor or my own feelings of happiness or despair.

Only the dead remained in El Burro Borroso.

The living had been absorbed into the night of La Ciudad.

Sanchez and his men had left the club as well. They weren't trained
investigators, so it wasn't like they would have obtained any more
information. And the cops were staying clear of the place, at least for a

few hours more. They didn't want to accidentally stick their noses into a crime scene, into the business of the samurai.

The decapitated body of the unfortunate donkey man still lay in the arena's sand, on top of its own head, the plastic mask slowly collapsing under the weight of the body.

The blood was becoming dry and thick.

A hand moved ever so slightly. Could some random nerve still have a bit of a charge after that much time had passed?

No, it wasn't that, because after a few seconds that same hand clenched into a fist, tightly, before opening again. Then the other arm raised up for a moment, the fingers moving stiffly, before passively falling back down.

For a few minutes, nothing else happened, not until the body sat up with a sudden lurch, making the head roll a couple of feet over. It sat on its butt, as if trying to get its bearings; then it slowly turned and began to feel around for its wayward head. When it finally found the bloody and battered donkey mask, it raised it up and let the cranium fall out and plop grotesquely back to the sand. There didn't seem to be anything special about that head, just the slack, dead face of what had been an ordinary-looking man, perhaps with just a fuller mass of hair than most men were gifted with.

The donkey mask was promptly tossed to the side, and then the body had to feel around again before finding its real head, one hand getting a good grip on that hair. Then the body tried to stand up—and fell back on its ass. It tried again, this time flailing forward to a hard knee landing.

Without hesitation, that body then began to crawl, dragging the head, letting it bounce along roughly. The process was slow, ridiculous, and horrid. But eventually, the animated corpse, along with its cranium, found its way to the street outside.

No one was in sight, no one to see that impossible escape, as the free hand located and opened a service cover. There was no one to see as the body let itself plummet into the sewers…no one but me…and only in a dream.

Homero Maldonado was a scrawny, pockmarked weasel of a man. A bit bucktoothed and with bloodshot eyes, he constantly wiped his runny nose with his forearm. He was very nervous…nervous beyond nervous…

because he had been called before Samurai Sanchez. Of course, "called" probably wasn't the right word. He'd been grabbed by a couple of the samurai's entourage and escorted into that man's presence. Homero didn't even have a chance to make things more difficult for himself by trying to escape, assuming he ever would have found enough courage to try.

Sanchez sat in a comfortable restaurant booth. Homero had been given a rickety stool that somebody had found out in the back. He had tried just standing, but his host had insisted.

"Do you know why you're here, Homero?"

"No, Señor."

Sanchez snorted. "Normally, when I invite someone for a chat, they know exactly why they're here."

"Truly, Señor, I don't know." He seemed ready to weep.

"This is one of those very rare times when I believe it."

Homero, for a moment, allowed a trace of hope to show in his eyes.

"All I need from you is some information…just a little info, mi amigo. You wouldn't begrudge a man just a little bit of information, would you, Homero?"

"No, Señor, of course not!"

"Very good. Very good." Sanchez was grinning. "Would you like a beer? Some good tequila? Both?"

"Yes, Señor!"

"Bring the man both."

The service was the fastest in La Ciudad.

Sanchez waited until his guest had indulged himself before continuing.

"So, Homero, I hear that you have a stepdaughter named Paloma? I also hear that you…shall we say…loaned her to some of my colleagues in the local entertainment industry?"

Homero choked on his beer. "Señor?" He was all of a sudden very nervous again.

Sanchez stood up and loomed over his guest. "Allow me to be clear, mi amigo…if you don't answer my questions honestly…well, if you leave here at all, you will be leaving some pieces behind." He let that sink in. "Now, do you have a stepdaughter named Paloma?"

"Yes, Señor."

"Did you sell her to that idiot Cristobal?"

Just a moment to look for an out…and not finding it. "Well, yes,

Señor. But it was more of a trade. And the girl was useless…useless…a tramp and an addict…always causing her mother so much…so much—"

"Shut up."

Homero immediately did.

"I'm not here to listen to your explanations or your reasons. You did some business. That's okay. In the end, we all work for the same people. All I want is for you to answer my questions…and only the questions I ask. Comprendes?"

"Yes, Señor."

"Does Paloma have any good friends? Friends who would get her out of her 'contract' if they could?"

"I suppose so, Señor."

"I'm going to describe someone to you." And Sanchez had no problem tracing a verbal drawing of Lupe. People had described her to the enforcer so many times that he almost felt he had seen her with his own eyes.

"Is that one of those friends, Homero?"

"Yes, Señor. It could be, anyway. There's a good chance it could be one of Paloma's friends."

"What is her name?"

"Guadalupe—Guadalupe Castaneda, Señor."

"Very good. Very good. Now, Homero, you are going to take me to visit her family."

Homero hesitated for a second, perhaps thinking about lying, saying he didn't know where Lupe's family lived. But then he must have realized that Sanchez wouldn't believe him and that the brutality would commence with a quickness.

"Yes, Señor."

I sat in one of my bars, feeling as drowned as the damn scorpion drifting at the bottom of my half-empty mescal bottle. It was definitely half empty, because I wasn't feeling like a half-full kind of guy.

The thought of another Flor blooming in my life, being important in my life, was too much. Too much because of those dreams I had been having. Too much because of the burden of loss, and of memory.

No choice, though. No choice because I wanted in. I wanted to approach the mystery of the girl who is Death, the girl who had risen up from the grave to unleash her havoc.

So, I poured myself another shot, hoping to drown the anguish that had risen up inside…me.

Later, in another bar, there was another man, also drinking mescal. It's hard to say what his mood was, but it wasn't as bleak as mine.

Samurai Sanchez had an appointment, a contact inside the army, a guy who was said to know things most people weren't supposed to know. The cartel enforcer wanted some technical advice before going after Lupe and her family.

The man was slight and nondescript, dressed as a civilian, not wanting to draw attention to himself.

Sanchez served his guest a drink. They toasted. Then Sanchez laid it all out for the guy: all the stories, accounts, and descriptions of Lupe Castaneda and what she could do.

The guest listened quietly, without interruption and with full attention. Only at the end did he ask a question.

"This is for real?"

"Real as the cash you're going to get if you can tell me how she does it, 'cause it has to be some kind of military thing, some top secret shit. No other explanation."

The man sat back, thinking…and thinking. His eyes drifted to the envelope full of money that Sanchez had slapped on the table at the beginning of their talk. Then he reached a decision.

"Yeah, top secret shit. It's gotta be something from El Norte. CIA or some other Special Forces operation. I know the gringos have permission to try out covert tech on you guys—you narcos and smugglers and border criminals."

He went silent again, thinking again.

Sanchez began to get eager and impatient.

"I knew it! I knew it had to be something like that. But what kind of weapon? That's what I need to know!"

"Body armor. It's got to be body armor."

"She ain't wearing any armor, amigo. Plus, her head isn't covered by anything, and she's taken shots in the head and the face."

The guy managed a knowing smile. "It's called Operation Crystal Knight. It's transparent body armor, clear as glass. It's bulletproof plastic with built-in power to enhance strength and speed. They're testing it closer to home, on you all, before they send a bunch of 'em off to the

Middle East."

"You're sure? Now I gotta ask you, are you sure that shit is real?"

"Yeah. They've been workin' on it for years."

Then it was Sanchez's turn to consider things. "Yeah…yeah… that makes sense. That fits everything that's been happening. Fucking assholes! They take some trash barrio chica and turn her on us! The girl's family reported her missing…like she was one of those putas they keep killing around here. But she was really recruited by those fucking gringo secret agents! What better way to make us look like fools! Having some girl knock us around and bust our balls!"

"That would be my assessment."

"Okay, okay, but what would we need to wipe her out?"

The guy scratched his chin. "Maybe a bazooka. No! Better yet, a flamethrower. You could fry her to death inside the armor."

Sanchez grinned. "That's easy enough to get. It takes just one call."

The man nodded.

"Then we're done! Thanks, amigo." Sanchez got up quickly and left the bar, the envelope still sitting there on the table. The man watched his host leave and took another free shot before taking the cash and quietly leaving, looking a little nervous, a little bewildered.

He had just made a lot of money selling a major cartel thug a load of bullshit.

Should I confess that it's hard for me to have an orgasm, that I've never had much of a sex drive? Not that it matters that much, because for me it's a do-it-yourself kind of thing, anyway. I never had any sort of real relationship after Flor left, because…well, she was Flor and nobody else was. Maybe you can understand that, or at least understand it a little bit, enough to have some empathy. Or else you think I'm an absolute fool, a sucker, and a weakling.

Either I'm a glorious romantic failure…or just a failure. In the early days, after she vanished, I felt like the former. As time went by, I became the latter.

I'll even tell you a sad story.

As a melancholy, aging man who makes the rounds of the bars, muttering to the worms and scorpions in the bottom of mescal bottles, I often get approached by working girls. I'm fair game and prime prey: a guy who looks like he might have enough cash. A guy who doesn't look like he would be up for anything rough, unpleasant, or dangerous. A guy who might even give you a little extra out of gratitude.

I always waved them away, sometimes angrily.

But there was this one time....

The girl looked so much like Flor that I almost...almost might have believed it was her. But I could tell she was way too young. Still, I had her sit with me. I tried to talk to her...about things I would have talked about with Flor. The girl didn't have much to say. Yet the fact that she so much resembled my lost love—well, that made me feel things I hadn't felt in a long time. And I was drunk enough to think that somehow that girl sitting with me could redeem me.

So, I took her to bed and swallowed some more mescal, hoping to fool myself into thinking it was her, that it really was Flor. It didn't work. The girl didn't seem enthusiastic about her work. And I couldn't make anything work on my end of it in my body, mind, or soul.

I paid her and sent her on her way.

That was the one and only time that I really thought about putting a gun to my head.

I didn't really want to meet a new Flor...this Ms. Murakami-Martinez.

Juan had become solid again, or at least it seemed like he had become solid again. He found himself walking on the sand; he could feel it under the weight of his deformed feet. Yet somehow it wasn't the right sand. The area, the geography, around him...it looked like the territory he knew, but it wasn't quite the right territory. For one thing, the sand was white, like salt crystals.

And the sun...the sun was too bright.

Then he realized he was casting no shadow.

He shielded his eyes and looked up into the sky, seeking the sun that had to be there.

He didn't find it. The entire world was infused with light, with a blazing clear light. But it was coming from...everywhere. There was no obvious source, no blinding disk anywhere above him.

Juan began to notice the stillness...the lack of any motion in that world around him...the quiet. There was no wind or even a breeze. The air was static. There wasn't a hint of a cloud, and no bird flew anywhere in the luminous, blue, and vacant sky. The desert vegetation that one would expect was present, but there were no signs of any animal life, not even an insect.

In his heart, if he still had one, Juan immediately sensed what had happened.

He fell clumsily to his knees, as they resisted bending, and screamed up into that sky, "You promised me the girl! Why did you take me to this other world? This is not my world!" He could hear his own words, but the inert air quickly consumed them.

Nothing answered him. There was only that absolute silence.

He stood up again and continued to wait, as if hoping the answer he wanted was simply delayed, forcing what had once been human hands to clench into fists. When it seemed obvious that there really would be no response, he screamed again, this time with no words, only rage.

He glared at his own hands. "Bitch, I'm not your puppet! I'm not going to be tricked and trapped in this crystal-clear hell. I demand you speak to me! You will speak to me!"

And again, there was only that silence.

"Oh really? Really! We will see about that! You will answer. I will not be ignored!"

Possessed by his own fury, El Bautista raised a wrist to his mouth and bit into it as hard as he could. If he felt any human pain, he disregarded it as he tore through his melted plastic skin, exposing the glowing veins that pulsated underneath. Like a vampire craving his own blood, he tore into himself and sucked his own substance down into his throat. Then he threw his head back and blew out a huge cloud of blood-red smoke.

The stillness seemed to preserve that cloud; it drifted slightly but didn't dissipate. It just hung in that dead air like a bad omen.

More crimson vapor continued to hiss and bubble out of the hole he had made in himself, forming a red ribbon that also preserved its shape. Juan's anger almost turned to glee, and he began to move his wounded arm, began to trace patterns, began to trace symbols he'd probably seen somewhere, in some book on the occult. They also floated sluggishly in the air, taking a long time to lose the forms he had given them.

"I summon you. I bind you to my will. I summon you. I bind you to my will. I summon you. I bind you to my will. I summon you. I bind you to my will. Come forth, I command it. Come forth, I command it. Come forth, I command it."

Juan repeated that conjuration again and again, making it a mantra until that wound he had ripped in his own wrist stopped gushing the blood smoke. He swayed on his feet, dizzy from losing too much of whatever flowed in those destroyed veins. But still he raised his other wrist to his mouth, ready to do more damage to himself so that he could continue his improvised rituals. His teeth were about to find his altered flesh; then he hesitated when he became aware of the buzzing.

At first so very faint, so far in the distance, but that sound was rapidly growing louder and getting closer. For a moment, Juan was confused. He lowered his hand and looked around, trying to find the source of the noise. He didn't see anything, but what was left of his expression still began to show a sly contentment.

His antics had obviously earned him a response from…something. He could feel it, he could sense it.

The buzzing grew louder.

Juan managed to make his mouth grin. "I knew you couldn't ignore me. I am the one who summons, you cannot deny me when I call!" His tone became angrier: "You can't just play with me! You can't just fuck with me! I have some powerful mojo, too!"

The noise grew louder.

Juan waited, smiling and expectant.

And the noise grew louder…louder.

Juan's smile began to fade.

And the noise grew even louder…becoming like the roar of a jet as everything, the air itself, that entire world, began to vibrate.

Juan's smile vanished as a glint of fear began to show in his eyes.

The vibration turned into shaking. The ground quaked under El Bautista's feet. That clear and static sky began to blur as the noise became something beyond deafening, as though some invisible storm had taken control of that world.

El Bautista's gloating confidence was gone as he was forced to put his hands over the remnants of his ears. He was forced to fall to his knees. He screamed in fear, he screamed in anguish, but nobody would have heard it over the din. Even his body began to tremble and quiver as small cracks appeared in his hardened flesh, causing the release of little puffs of more smoking blood.

But just when it seemed like the cacophony was going to completely crush Juan, it stopped…stopped in an instant. That world was immediately still again, immediately quiet again. The only noise came from his groan as he lay on his back, his eyes closed in agony.

No, wait…there was still a faint buzzing, very local, very close.

Juan forced his eyes open and found the source of that sound. A hummingbird, shimmering and brilliant and metallic green, hovered above him, watching him. Its eyes filled with an emerald glow that somehow conveyed a sense of anger.

The man on the ground stared at it, unable to find words. And for a moment, just for a moment, it lost its avian form. For a moment, just for a moment, it seemed to be some grotesque insect, something like a fat and misshapen bee with the multiple eyes and fangs of a spider riding on reptilian wings.

Juan blinked.

And it was a hummingbird again.

The buzzing, the vibrations, began to grow stronger again. Juan cringed. But this time the volume leveled off, gradually becoming more focused, becoming coherent, forming a voice. It was the voice of that woman, the voice that had ordered the man in the bunker to leave Lupe alone, the same voice that had spoken to Juan from the severed head by his fire.

"I didn't take you for such an idiot. You slip in between the boundaries of your realm, and then waste your essence and solidity thinking you can force me to come to you?"

Despite everything, El Bautista became irritated as he started to get back up. "But I did summon you and you came!"

"By my own choice, you dolt, not by your will. You were dissipating yourself, and you would have ruined my plan if I hadn't used my own forces to arrive here. It takes effort, you know, it's not easy. I'm still a long way away. It is easier to project myself here, in the in-between. I had to use much, much, much more effort to reach all the way into your real world to modify you. But it still would have been nice not to have to exert myself more just to make sure the power I've already invested isn't squandered! I could punish you for this, but that would just be a waste!"

Juan wasn't used to being talked to like that. Not even the Boss had talked to him like that. Even as an ordinary human, he had become used to being treated with a bit of fear and respect, even by other narcos. And it wasn't like he was emotionally stable, anyway. So, the words and the tone of the green hummingbird caused his anger to explode into a tantrum. He leaped at that strange bird, bringing his hands together, trying to catch it and crush it. But it easily shot out of the way, and his hands did nothing more than clap together as he landed clumsily in the white sands.

It took a while before he relented. He still tried to jump up and catch that creature a few more times, but it simply fluttered higher and completely out of his range. Finally realizing he wasn't going to succeed, he remained on the ground, yelling and screaming obscenities.

The hummingbird circled slowly, no longer forming words, as it waited for Juan to regain any sort of calm.

That took some time. Even when he stopped yelling, he still had to violently kick at the sand and rocks around him. Only after doing that did he stand still, with his fists clenched defiantly.

The little bird had simply watched his antics as it rode the blur of its wings. After he was done, the buzzing formed into words again: "The powers I have given you, those powers have taken you out of your world. I knew that was possible, but I'd hoped it would not happen, because you are a native of your own realm. But even that wasn't enough to keep your world from temporarily rejecting you. The conditions are still not right for a hybrid creature like you."

This time El Bautista listened with some patience before asking, "Then what about the girl? How can she be in the real world and just do whatever the fuck she wants?"

"She's…different from you."

"What is she, then? Who gave her all that power?"

For the first time, the woman's voice hesitated. "We've already discussed the girl and what you need to do about her."

Juan decided not to press the question. "Well, I can't do anything about her now, not if I'm stuck in this weird place!"

"Yes, that is unfortunately true." There was almost a sigh. "I've already invested too much effort and time in you. I can't just let you remain here in this in-between place. I will have to project even more energy across the void just to return you home, even though that will hinder and delay me longer. And you've already wasted so much of what you've been given, so I'm afraid there will be a process, a transition. I'm afraid you're going to be a ghost for a while!"

"What do you mean?" Juan's tone became demanding again.

The bird laughed. "Time's up! Just remember what we agreed to, what you promised, and I promise that your chance will come."

Juan tried to speak again, but no words managed to escape his mouth. Rapidly, very rapidly, he was becoming transparent.

Within seconds, he had vanished.

For a few more moments, the hummingbird hovered over the footprints he'd left in the white sand.

Then in a blink it was gone too.

"Fuck!"

The shout of Samurai Sanchez filled the air and area surrounding the hovel that Homero had led him and his squadron to. One of those men had even been equipped with the required flamethrower.

Empty.

Guadalupe Castaneda's family had vacated the place.

"They left…didn't say where they were going. Please don't hurt my family, Señor. I swear we don't know anything!" Sanchez already knew that would be the uniform response of the neighbors. And he was inclined to believe them…in advance. Why would a family tell their neighbors where they were going if that family knew the cartel was on their own tail?

Sanchez gave Homero a sudden punch in the gut. Not so much because he blamed his informant, more just to vent his rage. Homero fell to the ground, groaning, and lay there, hoping that total submission would spare him from further aggression. Perhaps he even thought about how his stepdaughter, Paloma, had tried the same tactic with him when he vented his rage on her…and how it had never worked.

But Homero had more luck with Sanchez than Paloma had ever had with Homero. The enforcer was quickly distracted by another angry impulse.

"Give me a grenade."

One was quickly offered. Sanchez pulled the pin and tossed the little bomb through the open doorway of the shack. He and his men turned and walked away as the place behind them ceased to exist.

Homero lay there, covering his head and hoping they would forget about him and leave him behind.

They did.

Stunned and showered with dust and debris, Homero lay there, quiet and still, waiting and waiting until he was sure Sanchez and company were gone. Finally, stiff and sore, he slowly got up. He didn't dust himself off or look for open wounds. He just wanted to get the hell out of there.

Maybe he would have checked his pockets to see if he had enough money to buy a drink somewhere because he'd gotten no reward from the samurai. But before he could even do that—

No warning.

Somebody was all at once behind Homero. He found himself lifted up in the air and let go, to drop back down to the ground…the wind pounded out of him again.

The attacker allowed him to regain his breath. "Please, Señor, it's not my fault. I didn't know they were gone. I wouldn't have wasted your time if I'd—"

The words choked and died in his throat. It wasn't Sanchez. It was Guadalupe Castaneda who stared coldly down at Homero. She grabbed him by the arm and pulled him to his feet as if he were weightless, her grip so powerful that he felt something rupture in his bicep.

With irresistible force, the girl alternated between dragging and shoving Homero down an alley. There was garbage everywhere and the stink of feces. He wanted to collapse, but every time he tried to let his knees buckle, Paloma's friend would apply painful strength to keep him upright.

"Buenos Dias, Señor Homero, Señorita Guadalupe!" called out a girlish voice from one of the hovels. She was laughing…laughing at him. He intuitively realized it was someone who knew what he had done, someone who knew that a day of judgment had arrived.

"Better pray to Jesus or the Virgin, Homero, because this Guadalupe has no mercy!" another woman shouted gaily.

In a neighborhood like that, it was no secret what Homero had done to Paloma. And all those folks who watched as they hid from Sanchez's sight knew Homero had sold out Lupe's family to the cartel man.

Nobody would have helped him, even if they could have.

He found himself facing a crudely made enclosure. The girl who is Death picked him up and tossed him over that fence. Another rough landing. He heard a bray, rolled over, and looked up at a startled donkey as Lupe's shadow fell over him.

A real donkey?

The message was clear.

I remember. I remember what you did to my friend, just in case you had any doubts.

Homero lay on his back and waited…tears welling up in his eyes. There were, however, no words…no words to beg for his life. Maybe he knew there was no point. Maybe he was even a little glad that his miserable life had at last run its course.

Lupe put her foot on his forehead and slowly crushed down with the pressure of a tank tread.

◈

Aleister Crowley sat alone at a chess table, lost in arcane contemplation. When he became aware of my presence, he looked up and smiled as he made a gesture of invitation, welcoming me to play with him.

I ignored Crowley because I saw Flor just a little farther beyond him, staring off into the darkness. That darkness was all around us, so black I couldn't even tell where we were located, just like in my previous dream before the chessboard.

Realizing I was at her side, Flor began to speak without bothering to look at me.

"When I left, you were already old. Now you're even older. And death is beginning to strip you down."

I shrugged. "That's all I've been doing since you left…just waiting to get stripped down by death." It seemed like a matter of fact, no reason to deny it…or get worked up about it.

"But you are going to be the one who sees. You're going to be the one who tells this story. And it's going to be a longer story than you think!"

I nodded.

Then I woke up.

Groggy and staring up at my ceiling, I found myself deeply relieved that Lupe didn't look anything like Flor. The latter woman had been shorter, with a wider build. Just her body type…she wasn't fat. And she had a beauty that you didn't notice right away, a beauty that caught you by surprise.

Somewhere…years ago…it had caught me by surprise.

My cell phone buzzed.

"Speak to me."

"Señor Castillo-Cruz."

"Ms. Murakami-Martinez."

"It's time."

◈

I had also dreamed of him again. The Boss. The Boss of the bosses…

sitting and brooding in his fancy office in his fancy club. He had worked hard to be the master of La Ciudad, as much of a master as a place like that could have.

He had fought so many battles, killed so many people, ordered so many more killed. The top dog, who had driven off the other dogs, who kept them at bay. The top dog, who kept the scavengers in line and out on the fringes—because there were always scavengers, and you didn't want one of them grabbing a big chunk of meat and running off with it.

He was the one who really controlled the packs of rabid animals who snarled and snapped in my city, pulling the strings of all those minor gangs and small operations. He let them fight over this street corner or that one, let them kill each other in horrid ways over an inconsequential square of turf. Murder City, some called it. One of the most deadly places in the world, even compared with combat zones. And all of it was just a cover, just a mask, just a diversion from the big operation: his operation. And that was his multinational, multimillion-dollar drug smuggling business, which ran relatively smoothly beneath and below those surface waves of violence.

The very best men worked for him. Men like Sanchez. Men like Barreno. His enforcers, the guys nobody wanted to mess with.

This was the gang that had kept him in control for a very long time.

But he was starting to lose that control.

And he wasn't happy.

True, the girl hadn't struck at his main source of wealth and power: she hadn't touched the drug trade. And that was critical because it left the true foundation of the cartel intact. But there were…intangibles. The very existence of that girl, who could strike at will and destroy whatever got in her way, or that she wanted to put in her way, didn't that automatically undermine his authority? The very fact that he couldn't seem to crush her or even find her—didn't that make him look weaker to all those scavengers out there? And she was striking at secondary sources of income, including moneylending and sex, local things that he got a cut of, things that helped him control La Ciudad.

He'd kept it to a whisper, but that girl had a way of showing up when a pimp was trying to keep some putas in line, with unfortunate results for the pimp. She'd destroyed a loan shark operation and wiped out Cristobal's donkey show scam, both supposedly under his protection.

And she had even killed one of his elite: Barreno.

It needed to end. It needed to end soon. Sanchez kept promising, kept saying he would get it done, kept saying he was on the trail. Well, the samurai was about to have a clock counting down on him. If Sanchez didn't get results soon, if the local talent didn't get results soon, then it would be time to rent some heavy artillery. Some really heavy artillery.

My contact stared at me, studied me as though I were some math problem he had to figure out. Was I really that much of a puzzle to solve? Old, tired, probably could be diagnosed as a chronic alcoholic…and a sellout. That seemed to sum up my equation.

He was one of those guys that you knew you had seen around. If I'd wanted to pin it down, I'd have to say that he'd been in some of the groups of bystanders hanging out on the edges of Lupe's aftermaths. Like maybe outside Lucio's bar. Or maybe even hanging out in one of my bars, maybe watching me drinking and smoking and talking to people. My mysterious new Flor definitely had some kind of interest in me. And it had become obvious that she had assistants. Like the guy who was supposed to meet me in that bar and take me to see La Señorita Murakami-Martinez.

So why the unrelenting staring, the silence, the untouched drink?

"Am I that pretty?" I finally asked. "Can't take your eyes off me?"

"Just trying to get a read on you."

"That hard to do?"

"You're a loser who really wants to chase little green men and chupacabras. Instead, you write vague whitewash stories about the loco local crime wave."

"Close enough." I nodded and took another sip of my drink.

"What I don't get is why she wants to meet you, why she wants to include you in this."

I made a noncommittal noise.

He seemed to be getting frustrated by the fact that I was indifferent to his objections.

We ended up sitting with a silence between us again. So, I just kept working on my cigar and my mescal.

"Well?" he finally asked.

"Well, what?"

"Tell me what she sees in you. I would really like to know."

"Maybe it's just time for another flower to bloom in my life."

He said he was going to take me to a house.

The way he was acting, I was sure he was going to say he had to blindfold me. But he didn't.

What he did insist on was that we go together and that we take his car. I didn't like that part. I didn't want to be dependent on that guy to bring me back from…wherever. But my intuition told me that I would be all right, that I wasn't in danger. So, I decided not to add any extra drama and I rode, just watching my sad city pass by my gaze. It wasn't as though that guy was getting more talkative.

At least he had a working air conditioner.

The skull was real and so was the rest of the skeleton, but it looked old. That led me to assume no recent visitors had been sacrificed. They had given her a wig of long black hair, elegant and expensive, probably real hair. She wore a black veil and a black dress, both also first rate. I had seen many like her before, but never all decked out in that one color. This was a high-class incarnation of La Santa Muerte, the Holy Death, Saint Death. Depending on who you asked, she was a holdover of the old and mysterious religion of the bloody Aztecs…or else she was a postmodern recreation fused with a whole bunch of New Age mumbly-jumbly. Maybe mix in some voodoo and Santeria seasonings, depending on who was doing the mixing.

It wasn't a religion that had been standardized. Many of the people brought a lot of their Catholicism when they worshipped her. But the Catholic Church condemned her as heresy and Satanism, anyway.

And the black Santa Muerte…that was the one you turned to when you were dealing with serious shit, either giving or receiving. She was the one you kept private. Normally, a stranger wouldn't be invited into her presence when she took her darker form. If you wanted compassion, you dressed her in white. In matters of the heart, she wore red. And there were other colors too, each with their own meaning. But I knew what the black meant: it was vengeance, the elimination of enemies, the destruction of the opposition. Like I said, you wouldn't normally invite a reporter to hang out with you when you were messing around with that color.

The altar was clean and orderly, tactfully sparse compared with the ones you normally saw. She didn't even hold the scythe or the globe. Her right hand rested in her lap, and her left was raised, with the palm facing out. One big black candle was burning in front of her, with a few others elsewhere in the room. The only other offerings were a bottle of fine mescal and an expensive Cuban cigar. The same offerings I would want if I were a deity.

That austerity made it more impressive.

The guy had left me alone in there. The room seemed to be soundproof, giving it the same quiet that a tomb might have. Was he still trying to make me nervous? Did he still want me to feel intimidated? If so, it wasn't working. I actually felt a strange ease and a comfort in that place. It soothed me. I didn't mind the waiting.

"Señor Castillo-Cruz."

Even in the silence, I hadn't heard her enter. But I wasn't startled. I turned to look at her in that candlelight.

"Señorita Murakami-Martinez."

Her name had implied that she would be of Japanese and Mexican descent, a relatively rare combination—and that hypothesis was supported by the facts. Delicate Japanese features but with a darker tone of skin than I usually associate with Japanese people. Glossy black hair flowed down over her back and shoulders, identical to the hair on the Santa Muerte. She wore a red robe, but I could tell she was very thin. This was an almost fragile-looking Flor. And there was something elfin about her, something ethereal in her energy, something touched by magic in that slender being.

And I let out a sigh of relief because nothing about her reminded me of my Flor, my lost Flor. My Flor hadn't been fragile. And she could be delightfully vulgar, the kind of girl who would deliberately spit on the ground while she talked to you and wasn't afraid to down a shot of tequila or mescal, including whatever bug they had at the bottom of the bottle.

Even at this first meeting, it was almost impossible to think of this new Flor doing those kinds of things. And that made me smile as I gave her a little bow, because I was pretty sure that, no matter what else was in store, I wasn't going to be falling into that kind of love with her.

She had been examining me just as intently, just as intensely, as I had been examining her. A light smile had formed on her lips. Her heritage gave her eyes a different shape than those of my Flor, but they did share the same depth of vivid brown. It was just enough to make me feel a pang of my usual pain. I turned away to look again at the skull of Santa Muerte because I suddenly didn't want that old despair to permeate that rendezvous.

"You are my brother," she said, her voice emerging from a profound silence.

"Pardon?"

"You. You are my brother."

"I'm sorry, but I was an only child. And even if there was something I wasn't informed of, you're way too young to be the child of either of my parents."

She laughed. "Don't pretend you don't know what I mean, mi hermano, Cervantes! You are my lost brother, the brother who was exiled. One of the things I am supposed to do in this life is find you!"

I looked her in the face again, and she read the question in my eyes.

"Well, Cervantes? Aren't you lost? Aren't you wandering in exile in these wastelands, as well as in the wastelands of your own life?"

"Yes." I felt no need to lie.

Then she looked toward the altar and seemed to fall into a meditation. The silence returned. I still didn't feel uncomfortable. The moment seemed powerful and full of significance.

When I looked at new Flor again, I saw a tear running down her cheek. When she saw I had noticed, she wiped it away with the back of her hand and let her smile return.

"It was very important that I find my brother. And I wasn't sure I would be able to. So, I am very happy I have found you."

Then she hugged me so firmly, so warmly, that I really could believe that I was a long-lost sibling she had never expected to see again. And then we talked and talked some more. I did feel as though I had known her, that I had known her for a long time. There was an immediate sense of trust.

I even told her about my dreams, about my visions.

Later I would dream of him again, see his anger and also see his fear. But I'm sure the fact that he felt fear only made him feel more anger.

The Boss of La Ciudad was looking at the ruined mess of his very expensively furnished office. Then he looked up at the hole that Lupe Castaneda had made with her bare hands after she'd landed on his roof. Not something easy to do since he'd added plating to the ceiling and walls to protect himself from surprise attacks. But that attack had been too much of a surprise—an unbelievable one. Yet he had no choice but to give it credence, because he'd seen the footage from his own security cameras with his own eyes, footage to which only he had access.

He'd watched that blurry feminine form rip her way in. Then she'd smashed the place up, not even seeming to be looking for anything. She had just wanted to smash the place up.

The attack had happened in broad daylight, probably while I was meeting my "sister." The club and restaurant weren't open for business; it was a nightlife establishment. But there had been employees present, preparing for the evening, who had fled when they realized the place was under attack. There had been no armed guards or narco men around, because the Boss hadn't been there, and his men always went with him.

Did he wonder what would have happened if he had been there when Lupe knocked? Did he think he had missed his chance for a quick victory? Or did he realize that he'd been extremely fucking lucky that the girl had missed her chance to give him the death that he deserved?

"Or else did he realize that Lupe had been watching…waiting for him to leave before she struck?" Flor Murakami-Martinez would ask me after I told her about that dream. "Did he know, or at least suspect, that she was teasing him, playing with him? He's the mouse and she's the cat!"

"I doubt the Boss would see himself as the mouse."

"But deep in his mind and soul, he would know it."

"Maybe. I don't know if it could sink in that fast. He's used to thinking he's the king of the world."

One thing was for sure, Sanchez would be getting a phone call. Your time is almost up, Samurai. Find her. Kill her. Or leave town.

Night had fallen.

Marco was only a little bit drunk. If he had been asked, he would have said that he knew he was only a little drunk because he had left the bar on his own two legs, wobbly as they were.

Not such a good idea for a drunk of any sort to be staggering down the street alone in the dark. Nothing to worry about, though…he was out of money…that was why he had left the bar. And he had nothing else valuable in his possession. The alcohol had made him forget that a robber wouldn't know either of those things until he found out the hard way, meaning it would be hard for Marco.

A burly man with a shaved head and goatee quickly walked past Marco, going in the opposite direction, looking nervous. If that man had wanted to rob Marco, then Marco would have taken the hit and gone down. He would have been forcibly searched. And he wouldn't have resisted, because that would have been his only chance of not getting the shit beat out of him. But that man seemed very nervous and just kept going his own way, leaving Marco to keep ambling the other way.

After another couple of hundred feet, Marco stopped cold. Something was in his way, something that didn't make immediate sense to his soaked-in-booze brain. It was some kind of upright object, and it was blocking the sidewalk. What was it? He edged closer and peered at it intently. Then, startled, he fell flat on his ass.

It looked like a young woman, upside down. She was doing a handstand, using only one hand. She wasn't moving; she was perfectly still and rigid. Was she dead? Had somebody propped up a body in that weird position to make some kind of weirder point?

Marco rolled closer, maybe thinking of trying to feel for a pulse or something. Instead, he was able to make out her face and her black hair hanging down. The eyes were wide open, following his every move. Her expression was coldly neutral. No sign of stress, sweat, or exertion.

Marco managed to get up onto his feet and run away, driven by sudden terror.

Later, when Samurai Sanchez's men came to check out that strange report, the girl was gone.

Virgilio was a tough customer, one of those men who had managed to carve out a street corner empire. He sold some blow and some smoke and ran a couple of girls. He paid the right people and managed to hold his own against the wrong people. His biggest ambition was to have the chance to do "the favor" for somebody who really had connections, somebody who could move him up in the world. Why couldn't he be the next Samurai Sanchez?

One way of earning a little extra cash was to charge a toll if you wanted to walk across his little piece of the pie. At least a dollar or two, if he was lucky, but pesos could be negotiated as well. If things got a little more difficult than expected, he had a few friends around for backup.

And if you were a pretty girl...well, maybe you could have the option of giving Virgilio a kiss instead of cash. Not that there were that many pretty girls wandering around loose in that neighborhood who didn't know what areas to avoid. And every so often, some even found him roguish with a bit of bad boy charm. Or at least that was how he liked to think of it.

That night, things had been slow. Virgilio leaned against a wall, smoking a cigarette, restfully alert. Then, just like that, this girl came around the corner. Reflexively, he promptly stepped out to block her way. She was a bit disheveled and definitely needed a bath, but she was still better than "better than nothing."

With an evil smile and a seductive voice, with just a hint of threat, "Hey, hey, pretty baby. You can't just walk past me without—" and then the words choked in his throat.

You see, Virgilio had heard the stories. Everyone on the streets had by that point, but he didn't really believe that impossible shit. Not until he saw this girl glare at him, not until he saw that darker than dark in the depths of her eyes. Then, in that instant, he believed. More than believed. He knew.

"Ha, Señorita, just a joke. Of course, you can pass. It's a public street, after all!" He made a sweeping bow, pretending to some sort of gallantry. Then he stepped back out of the girl's path.

Guadalupe remained motionless for a few seconds, making her decision.

Not worth killing.

She kept going.

Virgilio watched the night welcome the girl.

Then he fell to his knees to thank whoever he could think of to thank for his life.

Flor Murakami-Martinez also told me part of her story. She had served me dinner, or should I say, had that guy bring us something to eat. The only alcohol she had available was red wine, but I could make that work. She'd mainly listened to me telling her what I knew. I'd even told her about the first Flor manifesting in my dreams. Then as night fell, she began to get more serious about her side of it.

"I knew something big was going to happen, that something was coming. For weeks there had been voices…voices in my dreams, voices from the in-between places that were bringing me news. But even though

I'm a bruja, even though I know the world of dreams and visions, I could never clearly remember the words when I woke up because they were strange words, spirit words that I had never heard before.

"Sometimes I had those visions and dreams without any voices. Sometimes there would just be darkness...or a blasting and raging of black clouds that obscured everything...a storm that was about to come down on all of us. Maybe there would be a glimpse of things in the distance, so far away. Horrid creatures...or a strange woman with the whitest white skin and green hair...but I could never get a clear impression of who or what they were...only that they were concealed in that storm.

"Then there were times I saw you, Cervantes. And I knew that I knew you from a deeper place, a deeper place of reality, a deeper place of being. Sometimes you were watching two strange gringos playing chess. But usually, you were with a woman of la raza...you would be talking to her...or just watching the black storm brewing. One or two times, in one of my dreams, I saw what must have been your woman friend by herself, shuffling a tarot deck. I tried to approach her. She saw me. She seemed to smile at me, but then she went away, and I couldn't see her anymore."

"Yeah, she has a habit of doing that." I couldn't hide a trace of bitterness.

"Is she somebody you know only in your dreams? Or is she somebody that you also know in the life we call real life?"

"Both. She told me that I'm going to be witness to this story, that I'm the one that's going to tell it."

"Do you really think they will let you publish any of this?"

"Maybe as a novel."

She laughed...and that laugh was one of the few things that reminded me of my Flor, the Flor long gone.

New Flor could read the depth of my emotions, the depth of my thoughts, not that I was surprised. "I don't believe that she is with us anymore...here...in this world."

"Probably not," was all I said.

She saw I wasn't going to say more and knew it wasn't time to press me. She said, "One night I made an offering to La Santa Muerte, here, at this very altar. I directly gave her some of my essence and looked into the hollows of her eyes...and I fell into a vision trance. I saw the desert and I saw this storm that tore the sky open, revealing nothing but an even vaster void. And the storm had become a black tornado, a vortex, spinning madly above the sands but not touching down, directly above the corpse of a young woman. She was exposed in a shallow grave and looked almost like a mummy. All at once that tornado seemed to be transformed into a liquid, a tide of blackness that flowed down into that girl's body, becoming completely absorbed into her, all in seconds. Then the night in my vision was at peace again. The gash in the sky was suddenly gone. The stars shining again. Nothing moving. Except that girl. She had been given her life back. She rose up from the sand. She rose up from death itself. Her skin, her face, and her form took the tone of the living again, although she was too thin—starved. Then I knew her, knew who she was. She was Guadalupe Castaneda. Her mother had even asked me to look for her. I'll tell you more about that when the time is right. She appeared bewildered and afraid. But then she seemed to hear a voice, something whispering to her, something I wasn't allowed to hear. Whatever she was hearing, it made her smile. She looked at a nearby hill, started walking toward it, and began climbing it. And then the vision faded.

"I found myself back here, staring into the eyes of Santa Muerte, knowing that our world, this world, had changed in ways that not even I could have imagined it ever would."

Yeah, there was a lot to talk about. Somewhere before sunrise, I ended up sleeping in a guest room.

At dawn Samurai Sanchez and a squad of smoke-windowed and bulletproofed SUVs roared into the neighborhood, that ramshackle barrio that was the only place they could think of to look for Guadalupe Castaneda, the only place they knew of that she had ever called home.

The caravan came to a stop with a honking of horns and a shooting of pistols up into the sky. Sanchez himself tromped up into the late Lucio's bar and raised the bullhorn to his lips.

"Hey, all you lazy donkey fuckers! It's me, your favorite person in the whole big, bright fuckin' world! Hope you all got a good night's sleep, because today is the main event. Hope you all are awake and paying close attention. Because, Señores and Señoras, Señoritas, Chicos and Chicas, Niños and Niñas, if my girl Lupe doesn't show up in the next thirty minutes, we are going to start rounding you all up for some fancy target practice!"

Up until then, it seemed like I dreamed of things *after* they had happened, and sometimes in pieces and incompletely. Sometimes things were very out of order, and it was hard to tell exactly when they had happened. I wouldn't even know about Juan El Bautista at all until much later, when a certain critical moment arrived. But those moments with Sanchez, I'm almost certain that I saw them as they happened—vividly, while sleeping in Flor's house.

Sanchez paced back and forth, smoking cigarettes one after another, waiting for the thirty minutes he'd imposed on himself to expire.

His men deployed themselves around the abandoned bar, ready to lay down fire on anything that raised a challenge…or anything that their chief wanted eliminated. Any peasant who made a move to leave his house was told to get his ass back inside. "And don't try to get away again, unless you want to be first in line when triggers start getting pulled!" The man with the flamethrower waited patiently inside an SUV.

And that's how the time passed.

And passed.

At twenty-eight minutes, Sanchez's phone gave him a buzz.

He answered, listened for a few moments, and then said, "Seriously?"

He called over a couple of his men. "Go around that corner and then down a block and come back and tell me what you see."

They immediately obeyed.

The countdown ticked past the thirty minutes as Sanchez waited, still and silent, with a strange look on his face. He stopped smoking. Instead, he played nervously with the handle of his sword.

Before long, the two men came rushing back. "I think she's here, boss," said one of them. "I think it's her."

"She's coming?"

"No, boss. She ain't moving and she's standing weird."

"Where?"

"Just down the road there, pretty close, in the direction you told us to go."

Sanchez looked at the ground, watching his foot grind one of his cigarette butts into the dirt, considering his next move. Then he sighed. "All right. Let's get this finished."

Some of the men were delegated to approach on foot, some to get back in the vehicles. Sanchez himself took the wheel of the SUV with his flamethrower man.

Not that it was a very long drive. Sanchez saw his target as soon as he rounded a couple of hovels and something that was supposed to be a fence. Finally, Guadalupe Castaneda's ardent pursuer had found her, had gotten her to reveal herself to him.

His men were fanning out and taking their positions as Sanchez got out of his vehicle. They were lining up to confront the girl as she simply watched them. He made sure his sword was secure in its sheath and ready to go. He wasn't hiding the fact that he hoped that blade would deliver the coup de grâce.

Sanchez stood almost at attention and regarded Lupe. They weren't far from each other, maybe half a block. And she was indeed standing weird…firmly on her left leg. The right was raised up so that the bottom of that foot was planted against the left's thigh. The balance was perfect. She didn't move, didn't wobble. Her hands were in a prayer position in front of her chest.

She was looking straight at Sanchez, her expression coldly hateful and disdainful, lacking any trace of fear.

Yeah, Lupe's battle with Sanchez was the most coherent, the clearest dream I'd had up to that point. It was as if something had changed within me, as if I had also reached some turning point.

It was like having a front-row seat. I saw the events as if I were there, a disembodied spectator.

Usually, I would have to fill in much of the story by talking to witnesses.

This time, I was the main witness.

But I was still a reporter. So, I ended up confirming many of the details with some of the people who had been there physically.

Some of Sanchez's men sought cover as they fanned out. Others lay down on the ground or simply kneeled as they double-checked their heavy rifles and machine guns, all aimed at Guadalupe.

She just maintained her odd stance.

Sanchez continued to examine her: a straggly little street bitch. Nothing…nothing about her seemed remarkable. Nothing…except the fact that she continued to stand on one leg, perfectly balanced and showing no sign of fatigue, as seconds kept turning into minutes.

Lupe was facing him, but he couldn't tell if she was still looking at him. Her expression had become almost frighteningly neutral and her gaze absent.

His men, on the other hand, were agitated and nervous, sweating, squirming. It made Sanchez think that she was using psychological warfare on them. That damn girl was using her reputation and her weird behavior to freak everybody out, keep them on edge, make them afraid.

And it seemed to be working. Didn't Sanchez himself feel a little… uncertain?

Without thinking, the samurai lit another cigarette. It was easy to read what was going on in his head, the questions he was asking himself. Was this really going to be a problem? Was it really going to take twenty well-armed men to bring that chica down? Would he need his secret weapon? At that thought, he signaled the flamethrower man to get out and get ready. The guy had to struggle a bit. He was a soldier on leave, trained to use that kind of weapon, but it was still hard for him to fully deploy out of a civilian vehicle.

When Sanchez looked back to Lupe, still in her yoga pose, he could tell that he had her attention again.

I didn't know it at the time, but while most of my mind was at the battlefield, my body had gotten out of bed and ambled back to the chamber of the black Santa Muerte. I sat down at her feet, trying to get into a Lotus Pose of my own—and failing miserably, as could be expected. So, I just stared up into the face of the goddess, my jaw slackened and with a bit of drool escaping.

But what I really continued to see were the final minutes in the life of Samurai Sanchez.

Freeze that moment. It would have seemed absurd to any random pedestrian wandering by, not that a casual pedestrian would be wandering anywhere near all those guns. But why all that weaponry and all those men just to execute what looked, at first glance, to be a mentally ill, homeless girl doing yoga in the street?

"Let her have it," ordered Sanchez, not shouting, just loud enough to be heard. He wanted to be seen maintaining his calm.

Maybe invincible but not immovable: Lupe was the target of all that concentration of perfectly aimed firepower. She was blasted back as she hopelessly tried to keep her footing, and then she was flying and bouncing and rolling until she vanished into a ditch surrounded by rubbish and refuse. And the whole time she had maintained her strange pose.

Silence again, the cloud of gun smoke dispersing in the weak breeze. Nobody moved.

Sanchez just waited. And his men waited.

Was it over? They didn't lower their weapons; everybody knew that girl was full of awful surprises.

Sanchez figured she had never been hit that hard before. If she was wearing some invisible, high-tech exoskeleton, maybe it had been cracked. Maybe she was dead. Or maybe she was trapped, just lying there in her broken battle suit. And how much would that armor be worth if he could get it off her, if it was intact? Or better yet, was there any way he could get it repaired and fitted for himself, for Samurai Sanchez? Then who would they be afraid of on the streets? Then who would become a legend?

It was a hot day. The sun was burning and searing and blazing down on the scene. Silence continued to be in command. The smoke of the barrage slowly finished drifting away. Samurai Sanchez and his men maintained their positions, waiting for any sign of life to emerge from the ditch that concealed that girl, hiding whether she was alive or dead.

All at once, something shot up into the air with a *whoosh*. Something human sized and human shaped seemed to be hurled above and over the line of the men with guns. Everyone turned their heads to follow the object's flight as it reached its apex and then plummeted down behind them with a loud metal drum thump as it crashed on top of an SUV.

And there was Lupe, sitting there on the vehicle's roof, her clothing shredded by bullets, looking back at them with a little smile on her lips. She hadn't collapsed the top of the SUV very much, probably because it had been reinforced for urban narco combat situations, even if they had never expected a superhuman young woman to vault down on it.

Before any more triggers were pulled, she rolled off and dropped down out of sight on the other side of the vehicle.

"Shit! She's gonna get away!" yelled Sanchez, totally misinterpreting Lupe's intentions.

Then the SUV began to rise up off the ground, slowly and a bit awkwardly, as the girl struggled to keep her balance as she lifted it over her head. There was the sound of metal plating crumpling in her grasp... an unpleasant, harsh sound that caused some ear pain.

Sanchez and his men, each one of them, froze in slack disbelief as Lupe tossed the vehicle straight at their left flank. The impact crushed four men without the SUV itself taking too much damage, although it was upside down and resting on the smashed bodies.

"Fuck! Fire! Fire, you shitheads!" screamed Sanchez, for the first time his voice and manner conveying fear and panic.

"He didn't really believe until he saw," Flor would say when I told her all I'd seen.

"That was true for a lot of people, though. And some of them probably still didn't believe it!" I said and laughed.

No hesitation anymore: the firing squad was let loose again. Once more, Lupe was knocked and blasted back for almost a hundred feet because she couldn't find a way to use her strength to brace herself. Finally, she just lay down on her stomach. Some of the bullets still struck that harder-to-hit target, but she dug her hands and feet into the earth and held firm.

"Flamethrower! Flamethrower! Get it ready!"

The man with that particular weapon had lost his poise. He was visibly trembling and his hands were shaking as he prepared the device. But his training prevailed, and he managed to make do.

Meanwhile, everyone else had exhausted their magazines and were hurrying to reload, many of them also clumsy with fear.

And Lupe launched her own counterattack. Could it be called crawling? She began pulling and pushing herself along on the ground but rapidly, like a giant lizard or insect, closing in and presenting such a small, low target that the renewed gunfire wasn't doing much to prevent her advance.

Some of the men looked like they were preparing to run.

"Use that fucking flamethrower now!"

There it was: a huge gout of liquid fire, a demonic orgasm, a dragon's breath. It was a geyser of flame that rushed over Guadalupe Castaneda. She stopped moving as it covered her, poured over her, and hid her from sight. It flared and flared and flared until there was no fuel left.

The area was so barren that only a few things were burning after it was over. And there seemed to be nothing left except for a huge area of blackened, scorched, and desolate ground.

"Where is she? Is she finally dead?"

A mound of that earth rose up to answer Sanchez. Lupe stood up. Every fiber of clothing had been burned off her. She no longer had any possessions. If she'd still had Barbarossa's whip, then that was gone too. She was black as charcoal, covered by a carbonized layer of soot…but her skin was still smooth…not even seared or blistered. Every hair on her head was intact. And under the brightness of the sun, in her unharmed eyes, there lurked something even darker.

She took a couple of steps forward, clenching her fists. Then she stopped and grinned at her enemies, her teeth standing out against the pitch color covering her lips and face.

At that point they ran, scattering in all directions like cats in a lightning storm. Only Sanchez stood firm. He couldn't run. It would have been the end of him, the end of everything he believed himself to be. So the samurai watched the soldier hastily trying and failing to discard the useless flamethrower as he fled the scene; then he turned and looked Guadalupe Castaneda straight in the eye. He took a deep breath and drew his sword. He took his stance…and waited for her to come to him.

Even though Samurai Sanchez was trying to live up to his nickname, poised with his blade and ready to strike, Lupe seemed to suddenly be more fascinated by her naked and blackened skin. She rubbed her forearm with one finger, revealing the natural brown tone underneath the dark layer of carbon.

Was that the moment when Sanchez finally realized that there was no space-age sci-fi armor? Was that when he realized that Lupe was invulnerable in and of herself…without the assistance of any kind of technology…without any kind of explanation?

The girl seemed to continue without caring that Sanchez was even there, waiting to fight with her. She looked around, watching the gunmen disappear from her view. She watched the flamethrower man as he finally managed to ditch his equipment and sprint down the road.

Deciding to let them all escape, she finally turned her attention back toward their would-be leader. Sanchez and Lupe both stood very still for a few moments. Then she pointed at his sword, opened her hand, and held her palm out. A bit of avarice seemed at play in her expression. The message was clear: "Give me that. I want it. Imagine what I will be able to do with it!"

Sanchez maintained his poise. "Come and get it then, puta!"

Starting from at most twenty yards away, Guadalupe began to stroll toward her challenger, making it look so very casual. Closer and closer, just walking, but coming straight at Sanchez, like she planned to just walk through him, like she didn't even care that he was there.

So, the samurai just waited…waited as she got closer and closer and then close enough. Then he aimed a perfect, arcing slice directly at her neck, going for an instant decapitation.

In the same instant, Lupe raised her arm and took a step back to brace herself, taking the blow just above the elbow. Nothing about her gave way in the slightest. The sword didn't sever her arm; it didn't even scratch it. And the force of impact didn't make her lose her balance or move that limb even a millimeter. Instead, all that kinetic energy was driven back into the hands, arms, and body of Sanchez. No ordinary human, no ordinary mortal, could absorb that. The sword was let loose, to go spinning away as Sanchez howled in pain.

Such a perfect weapon—even though it was useless in that situation. For Sanchez, it was also a major part of who he was. He couldn't lose it. So, by intuition as much as by will, he turned and tried to dash to where the sword was landing, in a blind panic at the thought of losing it. But Lupe easily leaped up and vaulted over him, landing between the two, facing the man, her back to the blade.

Sanchez reflexively took a combat stance and fired a kick directly up and straight into Lupe's face. That time she wasn't ready to counter the basic laws of physics…and fell back hard. But she still maintained her weird rigidity, making it look like a statue had been knocked over. Then, with a slight push of her hand, she was right back up and standing in front of him again. So, he launched what should have been a killing blow directly into her throat. That time, one of her bare feet was moved back to prop her up. She slid back only a little bit as some bones cracked in his fist. There had been no give in her flesh. Sanchez gripped his injured hand and bowed down with the pain. Lupe suddenly kicked his legs out from under him with such strength that he ended up with head under heels, his feet spun straight up and his head almost pointing downward. Only his training allowed him a measure of control, and he was able to roll with the fall instead of landing on his head.

In that moment, though, Lupe would have been able to inflict just about any damage she wanted. Instead, she let him be and turned around to go get the sword. She looked too thin, too frail, to be able to wield a thing like that. But of course, her appearance was deceiving. It was easy for her to raise that weapon above her head and hold it with one hand. And she just held it there…and held it…and held it…without moving.

Sanchez, stunned, just sat on his ass and gaped at her.

"All black like that…pitch as coal…naked…eyes like onyx. And with that sword…it makes me think of that goddess from India…what is her name?" Flor would ask.

"Kali."

"Yes, that's it! Kali!"

Lupe began to slowly approach Sanchez again, exaggerating her steps into an almost cartoonish tippy-toeing, as if she were trying to sneak up on the narco, even though he was watching her every move, wide-eyed and unblinking.

With the sword haphazardly over her shoulder, she stopped right in front of him. Then…nothing. She just stood there in silent waiting, like she was carved out of black stone, except for her hair, curled and wild in the arid breeze. Her pose seemed to ask, "How do you want to do this? How do you want to go out?"

In reply Sanchez groaned and pushed himself up onto his two feet with a grimace of pain. He swayed like he might fall down again. But that was just for show. Suddenly, he had lightning in his leg: a kick that could have shattered a cement block struck Lupe in the knee. She wasn't prepared that time and ended up flat on her face. Yet she was still unbending and still holding the sword, with the blade pointing up in the air behind her shoulders. Sanchez brought his boot heel down precisely on the back of her neck. Nothing gave and there was no snap. With her own quick move, she seized the bottom of his pant leg with her free hand while she still lay facedown. He tried to pull free, jerking and kicking and pulling. But he couldn't make the girl let go. And his jeans couldn't tear easily. From a greater distance, it probably looked like he had a dead body or a mannequin tied to his leg that he couldn't shake loose from… because after grabbing on, she hadn't moved a muscle. It looked almost comical.

Sanchez took a pause and then he used his free foot to start stomping on the hand and arm that were holding him. It didn't do any damage or any good. But he kept going and going at it until he wore himself out and had to stop to rest, breathing heavy, stooping over a little. His only accomplishment had been to add some footprints to the layer of carbon on her body.

Lupe began to shake. The samurai was confused for a second. Then he realized she was laughing, silently laughing.

"Fuck," he said in a flat tone of resignation.

The only action he could think of? Walk awkwardly backward, pulling the girl with him over the rough ground.

"Do you have any idea why she can't talk or make any other vocal sounds?" I once asked Flor.

"I think it's because you have to leave something behind when you've been to places beyond your grave and then come back. She must have left her voice."

"She does have that horrid scar on her throat, the one thing that wasn't restored when she came back to life."

Sanchez dragged laughing Lupe about a hundred yards down that thing that passed for a road, back toward Lucio's bar. Her strange, noiseless giggles slowly faded as she became nothing but deadweight again. Sanchez had to stop again, bending over to catch his breath, hands on his knees, staring down at the back of the girl's head.

"Fuck," he whispered.

"Fuck," he said out loud.

"Fuck!" he shouted, trying suddenly to jerk his leg free, and failing, but still raging. Then he reached back and pulled a pistol out of a holster and emptied the clip with the barrel six inches above the back of Lupe's head. The bullets ricocheted harmlessly off her skull. Some of them ended up hitting the abandoned SUVs, leaving dents in the armor of the vehicles. But they left no mark on the girl's head.

Instead of reloading, Sanchez began to use the empty weapon to pistol-whip the hand that continued to hold on to his pant leg. That didn't last long either, as he dropped the gun and tried to shake the pain out of his hand again.

Lupe decided to move, just a little. Not releasing her grip on the denim, she lifted her hand up, forcing her opponent's leg about a foot into the air. Then she froze herself once again into perfect immobility. Sanchez was forced to stand on the other leg. The girl's grip was implacable, not allowing him to move his trapped limb up, to the side, or down…as he tugged on his pant leg. It looked absurd. He looked foolish.

"Shit, bitch. You're gonna have to do…something," growled Sanchez as he yanked out a switchblade, popped it open, and promptly cut himself loose from her grip. Then he started to run, leaving Lupe's hand up in the air and clutching only a piece of denim. But his running was clumsy and stumbly because he kept looking and looking and looking back over his shoulder to see what she was going to do. But she wasn't doing anything. She just kept on lying there, facedown, as Sanchez put more and more distance between the two of them, giving him hope.

But his hope was false. More like some predator than a human being, Lupe was up in a rushing flash, bounding across the space that he had gained. Sanchez barely had time to register what was happening to him as she caught up to him in an eye blink and gave him a shove that sent him sailing and crashing into an old VW Beetle that could almost have been mine but wasn't.

When Sanchez was able to open his eyes, was able to reactivate his consciousness, he found that Lupe was crouching over him, still all blackened and naked from the useless attack he had been so proud of arranging. He felt like he'd been unconscious for a long time but couldn't be sure. He moved his head, trying to look around to see if anyone had come to help him, if anyone had called for reinforcements. But there was nobody else in sight. The locals remained sealed up in their homes, and Sanchez's troops had abandoned him.

He turned back to face the girl and could see the depths of night in her eyes.

"What are you?" he mumbled.

No answer. Instead, she just started to admire that sword she still held.

With a deep breath, body shot through with sharp pains, Sanchez sat up. The girl didn't try to stop him, didn't really seem to care.

"Well, are you going to kill me?"

She shook her head no, still without looking at him.

"Are you going to let me go?"

Another shake no.

Sanchez was baffled. "Then what? Are you gonna fuckin' marry me?"

A small smile, a very small smile, seemed to appear on Lupe's face. But if it did, it vanished almost immediately as she looked toward the horizon. She got up from her crouch and stepped back a couple of feet.

Sanchez tried to stand up, but something wasn't right in his body, and he had to give up and remain seated on his ass. Neither of them moved for a while, letting silence dominate their interaction.

Then the quiet was broken, but not by Sanchez or by Lupe. It came from the neighborhood around them, from those homes, which had seemed almost abandoned or at least dormant for all that time the one-sided fight had lasted. There was movement everywhere, as if there had been some sort of sudden awakening. From out of the hovels and ramshackles and shanties, the people began to emerge. One had a baseball bat. Another held a broken bottle. One had an old, rusty chain. Another had a jagged knife. They came from all directions and began to surround Sanchez.

Lupe walked away.

Sanchez watched them. He watched those people whose lives he had threatened approach him carefully. There was no real expression on his face. But his lips twitched a little bit.

Then he closed his eyes and waited to die.

I came back to myself, clumsily sitting on the floor in front of that black Santa Muerte, stiffness and pain having overtaken my legs and traveling up into my back.

Flor's hand was on my shoulder.

Words tried to spill out of my mouth, trying to tell the story right away, but they were garbled. I felt a rush of fright until she began rubbing my neck and shoulders, causing me to relax.

"I know, Cervantes. It's hard being a seer!"

A couple of days later, Flor was visiting me at my house. I'd been strangely full of energy, barely sleeping and not even drinking that much. I'd been jotting down notes, almost constantly, about the things I'd seen and heard, both in reality and in visions.

"I'm mostly caught up now," I said. "At least with all the info I have so far."

Flor laughed but didn't say anything as she peeked out my window.

"They say that the Boss is going to throw Sanchez a huge public funeral, that he wants to show he still has the power, that he's still in charge of this town, that he's not afraid," I said.

"Are you invited?" she asked, still looking outside.

"I suppose. I am a local reporter…sort of. And somewhere up the line, *he* is my real employer."

"Doesn't that bother you?"

"Well, it's not a question of making a living; it's a question of staying alive. You know what they've done to reporters who don't play the game by their rules." I sighed. "But yeah, it bothers me."

Neither of us said anything for a bit.

Then she turned away from the window and looked at me. "Maybe you could take a date to the funeral?"

"You?"

"No. Lupe."

Flor just kept looking at me, amused, while I went through the process of recovering from my shock.

"You're serious?"

"Why not? She's probably going to put in an appearance, anyway."

"Why? I don't see her as being obliged to go wish ol' Samurai bon voyage."

"True. But she might have another reason to go to that funeral. It's possible that the man who killed her will be there."

"How do you know all of this, Flor?"

"I'm a bruja. I see visions, remember?"

"I remember."

"Are you ready to meet Lupe? I think it's time."

I got up and grabbed my car keys.

Juan El Bautista didn't immediately realize where he was or what had happened to him. At first, he thought he was standing at the base of a cliff, a polluted stream flowing at his feet. He was disoriented, his vision didn't seem quite right…gigantic forms filled some kind of sky, moving… some from the right, some from the left…he couldn't get them in focus, he couldn't make out what they really were. There was noise, so much noise, but his hearing was muffled and all the different sounds somehow mixed together.

Wait, the cliff was too smooth, too regular. And it was made out of concrete. Was it a wall or a dam?

Something floated past him, in the river. It looked like…a gum wrapper. But it was huge, at least ten feet long.

Things snapped into better focus, and that was when he figured it out.

The cliff was really a curb. The river was water in a gutter. The vast shapes were just humans going about their business.

He was tiny, a tiny creature in that gutter, maybe two inches tall.

"Fuck!"

"You're the one who wasted your own substance. It will take you time to get it back."

Juan spun around. Not so far away was a crumpled mass of paper, perhaps an ad from some magazine. There was a half-visible picture of a blonde woman wearing a bikini. The eyes seemed to have life in them, they seemed to regard him, and those eyes were green.

"Why did you do this to me?" Juan asked, stuck between anguish and anger.

"I didn't do any of this, not intentionally. The way this place works is…complicated. Still, that's what makes it worthwhile! I admit I didn't know that there would be an adjustment period, that your new being would be out of phase with your own world for a while. I didn't know that you would be pushed out and into the in-between place. But with time, you would have gotten back into alignment. You almost ruined it by tearing into yourself and releasing your essence just to get my attention. You almost lost yourself out there forever. Still, even though I am much farther away than the in-between, I managed to get you back here. It took some effort to find you, because you ended up a few steps into your own future. Not much but some. It took some of my own passing time to figure it out. At first, I thought I had lost you. But no, here and now is where you are. You're still intangible and you're small—there's not much of you left—but you can restore yourself. I've done as much as I can for you. Our deal still holds. You can accomplish your goal and mine. Just remember, your essence is fire!"

"How can I do anything when I'm like this? How can I restore myself?"

But the woman's voice was fading, the green eyes in the photo were losing their color. "Goodbye, Juan. My connection is breaking for now. Remember, your essence is fire."

After that, she was completely gone, leaving just that inanimate paper.

Juan stared at the picture of the woman in the bikini, as if hoping she would speak again, even if he knew that she wouldn't. If his alien benefactor did speak again, it would be a while and it wouldn't be through that photo. Yet he continued to stare, letting the shock of what had happened wear off.

"Now what?" he finally said to himself, lifting up tiny, transparent hands.

As if to answer that question, one of the giants passing by tossed a cigarette butt down into that gutter. Still burning, it hit the ground with what seemed to Juan an immense burst of sparks as it came to a rest not so far from where he stood.

El Bautista's eyes grew wide as he gazed in rapture at that smoldering remnant that, from his perspective, was almost as big as a barrel.

And he felt a craving, a hunger…not in his gut, but in his entire being.

More by reflex than thought, he dove to plunge both of his hands into the intensity of those embers.

He felt it, he felt that heat flow into his body. In an instant, that cigarette became cold as Juan absorbed all of its energy. And he grew. Not much, but he could feel his body enlarge just a little bit.

And he felt…better.

Then he laughed. "Yes, now I understand. My essence is fire! I need more! Give me more!"

He approached the concrete curb, which was still a cliff for him, and he reached forward. Still incorporeal, his hands passed into its mass, just like the hands of a ghost would be expected to do. Yet there was a small amount of resistance, a little solidity, a little bit of something he could feel. And he was able to grab just enough of the substance to climb up onto the sidewalk.

Uncertain what to do next, he dodged the footsteps of the giants and ran into an alley.

We puttered along in my old Beetle, passing the desolation of La Ciudad. Or was it passing us? It was hard to tell.

There was this feeling…the feeling that I was finally leaving this world behind. I wasn't even dying…other than by the long and drawn-out murder of aging. But I was still on a journey to the other side, the side where there is mystery, the side where there are forces and magics that can't be explained rationally.

My life had been a waste. It was just as ramshackle, just as much a shantytown, as Lupe's barrio. But I knew that if I could see her, meet her, maybe even touch her, and if I could see for myself what she could do, then that life of mine would suddenly be worth it. I'd never seen a UFO, a chupacabra, or a Sasquatch back in those days when I had truly tried to investigate such things, back when my Flor was still around. But none of that mattered anymore. Not if I could experience the reality of Guadalupe Castaneda in person. Because whatever she was, it was more unique and concrete than all those other things. All I had to do was complete the process and see her in the flesh. Assuming she was still flesh in the way I was, in the way the new Flor was, in the way Sanchez had been. Then and only then would I enter into the realm of those who know and leave at my back the desperate land of those who only believe.

Now I was trusted. I was with La Señorita Flor M-M. I didn't need an intermediary to meet me and drive me to her. I was able to know where she lived and did her work, a classier-than-usual storefront that offered her services: divination and curanderismo—fortunetelling and healing. It wasn't so far from Lupe's old neighborhood, from where she'd had her confrontation with Sanchez.

There was a large and more standard effigy of La Santa Muerte up in the front, but not as large, as real, or as impressive as the one farther inside, in the places where not everyone was allowed to go.

And, of course, those were the places we were going.

One would never have suspected that it had been transformed into the true Holy of the Holiest, the center of the world, the place where something beyond nature was going to reveal itself to a humble and unworthy pilgrim. After all, even if it was relatively nice, it was still a nondescript building in an out-and-down part of town.

That guy, the one who had first taken me there, was sitting and guarding the door to the back. He didn't seem hostile anymore. But he still hadn't given me his name. Maybe I wasn't supposed to know it. Flor M-M had a lot of things going on and the less I knew about some of them, so much the better. Not because I would blab or sell her out, but because somebody could always inflict enough pain to make me talk if they knew that I knew things. He stood up and aside as Flor unlocked the door and let me follow her in.

We didn't go to the chamber of the black Santa Muerte. Instead, we went down a hallway that led to even more rooms.

Another door was opened.

The Mystery was sitting there…watching a beat-up old TV.

"Lupe, this is Señor Cervantes Castillo-Cruz." Then to me, "Lupe has been staying with us when she hasn't felt like going out on the town."

Guadalupe Castaneda turned to look at me, smiled slightly, gave a little wave, and turned back to the TV. Her skin was still covered by the black carbonization. That was the only thing that made her look any different from all the other poor and young women of La Ciudad who could have been watching that same program.

She was apparently enjoying one of our relentless telenovelas. A thuggish businessman—or was he a mobster?—had grabbed a hysterical lady by the shoulders and was shaking her, roughing her up, threatening her. He wanted her to keep silent about some financial or sexual irregularity that he had engineered, that she had stumbled upon. I watched Lupe watch the show. Her expression was flat, but there was an intense glinting and shimmering in her brown, human eyes that gave a hint of that absolute blackness that sometimes filled them. I knew she was imagining what she would do if she were in that female character's situation.

That would have been a soap opera worth watching.

Perhaps even a soap opera worth writing!

Maybe someday, if I couldn't just tell the truth straight out, I could make it a script for one of those shows, overwrought and melodramatic and supposedly fictional.

Something brought me back from my daydream. It was a sort of electricity, a subtle and warm vibration that caressed the skin of my face.

When I became aware of it, I tuned into it and realized it was radiating from Lupe. I could almost see the heat waves pulsing on the pavement under the blazing sun.

At the beginning, it felt oddly pleasant. But then, in a sudden burst, it seemed to tear at my skin, like it was trying to strip that flesh from the bone. I was about to step back, but before I could, Lupe's program went to commercial—and that broke the spell. The black faded from her eyes, along with her interest in what she was watching and along with that field of energy.

Flor, my lost Flor, had claimed to be able to sense the auras of people. I never had, not until I was near Guadalupe Castaneda. But I don't know if it was due to any talent on my part. It was probably because the source of that particular aura was so powerful that even a stump like me could pick up on the frequency.

Strangely, when that energy, or at least my ability to feel it, faded out, a sudden drowsiness swept over me. There I was, in front of my personal Holy Grail—that invincible young woman who proved there was more to this world than modern humans were normally able to believe—and I wasn't energized; instead, I was sleepy. In fact, I was so impossibly tired that I collapsed onto a couch and fell asleep, no longer caring about the presence of Lupe or of Flor M-M.

And then I was…somewhere. I was the one watching TV. What was the program? I couldn't make it out at first; the picture was distorted and grainy. In desperation, I leaned closer, trying to make sense of the images dancing inside the screen. Yes, there it was: a girl was walking alone alongside a makeshift dirt road. It was twilight…or was it sunrise? I couldn't tell for certain. The image became more clear. The television seemed all at once to become larger and more modern, a transformation that let me know I was dreaming. But I didn't care, because that was when I could tell that the girl walking was Guadalupe Castaneda. But it was a Guadalupe with a rounder, fuller face, a Guadalupe with a little more weight on her, more natural. It was a Lupe that was still a normal, living human being.

An old brown van, so average and so nondescript, so incredibly normal for La Ciudad, came bouncing along and slowed to a stop next to Lupe. The driver said something. I couldn't make it out, but Lupe drew closer to the van. Why the trust? Did she know the driver? I couldn't see him…I couldn't make out his face…he was just a shadow. And it was all a mistake…a fatal mistake. With a strange dexterity, that man slid into the back of the van. Then the panel door slammed open with a bang that almost seemed to be a gunshot. Lupe tried to back away, wanted to turn and run. But a huge hand at the end of a powerful arm reached out to grab her by her hair, to yank her brutally into the van. As soon as her kicking feet disappeared inside, the door was closed as quickly as it had been opened.

Then the van continued its journey, trundling along, not too slow, not too fast, not like anything special had happened. It passed on out through the barrios and into the more established part of town, into neighborhoods that seemed more prosperous and middle class, more respectable.

It almost seemed random when that vehicle pulled into a driveway, an automatic garage door going up and then coming down behind it, out of sight of any possible witnesses. But the view of my television continued to follow the whole series of events. A man was waiting, a man I knew even though I had never met him. He smiled as the shadow of the giant hopped out of the van, pulling a Lupe who had already stopped fighting.

They took her to the basement.

What I saw next was the horror.

I'm not going to share what I saw.

But I woke up. The atrocity of it had driven my mind back to the surface.

Lupe was staring at me. Our eyes locked. I was weeping for her, for what had happened to her.

I almost felt I could sense her thoughts. "I couldn't remember it all…I wasn't allowed to remember it all until now…until you dreamed it!"

The night in her eyes was hurting me.

I felt like I was going to vomit.

Instead, I passed out.

Awareness returned…yet it was like trying to see through melted glass. There was something like a face hovering somewhere up above me. I blinked once. I blinked twice. Things became clear enough for me to know that it was a woman's face.

"Lupe?" I mumbled.

"Flor," responded that floating visage. The mouth seemed out of synch with the words.

"Flor?" In that moment I could think only of my lost friend.

A sigh…I felt the breath. "Not Flor from the good ol' days. You really need to get over that one. It's me, Flor, from the here and now!"

"Sorry." My vision was clearing, along with what passed for my mind and my memory.

Flor Murakami-Martinez didn't say anything more on the subject. She just stood there with her arms crossed and looking mock-irritated as I sat up. Same room. The TV was off. And there was no Guadalupe Castaneda.

"That was a neat trick, though. You shared a vision with Lupe. That's something even I haven't been able to do. The first Flor must have taught you well before she took off."

"I could almost think you were jealous."

Flor snorted slightly. "Maybe I am. Or maybe I just want to see you get over your shit."

"Either way, Flor didn't teach me that. I've never had anything like that happen to me. And I don't want to do it again. I saw it…saw what they did to her. Horrible." I started to feel sick again…took some deep breaths. "Horrible."

"You saw who killed her." Not a question.

"Yes."

"And you know him."

"I know who he is…it's *his* son…and he's a sick fucking psychopath… and that doesn't even begin to describe it. Where did Lupe go? Did she go to get him? Please tell me that she's going to get him!"

"She'll get him—but not yet. There are patterns of destiny that I can make out only dimly, but I can see that they demand that her vengeance be delayed. I know that much."

I sat there, still recovering.

Flor stood and looked at the inert television, like she was watching a show I couldn't see. "Some secrets have been whispered to me before the altar of La Santa Muerte. I was told that Lupe could not clearly remember how she died. I was told that when the time was right that you—and only you, Cervantes—would be able to unlock her memory. But I didn't know it would be in such a blunt…and psychic manner. And now she will have to suffer the ordeal of her memories, just like you had to suffer them with her to bring them forth. It's all part of…something…a prelude of some sort."

"Why couldn't she remember it? Why did she have to wait for me? What do I have to do with any of this? I've never had anything to do with anything like this before. I always sought it—but I never found it!"

"Well, now you have found it…or it found you. And we had to wait for you. We were told to wait for you—because you are the storyteller!"

I didn't know how to take that. It was all too much in that moment. I couldn't shake off what I had seen. "I need a drink, Flor."

She looked at me funny for a second and then said, "Okay."

Fire had been easy to find. There were small fires everywhere in La Ciudad. Juan was still intangible, still invisible, so he could go anywhere he wanted to find it: restaurants, backyard barbecues, kitchens. The people there might have been surprised when a flame suddenly extinguished, but they didn't seem to suspect anything unnatural. And even if they had suspected it, what could they have done?

El Bautista even found a couple of guys who were trying to copy his old tricks, pouring gasoline on a still-living victim and trying to light it up. It was a messy process because Juan forced them to try five times before he stopped consuming the fire and let them finish the guy's life.

After that, he seemed to be about three and a half feet tall. He'd regained more than half his height, although sometimes it was hard to tell because his form wasn't always clearly visible, even to his own eyes. And he wasn't sure how much time had gone by; his sense of it still seemed scrambled, especially since he showed no sign of having to sleep or even rest. All he did was seek the fire that was his essence.

He had no problem passing through wood or stone. Maybe he felt just a bit of friction, but he was still almost totally immaterial. He would mutter to himself, but no one heard his voice. He was truly a ghost until something happened that ended up giving him great pleasure.

Passing through a brick wall, El Bautista found himself in someone's backyard. A big dog was chained up to a post and immediately began snarling and then barking at him. He stepped to the side, and it moved to follow as best it could, its eyes still on its target.

"You can see me?"

In response, the beast charged at Juan, coming close and coming up short as the chain snapped tight and the dog's front legs were yanked into the air.

Juan leaned in just a bit closer to tease the animal. It began snapping wildly, hoping by some miracle to get a piece of its tormenter.

"You really can see me! But it would be nice if you shut up now."

Impulsively, El Bautista extended a hand into the dog's slobbering maw, which immediately slammed shut, trying to bite that hand off, but finding nothing to tear into as the phantom fingers passed on through the roof of its mouth and into the core of its skull.

Once again, using intuition more than deliberation, Juan released a small sample of his essence directly into the animal's brain, feeling himself shrinking slightly as he did. The effect on the dog was dramatic. It whimpered, became completely rigid, and fell over, dead as it hit the ground.

It was far more than Juan had expected.

After that moment of surprise, he began laughing uncontrollably as he continued walking—walking through another wall.

I woke up later in a bed. My own body odor was…disturbing…even to me. Much to my surprise, Flor M-M was deep breathing, asleep, next to me.

Still in my sweat-stained and rumpled suit, I sat up and remembered that I was at her place. Then all the horrid visions I'd shared with Lupe Castaneda came rushing in on me. I felt woozy…and lay down again. It wasn't like falling asleep; it felt different. But the end result was that I lost consciousness again.

I couldn't tell if I was awake, asleep, in a trance…or somewhere in the center of all three of those things. But there I was, still on that bed, alert and aware, feeling like I was starting to float up a bit.

The first Flor, my vanished Flor, stood near and looked down at me. She met my gaze again, and I sank into those big brown eyes that I remembered so well…even after so many years.

She didn't say anything. I didn't say anything. Her expression seemed to be one of concern. Mine was probably one of joy. I could see the vivid textures and deep tones of her skin…the lines in her full lips…the very light traces of age around those eyes…the neck that was more slender and fine than one would expect at a first glance…the bosom that was a little more bountiful than she usually allowed others to see.

For the first time, for the first time in a very long time, I felt just a glimmer and just a tiny, shimmering twitch of a true erotic desire.

Her expression seemed to soften.

Then she faded away.

I woke up again or at least switched to the state of mind that we usually call being awake. My body was heavy and smelly once more.

Flor Murakami-Martinez still slept beside me, still breathing deeply in the depths of her own dreams.

After finding some of Flor's red wine, I slept again and my dream vision was pulled away and far into the vastness of some primordial redwood forest, mist shrouded and greenly deep. I couldn't tell where I was, but it wasn't a landscape found in La Ciudad.

And I saw Lupe Castaneda, curled up and fetal, silently sobbing. Was I in the present? Was she suffering from her memories, from the recollections of the brutal death that random fate had condemned her to? Thinking of those events, those memories of hers that I had also seen, made me shudder again, and I wasn't even sure I was in my physical body.

"Cervantes," a voice whispered at my back. I knew it was Flor the first, back again.

"Look!" She was at my side, pointing into some shadows among the trees. Something was there, the pale form of a man. When the vision became clear, he smiled at me. Fangs glinted. A vampire.

"And over there." She pointed in another direction at a huge and looming figure, almost a giant, towering on two feet and standing like a man, bigger and taller than any human male, with only one huge eye. The Cyclops.

"And there." Lurking in some underbrush, another strange creature was hunched over. A hairy creature growling with menace. A wolf that was far too large to be a normal wolf. A werewolf.

From their three directions, those beings closed in on Lupe. She seemed unaware of them as they stalked closer to her. She was still lying there with her face plunged into her hands, writhing and wailing, still without making a noise. I wanted to warn her. But I couldn't move. I couldn't talk. Flor put a hand on my shoulder, seeming to want to comfort me, and to tell me to stay out of it and watch.

Soon the three stood over Lupe, staring down at her and her apparent helplessness, each with his own particular spark of hungers and appetites gleaming in his gaze. They seemed ready to tear her to pieces. Then Lupe became aware of them, and she removed her hands from her face to look up at them with an expression of loathing, her own eyes like blazing voids. The wolf leaped back. The vampire half-flew and half-climbed up one of the tall trees. The Cyclops backed away slowly and kept retreating as Lupe stood up with her fists clenched. All three creatures continued to follow paths of withdrawal into misty vanishing points.

Lupe watched them go, then sat down, seeming to want to continue her mourning.

"Think, Cervantes," said Flor. "A being like Lupe, so powerful and alien here on planet earth—how can her presence here not open the way to other beings that shouldn't be here…that have never been here…or haven't been here in a very long time? There will be struggles and battles between beings that have not been seen since the time of myth! These three, they are just shadows, premonitions."

I could have asked a thousand questions. But I didn't ask even one.

Lupe was looking at me, noticing me there for the first time. She smiled and waved. I smiled back.

And yet again I was awake, to find Flor the second almost glaring at me. She seemed perturbed, annoyed.

"Were you dreaming with her again?"

"Yeah," I said with a grin on my face, still groggy, some serenity restored to my soul by the first Flor.

But Flor M-M rolled her eyes.

"Why does that bother you?"

"I want to be the only Flor in your life."

"I'm probably older than your fuckin' father!"

That made her laugh and the touch of anger in her eyes fled like those creatures had fled from Lupe. "It's not like that. I already told you that you are my brother, and I don't like it that you're tormented by a lost love."

"Better to have loved and lost," I mumbled, still exhausted, still under the influence of too much alcohol. I dozed off again.

There were no more visions, no more dreams.

Later I felt recovered enough to go home. I wanted to go home. Flor wanted to come with me. While I finally took a shower, she got us a takeout meal.

We ate. We talked. Flor filled in the story some more, gave me more details.

"She was a good girl…or tried to be," said Flor. "She worked hard, wanted to help her family. They needed that help. She had to give up on school, never really learned to read or write. You know what happened to her father, that he couldn't work anymore."

"And I know what happened to the guy who did it."

We both smiled at that thought.

"She didn't party, even if sometimes she liked to go out dancing with her friends. Maybe drink just a little. No boyfriends, though. She was shy and hadn't met anyone she really liked. But mainly she worked a lot, so was too tired to do anything more than work and go straight home. That was when they got her, wasn't it? Probably when she was walking home from work."

Our smiles faded into melancholy. "Yeah, that would fit with what I saw, maybe walking home after a late shift. She sure wasn't dressed up for a night out."

"I knew her family. They came to me for cures, and they wanted me to tell their fortunes. They made offerings to La Santa. I never saw anything good for them. That's how it is sometimes. So, you just have to be vague and tell them to have faith. That's usually what people need to hear. That's part of the business. That's also why there can be so many fakers, but that's the price you pay when those of us who really have the spirit sight know when not to tell what they have seen. One day Lupe accompanied her mother, and I saw her death coming. Sometimes I can see a way for a person to avoid their ending, at least for a while, but this was not such a time. I could not help her avoid her death, so I kept silence. A few days later, she vanished. Of course, the police were no help, so the mother came to see me. I hoped I could at least help find the body. Instead, I saw only a darkness that terrified me. So, I told her mother that my powers were dim that day, even though that was another lie, and I promised to try again the next day, and the next, until I could tell her something. The mother left me with her sad gratitude. It made me more determined. That was when I made magic with La Santa and had that vision that I already told you about, when I saw Lupe return, her return as something no longer human, as something not even alive anymore, at least not in the way we are."

Flor paused for a few moments.

"At first I didn't believe it. I knew there was magic in this world, mystery in this world. But I didn't think that anything like what I'd seen in that vision could happen in this reality! But then things started to happen. A lot of things that you already know about…some that you've seen for yourself…at least the aftermath. Things and events that were undeniable. I continued to have visions, to see some of these events as if I were there in the flesh. I soon had to admit that Lupe was genuine. I was awestruck, amazed. I'm sure you felt the same way when you understood she was actually doing…what she was doing."

I nodded. I didn't want to say anything because I wanted her to continue.

"And it didn't take a psychic to see that the narcos would eventually find out who she was. And you didn't have to be a genius to know that if they couldn't stop her directly, that they would try to threaten her family."

"So, it was you who made her family disappear before Sanchez tracked down their house?"

"Me and my little group of followers. We have our own network that can help people. It's not a huge operation, but it's a good one. Lupe knew she could come to me, that she could hide out with me when she wanted a break from her vengeance trek. She can get a change of clothing here. I can get her guns if she wants them. She also knew not to go home, that she might expose her family to danger. So, I brought them here: they needed to see what had happened and they needed to see that they had to leave. Do I need to explain the joy and the fear that they felt—joy at seeing their daughter, fear of what she had become? They knew that they needed to leave."

"Where did they go?"

"We got them all to safe places in El Norte, even her friend Paloma— the one she rescued from that hellhole of a club. It's probably better if you don't know exactly where they went, at least not yet."

"Probably."

Then—

Then nothing. Sanchez had his big funeral. And I went. But I went alone. The idea of me attending with Guadalupe Castaneda didn't go anywhere; that was because Guadalupe Castaneda wasn't showing up anywhere. There were no longer any reports or sightings. There were no deaths that could be attributed to her.

One week passed.

Then a month.

Without that stark and daily proof of her existence, people began to speak of her as if she were already a legend. She was beginning to seem like all those other strange and unworldly things I had chased after in the old days. She was becoming another weird and unbelievable story that could never be truly proven or disproven.

My only consolation was that I had actually seen Lupe, seen her with my own eyes, in whatever her flesh had become.

Where was she? I'd seen the truth. I had shared that vision of what had happened to her, what they had done to her. Her revenge wasn't complete; it hadn't even truly started. None of the people she had killed in her rampage had been involved in her murder, at least not directly. If Flor was right, Lupe hadn't even remembered who her killer was until our minds met in the house of La Santa Muerte. But instead of going after him, it seemed like she had just gone.

Then the third week passed.

Juan El Bautista didn't feel the passage of that time. He never slept, he never stopped moving, continually seeking fire to feed his restoration. It seemed that he had regained his original height and his original size, but he was still invisible to human eyes and still intangible, still able to slide through any solid matter that tried to be an obstacle.

That was when he began looking for her, looking for Lupe.

He wanted to murder her. He wanted to try to kill her, the way he'd killed that dog.

He didn't know that she had vanished from the scene.

He restlessly searched La Ciudad, hoping to find her. Only his other need, his need for fire, distracted him. Sometimes he found and shadowed his old associates, hoping they would find the girl—or that the girl would find them. Some of them he loathed. Some of them he would have loved to have seen dead at his feet, the result of a series of perfect crimes. But he didn't want to use his essence and consequently shrink again. He would do that only if he could kill that girl…the girl he couldn't find.

So, he continued to prowl and prowl the city.

And sometimes, especially in the dark of the night, he would call out, "Where are you? I know you're there!"

But he never received an answer, not even from something with green eyes.

"No one knows where she is," said Flor. "And I have had no dreams or trance-sights of her. Have you?"

The question surprised me. I still wasn't used to thinking of myself as any kind of psychic or visionary. All that ability that had woken up in my brain had fallen back asleep when Lupe took off. "No, nothing."

We sat together in my kitchen drinking coffee. For once I was up before noon by my own choice. I hadn't seen Flor M-M for a few days. But she did have other business to deal with. She came and went as she pleased. I let her have a key to my house. I couldn't really tell you for sure what our relationship was. Sometimes she would stay for days, and it seemed like she lived with me. But we weren't lovers. And I didn't feel like a father figure. Maybe she was right when she called me her brother—a very much older brother.

"I may not know where she is," I said after watching my hand stir my coffee for what seemed like a few minutes. "But I know why she's there."

Flor watched me intently.

"Lupe knew that an atrocity had been committed against her, knew that she had been murdered. But she couldn't remember it clearly. All she knew was that some evil asshole had killed her. So, she went out to take action against all the evil she knew, all the evil she could find. Then when you took me to meet her, something happened. She remembered…and I saw it in my mind too. Now she knows exactly what happened to her, and she knows exactly who did it. So, either she is planning a special revenge, biding her time. Or else that memory has driven her insane."

"Or maybe even both," said Flor quietly.

"Or both."

Then came the night when I dreamed again.

I dreamed that I was in a nightclub, a gentleman's club, a strip joint. The place was full of the smoke of cigarettes and cigars, the scent of sweat and thwarted desires. Even though I smoked, and even though my body wasn't really there, I felt like I was choking.

And why was I there? I didn't want to be in that dream. I struggled to wake up.

Then I saw the woman who slowly turned around onstage, half-hearted, not really into it.

My lost Flor.

That was why I was there in that dream.

So, I settled back down to dream with her.

Mi Florita Pérdida seemed not just bored but annoyed by her presence in that place. She moved slowly up there, clumsily trying to spin around the pole, only feebly shaking her hips. It wasn't her scene. It never had been. But my vision was so clear that I could admire those pretty legs that I could still recognize…a memory buried somewhere deep in my old and mescal-washed brain. And I felt it again: the possibility of something like a spark of desire pushing its way down along my spinal column and toward my genitals.

I didn't get a chance to see if the spark could actually ignite, because in that moment Flor let her gaze drift out over the crowd of dead-eyed men, who seemed almost like props in the real show, and she saw me. A lopsided scowl took over her expression as she hopped offstage and advanced toward me.

"Cervantes! You must really be mad at me for some reason, making me appear in a place like this!"

"Me? *You're* trying to hurt *me*, making me watch you in a place like this."

She just shook her head and suddenly I was up and we were heading out the door. She seemed to be pushing me along. "Whatever. Whatever. I still have to show you what you need to be shown."

Outside there was only desert…and night. La Ciudad wasn't there, and the strip club didn't seem to be there anymore, either. But I became aware of figures in that night. People sitting oddly on rocks or lying in the sand. Their positions and postures didn't seem quite natural; there was something off about those quiet and motionless beings. I didn't want to approach any of them. I was afraid for some reason, even though none of them gave the slightest indication that they were aware of my guide or me.

"Over there." Flor pointed farther into the darkness, then took my hand and pulled me along against my will. She seemed agitated and hurried.

We passed among those people in the shadows. There were far more of them than I had perceived at first. None of them acknowledged us, but when we were among them, I could see that some of them were moving after all. There was twitching, shaking, nodding to nobody in particular, twisting and untwisting of hands, rocking back and forth. I was aware of a slight hiss or buzzing in the air, but it didn't seem to be coming from any one place.

Only after most of those beings were behind us did I see Lupe. She sat cross-legged at the base of a rock that was nothing more than black shadow. That darkness was so deep and profound that I realized I could see her only because I was using my dream eyes.

She was very still…frozen…her face buried in her hands again…the thick black hair hanging down like a shroud.

Flor and I stopped there and stood right in front of her. She didn't give any sign that she noticed either of us.

"Well?" asked Flor, after some timeless moments.

"Well, what?"

"What are you going to do?"

"I thought *you* were going to tell *me*!"

Flor didn't say anything else. She just kept watching me, remaining as silent as Lupe.

"Find her," I finally said. "Find her in the real world."

That was when I woke up.

Yeah, I knew where Lupe was.

Flor M-M didn't happen to be visiting, so I called her.

Somebody, somewhere, once said to follow your dreams. So as the sun beat down on my old ass, Flor and I got into my ancient Beetle. I even held the door for her; always good to have a little chivalry when one is on a quest. Then we bounced off into the desert, so that I could follow my dream. I was pretty certain it had given me specific directions.

Flor M-M always seemed amused…maybe even a little delighted by my old car. I couldn't help but wonder if she would have been so happy with it if she had known that the main reason I kept that car for so long was because it was the same vehicle that I had given the first Flor rides in. Mi Florita Pérdida.

I certainly didn't plan to be bringing it up in our conversations.

This time I was taking us out in the opposite direction, out the other way from where Lupe had risen from the dead.

"You know where we're going for sure." No question mark.

"I think I do. I think the place I dreamed about, where I dreamed Lupe is, it's a real place."

"Care to share?"

"You know the place they call Los Locos?"

"That's a place I've never been, that I don't really know."

Flor was captured by her thoughts for a few seconds before speaking again.

"So that's where she is, Cervantes?"

"I think so. I hope so. If we can't find her, if we can't bring her back, then the situation will just revert to the same old shit."

"That's a lot of shit, Cervantes. And not even Lupe Castaneda can clean all of it up."

"Well, at least she can kick it around in ways that nobody else can."

La Ciudad was a place of casualties.

Some were obvious, like the body of a gangster found with a bullet plugged into the back of his head or that of a woman who had been raped and had her throat cut.

Then there were others who weren't as obvious. These were the casualties who were still standing on their own two feet, still moving around and walking. They were people who hadn't lost their lives, hadn't lost limbs, hadn't even been maimed. No, these were the people who had lost their minds, perhaps even their souls. Victims of a thousand forms of personal horror, many were ragged and homeless, living on the streets, begging, picking through the garbage. They were mostly invisible. Once in a while, they would still be brutalized, but mainly they were left to their own scant devices. It was as if the evil in La Ciudad were content with its victory over them, as if it had accepted their surrender. There was really hardly anything left to be taken from them.

But there were still others, those who were so broken, so traumatized, that they couldn't even manage to eke out a scavenger's life. And many of them ended up in the place that was called Los Locos.

That's how I explained it all to Flor.

She just listened.

So, Flor saw it for the first time, out in the desert, at the end of our road, seeking shelter at the base of some small hills: a collection of huts and tents. Despite all of the disruptions in La Ciudad, things still seemed the same. It was still the realm of lost souls and damaged spirits. Some still found their way to that place on their own. Some were brought and left by friends or family. Many were brought by what passed for authorities of some sort.

There weren't enough real huts or tents to shelter all of them, so the homemade, shapeless little structures thrown together with blankets and pieces of metal, wood, plastic, and cardboard continued to exist. These improvised homes far outnumbered the habitats that had been planned, and they seemed to spread out at random over a far greater area. But that was to be expected. I didn't think that Eduardo's resources had suddenly increased in any dramatic way.

I had to slam to a sudden halt when a human scarecrow half-flew and half-jumped in front of my car. A withered and emaciated old man, nude except for a tattered Mexican flag that he wore like a cape, blocked our way. One foot was bare, the other covered by the remnants of a shoe. He kicked my bumper with the bare one and screamed at us.

"Friend or foe?" asked Flor.

I just shrugged as the man kicked my bumper again. I wasn't sure what I was going to do if he started to do any real damage.

"You really hang out here, Cervantes? It doesn't seem like your kind of place."

"I have a friend here who sort of runs the place, as much as it can be run. But I hope he doesn't find me here this time. I want to keep him out of this if I can. I even tried to help him out by writing a couple of stories about Los Locos, until somebody decided it made the town look bad, that it wasn't good for La Ciudad's rep."

"I see. Yes, this is the reason our city looks bad," she said with a smirk.

The man kept screaming and flapping his flag like he was a big, weird bird with broken wings. He was still in the way. But he didn't make any other hostile moves and he'd stopped kicking. I decided to wait, see if he exhausted himself, got bored, wandered off.

It wasn't long before his voice went raspy, hoarse, became a painful whisper. Soon he was silently opening and shutting his mouth at us… angrily.

Flor made a face at him. He didn't seem to notice. Then he kicked the bumper one more time. Definitely crazy. Otherwise, he would know that in a place near La Ciudad, there was a good chance of getting shot for doing shit like that.

"Should I do something?" Flor asked.

"Not yet," was all I said. Not "Like what?" I had no doubt if she chose to do something, something would happen.

In that moment, the man suddenly looked to his right, then wrapped himself up tightly in his flag and bounded away, leaving behind him nothing more than the sight of scrub and rocks.

There was a new arrival, and he had apparently scared off the flag man. This one stood calmly, watching Flor and me, waiting. But he was watching us with only one eye. In the place of the other there was a destroyed and empty socket. He formed a strange symmetry with my last visit, because he was missing the opposite eye to that of the woman who had greeted me then. Half his face had been burned. The mouth was twisted and the jaw hung half open. Saliva trickled from the lowest corner.

He was dressed in the dirty and worn robes of a Catholic priest.

I smiled…it was a sincere smile…as I got out of the car and approached the man.

"Padre Guzman? That is you?" I extended my hand. Much to my surprise, he took it, giving me a firm handshake as he nodded. He didn't say anything. He couldn't: they'd taken his tongue.

"He really is a priest?" Flor, following my example, had gotten out of the Beetle.

"Is…was…I don't know how all of that works. All I know is that he tried to speak out against the narcos…and he ended up here…like this."

It was actually Sanchez who had carried out the deed, being overzealous. The story was that the Boss had reamed him out over it. You know how it is, some of those guys really believe they're still good Catholic boys. Maybe the Boss was; he'd forgiven Sanchez his sins enough to throw him a fancy funeral.

But Lupe hadn't.

Speaking of that, the three of us stood a bit uncomfortably for a few moments. Then I described Lupe to him. "Padre, do you know if this woman is here?"

His damaged features were still able to display fear. He began to back away from me.

"Padre, please, just point the way. That's all I ask: just point the way."

There was a hesitation that dragged out long enough that I began to think he wasn't going to respond. But then his trembling finger rose to indicate a trail that led away from the road. After Padre Guzman was certain I understood, he quickly headed off in the opposite direction.

"I guess that means she's here." Flor shielded her eyes to look down that path that our reluctant guide had shown to us. There were some of those makeshift shelters in the distance, but no sign of any human beings. And to tell the truth, it really wasn't much of a path either. Yet neither of us wasted any time in starting down it.

Progress got slow, mainly because of me. As soon as we passed the semi-tents, we had to thread our way among rocks and brambles and go up. That meant I had to frequently stop to catch my breath, fan myself with my hat, wipe away the sweat, continue on for a bit, then repeat the process.

Then we found the first body. I didn't even notice it—until I startled its shroud of flies into angry flight. The corpse seemed to have belonged to a chubby, nondescript man. Neck broken, head facing up in a way that didn't match the fact that he was belly down. His pants were also partly down, exposing his ass.

"I'll bet he tried to rape her," I said flatly.

Flor chuckled.

The man's smell wasn't nondescript, so we kept it moving.

Then a second body.

And then a third.

All positioned the same way: stomach to the ground, broken neck, scavenged eyes looking up into the blue sky. She'd killed like that before.

"Idiots," said Flor.

"Just like everyone else who tried to fuck with her"

We kept going. It kept being hard on me.

Then we came to a blanket that seemed to have been thrown on the ground by chance. But then we saw it was draped over something that didn't move.

"Hello!" I called out, in case it was a living person finding protection from the sun.

"It's her," said Flor.

"You're sure?"

"Yes."

"What should we do?"

"That's up to you."

I didn't question her. I didn't question anything. Instead, I did something stupid. I didn't consider it beforehand. I did it on impulse.

I yanked the blanket off Guadalupe Castaneda.

And it was indeed Lupe, sitting with her legs crossed, bending over, with her elbows on the ground. As in my dream, her face was buried in her hands. She didn't react, didn't move, didn't twitch a muscle.

All I could think to do was plop my ass down beside her and harvest more sweat from my brow with the handkerchief. Flor remained standing, glancing up at the sky every few moments. I became strangely aware of the ticking of my watch. Lupe continued not moving, not in the slightest. She didn't make a sound. She didn't even show signs of breathing. Did a being like her have to breathe? I didn't know.

It wasn't long before I started to feel dizzy. My fat rolls were beginning to bake inside my rumpled suit. I was thirsty as hell, but I didn't have anything to drink, not even water. I needed to eat soon too. If I had thought ahead and brought some stuff, we could have had ourselves one really weird picnic. I was fading fast; I wasn't going to be able to stay there much longer.

Flor was strangely quiet as well, looking around, looking at me, showing what seemed to be a hint of concern. She also seemed to be waiting for something. I wanted to wait too. I didn't want to leave Lupe there like that. And yet, what was there to do? Pick her up and carry her back down? Put her in my trunk? In those old Beetles the trunk was in the front, so she might have fit. But even assuming she didn't resist, it felt disrespectful to do something like that to her.

A wave of wooze began to swamp me. I felt like I was swaying…that I was going to fall backward…or forward…I couldn't tell which. Then a few words popped out of my mouth. It was my voice, but I didn't feel like I was the one saying them.

"She's not ready. It's not time. She can be here."

Then, without willing it…without meaning to do it…I struggled up and staggered back down the path toward my car, like a big, old drunk. And I guess I could be called a drunk. But I hadn't been drinking that day, at least not up to that point.

Flor followed me, still silent.

I began to feel a little more in control of my movements, so I looked back over my shoulder at Lupe. And I could have sworn that out behind her, and higher up the slope in the distance, I could see a woman waving to me. The first Flor. Then she vanished…swallowed up in the waves of heat.

Somehow, I managed to make it back down to the road and to my vehicle. I also began to regain more of…myself. I found my voice again and asked Flor M-M if she could drive.

Still quiet, she took the keys that I offered her.

Time passed.

I would often think I should go to Lupe. But some little voice would whisper in the back of my brain that it still wasn't the moment.

The hammer of summer continued to strike the anvil of La Ciudad.

My life became more sane. Flor the second came to visit me often. We would talk late into the night about the arcane and the mundane. I drank less because those long conversations distracted me, kept me from going to the bars as much. Sometimes she would cook something for us to eat, so I was eating better, at least a little. Sometimes it felt like she could have been my daughter. Sometimes it even seemed like she could have been my wife if our ages hadn't been so out of synch. But in our closest moments, in the most intimate points of our talks, she still called me her brother.

As if by some agreement we had never actually made, we hardly ever mentioned Lupe. I don't really know why.

And those dreams, those visions, of my first Flor stopped blooming in my mind.

In the blaze of those desert days, the city itself began to lose what little shine of sanity it still had. As Lupe began to fade into memory and urban legend, the kill rate began to rise beyond all reason. The public at large had never known her name. But it was as if the presence of that unknown girl had repressed some of the madness, stomping it down with her invincible and unworldly power. And once she was gone, that dam had burst, and all the foulness came flooding back with a vengeance.

Of course, what everybody knew and nobody said was that the Boss liked it that way. He liked that the little fish were constantly struggling for survival, that they were always being eaten by the slightly bigger fish. Back in the day, the old Bosses liked to have the city under control, a city where nothing could happen without their permission. All the little gangs and wannabes didn't move without asking. The police were paid to look the other way, and those little fish did the dirty work.

The new way was different. Let them fend for themselves, go wild, tear each other apart over the scraps. More and more money, and more and more drugs were passing through. The little fish were too unprofessional, too untrustworthy, when it came to that level of commerce. They could run wild as long as they didn't interfere with the real business. This Boss would use the chaos as the cover for his operations. A lot of cops were still paid to look the other way or were just afraid not to. Others got paid even more to do some of the dirty work. And true professionals were integrated into that corrupted force to do the really dirty work.

La Ciudad, that violence-ridden, devastated city, was nothing but camouflage that concealed the mechanical and leisurely flow of the narco traffic.

It was clever. It was too clever. It made the national government look bad. It was embarrassing them too much in front of the gringos. El Norte was unhappy. That would change the game.

Heavy shit was about to come down.

A new president wanted to impose his own order. He wanted to show the narco lords who was really the Boss. He wanted to wage his own high-intensity war on drugs, even though the old one had been lost a long time ago.

So, there was my home, La Ciudad, that festering sore of a border town that oozed horror, with all its dead women and all its dead men. That was definitely a place that desperately needed to have a heavy boot on its throat. That would be a very good place to make a show of power. That would be a very good place to start.

It would show his power. And it would please Washington, DC.

The president was going to send in the army.

I know for sure that the Boss and the general met in person, face-to-face, only because I dreamed it. On the streets there were only rumors that they had met, thirdhand gossip from the fourth mouth that managed to get to my ears.

And it was good that those two villains met, because it does make the story better.

In my dream, I saw them meet at the Boss's estate in Narcoburbia, that strange and upscale neighborhood that wasn't supposed to exist for the rest of us. A peaceful and clean place, with big yards and big houses, plenty of electricity, plenty of clean water, and a great sewage system. The American Dream torn—stolen—from El Norte and planted somewhere outside La Ciudad. It was where the high-level narcos lived. We all know about it but pretend we don't. People like me don't go there unless we're invited. And we're never invited.

If I wrote about it publicly, I would probably be a dead man.

But in my vision, there they were, sitting in the Boss's big, fancy office in that mansion. I could see them as they smoked the most expensive cigars and drank the most excellent tequila.

That was how men like that made their deals.

First, they got comfortable, showed a human face, made small talk. Weather. Sports. Women. Some pleasant and whitewashed stories about the family. Amusing anecdotes about what they liked and hated about their jobs. They even allowed themselves a comparison of each other's favorite mistresses. After all, they were drinking the best tequila and smoking the best cigars. And they were men of the world who understood how that world really worked.

In the end, though, they had to get around to drawing a bottom line, a line drawn by the general.

"We keep your organization in place. You keep moving your product, as quietly and as invisibly as possible. But all the payment for protection, that will now go to the army, to me. All those little gangsters, all those corrupt cops, all those scavengers you are pitting against each other, you need to cut them loose."

"If I cut them off, they'll start to turn on me instead of each other. I will have to fight them, General."

"No, I will have to fight them. I was sent here to clean up this city. The minor gangsters, the cops on the take, and the scavengers are the ones who make things look bad to outsiders. You do your job and I will do mine. I will create the order the capital sent me to create. I will keep that order. And you will get your money's worth!"

Getting your money's worth.

The new order.

Meet the new boss….

For me, it started when I was ambling down the street and saw an armored personnel carrier drive by. It was probably a gift from Gringolandia, an iron fist for the war on drugs. I didn't pay too much attention to that **APC**, or the guy on top with the machine gun. I had a feeling right away that it would be best to treat them like the narcos: pretend they aren't there and go on with your business.

When I saw another one of those vehicles rounding a corner, I decided to cut through an alley and head toward the office. I wanted to get a feel for what was going on, see what my peers in the news biz had to say, what they knew, whether anybody had given us direct orders on what to publish or not publish.

What I found was an army captain briefing an assembly of reporters, editors, and managers. I wasn't that late…considering that nobody had bothered to invite me. But nobody said I had to leave, so I took a seat and listened. It was simple: the army would very much appreciate any good work that the press could provide in supporting its efforts as it attempted to restore the dignity and safety of La Ciudad. The captain himself would always be available and willing to provide any reporter with the most accurate information about ongoing operations. He certainly didn't want us to have to resort to the gossip and rumor of uninformed civilians.

So, yeah, the message was clear.

There's going to be some nasty shit going down. Hold your nose and look the other way.

In a dream I wanted to find Flor, my lost Flor. I sought her in the bleak desert in the night. It was important that I find her, very important.

But she wasn't there.

I woke up and went into my living room. Flor M-M was there, performing a beautifully choreographed dance with Sanchez's sword. A display of the art of the thrust and parry of a trained martial artist. It looked perfect to my eye, anyway.

She saw me watching her.

"I am truly Japanese," she said.

"Only half," I joked.

"That's a lot more than Sanchez was!" She smiled wickedly. "But he did have an excellent and authentic sword. I've always wanted one and I doubt Lupe would mind that I borrowed it; she left it at my place."

"You never did tell me how it happened that you have a Japanese father."

"You never asked. A remarkable oversight on your part, Señor Reporter," she said and laughed. "He was Japanese mafia…yakuza… came over here to negotiate some narco business. Part of the deal was that he had to stay here for a while. And he couldn't resist doing some dirty work for the old order. And he couldn't resist my mother, either. She was also a witch."

"Like mother, like daughter."

Flor suddenly put the sword over her shoulder. She gave me a strange look and then her expression froze. I had the trace of a thought that maybe I had said the wrong thing.

"You dreamed about her again." Not a question.

I couldn't contain a nervous chuckle. "More the case that I dreamed that I wasn't dreaming of her."

"You still drag her around in your soul, even though it only makes you suffer and pulls you under."

"True. I can't disagree."

"Why do you let her haunt you still?"

"Because I was supposed to be with her. I knew it. I know it deep within myself, a knowing that comes from a deeper place of being. Back then, it wasn't a feeling that I asked for. I never really had a choice. It was actually terrifying…and exciting…and overwhelming. It wasn't just the usual combination of love and lust and desperation and joy, even though that was a good part of it. No, it was more like an intrusion from some other world…some other…something."

She kept giving me that strange look. "And yet she left."

I allowed myself a bitter smile. "Maybe she felt something too—and maybe it was too intense for her."

"Did you tell her how you felt?"

"Sort of…I tried…I came close…I approached it. But the emotions were so strong. And I was never good at that kind of shit, anyway. Besides, I thought I had plenty of time to figure it out."

"Then suddenly she left without telling you…and without ever contacting you again."

"Like I said, maybe it was too intense for her…or maybe she got tired of waiting for me to man up and tell her how I felt."

"Or maybe she didn't care."

That knocked me silent for a minute…having to hear out loud a possibility that I barely even admitted to in silence. We'd talked about this before, of course, but she'd never been so…blunt.

"I prefer my interpretation," I finally muttered.

Knowing that she'd made her point, Flor just resumed her elegant sword dancing exercises, the blade slicing through the subject that had been left hanging adrift in the air.

APCs kept rolling down my street, down all the streets. So, I kept the shades drawn. I didn't think they were trying to intimidate me personally. I didn't think they cared at all about me. Maybe they didn't even know I existed.

But I still kept my shades down.

The new order had been imposed. Not even cops were safe. The army had to show that it was serious about cleaning up all that corruption, after all. And if the army thought you were a problem, or that you resembled one, then you vanished. Maybe forever. Or maybe your corpse showed up after a while—and not in mint condition.

The new order.

Needless to say, a lot of shades were drawn.

"I really wish we knew how Lupe came back from the dead," I said to Flor one afternoon. The same topic we'd often discussed.

She had been sipping tea and she set the cup down. "I still have no idea. But I haven't given up. I try to use my spirit sight. But there's always that boundary that I can't look beyond, only that darkness that I've never been able to peer through. I can see Lupe rising, but I never witness what caused the rising. You know…you've seen things…you've dreamed things too, Cervantes."

"And I've never seen anything to explain it either."

"Your little friend didn't give you any info?"

"No. And she doesn't even come to me in my dreams now. I hardly dream at all anymore." I couldn't bring myself to admit to Flor M-M that I still dreamed I was looking for the first Flor…but that I could never find her.

If the second Flor could tell I was hiding that from her, she was nice enough to let it go.

"Only La Santa Muerte…only La Santa Muerte could have done it," she whispered, as if she were afraid that ears other than mine would hear.

Oddly, my work became less tense. Under the old regime, I had been a crime reporter who had to cover up any facts that would point toward the real criminals. But things had been so crazy that even if I thought I was following the script to the letter, it still seemed like there was a chance that somebody would get pissed off at me. So, I was always alert to the possibility that certain individuals would be less than satisfied with my work.

With the new order I wasn't fed stories anymore. Nobody talked to me "off the record" to tell me anything, true or false. I wasn't asked to write anything. I wasn't sent anywhere near the scene of a crime or of a military action just to make it look good. That captain just gave us stories already written up, and the paper was supposed to publish them exactly as given, which it did. Nobody dared show any initiative to do more than that.

But somebody was still paying my salary. And the paper sure as hell wasn't going to fire me without being told to. So, I put myself on the local human interest circuit, sniffing out the most innocuous and harmless bits of news. Elaborate gardens, stamp collections dating back a century, model ships made out of beer cans: that was the stuff I was looking for. And that was the stuff I was glad to find. I even felt more like a real reporter than I had when I was on the crime beat.

"That's an incredible replica of the *Bismarck*, Señor. Is there a particular brand of beer can that you preferred using?"

And the APCs kept rolling by.

And people kept vanishing.

One day Flor came in through my back door. Her face was filled with worry, an expression I wasn't used to when it came to her.

She read the questions on my face before I could form the words. "I have to leave town. They'll be coming for me soon; perhaps they already are. They found out that a priestess of La Santa, or a witch of some sort, is a focal point: a person who can draw forth things they don't want brought forth. They know I run some sort of underground and independent organization that does clandestine things. I'm a perfect scapegoat. I smuggle only people, not drugs or guns…but we both know that the reality doesn't matter. So, it's best that I go away for a while and have everyone else close up shop, hide, or leave."

I nodded. "Should I go too?"

"No. I can sense that you're not caught in their web. Besides, you need to be here. You need to be near Lupe."

"I guess another Flor is about to leave me then. But at least you've told me; at least I know why."

"Unlike that Flor, this one will be back. I won't forsake my brother!"

We hugged, a strong, long hug. Then I stood in the doorway and watched her leave. An old, beat-up car was parked in the alley behind my house. That guy, the one who had first taken me to see her, opened the door for her and then got in on the driver's side, giving me a quick nod.

Then they were gone, leaving me with just the slight scent of burning motor oil to remember them by.

Soon after Flor left, my age began to creep back into my body and make itself felt. I began to feel all my despair again, too. And, despite what Flor had said when she left, I began to feel a cold fear. Reporters were disappearing, too. And I had been a small part of the old order. That was a fact, no matter how trivial I was trying to make myself. I shut myself up in the house more and more.

I hardly went to the office.

I hardly did any reporting…about anything.

I hardly ever went out to the bars, instead doing my drinking in private.

I even hired a woman to bring me my groceries and booze.

And days became weeks as my self-imposed imprisonment entered autumn.

Sleep came in fits and starts…almost a trauma. There were no dreams. I missed my dreams. When I did manage to sleep deeply, I could tell that I was seeking them out. I wanted my dreams. I wanted the first Flor to return to me in the only way that she could, or would.

And I wanted the second Flor to return to me in the waking world.

In the end, there was nothing to do but drink mescal and watch television alone, trapped in my own anguish. I guess, in my own way, I was like Lupe, sitting in my own hell.

Then at last a dream.

I was making love to my lost Flor. No, I was fucking her. It was passionate. No, it was savage. I was young again, thin—or at least thinner—full of energy and lust and love. Had there ever really been a time in my life when things had been so ecstatic, so aggressive? It was magnificent. I had reclaimed my youth and I had reclaimed Flor.

It was lasting forever…I was lasting forever…and I wanted it to last forever.

Then her moans turned into giggles. She began to laugh at me, harsh and mocking.

I suddenly realized it wasn't Flor. It was the prostitute I had tried to use as a substitute all those years ago. She pushed me away, her face full of cruelty and contempt.

I found myself running in the desert, in the dark. The lard was refilling my body…the age and wrinkles had returned…terror slapped my heart. Why was I so afraid? Because the phony Flor had tricked me? No, something awful was behind me, and I had to keep running, running. I stumbled several times as I tried to keep up a pace my body could no longer maintain…until I fell and hit hard.

Managing to get up on my knees, I saw that I was in front of Lupe. She was sitting on the ground just like I had last seen her in the waking world, in Los Locos. Her face was still hiding in her hands. She didn't seem to even be aware that I was there.

"They're not going to leave you alone for long—they're almost here," I said to her quietly, as though I were afraid someone else was listening.

And then, finally, she let her hands fall away and she looked at me. I recoiled from her. There was such total hate in those inferno eyes.

My only comfort was the fact that I knew her hatred wasn't for me.

Then I woke up, finding myself back in my world of sweat and nausea. I felt sick and weak in my body. But in my spirit, I felt strangely better.

Guadalupe Castaneda was finally waking up.

Hours later, I was trying to sit up and watch television, trying to drink some water, when my cell phone buzzed. I was zombiefied and hung over, and nobody had called me in so long that it took me a while to realize what was happening. By the time I fumbled the phone into my hand, the caller had long been exiled to voicemail. The call had come from Eduardo's phone, and a message had been left.

I hit the right buttons.

The voice I heard wasn't Eduardo's: it was the panicked voice of Gustavo, the young assistant.

"Señor Cervantes, the army is here. They say that Señor Eduardo is hiding criminals, that he's dealing drugs. They are arresting him, they are searching Los Locos, rounding people up. They're probably going to find…*her*."

End of message.

It didn't surprise me that the boy and Eduardo had known all along that Lupe was hiding there.

And it didn't surprise me that they hadn't told anyone.

Why did I go to Los Locos? I knew I would be risking my life traveling to a place where the army was conducting a dubious operation.

But I also knew that Lupe was there. I had to know what had happened…or what was going to happen.

At least I was smart enough to go around a back way, which was almost too much for my Beetle. I was afraid there would be helicopters circling, but there weren't. I was surprised that I could walk all the way to Eduardo's cabin without seeing any soldiers, without seeing anyone at all.

Young Gustavo came running up to me as I cautiously got out of my car. He must have been hiding nearby and seen my arrival. He still had Eduardo's cell phone in his hand. We were both breathing heavily. But he was doing so because of exertion. I was doing it because I was tense as hell and still feeling like shit.

"It's horrible, Señor Cervantes! They've taken away Señor Eduardo, and they were taking away a lot of other people too, when they found…her…and they wanted to take her away too!" Then he seemed to lose his words.

"What happened?"

Instead of answering, he gestured for me to follow him, leading me on a convoluted route behind a cover of rises and ravines, a subtle maze that concealed us, one that only a person who had lived there, played there, explored there, would have been able to find a way into.

We ended up near the remains of an old stone wall. Gustavo got down on his hands and knees to go the rest of the way. I felt like I had to imitate him, and I let my trousers and legs pay the price.

Peeking over that wall, we saw the carnage. An APC was upside down, a hole torn out of its side. I suspected it had been torn by hand. Half a dozen apparently dead soldiers had also been randomly arranged to help highlight the scene.

"I saw it, Señor Cervantes. She was just sitting there like she always does. The army men came…they were taking some people and making others run away…they were snooping around. Two of them found her. They were rude and vulgar. She ignored them and they got mad. One of them grabbed her arm and began to pull her up. She pulled away easily and just sat back down. That really pissed him off, the one who tried to take her. The other one laughed at him and made fun of him, saying he couldn't handle some half-starved crazy girl, so the first guy lost his temper and hit her in the head with the butt of his rifle. And, well, that was it…I couldn't tell exactly what she did…too fast…then both were dead. Then she started walking…walking toward the armored car and some other soldiers. I ran the other way. I didn't want to see her kill all those men, even though they were not good men. But I heard the guns… the yelling…the screaming."

Soon there would be dust clouds and the sound of motors approaching. Because most likely the army would be sending reinforcements, either to investigate what had happened or to hunt down the enemy.

"So, you don't know where Lupe went?"

"No, Señor."

"We'd better get away from here. Do you want to come with me?"

"Yes, Señor."

I was worried on the way home. Soldiers had been killed; an armored vehicle had been destroyed. Would there be roadblocks? Would they be laying down total martial law? Would I be stopped and detained if they thought I had seen the evidence of their defeat? But the presence of the armed forces was sparse. I reached my house safely.

"Go ahead and find something on TV." I figured Gustavo wasn't a kid who had seen much television, so any old crap might amuse him for a while. I sure as hell didn't know what to do with a kid. I was already old enough to feel like I could have been Flor M-M's dad—so now I had to feel like a fuckin' grandfather?

He asked for candy, soda, and snacks. I didn't have any of that stuff. So, I offered him a shot of mescal. It's not like a street kid from La Ciudad wouldn't have ever tried it before. He accepted it like it was nothing, which was what I expected. Within twenty minutes he had passed out on my couch, TV still on. Hell, maybe I did have it in me to be a grandpa.

I knocked some back too and dozed off for a bit myself. I wasn't worried about the kid. I didn't think he would steal anything, and even if he did, I didn't have anything all that valuable. And I didn't think he would take off, but if he did, well, it wasn't like he was my prisoner.

No dreams. Just a fleeting glimmer that I wanted to dream of lost Flor. But I didn't.

I woke up. Gustavo was still asleep. The sun was going down behind the drawn shades. I knew I was probably going to be expected to come up with some sort of dinner…so I forced myself up and started to lumber into the kitchen.

That was when I heard the explosion.

That was when I felt the house shake on its foundation.

I hit the floor in a panic. Was I under attack?

No. The rumble was farther away.

I peeked out the window; a huge cloud of raging black smoke was rising up from probably several blocks away.

Gustavo was awake and frightened.

"What is it, Señor Cervantes?"

"I don't know. But it's not close."

Then, to make me a liar, a chunk of smoldering metal landed in my yard. We were both staring at it, peering out from underneath my shades.

A military jeep drove by.

Then a truckload of troops, their faces filled with shock and fear.

They were all headed away from the explosion.

"It looks like our proud army might be having a problem they can't quite figure out how to deal with."

"Yes, Señor."

As it became night, there was suddenly a curfew. It was announced on the television, on the radio. And it was announced through loudspeakers haphazardly mounted on various army vehicles. Or just by a guy with a bullhorn in the back of a truck. Be inside and off the streets by 10:00 p.m. or else you will be detained.

Why were they trying to control the night when Lupe had fucked them up in broad daylight? Who could say? The logic of the military mind often eluded me.

I never did find out for sure what had exploded that day. But whatever it was, it was just a footnote to what was about to happen.

"I need to find Señor Eduardo," Gustavo announced the next day. Was it loyalty, or just the fact that I didn't have anything good to eat…and I wasn't showing any signs of going out for supplies. I had tried to call and see if anybody would deliver anything to me, but nobody was answering. A lot of lines were busy. Maybe the army had sabotaged the phone system. "Do you know where he is?"

"No." It was true. At that point, I had no idea where the army was holding its prisoners or what it intended to do with them.

"I will find him," the boy said, and he prepared to slip out my back door, just like the second Flor. Only Gustavo didn't have a car and driver waiting for him. I didn't try to stop him. I honestly didn't know whether he would be safer with me. And I didn't think I had any right to stop him. So, I just gave him a few dollars and told him he was welcome to come back. He nodded a thanks and was quickly gone.

I decided it was loyalty. Eduardo was probably the only one who had ever looked out for him. And he was a street kid. He would know how to get by. I doubted that the army would be interested in rounding up homeless boys. They were about to have their hands more than full with one homeless young woman.

And the army was still trying to figure out what to do about the cops. Which of them could be controlled properly? Which of them should be eliminated? You couldn't just make an entire city police force vanish; you had to be more…surgical. The cops were implanted in the local corruption and trafficking, and they knew the scene much better than the military, so they definitely had their uses. But they couldn't be trusted and they couldn't be given free rein anymore. Their cut of the power and the profit would have to be reduced. So, they had to be pushed around and shown who was in charge. A disappearance here…a torture there…a brutal execution in the middle…even some normal detentions.

It was all part of the new game. Make it look like you're cleaning up a dirty police force; meanwhile you're keeping the most valuable players on the field, the ones who really know how to play ball.

Soon a lot of cops were staying off the street, or ducking out of sight, when an APC or jeep came rumbling down the road. And that absence of the old order opened up exciting new opportunities for the men of the armed forces.

For example, the first night after Lupe's awakening, troops harassed some of the street talent—La Ciudad's young ladies of the night. A truckload of enlisted men pulled up to the curb and wanted to exert their newfound prerogatives by demanding freebies.

A few of the young women didn't understand that they were supposed to comply and keep their mouths shut and their legs open, instead choosing to make a scene, choosing to argue. But these weren't boys from the neighborhood. They had no sympathy for those girls; they just wanted the job done. So, things got rough quickly. One of the soldiers whipped out some pepper spray and used it. Two girls screamed and fell to the ground, and then got grabbed by a couple of the other men. The rest were about to let themselves be loaded in the truck.

Then one of the hookers pointed and joyfully yelled, "The holy girl!" It could even have been the very same prostitute who had talked to me about Lupe on that very first night. But no, it probably wasn't.

I don't think those army guys had even heard about Guadalupe Castaneda. An occupation force usually doesn't get to hear the best stories the local population has to tell. I doubt that the Boss even told the general. Who would believe that kind of story? It would only have made the Boss look crazy. And nobody had even seen Lupe in a while.

It was the guy with the pepper spray who actually bothered to turn and look. And there was scraggly and dirty Lupe, who had just walked up on the whole thing. He checked her out and gripped her by the arm. "You can join the party, too. We'll just hose you off first!"

Lupe easily pulled free, surprising the man, who immediately sprayed her in the face. None of the survivors saw if she even blinked. I doubt she did. She probably just stared at him expressionlessly for a few moments, giving him time to realize that the chemical wasn't bothering her, giving him time to realize something was very wrong. Then she took him by the wrist, crushed the wrist, and took the spray away from him as he fell to his knees in shock.

Another soldier, obviously not knowing who he was dealing with, came to the aid of his wounded comrade. All he could tell was that a homeless beggar had done something nasty to his peer. Direct action was called for. So, he slammed his rifle butt into her head. But Lupe was braced and took the blow with hardly any give. Her hand shot out, took the rifleman by the throat, lifted him up off the ground, and squeezed just slowly enough for him to fully realize what was happening to him as he died. Then she gave the kneeling man a slight kick to the head that shattered his skull and snapped his neck.

At that point, the rest of the troops stopped bothering prostitutes and turned to confront the threat that didn't look like a threat. Lupe dug her fingers into the container she held, and pepper spray exploded everywhere. The girls scattered in all directions since nobody was bothering them anymore. The men had to back away quickly from the noxious cloud.

In the confusion, Lupe reached under the side of the army truck and flipped it over. Then she turned and walked away without even looking back into the fog she had created. Nobody tried to stop her. When the cloud faded, the holy girl had vanished along with it.

The real war had been declared.

Juan El Bautista had felt only rage when the army stormed into La

Ciudad. He had watched helplessly as the old order of things was crushed under military boots, that old order that had once been so important to him, that he had helped create, that he had helped maintain. Yet as time went by, he couldn't help but enjoy his ringside seat at that supposed restoration of the rule of law, especially when the local cops took a pounding for their corruption. Juan had sympathy for the street thugs and bottom feeders, who were taking the brunt of the army's operations. But those cops, always on the take, most of them not having the balls to do any of the real work and just taking cash to look the other way—it was fun to see those guys sitting in cells, getting slapped around, getting the shakedown, begging for their lives.

The soldiers also disgusted Juan. Weren't they just cops with better weapons? Weren't they just trying to take over the operations of the stupid police? As the army took more and more control, Juan's initial fury began to return and began to turn into pure hate, a hate that seemed to create its own fire within his heart.

That fury finally broke loose when Juan came across troops in the process of extracting cash from street talent…taking privileges that rightfully belonged only to the cartel. He'd already seen this many times, during that time that he still lost track of. But this time, his hatred burned so hot that El Bautista actually thought it was feeding him, making him stronger. He could spare a little of his own fire, couldn't he? He could afford to slide his hand into a soldier's chest…into his heart…and fry it like he'd fried the dog's brain, couldn't he?

Then he had a better thought. What if he reached into their bodies and instead of spending his own flame, he took theirs? What if he could take their fire, their lives, and feed off it rather than wasting his own essence? He had gotten good at absorbing energy from fire; he knew how the process worked. Why not try to reapply that knowledge?

The so-called criminals were cuffed and sitting on the curb, maybe even the same curb that had once seemed like a cliff to a tiny phantom. One of them had already been taken away to get a ransom that might or might not get them all released, might or might not save all their lives. Bored troops stood guard.

Juan came up close behind one of those soldiers, so close that the man could have felt the breath on his neck, if the ghost had breath that a normal man would feel. He stared at his translucent hands, gathering his will to try to take the fire of the living.

Slowly, carefully, he passed his left hand into the core of that soldier's body. He was able to feel the warmth and the beating of the heart. At first, by reflex, he almost did discharge some of his own lethal energy. It was a struggle to restrain it. He had to remember how to take, to consume, in the same way he consumed ordinary flames.

Then Juan felt it: something warm and almost oily that slid and flowed through his arm and all the way into the center of his own body. Yes, he could instantly tell it was making him stronger.

The soldier's body contracted slightly as he made a choking noise, his face wrinkling and shriveling as he collapsed to the ground.

El Bautista let the strange power surge around inside himself. Was this what a light bulb feels like when it is turned on? It was far more… delicious…than absorbing simple flames. And he definitely felt more powerful.

He laughed as the military men tried to come to the aid of their comrade. It was tempting to take those lives as well, but he decided to be cautious, at least at first. Maybe it wasn't a good idea to be too conspicuous. Maybe it wasn't a good idea to reveal that there was an invisible killer on the loose…not yet.

Juan kept laughing as he began to walk away, even more amused by the fact that no one else heard his laughter.

Then he froze, the merriment dying in his throat.

Far down the street he saw her, he saw the girl.

There was no doubt, no doubt at all. He would recognize her anywhere.

Then she was gone.

Juan decided not to follow her. He wasn't sure he was ready.

And he wanted to be ready.

I knew there was no hope of Flor the first returning, not in the flesh.

And I didn't want to give in to the hope that Flor the second would return.

So that left me with allowing myself the hope that Gustavo would return. It wasn't that I really wanted to share my time with a kid. It was more that I just wanted to have something to hope for that seemed… reasonable.

On the television news and in the papers, for those first few days there were just stories about the army having violent confrontations with the narcos and kicking ass. There was no mention at all about a juggernaut in the form of a frail-looking young woman who was kicking their asses right back at them. But the people saw…they knew…they whispered it. And too many military guys were ending up in the morgue, way too many.

I was still enough of a journalist to wonder what would happen when the general's staff started getting all those reports about Lupe. How long would it take for the truth to be accepted? Would they try to hide such an impossible story from him? If so, who would they blame such excessive casualties on? In private, they couldn't blame the cartel, because they had an arrangement with the cartel.

Yeah, I wish I could have been there for that—or at least had a good source or a dream to tell me how it went down.

I knew those commander types. I'd talked to quite a few back in the day. They were the ones who always denied even the most credible UFO reports, refusing to budge an inch even when you had a pilot or officer as a witness. Didn't matter. Didn't exist. Probably just a balloon.

But Lupe wasn't going to just shoot off into the sky, leaving nothing more than a brief and tantalizing hint of mystery. She was going to keep tearing them apart; no skepticism allowed.

The highest of high noons came a couple of days afterward. Some troops decided to harass the street vendors. They wanted free food and drinks and immediately got tough about it. It wasn't like the vendors wouldn't have given them whatever they wanted almost immediately. It was already known that the army men had no honor. And the folks of La Ciudad were already well trained to submit to the cops and the narcos.

The leaders of that little display of power had pushed a couple of victims down, to a round of laughter from some of the other soldiers. A bunch of them began to help themselves; others waited to be served like they were paying customers. Then there was a loud crunching noise and a sick gurgle. The vendors were all looking wide-eyed behind the mass of greedy soldiers. How could they not turn around to see what the deal was? They did—and there was Lupe, holding the body of one of the soldiers' comrades over her head with one hand, blood dripping down on her from that limp corpse.

With her other hand, she was pointing a pistol at the soldiers.

Once the soldiers were fully aware of the situation, she emptied the clip. It was close range; hard to miss. Six men went down. Fire was finally returned. As had often happened in the past, the girl who is Death was knocked flat by the force of the bullets as she let go of the body she'd been holding, and which certainly hadn't helped her balance. Then she immediately sat back up after being hit by those dozens of rounds and switched clips and opened fire again. That time she didn't get as many because they were scattering, running, diving for cover. The civilians were also escaping as fast as they could. Lupe stood up and was changing over to her third clip of ammo. From what they thought were more secure positions, some of the soldiers prepared to return fire again. But before they could manage it, she took a sailing leap up and over, landing behind those positions. Three more dead as she got the drop on them.

From a safe distance, applause could be heard. It came from some of the vendors and other residents who had seen what was happening. Then, fearing the attention they might draw, they slipped away.

An almost dead silence after that as the gun smoke hovered in the equally dead air. It was broken only by the frantic sergeant on a radio calling for reinforcements. Lupe stared at him, not moving a muscle, not even blinking. It would and should have been obvious that she wanted him to call for more victims, more soldiers, to feel her wrath.

"Under attack, under attack, dead, dead!"

Then she saved him the embarrassment of describing who was attacking his squad by shooting him in the head.

Guadalupe Castaneda had lost her sense of humor. She had become more merciless, more brutal. She was a perfect whirlwind for all the overlords of La Ciudad to reap. She was also a living scythe, more than ready, more than willing, to do that reaping.

Backup came immediately. A helicopter roared in the sky, descended toward the scene of the massacre. It had been up there the whole time, but in the distance. By that point, the general had to know that something wasn't right, that something was fucking things up for him. Maybe he didn't yet know exactly what the nature of that something was, but he intended to set things up so that he could start fucking things up for his enemy. And having some helicopters deployed for immediate response and counterattack seemed perfect for that sort of thing.

It was a ridiculously short battle.

Lupe turned and looked up, changed clips again, raised her pistol, shot at the aircraft. But there was no way she was going to take out a military chopper with such a relatively light weapon.

A sharpshooter in the copter returned her fire. Lupe took a direct hit in the head, maybe two, maybe three. But she'd seen it coming, and she put one foot way forward and one way back, bracing herself so she wouldn't go down again.

Probably not able to believe that the young woman's head was bulletproof, the gunman couldn't resist the temptation of checking his rifle to make sure it was functioning correctly. The helicopter pilot maintained position about a hundred feet above and back from Lupe, also most likely wondering what the problem was.

Lupe took those moments to seize a vendor's food cart and throw it overhand, straight at the chopper. It struck the blades.

And that was that....

Metal flew in all directions as the former flying machine dropped like the spinning deadweight it had become.

Fortunately, all the potential innocent bystanders had already given up their bystanding and fled the area.

Lupe used the billowing black smoke as cover to leave the scene as well. Maybe she'd had enough action for a while.

Once he'd fed on human life directly, absorbing that sustenance straight into his being, Juan lost all appetite for fire. And the entire city became a temptation. It was very difficult not to just slide his hands into every passerby that he saw, very difficult to restrain himself from committing a sort of feeding frenzy genocide. But caution kept the upper hand. He didn't want anyone...or anything...to even remotely suspect that something like him existed. He didn't want to attract the attention of some other unknown being that might have its own angle, its own agenda. He also knew that sooner or later he would come back into phase with the world...and that would be the time to proclaim himself.

No, for now he had to kill with stealth, choose his targets with care, usually from among the victims of the army, those who were about to die anyway. Maybe there was a gun to their head, the trigger about to be pulled. Maybe they were being beaten and tortured in military custody. Maybe they were about to be caught in a crossfire. If there was an angel of death, El Bautista's goal was to cut in front of that celestial being with just seconds to spare.

That was how he fed, that was how he became stronger.

He knew that the girl was confronting the army. Perhaps those soldiers were really there for her, or perhaps she had just gotten in the way of what they really wanted to do: take over La Ciudad. Either way, the first battles hadn't gone well for them.

Every time he spotted her, Juan would watch the girl, study her from a distance, seeing if he could learn something new about her. Then, one of those days, he was closer than he intended to be. She was stalking down an avenue. And he could have sworn that she saw him, that she fixed her gaze upon him for a moment, that she pretended not to see him while still altering her course to approach him.

In a reflexive panic, Juan ran through several walls and then dove underground and hid for a couple of hours.

His intuition had told him that he wasn't ready to face the girl again.

But it also told him that soon he would be ready.

I saw them meet again. They had to meet again. They were at the Boss's mansion. It was a secure place, a place where nobody would dare pry.

The atmosphere was just a bit different this time. Before, the general had come to lay down his law. That time he could have swept it all away and really cleaned up the town. He could have taken the Boss down. Instead, he'd gone for the payoff. Most of the cards of power were still in his hand. But this time he was at a disadvantage: his strength no longer seemed absolute, things had gotten weird. There was a joker in the deck.

Yet he knew that he still had the upper hand. The Boss would have to be cooperative. Only the general stood between him and a "personnel change."

He showed the Boss the recording of a video feed from the copter, before that blurry, indestructible chica brought it down.

"What the fuck is this shit?"

But the Boss did want to play it out just a little. He sat back, lit up a cigar, and took a sip of his very fine tequila, knowing that he could take it just so far. He had to be attentive to the rage building in his guest.

"That girl can't be killed or even hurt. And she kills whoever she wants. She's wiped out some of my best men."

"You're serious?"

The Boss shrugged. "Did you watch your own tape?"

Silence. Then, "It's gotta be a fucking trick…some kind of gimmick!"

"That's what one of mine thought. He had her hosed with machine guns. He had her flamethrowed. He even used one of those fancy Japanese karate swords on her. And she was the one who walked away… with the sword."

More silence.

Then, "One little, fucking, piece-of-shit bitch can't take on the whole fucking army! We will destroy her!"

The Boss just offered to refill the general's glass.

"You really don't believe me, hombre?"

As an answer, the Boss just raised his own glass and offered a toast: "To your health, mi amigo!"

Then began the phony war, a strange stalemate, the game of waiting.

La Ciudad was now truly under martial law. The army was everywhere with its patrols and checkpoints, everything on a smooth lockdown. The town actually seemed to behave itself. The general and the Boss agreed: no violence, no feuds, no distractions. Any violation would actually be greeted with a proper arrest. No bribes would be taken for a quick release. And nobody would be pounded down or shot in the back of the head for not taking bribes if they were offered.

Wrapped up and nailed down. Watertight. Airtight.

I felt a little better and a little more secure. I made it out to the bars now and again. I lifted a glass of mescal to toast the peace of La Ciudad, even though I knew we were only having an intermission, a little break.

And Lupe was still there, out on the streets. Wandering aimlessly as those hours turned into days and we entered deeper into autumn. She didn't seem to rest; she didn't seem to stand still. Prowling and prowling and looking everywhere for—what? Something on which to let loose her wrath, of course. But nobody was attacking her. There was nobody being victimized for her to save. And in her heart, Lupe wasn't able to justify an unprovoked assault.

The people on the street would smile and nod as they got out of her way. Usually they were subtle about it, afraid they would piss off the authorities if they showed too much support. It might be easy to unwittingly provoke vengeance, especially if the army grew restless, tired of obeying the law. But sometimes the displays of affection were more overt. Sometimes people would pray as she went by. Sometimes they would even approach her, as if seeking to touch her, as if seeking a blessing.

And the army was watching Lupe. A man or two would briefly follow her. They would radio ahead and make sure the others knew her location. During that time, she never stopped moving. She didn't need to sleep or even sit down for a few minutes, that girl whose eyes would still sometimes fill with that deep darkness that was blacker than the night.

After a week of that, there was no one in the army who could deny that they were up against something that wasn't right.

They started to follow her from a greater distance. If she seemed to have the slightest interest in moving toward them, they rapidly retreated.

Those helicopters were always in the air, not flying too low, hoping to stay out of range of anything that she could hurl at them. There was no question that they were monitoring her day and night with all the fancy surveillance gear that the gringos had given them to use on the drug traffic—even if they were just tracking a blur on their cameras and monitors.

I had to wonder why Lupe didn't do anything more. I knew she still had at least one act of revenge to complete: getting even for her own horrible death. Was she playing it out? Was she actually glad for a break, even though she didn't seem to need one?

A week had passed…then a day…and then another day.

Then the general called an end to the watching and waiting game.

I had to admit, the way they started was clever. Take some snipers, arm them with .50-caliber rifles, and have them take shots at Lupe. But take those shots from such a long range, and from such concealed positions, that she wouldn't be able to figure out where the bullets were coming from.

She would be walking down a street, perhaps lost in her own unknown thoughts, when she would catch a shot. Usually it came from behind, aimed at her back. Even though no harm was done, the laws of physics still applied, and the impact would knock her forward and down. Sometimes she just hit flat; sometimes she caught herself with her hands. Or maybe the projectile would flip her leg up and cause her to fall. Or maybe the bullet would hit her in the torso. At first, they would sometimes dare a shot from the front, right in her face. Those shots were so powerful that they almost never failed to take her down.

But, of course, she would be right back up without a scratch. Maybe there would be a black mark she could easily wipe off. Either way, the only damage was to her dignity and to the clothing that she was wearing. Very soon, once it became more and more apparent to all of them that she was invulnerable, they would shoot at her only from behind.

People began to leave clothing for her on the curb and along the roads she roamed. They did it on the sly, of course, when nobody would see their support. When Lupe figured out the deal, she would pick out some and change whenever she felt the need or desire to do so.

Those first few days, she would turn and face her attacker, her expression one of rage. But there would be no foe in sight. She would stand and wait for another bullet, wanting a clue as to where her enemy was. No such shot ever arrived. Her waiting would drag on; she would just stand there and not move, challenging them to give her a chance to retaliate. Was it really surprising that they never took that second shot? They were probably watching Lupe through a high-magnification scope; they could see that the girl had been struck by the full intensity of their firepower. The .50-caliber was a bullet that could easily penetrate metal and stone. But all it ever did to Lupe was annoy her.

After Lupe figured out the game, she would just get up and keep going. If there was another shot, she would just get up and keep going again, not even looking back. Or sometimes she would just lie there for a while. Maybe just to take a break, maybe in the hope that they would come closer to see if they had actually hurt her. If that was the case, the soldiers never fell for it. And eventually she would get up and go on her way. Sometimes she would give them the finger. Sooner or later, they would have to crank up the game. Sooner or later, they would have to engage her with something she could get her hands on, something she could smash her fists into.

I knew one of those snipers.

A woman.

I'd interviewed her once, years earlier, when she was still a teenager. It was a human-interest piece for the paper, something that didn't step on anybody's toes. Back then, she wasn't in the military, but she was already a champion sharpshooter, winning trophies and putting the boys to shame. Now here she was, years later, on the scene in La Ciudad. I was seeing her in my visions, and I recognized her, even though she was now an adult and in the army, a lieutenant.

The general had requested her services.

Her name was Catrina Ochoa.

She thought that she'd been ordered to La Ciudad to help deal with the cartel. And maybe that was true when she first got the assignment. But the facts on the ground had changed that mission.

Catrina didn't find out the truth until she had set up her .50-caliber rifle in its first "nest." She'd just taken a swallow of water and was swirling it around in her mouth. When she was told what her mission was, she spit out the water.

"I'm supposed to kill a young woman? An unarmed girl?" She didn't normally question an order, but the shock had taken command of her for a moment.

"She's not always unarmed," replied a man, another officer. "And it's not like you're going to be killing her." He let out a forced laugh.

Catrina was only more confused. "I don't understand. You want me to cripple her?"

"Not that, either."

"What is it that I'm supposed to be doing, then? This isn't a toy gun. This isn't practice."

The man became more serious. "Listen, Lieutenant, take whatever shot you want: the head, the torso, an arm, a leg. Just make sure she's not facing you, for your own sake—and be ready to move quickly after you take that shot. Trust me."

"I don't see how I can be in any danger shooting somebody in the back from hundreds of meters away. It's not like I'm going to miss!"

"I know, Lieutenant; we don't expect you to miss. It's just that…you won't believe it. Just take the shot when you get the order, and then you'll see…then you'll know. Just get ready and wait for the moment. There's no more for us to say." And then he left, heading for his jeep.

Catrina took him at his word and didn't say any more. Instead, she sat down by her rifle and waited, and then waited longer…taking another swallow of water and spitting it out again. It was a way to trick her thirst, at least for a while, so that she wouldn't have to pee.

A helicopter flew high overhead.

For the rest of the day, her radio gave updates about "the subject" or "the target," always far from Catrina's position. How strange that the entire army seemed to be concerned with one single person, a girl walking around the city in an apparently random way.

Catrina's first day on the job ended without incident.

Sometimes Lupe would suddenly leap onto or over a building, as if hoping to catch some military vehicle by surprise. Sometimes she came closer than she realized, but she never quite managed it. But it was a fucking crazy game that the general was playing. I wondered if he was playing that way because he still couldn't believe it, because he needed to see that same proof again and again before he could truly be convinced that the girl was for real.

Lupe switched it up. She began to stop at random and just stand there out in the open, arms crossed, waiting. Or she would raise her arms up over her head, perhaps to see if they would accept a surrender. But they weren't that stupid.

There were times she would stand motionless, in her chosen pose, for hours. Nothing would move around her except the wind…or a stray dog, who seemed to know to get only so close. She dared them to take a shot. But they never did. They never took the shot while she was waiting for it.

Catrina had been ordered to set up her rifle on top of a three-story building with a good view down a long avenue. She still hadn't had any contact with the target, but her superiors seemed to think there was a good chance the girl might come down that street.

Once again, the radio gave updates on the subject, who was still many blocks away. This time the lieutenant leafed through a gossip magazine she had found. Not the most interesting thing to read but better than nothing. As she tried to decide what article to read, she munched on an apple, still attentive to every radio transmission.

And the day began to pass slowly.

Then, halfway through a story about an ugly celebrity divorce, the target changed direction and began moving toward Catrina's zone.

But there was still time to finish the article…and to start another.

And another.

The target was continuing to approach the lieutenant's position, getting close enough that it was time to put the magazine aside.

It was time to get into position. It was time to get ready.

Very soon, if the mystery girl didn't change direction, she would be coming into view.

Catrina put her eye to the scope, watching, waiting, and listening.

Her radio informed her that the subject was maintaining her course toward the emplacement. So, Catrina continued to watch the world in front of her through the scope. For the time being, there was nothing unusual, just the flow of people and vehicles.

But the radio was insistent; it told her that the girl was about to appear.

And up in that distance, something was starting to happen. The people were beginning to stop, to turn, to look, to get out of the way. Cars were even pulling over. A path was being cleared in a manner that showed way too much practice, way too much discipline. What was happening wasn't unexpected, not for those residents of La Ciudad.

Wait. Someone…one single person…was walking down the middle of the road that had been cleared. A single female figure entered into Catrina's field of vision—and into the range of her rifle.

A single female figure.

Why did her superiors have such an interest in this target? Why was everyone so secretive, so nervous? And why would the crowded street open the way for…a single female figure?

That young woman did walk with confidence, her head held high. The lieutenant couldn't help but evaluate the long, wavy black hair moving with her steps as it was teased by a gentle breeze. And yes, the young woman seemed to be unarmed.

Who was this young woman, walking slowly and proudly, offering a slight smile to the hundreds of people who let her pass, that looked at her with such…reverence?

Who was this young woman…coming closer, slowly closer? She wasn't so different from Catrina. Maybe a little taller, a little thinner, a little younger…even her hair was almost the same…the skin just a bit darker in comparison to the hand on that trigger.

Why did the general want her killed?

"I have her in sight."

"Facing you?"

"Yes."

"Don't shoot unless she turns away from you. If she sees where the shot came from, you could be in jeopardy. Do you understand, Lieutenant?"

"Yes."

Catrina wanted to say, "Why? It's not like I'm going to miss!" But she held the words, clenching her teeth to make sure they didn't get loose.

The young woman kept walking straight toward Catrina, almost as if they had an appointment, almost as if she knew the lieutenant was waiting.

But that was impossible, wasn't it?

"I'm really supposed to kill this girl?" Catrina thought, her mind radiating brightly for me as my mind watched her prepare for the ambush. "Maybe she has something to do with the cartel…the daughter of some kingpin." That would explain why all those people got out of her way.

A cocaine princess.

But why would she be alone, and on foot, wearing old jeans and a shirt?

And there was too much reverence. Some of those people were even kneeling and praying as she walked by.

Did they think she was some kind of saint?

It made no sense.

Now the girl was well within range and out in the open: no cover, nothing that could stop a bullet, and nothing to conceal her from the crosshairs. It would be so easy…so easy to finish it. Yet the orders had been clear: do not take the shot if the target is facing the shooter. And it wasn't as if Catrina wanted to take that shot. As a sniper, she had done quite a few things she wasn't proud of, but she'd never assassinated a young woman, possibly still a teenager, who showed no signs of being a danger or a threat.

This was basically going to be a murder.

If that order came.

The girl continued her slow march toward Catrina. If that march continued, would the lieutenant be told to retreat? She took a breath as she kept her finger on the trigger and her eye on the scope.

Yeah, it would be so easy, so easy. Besides, there was that feeling of power, that dark temptation to play God, to take the life. It wasn't the dominant feeling, but it was there. It was always there, and it helped make Catrina what she was. It honed her skills and gave her an edge. It made her feel impatient. If she was supposed to kill that young woman… well, let's get it done. There was no satisfaction to be gained by just waiting…waiting…waiting.

The subject kept coming closer.

Then…a man rushed forward and fell to his knees in front of the girl, blocking her advance. There were tears in his eyes, his hands were clasped together, he was imploring something. The girl seemed embarrassed, if only for a moment, giving a quick nod and helping the man to stand. Then she pointed back in the direction she had come from. The man nodded in return, looking grateful, and quickly retreated.

"Who the fuck is this chica?" Catrina whispered to herself, so quietly that she wouldn't be heard over the airwaves.

The girl began to advance again, continued to get closer.

Soon even a complete novice would be able to take that shot.

A few more steps and the target stopped…and raised her hands… keeping them high, as if she were surrendering to someone. The residents began to back away even farther.

Did the girl see Catrina?

No, that wasn't possible, and she didn't have her eyes fixed on the lieutenant's position. But she did seem to suspect somebody might be… somewhere. She did seem to suspect she might be in some sniper's crosshairs.

Way up above, one of the helicopters cast a quick shadow as it passed the sun. The girl glanced up at it for a moment, smiling as she kept her hands up.

A minute passed…two minutes…three. Those hands stayed raised high as Catrina's stayed on her rifle.

Four minutes…five…six.

A person couldn't normally keep their arms up for that long, could they?

Finally, as the fifteen-minute mark was coming up, that weird young woman shrugged and slowly lowered her arms…then turned around and began to walk away.

Her back was to Catrina.

"Take the shot," ordered the radio's voice.

There was still a moment, just a moment, of hesitation. After all, it was going to be an execution, a pure and simple murder. There was no way to deny it.

But it had to be done.

Orders. Well, they were called "orders" for a reason.

The lieutenant pulled the trigger…aiming for the back of the girl's head…that would be the most merciful. A body shot could deliver a few moments of pain, shock, awareness of death. True, the rule was to usually take that torso shot because it was a bigger, more certain target. But Catrina didn't have to play by those rules. She knew there was no way she was going to miss.

A direct hit, straight into the skull, just as she had expected. Yet that was the only thing that went as expected.

The cranium should have been destroyed. There should have been a blast of brain, blood, and bone fragments.

That wasn't what happened.

The force of the impact took the target off her feet, propelling her forward and down as she actually left the ground for a moment under the power of that bullet. Then she landed hard on her stomach.

But her head remained intact.

Even more incredible, she stood back up.

"Evacuate! Evacuate!" demanded the radio.

Catrina immediately obeyed. She grabbed her weapon and ammo, and then she ran down the stairs to the vehicle that awaited her. As she jumped in the back, the driver took off with a screech and then quickly lost himself in traffic.

Impossible.

It was impossible.

And yet it also made a certain kind of sense. It explained the mystery around the mission, the enigmatic statements. They knew Catrina wouldn't believe it until she saw it for herself...until she saw that girl survive, unharmed, as a .50-caliber bullet was shot straight at her brain.

Who the hell was that girl? What the hell was that girl?

Maybe now, since the lieutenant had seen it for herself and knew the unbelievable truth, she would be able to get some real answers. She saw the man at the wheel watching for her reaction in the rearview mirror, watching her processing what she had just experienced.

Catrina met his gaze.

"What the fuck was that?" Her question came out more calmly than she'd expected. Cold with a contained anger that didn't show any hint of the hysteria lurking underneath.

"Nobody knows, Lieutenant. All we know is that her name is Guadalupe Castaneda...or at least that's the identity of that body you shot at. Until recently, she was apparently just an ordinary chica...she was reported missing for a month or so. Then...she came back like that...indestructible like that. And she's killed a lot of people."

"Indestructible," Catrina repeated. "Indestructible."

"Exactly. That's why we're vague with new personnel. We've found that it's better to let them see for themselves. Maybe that's not very professional, but we can't even show them films of her. She shows up as just a blur in any video recording. So, we don't even have any good proof. Would you have believed it?"

Catrina paused for a moment, trying to gather up the thoughts running around loose in her spirit. "No. I would have assumed it was some kind of test, maybe even a psychological test, to see what information we were willing to accept from our superiors."

"Exactly," the man repeated.

"But it wasn't a test. I used my own rifle and my own bullets that I brought with me, and they were never out of my custody."

"Exactly."

After that, they both fell into a silence.

Catrina's hands began to tremble until she was finally able to will them to stop.

New orders came in. She was rushed to another location and told to set up for another shot, to wait and see if the bulletproof girl might come into her sights again.

Catrina wasn't really sure how long she waited that second time. Her mind was still in confusion after everything she had already seen. But she was eager, eager for another shot at that girl, eager for another perfect head shot. She wanted to see it again, wanted to watch as a projectile that should pulverize a skull actually did nothing, no real harm.

Yes, she wanted to see it again. She wanted to confirm that the impossible was possible.

But in the end, she wouldn't get another chance, not that day.

Lupe ended up taking a different path. Another sniper would get to take that next shot.

They told Catrina to pack up; the driver would take her to her quarters.

Were they trying to irritate her? Were they trying to bore her? Perhaps they actually thought that if they kept picking at her, without ever confronting her, that she would get fed up and leave town. I started to think maybe that was their strategy. Maybe they were planning some really big surprise for Lupe. After all, if they could get her to leave the city and go out into the desert, they could begin to drop some really heavy shit on her. It wouldn't look good to drop bombs on your own city. And it was right there on the border, too. The gringos wouldn't go for that.

But yeah, if they could get her to head out of town and into some wasteland…

Assuming the general was that clever.

But clever or not, I was glad our army didn't have any nukes.

With Lupe running around loose as the army took shots at her, and with the army running around loose trying to take its own kind of control in La Ciudad, nobody noticed the subtle deaths that Juan brought: those unseen hands that slid into the flesh and drained away the force of life just as a bullet was about to be fired, just as a fist made a brutal impact, just when someone was getting the shit kicked out of them while lying on the ground, or just as the cattle prod touched the genitals of a prisoner tied up in a cell.

Maybe there was even surprise that a victim had died, at least in the cases where that hadn't been the plan. But no one, no ordinary mortal, ever seemed to suspect that there was anything unnatural behind such deaths.

It was the cost of doing business.

And so El Bautista's strength grew.

Then the night came when Juan walked through a wall and into a bar. Two very big and very drunk men had gotten into a fight, a serious fight. There was already bruising and blood. In that moment, they were grappling, wrestling, trying to force each other to the ground.

The hungry ghost forgot his caution, impulsively reaching into both men at the same time to tear away what gave them life, causing both to crumple to the floor in their shared death.

And even before the taking of those last breaths, Juan felt the change. Something within him crossed a threshold, something ignited, a new level of energy filled him. His thoughts suddenly became more clear. The shabby world around him became more colorful, more vivid.

He could feel how powerful he truly was.

He immediately felt ready, prepared to take on the girl who is Death.

Still invisible to the world, Juan slipped through the next wall without even a second glance, without even knowing how the other patrons had reacted to the sudden and dual demise he'd left behind.

One night I dreamed again, dreamed deep down into whatever it is that you call the self—my self specifically, such as it is. I dived under my own surface and found a place where I wasn't a tired old body. I found a place where I was feeling and energy.

It was a place of love, of my love for the first Flor.

I tried to go down deeper. I tried to go down further. I knew she had to be there…somewhere. Yes, deeper and further into those feelings, into that energy. I found a path, my path, a path that was supposed to lead directly to her. It was a road that tore through all obstacles, a road that led straight and relentlessly to her. It was my road.

And yet somehow, I hadn't been able to follow that path to the end. I hadn't been able to find it.

I seemed to wake up, floating on the surface of my body and my mind, awed that a cynic, a broken-down old failure, could still shine with a love like that.

Then I slipped back into sleep and dreamed again.

I was in a white desert with the most pure sky and a light fueled by my emotions. It was a pristine place, not like the sands and rocks around La Ciudad.

I held a cell phone. I guess it was mine. I texted Flor. In waking life, I hated texting and never did it. But in the dream I did it, maybe because in that place hearing her voice would be too intense, too overwhelming.

"Where r u?" I asked, not really expecting a response.

But there was one: "I m sorry don't recognize ur # with whom am I txt'n?"

"Cervantes."

How much dream time passed before her response? "Oh. Hello. So, I gotta tell ya, I don't feel comfortable talkn to ya now that I've entered into this other place of being. I m gone."

Then a moment and an eternity later, "Things change, nothin ever stays the same. Take care Cervantes. May the Force b with u. Peace."

What could I say to that? My dream stood still in that crystal-white sand in a moment that might have been forever…or maybe it was seconds. "I miss u. If u need me I will b here."

"Thank u."

That was it. I knew I shouldn't say any more. And I knew she wouldn't be saying any more. And then I realized how alone I was in that place, as pure and beautiful and clear as it was. I stood there frozen until—

◆

—I woke up, fully embodied in my tired carcass.

I couldn't resist looking at my phone. There were no text messages, not from Flor, not from anyone else.

Yet every message I had sent to her in my dream had been saved to my drafts. Probably because there was nowhere to send them.

Weird too. They say you can't read in dreams. But I vividly remembered reading all those dream texts, both mine and hers. They seemed more real than the morning paper.

Nothing to do but down a couple of shots and try to doze off again. Yeah, I was so fucked-up that I was trying to send text messages in my sleep. But who gave a shit? It would have mattered only if I had somewhere to send them in the waking world. And it would have mattered only if Flor had sent some real ones back to me.

Never mind that she had vanished so long ago that there had been no cell phones or texting. Even if she was alive, she wouldn't have that number.

I slept deeply again.

There was no more dreaming.

La Ciudad was the city of loss. In my own way, I was like all of those others who had lost somebody. I didn't know what had happened to my first Flor. I didn't know if she was alive or dead. The most awful—or the most wonderful—things could have happened to her, and I would never know.

So how was I any different from the friends, relatives, and lovers of all those other women who had vanished from the streets of La Ciudad?

How was I any different from anyone else who had cried over a lost daughter, wife, or girlfriend?

I wasn't.

I woke up to an explosion, a rumble in the distance, a shaking of the ground.

I sat up. My mescal bottle was still in my hand. The scorpion in the bottom was sloshing around like my brain.

Daylight was pushing in on my head.

Yet somehow, I felt strangely refreshed, almost happy. I was feeling like I had finally gotten that "at least a goodbye" I had always wanted.

Flor had at least tried to say farewell.

In the background, another explosion, another rumble, another slight shaking of the ground.

I didn't know it yet, but the day of the rockets had arrived.

It had been a very interesting time for Lieutenant Catrina Ochoa as she'd settled into a more routine amazement. The days had been a blur of movement, rushing around La Ciudad, setting up her equipment, waiting to take the shot, hoping to take the shot, sometimes getting to take the shot, sometimes getting to see the impossible once again.

But she'd done her last shift.

The sniper strategy was being phased out; the shooters reassigned. As the best of the best, Catrina had been ordered to join the general's entourage.

She was certain to get a promotion.

And now she was getting to take a brief break.

She'd been provided a small apartment in the city, a place that was easy to deploy from; now she could finally take advantage of it.

It was strange to be at rest, to eat takeout food, to watch crappy television. She'd been running on adrenaline for so long, feeling the excitement for so long, that she'd almost forgotten what fatigue is. But now it was hitting her hard; it was time to sleep. She had to use willpower just to wash off in the tiny, low-pressure thing that some people might call a shower.

Brushing her teeth, she examined herself in the old mirror. Her eyes didn't seem like the eyes of a killer, but they were.

Yet they weren't the eyes of someone who had killed recently or the eyes of someone who had killed an innocent. No, they were the eyes of someone who had tried, who had fired the true shot, and who had failed only because the target was…impervious.

Catrina rinsed out her mouth and exhaled.

She was still in awe, just like all of us, just like all the people who had seen the truth that was Guadalupe Castaneda, a truth that was either sacred or unholy. Most of the folks in La Ciudad had opted for sacred, but Catrina wasn't sure that was the correct choice. No natural body could have stopped that bullet. It could have just as easily been El Diablo instead of Dios to provide that magic.

Nevertheless, a smile appeared on her reflected lips as the full realization of what she knew blossomed within her heart. A feeling she hadn't let herself fully experience in the many days of waiting and action. It was the same feeling that had manifested in me when I'd realized what Lupe was and what that meant: proof that there was still mystery, absolute mystery, in the world. It made Catrina feel a deep fear, but it excited her even more.

Catrina shivered, suddenly certain of a presence behind her…and also knowing that was impossible. Her one-room place was so tiny, she would have known if someone was there, if someone really was behind her.

It was definitely time to get some sleep.

Juan stood directly behind Catrina.

So close.

Close enough to kill.

And he desperately wanted to kill the lieutenant, to take her life into his invisible hands and make her death long and painful. He hated the army and he hated women, so there were no scruples to stop him. But he didn't do it. He exercised self-control because Catrina was causing problems for his main enemy, the one he hated most of all.

Lupe.

When El Bautista first realized what the military was doing, that it had set up a mobile network of snipers to harass the girl, his first impulse was to go after those shooters, just to cause chaos, fuck things up. He was able to fight that impulse, to resist that temptation, only because they were teasing Lupe, probably irritating her, frustrating her, pissing her off. That made it worthwhile to let those soldiers live.

After it was over, after Juan had become a god, he could deal with the army however he wanted. But for the time being, he would let the army hinder the girl without taking on the task of hindering the army.

Still, he wanted to find those snipers, wanted to watch them, just to know that he could do it, just to know that he could have killed them. It was easy for an invisible, intangible man to find those shooters, to follow them, to stalk them. He could get within inches. He could place the surface of his palm a hairbreadth away from their skin and maybe just get a little taste of their lives.

It was something to do, something that amused him.

Then he found out that one of them was…female.

He was especially drawn to her, especially repelled by her: a woman who could play a man's game, a woman who was a warrior, a woman who had better aim than any of her peers.

For a while, Juan only haunted Catrina. He especially enjoyed following on her heels to that tiny apartment, to stand there behind her, and to know how easy it would have been to murder her. If he'd still been in his normal body, he certainly would have had an erection in those moments. He was that kind of guy, after all.

He watched avidly as she undressed, showered, and prepared to sleep. And even though he no longer felt human arousal, human desire, he was still excited by the fact that he could invade her privacy, to know that she was at his complete mercy, to know that he had absolute power over her.

Juan kept watching as Catrina went to her bed and turned out the light, watched as she promptly fell asleep. Then he leaned down and close, as if to kiss her cheek or forehead, getting so close again but not actually making contact.

"You get to live another night, my dear," he whispered.

After that, he turned and left, striding through the wall.

That night Catrina would have nightmares.

It was also the time of the altars.

Never had the existence of Lupe been so public.

There was no denying her. No faith was required when everyone could see a young girl take a .50-caliber slug and then get up and keep walking.

The holy girl. That was what the young prostitute had called her that first night, the night when it had all started. And now that phrase was being whispered among the poor, tired, and huddled masses of the city.

As she paced the streets, seeking that confrontation she couldn't find, the people were more forthcoming with their affection. There were those who made a sign of blessing. There were those who would bow. There were those who would fall to their knees in prayer. More and more people began to do those things.

At first, Lupe was taken aback, almost frightened by their increased reverence. Then, when she got more used to it, she began to smile, nod, and acknowledge her worshippers.

Then she began to keep more distance, warning people away with her gestures if she thought they were coming too close or being too blatant. She was clearly becoming worried that they were putting themselves in danger.

The people understood.

That was when the street altars began to appear. Usually crude and hasty, a candle or two would burn in front of a small figure of a woman. Maybe it would be a doll, maybe a drawing, a clay sculpture, or some other effigy that was supposed to represent Lupe.

The folks were not only supporting her, encouraging her, they were making her a saint. La Santa Chica.

And that really began to piss off the army.

They began to smash all those little altars as soon as they saw them.

Then new ones would immediately appear.

Yeah, the army was really getting pissed off. The general was probably losing his patience.

"Tick-tock, tick-tock," said Juan to himself since none of the human beings around him were able to hear his words. "Time to kill a bitch!"

He was ready, he wanted to find the girl, he was certain his moment was upon him. Wandering the city, passing in and out of its buildings, walls, and alleys, he was suddenly having trouble finding her. She was on the move too, as her own battle with the army continued. Juan was attentive to sounds of gunfire and explosives, but when he did hear them, they were always too far away, and he always arrived too late to carry out his plan for murder.

Yet his eagerness only increased. He could feel his power, he knew his essence had become self-sustaining. He no longer needed to feed from either fire or from lives that were about to end. He was still invisible and still intangible, but he felt the energy within him, and he sensed its might. He knew that he was finally the demigod that he had always been destined to become.

But he realized he had to consume one more life, one more time. He had to feed on the girl's life if he wanted to reach his true apotheosis.

Once he absorbed…whatever that force within her was…he would be the god of this world, he would be the invincible one. And with her powers combined with his knowledge and connections with the criminal world of La Ciudad, he could truly rule, he could truly create an empire. All that girl could do was fuck things up. She wasn't worthy of being… whatever she was. Juan could command, Juan could inspire, Juan knew how to be divine.

They would all be fucking worshipping him. He would have them all at his feet and on their knees. Oh yes, if he wanted sacrifices, there would be sacrifices!

But only that one last sacrifice really mattered.

He needed the girl.

These were the thoughts that kept spinning in El Bautista's head as he searched, yet he was still taken by surprise when he finally saw her, saw that girl. She was coming down the street and straight toward him, walking aimlessly during some lull in her battle with the army.

The girl saw him too. There was no doubt this time because she stopped and stared directly at Juan.

They were perhaps two hundred yards apart, standing still and examining each other. He couldn't tell if she recognized him with his disfigured, seemingly melted form. Her expression betrayed only curiosity. She also knew she was facing something different.

Juan beckoned to her, challenging her.

The girl smiled slightly; then she advanced toward him.

Despite his impatience, El Bautista decided to wait for her to come all the way to him. It seemed only fitting that she fully present herself as the true offering.

There was no hesitation in her approach as she quickly closed the space between them. Closer and closer she drew to him. Her expression became more hostile as she clenched her fists. Maybe she did realize who he was—or at least she realized he was an enemy.

Juan reached out with his left hand, a grin of anticipation filling his deformed mouth. The strange fires sparked at his fingertips, his own energy ready to merge and mix with hers in that moment before he would consume her life.

At last! At last, he was close enough. Juan plunged his hand flat and straight at her chest, straight at her heart, ready for the flood tide of force that had to come, force way beyond anything he had ever experienced, power that would flow and feed him, exalt him, make him truly divine.

To devour that girl's spirit, to slay another demigod: wouldn't that be the absolute sin, the one he had always sought to commit?

There was only one problem, just a small one. His hand didn't penetrate. The girl's skin, her flesh: they were solid to his touch.

Was he suddenly corporeal again?

No. That hand and his arm, they were still transparent; he was still immaterial.

The girl had stopped cold, also looking down at Juan's hand just below her breastbone as he tried to push harder, tried to make it pass into her so that he could take what he wanted.

Nothing. Not a centimeter, not a millimeter. The sparks continued to dance uselessly around his fingers as those digits bent back under the pressure. In all of Juan's world, only the girl was concrete. He still couldn't fully accept it, he still felt confused. He pulled his hand away and studied it, as if it were some device that wasn't working right, something he could fix.

And in that moment, the girl swung her fist with her full strength toward Juan's chin. There was a loud crack as she connected perfectly. Juan's plastic-like flesh shattered as his jaw was broken and torn half off.

Yet because Juan was still intangible to the rest of the world, and because he was almost weightless, the impact sent him flying up into the air for a hundred meters or more, before finally dropping out of the girl's sight.

Juan was only slightly conscious, just dimly aware of what was happening to him, when he finally fell back to earth…passing through the surface and deep, deep into the ground, losing what was left of that awareness.

In the meantime, Lupe continued walking.

So, like I said, the day of the rockets had arrived.

Ah, Mexico, with your big and gringo-equipped military, which never had a real war to fight. So, it pretended to fight the narcos for a while. Then it suddenly found itself a real conflict: a battle with a wayward teenager, a girl who had risen from the dead.

Lupe was still stalking those same streets, probably expecting the usual .50-caliber greeting. The choppers circled La Ciudad, high and far away, just as they had ever since Lupe had taken that first aircraft down. She probably didn't even really pay attention to them anymore, thinking she'd gotten the best of them.

Close to noon, the city already barraged by the sun, Lupe was ambling in the middle of a not very busy road. Few people were near her. At least they picked a moment when they had less chance of causing collateral damage.

Those helicopters might have made themselves tiny, almost specks, up in the sky. But they weren't harmless. They'd just been holding back, waiting and waiting for that order to strike. Without warning, one of them dropped a laser-guided antitank rocket straight down the lane, aiming for Lupe's back. It arrived faster than the speed of its sound. No way to know if it hit her directly or just the ground at her heels.

The sudden micro-cataclysm left a crater, debris, dust, smoke, shattered windows, damaged vehicles, but no visible casualties. Not even Lupe, who bounced and bounced and landed at least a hundred yards down the street. Her favored outfit of blue jeans and long-sleeved shirt had been destroyed again. Yet she was instantly back up on her feet, unharmed.

She did seem taken aback for a few seconds. Then she grinned and lifted a middle finger up high and over her head, waving it back and forth.

A second rocket arrived in response, this time fired at her face. And considering that the girl stood motionless and defiant, and considering that you could probably score a direct hit on an ant from miles away with that technology, I wouldn't have been surprised if that second missile had gotten her right in the nose with its armor-piercing punch.

But that time, when the smoke had drifted away and the dust had begun to settle back to the earth, there was no trace of Guadalupe Castaneda. Gone with that smoke, but not with the wind—because the wind still blew.

A day passed, then a second, then a third. That empty space, that last place that Lupe had been standing, remained empty, a crater that could have just as easily been a giant pothole. It wasn't as if we didn't have those.

They had waited almost two hours on that first day, but finally some soldiers had come to check out the impact site. They had approached with fear and hesitation, found nothing, and left with visible gratitude and relief. Then the people had come to look, but they always kept a respectful distance from that spot where the holy girl had last stood. And during those next few days, they came there with candles and prayers, more and more of them, until the army finally forbade it.

But all over the city, the altars still appeared.

And the soldiers still destroyed them.

And then more would appear.

A week went by.

I stayed in my house again—all the time. I didn't dare go out. If the army thought they had gotten rid of Lupe at last, then there was no telling what kind of rampage they would go on. So once again, I paid people to bring me my booze, cigars, and food. I continued to keep the shades closed. No, I didn't trust that army. I knew they were keeping an eye on reporters—and probably an ear on them, too. I was sure they had tapped my phone line and had my cell phone monitored. Flor the second knew it too, so she never tried to contact me.

There were two options for a guy in my situation, guys who had been on salary for the old order. They would either want to recruit me or they would want me to keep my mouth totally closed. If not, they would decide on how extreme the measures should be if they had to close it for me.

Yeah, technically I still worked for the paper; I could keep writing my fluff pieces. But that wasn't the point. Nobody had called or shown up to actually tell me or drop a hint that I was in the new order. So that meant it was best that I lie low and indeed keep my mouth shut and hope that nobody showed up to make sure it was shut.

And still no evidence of Lupe. She'd decided to vanish again, for whatever reason. Did she want us to think she had been a dream, a dream that we all had shared?

No, friend or foe, we all knew she was real. It had all happened. Too much had already transpired for any of us to be in denial. Because when we woke up the next day and the next and the next, her body count was still there. People like Sanchez were still in the ground…a stark and unyielding fact to act as witness to her presence and her deeds.

Of course, just as I knew they would, during that time the army began tentatively, then cautiously, then confidently to resume its methodical takeover of La Ciudad.

How long was Juan El Bautista under the earth, drifting through the stone and rock, recovering from Lupe's attack? All he really knew was that his awareness was slowly coming back, that the fire of supernatural life that simmered within him was slowly healing him, slowly restoring him. He was mending from that blow that would have killed an ordinary man—would have killed ten ordinary men.

How long was it before his eyes fluttered open, only to regard the darkness of the underground that he floated in?

He didn't panic. He knew where he was and he knew what had happened to him. He was putting all of that memory back together as he was restored.

He needed to recover.

He needed time.

He just needed to let that alien essence that had been given to him do its work, to nurture him, to give him its secret blessing.

And he also needed that time to think, because it was his destiny to confront that girl—to destroy her. So, what had gone wrong?

It was obvious. He had been impatient. He hadn't allowed his powers to grow, to increase to the point where he could complete the mission that had been given to him, the mission that he had willingly accepted. But he could still feel those fires burning in his core. That woman, that green one, had fully stoked them, and the girl couldn't extinguish them. They were still working within him, transforming him into what he would need to become to truly defeat that girl, to totally annihilate her.

He only had to wait.

Still, with just enough materiality to allow him interactions with the surrounding matter, he was able to half crawl and half swim back up into the daylight.

◈

I don't know why the fear was so strong in me. There was no sign or indication that anybody really cared about my existence. I probably wasn't even enough of a bug to bother mashing flat. But I still acted as though there were a million-dollar bounty on my head. I finally started to think that the fear that paralyzed me, the fear that saturated my spirit, wasn't really just my own personal fear. It was the fear that coursed and pulsed through the veins of all the residents of La Ciudad.

After many dreamless nights and days of sleeping like a dead man, I finally dreamed again. I saw my phone, I was holding it. I could read that I had a text message.

"U ther Crvantes?"

"I don't recognize ur # who m I txtn w?"

"Flor."

"Flor?!"

"Not that flor u dummy…new flor!"

"Sorry."

"No prob. U have 2 find Lupe."

"How?"

"Dream ur way 2 her."

Then all at once I was with Lupe. But my body wasn't with me. I was just some hovering and weightless presence…kind of drifting at a height that let me look down on the scene…because I was there with her…there on the street. I was watching her as she flipped her middle finger at that helicopter…waiting for that second missile that was sure to come. And of course, it did. I already knew that it did. I was in the past, after all.

When the second missile hit her, it actually hit her in the chest… because in that moment of impact, she was jumping up. I flew with her as the force of the explosion, combined with her leap, took her up and over some buildings. She ended up slam landing on her butt in the middle of a street about three blocks away. She wasn't even stunned, just annoyed. I followed her eyes as she found a service cover just a foot or two in front of her. Moving quickly, she lifted it and let it close above her as she dropped herself into the sewer system of La Ciudad.

My dream self laughed—or at least tried to. I didn't really have a voice. Lupe must have truly had faith in her invulnerability if she was willing to go down into that nightmare! And she was taking me with her. I was following her without choice or thought.

I was afraid for a few moments that my sense of smell would be functioning in that place. Fortunately, it didn't seem to be. The sight of that place was nasty enough.

But how could I even see in pitch blackness? I was baffled. Then I realized I was seeing through Lupe's eyes. She was able to see in that utter darkness…and somehow, with her, I could see down there too. I had no control or possession of her; I was just in some way sharing in her sight.

And, horribly, her sense of smell did work. Up to her waist in sludge and crap, I felt her convulse as she gagged a few times. At least she didn't throw up. But then, I don't think she had to eat anymore.

She also realized, or remembered, that she didn't have to breathe. Moving air in and out of her lungs was just a habit that she could stop. Doing that finally allowed her to regain control of herself, and she began to wade forward, her face still twisted with distaste. At first, she tried to fight her way forward against the flow of the filth-saturated waters. But even with her strength it was hard not to slip, slide, stumble, and constantly be pushed back. She was probably trying to walk on a thick coat of slime. I found myself thinking that she could do it if she swam. But did she know how? And even if she did, maybe she didn't want to have to lower herself even farther down into the shit.

Instead, she decided to turn and follow the flow, half walking and half being carried along, still looking totally grossed out.

Becoming more aware that I was in a dream, I started to resist it. It seemed like it wasn't going to end. I didn't want to be stuck in some endless dream about Lupe floating around in the sewers below La Ciudad. But I couldn't break free. I was stuck there, dreaming with her.

"I don't want to be here. I don't want to be here," I muttered and mumbled. I even thought I could make out the sound of my own voice saying it in the present, where my body was still located.

"I don't want to be here. I don't want to be here!" I could have sworn that I heard Lupe's silent voice inside my own skull: the voice of a young woman that I had never heard before.

Both our monologues were suddenly interrupted when something erupted out of the muck directly in front of Lupe. A human—or at least a humanoid form concealed in sludge. Lupe was startled, actually frightened. Reflexively, she tried to jump back. Instead, she lost her footing and plopped even deeper into the crap, barely keeping her head above the surface. And before she could react, the thing had reached down and seized her by the throat. Then, with seemingly little effort, it raised her up. Still shocked, she didn't resist as it bent her head back, opening its mouth to reveal vampire fangs, trying to sink them into her neck.

Instead, it let loose its own surprised grunt when those same fangs failed to penetrate. Angered, and with a muffled growl, it tried to bite and tear even harder. Confused by continuing failure, it pulled its mouth away and stared at her. Apparently, the creature was able to see down there in that darkness, too.

The sludge and muck were beginning to fall and ooze off Lupe's attacker, revealing what looked like a corpse that had been mistreated and dead for a while. Chunks of flesh were missing, and a patchwork pattern of skull was evident. The eye sockets were filled with dead, withered eyes that still seemed to have the ability to move and function. The lips had been torn away to leave the teeth and fangs, oddly shiny and white, in plain view. What was left of that face seemed to mirror Lupe's own shock. Both of them remained frozen in their positions for a few moments.

It took me those same moments, but I recognized that creature. I had no doubt, even though that visage was now filled with evil intent and strange hunger, when before, it had been slack and lifeless. It was the face of the man in the donkey mask that Samurai Sanchez had killed, the man who had taken his severed head and escaped into those same sewers, back in a time that seemed so long ago.

Somehow, he had managed to get his head back on and gotten it to function again.

Lupe was the first to recover her poise, and she drove her right fist full-on into the thing's jaw, a blow that would have pulverized any normal human being's entire head. In this case, with a loud crack, the vampire's face ended up looking over its own shoulder, unnaturally dislocated and with half the jaw demolished and the whole thing hanging loosely. But its hands still held Lupe and were squeezing her throat with their own unrelenting grip.

She seized him by the wrists with her own hands and with loud snaps crushed the bones. But I could feel that she had to exert herself. It didn't seem to feel any pain, as it just took the damage. It was even somehow starting to make its head rotate back into place with a jerky, spastic motion. Below the surface, she kicked his legs out from under him…and she lost her balance too…with them ending up face-to-face with their heads barely above water.

Lupe managed to quickly stand back up. Her enemy was either unwilling or unable to match her. Instead, it stayed on its knees. Unable to fully return its skull to a facing forward position, it lurched and turned its torso so it could regard the girl with that immobilized head.

Before she could decide what to do next, it began to speak by emitting a raspy, hoarse, and croaking voice. "It must be you, then. It must be you. Finish it. Finish me. I arrived too soon; we should not be here yet. My master sent me, sent me as a harbinger to challenge the claims of the green one, the arrogant one who already claims victory. But my master, he is closer, and he will arrive first. He will make this place his own before all rivals. Even you shall fall, even you shall fall. But it is still too soon. I cannot be here yet, cannot survive here yet. It is agony. So, finish me! It will be a mercy!" Then he stared at her, waiting.

Lupe thought about it for a few seconds, then nodded, bent down, took that damaged head in her hands, and gave it a massive twist, turning it around two or three times, snapping and tearing it off. But again, she had to use a lot of effort, a lot of her strength, to do it. The body vanished below the surface. Lupe held the head in her hands. The milky, stagnant eyes still seemed to regard her. Then she slowly crushed the skull between her palms.

What splattered out of that cranium seemed even more vile than the swamp of shit that surrounded the scene.

Lupe was shaking it off her hands when an eerie moan seemed to echo in the tunnel. Then, with a roar, an unexpected high-velocity tsunami wave of sewage water filled the underground chamber up to the ceiling. And it swept Lupe away.

My dreaming didn't follow her that time.

Instead, I woke up pouring sweat, panting…my heart pounding like a jackhammer.

Had that been for fucking real? Had that truly happened? Had Lupe really confronted some undead thing down in the sewers? All I could say at that point was that it had seemed as real to me as my waking state… my staggering, trembling-hands state…as I struggled to get myself a shot of mescal. My heart still felt like an anvil and hammer. I might have some kind of attack, one that would be my finish, if I didn't get some calm into me.

I managed to drink, and instead of dying, I slowly, slowly regained some normality.

Breathing deeply, I took another shot and then slouched and slumped down into a chair.

My mind and body became more still. So, I just sat there. Then I started to wonder if I was dying after all. Everything seemed numb. I didn't feel like I could move the slightest muscle. And I didn't really want to. There was no panic. I just didn't care.

Then I saw Lupe standing there, right in front of me. She was clean and even smiling slightly. It was either a vision or a hallucination.

I tried to ask her a question: "Time to finish it?" But I wasn't sure if my mouth even opened, let alone if any noise came out.

Yet she seemed to understand, and she shook her head, losing her smile. Then she silently mouthed some words that I was able to comprehend.

"Will it ever be finished?" That was what she asked me in return.

Then I lost consciousness, knowing that Lupe was about to make her presence known again.

Juan continued to exist as a wandering ghost.

He didn't feed on the life of mortals anymore; he didn't feel the need. He could tell there was no more to gain by doing that. He could feel his power growing on its own as he recovered from the setback that puta had dealt him.

But he couldn't seek that girl, not yet.

And he couldn't watch her fight with the army; he couldn't risk getting close to her again. She could finish him if he got too close, too soon, before the time that was predetermined, the moment he had been promised by his benefactor.

He could watch the army locking down its control on the rest of La Ciudad, but Juan didn't find that interesting. In fact, he found it tiresome and irritating. He knew he was no longer the man he once was, yet he still hated to see the forces of the supposed authority ruining everyone else's fun.

So, all he could do was wait or maybe peek into the private

perversions and atrocities taking place behind closed doors.

But even that became tedious for someone who no longer had flesh, no longer had human desires.

And El Bautista was not a patient phantom.

That was when he began to be curious about what was going on with his former employer. How was the old man getting by with the army running rampant in his city?

Yes, perhaps it was time for a little visit.

Maybe it was time for a reunion with the Boss.

Everybody in La Ciudad knew about Diego "Dynamite" Dara. Like Samurai Sanchez and Barbarossa, he was part of the inner circle of the Boss's enforcers.

His particular nickname came from his own eccentric style of killing people.

Diego always managed to have crates of dynamite on hand. I don't know where he got them, but it was the kind you used to see in the movies, old-timey stuff, sticks with the kind of fuse you lit with a match. When he personally wanted to get rid of someone, he would have them rounded up and bound and delivered to his estate outside La Ciudad. Then he would forcibly insert a stick in some inconvenient orifice, whether mouth or vagina, light the fuse, step back a safe distance, and watch as the victim stared at the fuse burning down to the end.

Like the others, he'd been part of the hunt for Lupe. But fortunately for Dara, he had never come close to finding her.

So, when the army came to town, Diego still had his life, and he left. He didn't trust the new order, and he'd apparently set plenty of cash aside. Besides, if he needed money, there were more than enough potential employers farther south that could offer him a no-questions-asked vocation.

Diego had built himself a little underground bunker near his killing grounds. That was also where he stored the dynamite. When he took off from La Ciudad, he left behind some men to guard the place. But, one way or another, they also went away, leaving the place abandoned.

Yeah, everybody living in La Ciudad had probably heard about Diego and his dynamite. And if they thought about it, they probably would have figured he might have left some of it behind when he headed out of town. But the general and his staff...well, they didn't know the story. Nobody had remembered or even thought to tell them that there might be unsecured and unsupervised explosives in the area.

So, there was nobody around to care or even know that the entrance to Diego's bunker had been found and the door somehow crushed, twisted, and broken.

There was nobody there to know that some of that dynamite had gone missing.

Deep in the core of the night, only one helicopter was in flight. And La Ciudad seemed pretty well pacified. Nothing going on. Lupe had vanished. What else could have directly challenged the army? The other seven choppers of the squadron were back at base, on the ground. Sure, there was a high, razor-wired fence. Of course, there were guards on watch. Maybe they were awake. Maybe they were even doing their job, not gossiping or gambling.

But even if they had been fully alert, with all the motion sensors and night vision goggles that El Norte could have given them, they wouldn't have been able to stop the young lady who easily leaped over the fences as if she were flying.

And once she was over, how were they going to stop her from tearing open a copter's door, lighting a stick of dynamite on a short fuse, tossing it in, and then jumping over to the next machine as the first one was blown apart? By the time any kind of response, other than panic, was organized, Lupe was over the fence again and apparently gone into the night. That was actually an act of mercy on her part. There was nothing to stop her from committing a massacre.

The surviving helicopter, like a moth to a flame, descended and approached the burning wreckages, the pilot probably thinking there had been an accident. As the chopper drew closer, the pilot must have realized his error, that the base was actually under attack, and suddenly tried to ascend again. Too late. Something heavy and hard struck the aircraft and snagged in the propeller, and the copter dropped straight down into an empty patch of desert. Fortunately, there were no casualties—except for the crew.

My phone buzzed.

I'd heard the explosions of Lupe's attack from far off while I was in a drunken half sleep. And I'd had a vision, very vivid, of what she had done.

The phone pulled me out of it.

"Hello," I mumbled, not even checking who was calling.

"Cervantes, it's Flor. And don't even ask if it's back-in-the-day Flor!"

"Wouldn't think of it," I lied.

"I'll be returning soon. I sense the time of danger for me is about over. But can I stay at your place? Caution would still be a good thing. At my place, everyone would know I was back."

"Of course, Señorita! Why even pretend that you couldn't?"

She laughed. "Then see ya later, gator," she said in English before disconnecting.

All at once, I felt a lot better about life…or at least my life.

I wasn't so sure about anybody else's.

I didn't know if my dream had been for real. I didn't know if Lupe had really fought with that undead thing in the sewers. I didn't know about Juan yet, so I wasn't completely convinced that monsters were on the loose. But one thing was undeniable: Lupe had discovered that those disgusting catacombs were a perfect venue from which to launch her counterattacks.

At first, she came up only at night. And why not? If my visions were true, she could see in the darkest of dark places. All she had to do was randomly move around under the streets, then peep up by slightly lifting a service cover or peering out of a drain, until she saw an army vehicle or some unlucky patrol of soldiers. She could easily be on them before they knew it. The slaughter became methodical, most often hand to hand. She had become even more merciless; there was no teasing or hesitation. Lupe had become an avenging spirit incarnate in flesh that was no longer ordinary flesh.

If there were too many, and some were able to run for it, she might pick up a rifle or a pistol and take some more down that way. If some escaped her aim, she usually chose not to give chase, letting them go and jumping back down into the sewers. It probably pleased her not to give them any time to set up their .50-caliber irritation game.

With the APCs, she took two approaches. One was to rush the

vehicle, reach under, and roll it over and upside down. Or she would leap up top, get a grip, brace herself, rip the hatch off, and then drop in. If she chose the first method, you might get to live. If she chose the second—usually not.

The army stopped patrolling at night. The way things had flipped on them so suddenly, the way their air support had been so easily destroyed, seemed to have left them demoralized and off balance. They appeared to be unable to find a response to the way the game was being played. The sniper game was useless when the target could retreat underground. And nobody was volunteering to go down there after her.

Lupe began attacking during the day, using the same methods. Then the army reduced operations in La Ciudad even when the sun was out. No new helicopters had arrived. Was the general embarrassed to ask for more? Or had his requests been denied?

But they were up to something. Nobody was allowed to approach the estates of the narco lords. The army had created an iron security perimeter. Civilians weren't even allowed close enough to catch the envious glimpse that they had sometimes managed in the past.

And a lot of heavy equipment was coming and going, stuff that looked like it was for major construction and mining. I was hearing all this because I was going out more. But nobody who really knew anything was talking, not in the bars, not to me, not to the people who talked to me.

Juan El Bautista…he'd forgotten how to get there; he'd forgotten the way to the hidden realm of the narco lords. Well, maybe he hadn't exactly forgotten. It was just that he had become so disconnected from the world of the living—he'd been wandering randomly for so long—that he'd lost the habit of being able to find exact locations.

Or maybe it was because his brain no longer had a solid and physical existence that maybe it couldn't easily touch all those memories anymore.

But what was really worth remembering? All Juan truly needed to know was that he would soon become a god and that he had to destroy that girl. Nothing else mattered much.

Now, where was he going?

Oh yes, to find the Boss. That would be amusing.

Finally, he recalled the way.

All he had to do was drift across some sparse landscape, half-walking and half-floating, as he passed through any barriers that separated the narco mansions from the rest of the world. He'd had a place there once; perhaps he still did. He'd never sold it; he'd just left it unused in favor of the much more private ranch. Could somebody have declared him dead and confiscated it? That didn't seem likely, not with everything else that was going on in La Ciudad. And even if they'd noticed that Juan didn't seem to be around anymore, they probably would have assumed that he'd left the battlefield behind until the army finished its fraudulent business.

He half thought about going to that house, if only to see if there were any intruders or transgressors he could slay, just on principle. But then he got distracted again.

The old neighborhood wasn't what it used to be.

The army was there…lots of soldiers and armored vehicles…lots of other heavy equipment. They seemed to be digging up the place, working on some major project. Yet things seemed strangely…peaceful. The posture of the military people wasn't aggressive. Compared with the main body of the armed forces engaged in the La Ciudad operations, it appeared leisurely. Here and there, officers were supervising…whatever was going on. It was hard for Juan to care. Whatever it was, he was beyond it. But he couldn't help but notice that some of those "officers" were men he had once worked with, other narcos, men who definitely hadn't been arrested.

"All a lie, no surprise," said Juan out loud, even though none of those human ears would hear him.

He began to glide up a slope, toward the highest point and the biggest house in that exclusive suburb.

The citadel of the Boss.

But it wasn't there. Or, better said, it was half there, along with more specially-authorized workers and more equipment. They seemed to be remodeling it, reconstructing it. More of the mundane and boring work of mortals, nothing for Juan to worry about. All that mattered to him was that the Boss wasn't going to be there. Disappointed, he turned to go back down the hill, moving slowly since he no longer had a goal. And that was when he noticed the limousine, the private car of the Boss. That thing probably had better armor than all of those military vehicles parked not so far away. It was parked at another mansion, one that was still intact. Who owned that one? Juan still didn't care enough to recall. Whoever it had belonged to, the Boss had obviously ousted him and taken it over while his place was getting renovated. It was also under heavy guard, surrounded by soldiers and snipers. Juan even recognized that woman who had been taking shots at Lupe, the one he'd been oh so tempted to kill.

He suddenly felt the momentary desire to kill a few people and cause a commotion, maybe even take that woman's life. But no, it would be more fun to go find the Boss, to spy, to see how much grief that supposedly invincible girl was causing everyone. Besides, once he became a god, he would probably want those humans around. He would rule over them and they would worship him.

El Bautista slipped through the thick doors and down the halls of that other mansion. It seemed to be the base of operations. There were all sorts of people doing all sorts of things that would be of no real consequence in the long run.

It didn't take long to find the Boss. He was sitting in one of the back rooms, protected by sentries and chatting with a general. They were alone, sipping expensive tequila and smoking expensive cigars...very relaxed, very sure of themselves.

"Maybe I should just kill them. It would be so easy!" he thought.

But the ghost decided to just listen.

And when he heard their plan, all he could do was laugh.

As we advanced deeper into that autumn, the city seemed at peace. The army had pulled back from the main areas of battle to defensive positions farther out. And the criminal element that had controlled those streets before Lupe and the army arrived? Well, they weren't going to try to make a comeback when they would be caught between that hammer and anvil. The only moves they would make were to lie low and take an extended vacation or hit the highway. Anybody that Lupe might be able to take a hate to was lying low and crouching down. Even the holy girl herself was staying hidden. She had gotten used to the filth of her lair. It wasn't like it could do her any real harm. Whatever force had raised her from the dead wasn't going to make her invulnerable to swords, bullets, missiles, and flamethrowers just to let her be defeated by atrocious sanitary conditions.

Yeah, for a time, the regular folks were able to live a life that most civilized cities would call normal. People went to stores, took their kids to the park, went out to eat in restaurants, all without being harassed. No junior narco came to throw his weight around. No gang came to demand protection payments. No cop came up to you to charge an extra tax.

Of course, it was a false peace. None of that was going to last for long.

Juan spent his time haunting the realm of the narco mansions, watching the soldiers work, watching them prepare, watching them finish setting up for their plan. If he'd still cared about his human life, he would have been offended that so many of those narco-aristocrat castles were being used as lodging for soldiers and workers. He would sometimes lose control of himself, laughing at the thought that Barbarossa and the good ol' samurai were dead at the hands of the girl…laughing at the thought that she had also killed him, but that he hadn't stayed dead like the others.

He was going to be a god, very soon he was going to be a god.

A couple of times, he even heard those busy humans talking about him, wondering what had happened to him. Had the girl murdered Juan El Bautista? There were bodies found at his ranch, but not Juan's body. Had he escaped? Nobody knew. He'd just…vanished. Yeah, the girl had probably been out there and fucked up Juan's operation…that was their most likely explanation.

Juan had to laugh again. Yes, he had vanished from the sight of normal humans; that much was true.

Then he just continued to watch them work, to attend their meetings, to hear the latest news about Lupe. Sometimes, he would sit with them and watch television.

As the work approached its end, he made sure to eavesdrop on the latest plans.

His time was coming.

Yes, very soon.

And he intended to be ready.

There was a knock at the door, my front door. I peeked out and confirmed what I already knew: it was Flor. She was alone. I opened the door.

"Hello, stranger," she said.

Then we both reached out for the embrace. And we held it for a long, long time.

"You smell like cigars, mescal, and sweat," she informed me. But she didn't let go of the hug.

"You smell good," I replied. It wasn't like I was lying.

We went inside and sat down in my little kitchen, at the table, my empty bottles trying to form a barricade between us. We sat silently, just enjoying our reunion, being in each other's company again. With her there, it was hard to remember if it had been a day short of forever, or just a few short days, since we had last seen each other.

Flor didn't want to drink alcohol, so we sat at my table and sipped bottled water. I even cleared the scene of my mescal bottles.

"Have you found out any more about Lupe, about who or what she really is?" she asked.

I shrugged.

"You were dreaming with her, traveling out of your body with her, so I hoped maybe you had learned something more while I was away."

"I don't even know for sure if the dreams are true," I said, and I told her about my vision of that zombie thing, or whatever it was, in the sewers. "If Lupe exists, why not that thing? But if it does exist, wouldn't somebody else have run into it? Wouldn't we know about it if it was real? I guess I could ask somebody if the authorities picked up that guy's body at Cristobal's dump...or if it vanished."

Now Flor shrugged. "I do think that Lupe has changed things... that her existence has somehow changed the world." She fell silent. I just waited for her to gather her lines of reasoning and weave them together. "Deep inside each of us, concealed within each of us, there is something that is eternal, indestructible, and divine. Sometimes some of us can truly feel this thing that is hidden down in there. Sometimes it guides us, empowers us, and inspires us. But our bodies and our flesh never truly become eternal, indestructible, or divine. It always remains something that is in our spirit. But somehow...somehow Lupe has become that thing in her bones and skin and blood. She has become that thing in this world…in the here and in the now!"

"Eternal, indestructible, and divine?"

"Yes."

It sounded good to me, but it didn't really explain anything.

So, I asked, "What could bring something everlasting and invulnerable into this world, where everything is transitory and contingent?"

"La Santa Muerte."

I wasn't sure how to respond, unable to commit to being for or against that hypothesis. For all I knew, Lupe could be the Second Coming. I wondered if there was any way to know if she had taken three days to rise from her shabby grave.

Flor was looking at me, like she was examining me in detail…like she was doing some deep thinking. Once again, I didn't interrupt.

"Sometimes—most of the time—I thought you were kind of a doofus for pining away for that other Flor from all those years ago. But while I was gone, while I was away from you, I found myself thinking about it. And I had some feelings and some intuitions. It's like your nostalgia for her is a beacon that has and will draw her back to you, at least as a spirit. She doesn't want to come back, or at least is reluctant to, but she will have to. She owes you a debt. She owes you a goodbye. And I think she will have a task, a mission, to show you some things that you will need to know. I don't know for sure if you faltered and bungled the relationship. Or maybe she wasn't up for it either…maybe it was too much for her…maybe it was too much destiny. But I still think there is some destiny there. And I worry for you. And I am jealous too."

"I never told her…never told her that I loved her."

"Did she ever say that she loved you?"

"N-No, but maybe I was the one who knew—who knew that she was the one I was supposed to be with," I stammered. "Maybe I was the one who was supposed to say it. Maybe she would know that truth only if I spoke it out loud. And I fucked up. I didn't say it!"

She calmly and quietly studied me some more and then said, "Don't be so hard on yourself. You have to forgive yourself. And I think you have to forgive her, too. I highly doubt that she was perfect, either."

"I still should have had the balls to say it."

"And maybe she should have given you more time to say it."

As far as saying things, if there was more to say in that moment, it didn't get said. Instead, another explosion shook my house.

◈

We waited for something to follow that detonation. Nothing except silence. Outside, even the background noises had ceased. Inside, our conversation remained interrupted as we stayed quiet by unspoken consensus.

Finally, there was another explosion. It seemed to come from farther away.

I took the risk of getting up and taking a look from under my window shades. I saw a smoke cloud in the distance. Then there was a third explosion that sounded like it was even more distant. Then a fourth that was even farther. I went out on my porch. Flor followed. We stood out there, waiting for something else to happen.

A fifth explosion.

Time started to drag.

Then we heard the voice.

They'd found some old trucks. Why risk their good military vehicles? They'd mounted loudspeakers on them. They'd parked them, leaving them here and there around downtown La Ciudad. Nobody really noticed at first, not until the same hostile voice began to blare out from all of them at once, creating a threatening network of echoes.

"Señorita Guadalupe Castaneda! Calling Guadalupe Castaneda! You are most cordially invited to a festival in your honor. This festival will be held at the home of the man they call the Boss. Please feel free to come immediately…or at your earliest convenience. This invitation will be repeated until you accept it!"

Flor and I heard the whistling noise before the next explosion.

"Señorita Guadalupe Castaneda! Calling Guadalupe Castaneda! You are most cordially invited to a festival in your honor.…"

Then more shells fell. We didn't know it until later, but the artillery was definitely being targeted to deliver a death toll. Many of those shells were landing in Lupe's old neighborhood. One even finished off Lucio's bar, once and for all.

People were being killed. Officially, they would become collateral damage of the never-ending war that was either against or for drugs.

And the invitation to Lupe kept playing again and again and again.

A couple of hours went by. Artillery rounds kept being fired. But I wasn't really worried for myself. My part of town was just a little too upscale to be deliberately blasted. There would have been too many questions to answer later.

"Señorita Castaneda! Can you really refuse our invitation? We don't think so. That's why we are so insistent. That's why we will keep it up until you grace us with your presence!"

Then more shelling. At least they had changed their message.

"If she doesn't go, they're going to kill hundreds of people," whispered Flor, even though there was no one around to hear her.

"And it will all get blamed on the narcos," I added.

Then suddenly I felt something, a certainty that welled up from what could still be called my soul, a wave of intuition washing up on the beach of my awareness.

"She's on her way. Lupe is on her way."

Flor seemed startled for a moment. Then she smiled.

When Lupe did appear, she had cleaned herself up and found some fresh clothing, a white T-shirt and blue jeans. All the sewer filth was gone. Any remaining carbonization had been scrubbed off. Her hair was still black and wild, but she'd gotten most of the tangles out. She must have gone back to Flor's place again. That was probably where she'd gotten herself in order. That was probably what she'd been doing when she heard the army's message. If we'd been there instead of at my place, we would have seen Lupe in person.

For some reason, I wondered if she'd prayed or made an offering to Flor's black Santa Muerte. I found myself doubting it.

As far as the military and the rest of the population, they didn't know where Lupe had come from. For them, she was just suddenly there, out on the streets, walking along like a normal person would, except for the fact that everyone, civilians and soldiers, now hurried to get out of her way. She happened to saunter past one of those speaker trucks, still repeating and repeating its message, and casually reached down with one hand and flipped it over. The "invitation" sputtered and died.

A few minutes later, all the loudspeakers went dead.

And the shelling stopped.

Because the invitation had been accepted.

Lupe kept walking at a good and steady pace, but not beyond the limits of what a normal human being could have accomplished. Her expression was mainly impassive, with just a trace of determination. Once they'd adjusted to the latest events, the people began to line the streets, watching quietly from a safe distance as the silent girl advanced toward whatever battle was going to be offered.

And what the hell could they be planning to wield against her? Mexico didn't have the A-bomb. The gringos sure weren't going to give us one, especially not to use right on their own border.

Some of the spectators, and then many of the spectators, fell to their knees and clasped their hands. A few chose to salute. A few chose to wave. Some just kept watching. But all remained silent as Lupe approached the edge of town.

Outside town, stationed on a small hill, an army unit watched through their binoculars as Lupe strolled toward them. A couple of snipers also targeted her in the scopes of their .50-caliber rifles, but this time, they didn't take the shot. As soon as it was clear that the girl was headed their way, they promptly rushed to their jeeps and took off into the desert. By the time Lupe got to that place, there was nothing left but soil and footprints and dust slowly scattering. She might not even have known that anyone had been observing her.

Nobody seemed to be following her.

No other human being was in sight.

There was nothing to oppose Lupe's entry into the no-man's-land and nomad land between the rest of us and…them…that realm of the narco elite to which she had been invited.

Once they had finished, all the workers and construction equipment cleared out immediately and quickly. They'd left barely a trace that they'd ever been there. The narco mansions suddenly stood abandoned. Not that Juan had been left completely alone: the army still had a unit on-site to monitor things, to make sure all was going according to plan.

Yeah, everything looked like it had always looked. Nobody would know that all that work had been going on. Juan ambled up to the citadel of the Boss. Nobody would have been able to tell that it had been rebuilt.

He stood in the driveway, knowing that was where he had to wait. It was up to the army to deliver the girl to him. He would have to count on them, and he didn't like that…he didn't like that at all. It filled him with impatience, it made him want to take action, it made him want to run back to the city and confront the girl immediately.

But he couldn't do that; he had to stay near the mansion. He knew that was where he had to be.

So, he waited and waited and waited…not really able to track the time. His eyes seemed strange to him, like they weren't functioning the way they should. He wasn't even sure he could tell night from day, and yet he could still see everything clearly.

Then it hit him, without warning: severe vertigo…nausea…a certainty that he was going to vomit. The sensation was so unexpected and overwhelming that by impulse he stumbled toward the house, passing through the door and rushing toward a bathroom, forgetting that he was still intangible and that there was no food in his stomach. Only when he reached the toilet did he remember himself, just as the feeling began to fade.

"It's almost time. Your moment is almost here!"

Juan knew that voice. It was her voice, unmistakable, coming from somewhere above him.

Looking up, he saw a big green spider smiling at him. Yes, that was what it was doing…it was smiling…because it had a little human mouth. He could even see the tiny teeth and lips.

El Bautista found himself at a loss for words.

"I just thought I should wish you luck. It will be an excellent battle. You'll be the one who will have to make their stupid plan work. I don't think they can pull it off without you. They're idiots who have no idea what they're dealing with." Then that spider let out a cheerful laugh that still managed a sinister undertone.

"Are you the devil himself?" Juan blurted out.

"Himself? Himself? Is that how you talk to the ladies…at least the ones you aren't raping and murdering?" she said, her voice even more feminine, with an almost flirtatious cadence.

"The devil can take any form and use any voice."

"It seems a little late for you to be questioning me, Juan," the spider said, and sighed. "Sure, then. I'm the devil, as well as the master of irrelevant paradigms, when necessary!"

"What?"

"Never mind; get to work. I didn't put in all this effort just to chat with you about your religious beliefs. The girl is on her way here…now!"

Then the spider extended one of her legs. It was only then that Juan realized the creature had ten limbs instead of eight, as a door the size of a playing card materialized in midair in front of her. A miniature hand, a very human hand with five fingers and a thumb, took shape at the end of that appendage, turning the knob and opening that door.

Speechless, Juan thought he saw space and strange stars across that little threshold.

"See ya," said the spider as she leaped through that portal.

The door slammed shut and vanished.

Juan stood alone for a moment.

"That's some crazy shit," he finally said.

Then, as if the spider had given the cue, he heard an amplified voice from somewhere outside. It was a voice from a loudspeaker that was ordering everyone still present to take up their positions—or to vacate the area if they hadn't been given the specific order to stay.

"This is not a drill. I repeat, this is not a drill!"

"At last," said Juan. "At last!"

"Can you see her?" Flor asked me.

"I wasn't trying."

"Would you try?"

I nodded, letting my body fall onto the sofa under Flor's worried but eager gaze.

I was about to say there was no way I could do it so easily, but then all at once—or maybe twice—I was there, seeing the same scene Lupe was seeing as my awareness seemed to hover just a little above her head.

At first, it was all just the same desert landscape that I had known all my life. Lupe was attentively looking for the slightest sign of her enemy, still taking her time, still in no hurry. She knew that sooner or later they would have to do…something…that they would have to show their hand.

Then I felt a change of some sort: a chill in my soul that made my body tremble on the couch where I had left it. I could feel Flor touch my shoulder, and that feeling soothed my spirit.

Yet, the change in my perceptions remained. I could see…see strange forms, uniforms, deforms all around me in that desert. They were things that seemed to follow Lupe or to walk alongside her at a respectful distance. Some had eyes of ice and some had eyes of fire. Some seemed to have no eyes. All their faces were shadowy and obscured…even in the light of the bright sun. They didn't wish to clearly show themselves. I could tell they didn't want me to see them.

At first, I thought that it had to be something that the army had conjured up, as if they were some sort of brujos that could summon the non-natural to strike at the unnatural. But as soon as I thought it, I knew it wasn't true. Those things that I could only partly see had nothing to do with the human world. They were beings that were far from fully manifested. They were more like a potential, a hint, a suggestion of entities that could become real but had yet to achieve that status.

I could sense they were there only because of Lupe. They were drawn to her. It didn't even necessarily feel like they were either hostile or friendly. The general feeling was more of curiosity, even some nervousness.

I realized that even those denizens of…wherever…didn't know what Lupe was any more than I did.

I couldn't tell, not for sure, if Lupe was aware of them. She continued to walk as if she were alone, cautious but not excessively concerned.

Or maybe she had known they were there for so long that she was used to their presence. Maybe she was just ignoring them.

Then, ahead, on another rise, a new form seemed to congeal; it was still too far away for me to make it out clearly. But it seemed human and female.

Flor the first.

She was facing my direction, probably watching Lupe, just observing and not moving.

Forgetting for a moment that I was bodiless and merely trailing along in Lupe's wake, I tried to run toward the figure. The nothing that was happening with that promptly reminded me of my situation.

"Lupe! Lupe!" I tried to shout. "Do you see her? Can you go to her?" But Lupe continued to maintain her calm gait on a route that wouldn't be leading to where that misty figure stood.

And then that figure started to melt and fade.

"Flor!" I tried to shout again, only then realizing that I wasn't even hearing any sound. My voice was only a memory of having had one.

"Flor!" That time I did hear myself, as I jolted back to awareness on my sofa.

"I'm right here," said Flor the second, trying to soothe me. Then she saw my confusion and consternation—and then she understood.

All she did was roll her eyes, sit down beside me, and pat my leg without saying one more word.

Miles away from where I found my addled brain, Lupe continued her slow advance. She could have moved so much faster if she had wanted. Maybe she was trying to frustrate them, make them impatient. She came to a stop on another rise and stood there, unmoving. A strong and rising wind whipped sand in her face and made her hair look like a tattered black flag. She didn't bother to blink.

Still far away, away in the haze, it was barely possible to make out the shapes of some of the fancy houses that marked the boundary of Narcotown.

The wind grew stronger, the dust and sand more harsh, and still it didn't seem to trouble the girl. She continued to stare at her destination, apparently trying to see something, something that would give a clue about what her hosts had planned for her. There was no fear or concern in her expression, but perhaps a blend of curiosity and anticipation. And even hope? Hope that she would be able to do so much damage to them that they would finally leave her and La Ciudad alone?

Time passed. No challenger appeared.

The sun had long ago reached its peak and was beginning the process of lowering itself back down toward the horizon. Clouds of dust dimmed it and made it bleed red light.

And Lupe started walking again.

Feeling better, Juan went back outside.

Not exactly sure what to do, he decided to sit down in the middle of the driveway that led to the Boss's mansion. He sat cross-legged on the asphalt like some demented monk, floating on the surface as if it were water as he waited, waited for her to come.

And he could tell she was down there, see her with his own alien vision, walking across the flats. A tiny figure obscured by distance, but he knew it was her. He watched her reach the road and begin to ascend the slope, heading directly to where he sat. He also listened to the wind, half-convinced that hidden voices lurked within it.

Yes, she kept approaching at her mostly steady pace, getting closer and closer, but Juan still had no idea of how he was going to confront her, how he was going to destroy her. He could still see through his hands… he could still pass through matter…and he already knew that he couldn't fight her like that. So, what was he supposed to do?

His attention became more and more focused on Lupe, and on his desperation to find a way to hurt her. He no longer noticed anything else. His gaze had become a laser focused on his foe.

And in that moment, he felt something burst inside himself, something moving within his being, something that was beginning to change him.

But this time it didn't make him feel sick; it made him feel powerful.

She had to descend again, this time into an empty flatland. Once across that, there was a small ridge on which stood the first mansions built with the dollars of folly and addiction.

I could see it again, see it all. I was slipping and sinking back into my visions and trances. But this time, my astral awareness didn't cling to Lupe as tightly. Instead, my psychic eyes drifted and floated above her head, as if I were tethered to her, like a balloon. And it almost seemed like I was being tugged and bounced along, just a little bit behind and above her, bringing up the rear as a pointless, bodiless mascot.

In those same moments, I was also aware, dimly aware, that my body was still in the living room, being watched over by Flor M-M. But most of me was tagging along with Lupe as she crossed the flats at an unhurried pace.

And I began to be aware that something wasn't right. That place was too barren, too smooth, too empty.

"Lupe, can you hear me?" I tried to ask.

No sign that she could, not the slightest sign.

"Lupe!" I tried to shout.

If I had found a voice in that place, it would have been overwhelmed by the winds that tormented the sands.

On the ridge, a handful of remaining troops quickly vanished. Helicopters were still in the sky, way up high, out of range of anything Lupe could do to them. The general had managed to get himself a few more of those aircraft, and he probably wasn't going to take any chances with them. But they were drawing the girl's attention up into the sky.

Drawing her attention? Were they going to drop something on her? I almost began to think it was possible that they had gotten those crazy gringos to give them a nuke. Hell, maybe those gringos knew Lupe was for real, and they didn't want her crossing over into El Norte, where they would have to deal with her.

Wait.

Drawing her attention.

Drawing her attention.

It was just about distracting her. No attack was going to come from the sky. My thoughts of a mushroom cloud were just a brief attack of paranoia. And any remaining soldiers, hidden in prepared positions, knew that at best they could only be a delay and a distraction as well.

It was all about drawing her attention away from the soil that was immediately at her feet.

And there was nothing I could do but watch…watch and hope that she would understand any trickery in time.

I began to panic…my floating mind almost seemed to tremble. Did my body moan and call out back at home? Even if it didn't, I was sure it was soaking in sweat.

Lupe picked up her pace, fists clenched, charged up for battle. She prepared to brace herself for bullets and bombs. But no troops appeared to challenge her. And the helicopters above just continued to circle far, far above those arid lands around La Ciudad.

Suddenly, a strange sound. A monstrous gulp.

The world around me vanished into a void.

Then it came back.

But it wasn't the same.

I was alone.

There was no Lupe.

The terrain, the landscape, the geography…that was the same; but there was no sign of human habitation…no road leading up the ridge, not a single narco mansion on those heights. And everything was brighter and clearer, the light was dazzling, coming from all directions, casting no shadows, because there was no sun in that absolutely cloudless, blue, blue sky. There was only light, with no obvious source, everywhere.

The sand and the soil, all of it was white, like snow or salt. There was vegetation, the same scrub and cactus that you would normally find outside La Ciudad. But it was all pristine and perfect, no trace of damage from drought or insects. In fact, I saw no hint of bird, reptile, or mammal.

All of it was so still, in a stasis, as if even time had ceased to move.

That place was not the real world, at least not my real world.

And actually, there was one mammal…me, because something had provided me with a body in that world, that place. But even though I could see my familiar hands, even though I could tell I was wearing my usual rumpled white suit, even though I could feel the familiar hat on my head—I could tell that it wasn't truly my body.

I didn't feel the weight of my age.

I wasn't sweating.

My eyes weren't watery, and they blinked only if I willed them open and shut.

I wasn't even pretending to breathe.

That body, it was a facsimile.

I made it walk and it walked with energy, not the immediate fatigue that should have assaulted me. And it walked with ease. It was strange to move so effortlessly, to maintain a pace, to just keep going without the stiffness, aches, and pains that were my normal companions.

Where was I going?

Without any obvious goal presenting itself, I decided to keep following Lupe's path, the direction she had been going when I'd last seen her, toward the ridge. If nothing else, from a higher position, I might be able to see if there was anything in the area—if there was even any sign of La Ciudad. My feet almost glided, quickly and smoothly, over the white sand. I would have enjoyed that stroll if it weren't for the fact that I didn't want to be there. I wanted to still be with Lupe; I wanted to see what was going to happen with her and the army. I didn't want to be in that weird alternative world all by myself, with nothing to do.

Then a movement caught my eye, up on that ridge where the road should have been. One figure, alone, was ascending.

A woman.

At first, I thought it had to be Lupe. Had the army somehow brought her to this alternative universe? No, I might have believed in Bigfoot, chupacabra, and UFOs—but I didn't believe the Mexican army had interdimensional technologies.

And it wasn't Lupe.

It was Flor, the first Flor, the Flor of my dreams.

I tried to call out to her, but my voice seemed to be instantly absorbed by the total inertia that dominated that place, that complete stillness. So, she just kept going, without looking back.

I finished crossing the flats and began to climb. If I'd really been me, there was no way I could have done that kind of hiking. But I did it comfortably in that place, reaching the crest as if I were an athlete. Now I could see that there was definitely no road, not even a trail. And higher up there was no trace of any human activity, other than Flor, who, still with a good head start, was using that barren ridge to continue her own journey upward.

Since I had a better view, I took a few moments to scan my surroundings to see if there was a chance that anything else was going on. But there was nothing out there, nothing I could see in any direction. Not a hint of La Ciudad. No fragment of a civilization.

The only obvious thing to do was follow Flor, so that was what I did. The idea crossed my mind that maybe she knew I was there, that she didn't want me to follow her, that she wanted to get away from me. Yet there was really nothing else for me to do, as far as I could tell…other than wander aimlessly in the desert and hope to somehow return to the real world.

So, I continued that ascent. If Flor didn't want me to catch up to her, I probably wouldn't be able to. Or maybe I could anyway. How would she react?

Only one way to find out.

My physical form was still subject to some of the constraints of normality. It still took time to make that climb. I didn't have to rest; I didn't feel thirst or hunger, but I could still move only at a human speed, even if it was without the panting, the sweating, and the pounding heart that I was used to.

In fact, I didn't even seem to have a heartbeat.

So, I just kept going and going.

I'd lost sight of Flor, so I could only hope that I had a reason to keep moving.

The ambient illumination never changed in intensity. That bright, sunless sky never showed any sign that there was a night concealed within it. Perhaps in that world, time did not pass; maybe only the endless present was real.

I could only hope that I was outside the clock's domain. Otherwise, I was missing out on the real story: Lupe's moment of truth with the army.

But either way, time was mentally passing for me, in what seemed the usual way, as I went on with my strange journey.

And eventually I reached the site where, in the real world, the big house of the Boss would have been, where it should have been, dominating all the other mansions that were not there.

Instead, I found Flor sitting on a rock, watching me with a combination of amusement and annoyance.

Since I couldn't actually take a deep breath, I just waved awkwardly and began to slowly approach her, looking toward her feet.

"I thought we'd said goodbye—but here we are," I said, the words escaping my mouth without permission.

"Like I said, things change, Cervantes...and then they change again."

"But what about you? Where did you go? Are you alive or are you dead?"

She sighed. Did that mean she had breath in that world, or just that she could fake it better? "I don't know why I'm here. It makes no sense to me. I think I should be gone. But then I keep having to show you things because there's always another card to turn over. I believe you will see me again after this. Eventually. For now, I can answer one question, if it's one I can answer. So, ask one."

I finally looked up and gazed into those eyes I missed so much.

I knew by an immediate hunch that she couldn't or wouldn't tell me what had brought Lupe back from the dead. Still, there was something else I was newly curious about, something that could be very important. "Those beings, those presences that I could see watching Lupe: What are they, what do they want?"

"That's sort of two questions," she said flatly.

Then she suddenly laughed and said, "They are...powers...beings from beyond, that watch from their realms. Most of them are strange and ancient beings with the magical strength and will to project their presence, partially, all the way to earth, now that the way is open. But they are too far away to fully manifest themselves. They have a super clairvoyance, and they have sensed...a disruption...in the fabric of life here. That's Lupe. They want to see and they want to understand. But those ones that watch, they are not the problem, not the danger. The threat will come from those beings who dare to act, who will try to reach our earth in the fullness of their being. Lupe's...return, it shows them the way."

She fell silent.

I was still just enough of a reporter to try for a follow-up question. But before I could, she put a finger to her lips. "*Shh.*"

Then Flor faded.

That white world faded.

It was like nothing had happened, like a skip in a vinyl record.

It had been a vision.

I skittered back a few seconds, and I was trailing along behind Lupe again.

Nothing had really happened.

Lupe continued to cross that flatland unopposed.

She began to ascend the ridge.

She advanced....

By the time Lupe set foot up there, on the road that led to the mansions, nothing was left that even pretended to be a defense. There wasn't a single soldier, or any other human being, in sight. Not a cat. Not a dog. Just a frail-looking girl from the slums of La Ciudad looking at the fancy houses and citadels of the narcos. Many of those men had started where she had started. They were men who had made their own way to that place on a path soaked with blood and strewed with bodies and carnage. They were men who were nowhere to be seen, men who had run away. Men who were more than happy to have the army confront that girl while they stayed out of it.

Lupe took a defiant stance, almost like the star of some old gringo Western, playing a sheriff who awaited some final gunfight...a high noon...a showdown at the corral. And she just looked around, back and forth, slowly. She was still expecting something. Sooner or later, there would have to be some challenge, some attempt to confront her.

She looked back...back the way she had come from. Her face was unreadable. Could she have been wondering if she'd been tricked, that they'd just wanted her out of the city for some reason? Was she trying to figure out what that reason could be?

"We're waiting, Señorita Castaneda!" a voice burst out, cutting through the background noise of desert wind with a screech of feedback. It came from one of those speakers mounted on a beat-up van parked a couple of hundred yards up the road. "Keep going, all the way up, all the way to the biggest house!"

Lupe spun to confront that voice. Spotting the source, she advanced toward it, marching straight up the middle of what turned into a wide, well-paved road that was part of the privilege of living in Narcolandia.

She stopped in front of the vehicle…motionless again…waiting again. Maybe she was expecting it to explode and give her another chance to prove her invulnerability.

Time kept dragging on into the afternoon. The van remained mute. Finally, Lupe started to saunter up the avenue. Her gaze was now fixed and firm on the castle that was high above and far away at the end of the road. It was the dwelling that looked down on all the others.

The home of the Boss of the bosses.

Juan watched as the girl came closer and closer.

He was convinced that the girl could see him, that she had already spotted him waiting for her in the driveway. She was aware of him but was trying to ignore him as she advanced. He wanted to scream at her, to tell her that he knew that she could see him, that there was no point in playing games. But he decided to be patient and keep his own counsel. It didn't matter, anyway; she was coming right to him.

El Bautista didn't think the girl was stupid. She had to know the army had planned some kind of trap. What she wouldn't know was why Juan was there. Was he part of the trap, or was he just there to watch? That thought made him snicker. She was about to find out.

The power inside him: it had become a spinning vortex, a building pressure. He felt something come up into his throat, and suddenly he lost control of himself and coughed out a few thick plumes of red-brown smoke.

He gasped for breath…and this time his lungs actually grabbed onto some air and pulled it in. All at once there was a solidity to his body, a solidity he hadn't felt for a while…for a long time. He raised his hands up—and they were no longer transparent.

The girl was still walking toward him; now she was no more than a hundred yards away.

Juan stood up, almost lost his balance as his full weight and his full mass were returned to him.

He could feel the hard cement under his feet, supporting him.

He could feel the breeze on his toughened skin.

He laughed and blew out more of that reddish vapor.

He could feel the strength, the inhuman strength, that his deformed body possessed, the power that had been promised to him. He could feel that he was fully back in phase with the normal world.

And the girl was closing the distance.

"Come and get some, puta!" he shouted at her with more joy than anger, pulling back the hood of his sweatshirt, of that clothing that had somehow shared his strange journey, fully revealing his face, which looked like melted plastic.

But she didn't hesitate, didn't show any fear.

Higher up in the hills, far above the mansion in a carefully concealed emplacement, the general had been watching through binoculars since Lupe would be only a blur on video. He seemed pleased until he saw a figure appear out of thin air directly in front of her, insolent in its posture and prepared to challenge her advance.

Catrina was there in that moment too, watching through the scope of her rifle. She wasn't expecting to take a shot, not this time; it was just that she wanted the magnification the device offered her. She let out a gasp when she saw Juan materialize.

"Who the fuck is that?" demanded the general.

And he wasn't the only observer asking that question.

I asked it too.

Because that was when I first saw Juan, that was when he first appeared to me—at the same moment he was appearing to the general and to Catrina. Before that moment, he had been just as invisible to me as I was to everyone else. But I was just a soul floating along with Lupe. Juan was definitely something else.

At first, I didn't even recognize that melted, plasticized creature. I didn't know that it was El Bautista.

Then I saw his story.

It was strange, a sudden vision that burst into my mind. In seconds, maybe less than seconds, I saw his story, just as I had seen Lupe's. I saw his dark destiny and how it intertwined with all the other events that had been taking place, how it wove into the story I would have to tell.

I was taken out of time.

I was swept up in its implications of what it all meant. I tried to see what the army's plan was for Lupe, now knowing that Juan had heard it. But a flash of green light blinded my mind's eye.

And then I was called back when I heard Juan yell, "Come and get some, puta!"

That brought me straight back to the now.

It was time to do the unique job I had been given, time to see how Juan and Lupe's story was going to end.

Step by step by step, Lupe ascended to that dominating house, almost like a pilgrim approaching a most holy of holy places. There was still nothing that opposed her progress. Juan had fallen silent, standing like a sentinel, waiting for the girl to come to him. Nothing else presented itself that could suggest a possible opposition.

Any remaining troops were well hidden.

She just took her time, acting almost like a sightseer.

And so, she reached the entrance to the driveway.

There wasn't even a wall or fence for her to vault over or tear her way through. It was clear that the Boss had wanted to make a statement: he had wanted to make sure that the world knew that he didn't need fences, or walls, or any of that shit. Because nobody—anybody who ever dared to challenge him—would ever make it that far.

Yet there was Lupe strolling up his driveway with nothing but the force of the wind pushing back against her advance, along with some dust that might have stung the eyes of an ordinary human being. But she was no longer that. Still, once my disembodied mind, which was tagging along, paid attention, I noticed that she did blink every once in a while. And I wondered if it was just a habit, a reflex of mortality.

I let my invisible eyes float back toward the mansion. All at once, it seemed very artificial and fake to me, like a prop, a facade built for a movie.

Lupe stopped for a moment and raised her gaze to the sky, perhaps checking to see if an extremely large bomb was plummeting down on her.

Obviously, it was a trap. But where exactly was the trap and what exactly was the trap? That was what she was trying to figure out. I could tell now that Lupe didn't think Juan was part of it: he was there on his own and for his own purposes. So, what did the army have in mind? What did they think they had found that could destroy something that had so far proven to be indestructible?

But she had to continue, knowing that if she didn't follow through, they would renew the shelling of La Ciudad and killing people at random. It wasn't as though she had any fear: she trusted her power. But she was becoming annoyed by all these distractions being imposed on her; her mission wasn't yet completed.

She had yet to achieve her true revenge.

She still hadn't found her killer, who had, possibly not by any coincidence, grown up in that house.

In those moments, I was even able to skim the surface of her thoughts again.

The probably irrational hope was crossing Lupe's mind that the man who had brutalized her and murdered her, that son of the narco king, would be wrapped up and left for her inside the castle. A hope that the army might sacrifice the Boss's son to her as a gift, a bribe, to just go away after giving her that revenge on a platter. And for all I knew, once Lupe had consummated that vengeance, maybe she would go away… maybe she would die again and return to wherever it was that she had come back from.

Step by step, Lupe walked the rest of the way up the driveway. She no longer cared about Juan. All she cared about was reaching the house and getting past whatever the army had planned.

In fact, she was going to ignore Juan and breeze past him as if he were still a phantom.

But Juan was fully tangible again…solid…feeling and flexing his weight and his strength. His melted flesh had been re-formed and hardened into a sort of exoskeleton, a sort of armor, so thick that he was sure it was bulletproof.

And didn't that make him the equal of the girl in a battle?

Oh yes, he was finally ready for her.

Yet she kept walking like she didn't even care that Juan was there, like he wasn't relevant to her, like he was still that helpless ghost that had been no match for her. She was going to just pass him by without even bothering to acknowledge him or look him in the eye.

Did she seriously think he wasn't going to do anything? Did she think he was just some useless spirit that was haunting that place?

Yes, she was going to pass him…pass him within a foot or so.

Or at least that was what she thought.

Juan, still feeling a bit clumsy in his new and rematerialized body, swung his arm out and smashed Lupe in the face with an elbow. There was a loud crack, and she was knocked onto her back and sent skidding fifty feet back down the driveway.

"Ha!" El Bautista shouted triumphantly. "Finally, there's somebody who can give it back to you!"

◈

"Who is that fool?" the general demanded again. "He could fuck everything up!"

Catrina continued to keep her eye glued to the scope. "Should I shoot him, sir?"

It seemed like he was about to say yes; then he saw Juan take the girl down.

◈

Lupe sat up, staring at her attacker for a second. Then she stood up with ease, not harmed in any way. She didn't show any sign of worry. Instead, her expression vacillated between curiosity and annoyance.

She started walking back toward him.

"Want to take a shot, puta? I'll give you one for free!"

Lupe stopped three feet from Juan, face-to-face, examining that visage that when looked at more closely resembled something halfway between reptilian and candle wax that had hardened after melting.

"Go ahead," he said with a sneer.

Lupe launched a sudden punch right at her antagonist's face. He wanted to take her blow full force, wanted to see if he could. But he flinched, just a little, and the girl's fist glanced off his temple, not fully connecting. Still, there was another loud crack as Juan was spun around and began to fall. He managed to catch himself with one hand and moved to immediately stand back up.

A puff of red smoke emerged from a small fissure where he'd been struck.

But Juan still smiled at the girl with his malformed mouth.

He hadn't even been stunned.

Lupe paused, trying to figure out what to do next.

Juan didn't hesitate. He lunged straight at her, wrapped his arms around her waist, and tackled her to the ground.

After that, the two opponents began to wrestle and grapple in the middle of that driveway. Juan seemed to have the advantage at first, perhaps because he was more used to a real fight than Lupe was. He managed to get on top of her, his face above her head. Then he spat on her, a huge glob of red-hot and lava-like mucus. Some of it splattered on the ground and began to eat into the asphalt.

But Lupe's skin was unharmed as the mass of goo bubbled and steamed on her cheek.

All El Bautista had managed to do was provoke her.

With a silent scream of rage and disgust, she managed to get her legs into position underneath Juan so that she could propel him off her. It was his turn to be caught off guard, and he let out a shout of fright as he turned around and around in the air, finally landing on the roof of the next mansion down the slope.

For a few moments, he lay on his back. For a few moments it seemed like that roof his impact had damaged was going to hold.

Then it collapsed under him without warning, and he fell through.

Lupe was back on her feet, doing the best she could to wipe that loathsome slime off her face…that sizzling slime that would have left any other person without a face to clean. But for the girl, the only damage was to her pride.

Shaking most of the mess from her hand, she began to look around, expecting her foe to come rushing back to the battle at any moment, still uncertain of what the army was up to, or what they thought of Juan crashing the party.

She was trying to decide what to do next. No answer was to be found in the silence that had returned around her. No further instructions would be provided. She would have to make her own choices.

Then she decided. Whatever was going on, she would have to deal with Juan first. So, she turned around and began walking toward the house her foe had landed on.

"Shit!" roared the general. "She's leaving the main mansion to go after that thing…that asshole…whatever he is!"

Catrina was calm. "Don't worry, sir. Let them fight. If he kills her, we win too, right? And if she kills him, well then, we just tell her to go back to where we want her to go."

The general snorted and fell silent, not wanting to admit that a woman had reason.

And what Catrina hadn't said, even though she was thinking it, was, what would they do about that creature if he did kill the girl?

Juan sat up in the master bedroom, the hole in the roof gaping above him. He inspected himself to see if any of his substance was leaking out, to see if there were any cracks in his plastic-like skin, which had become more like a shell.

As far as he could tell, he was intact.

Without any more hesitation, he jumped up and charged out of the room, down a hall, and down a big stairway. From somewhere in that house, there was the sound of music playing. But Juan had no interest in knowing its source; he didn't care if the house had occupants or if a stereo system had just been left to play continuously.

Leaping down the bottom half of the stairs, he landed loudly on a marble floor and began to stride rapidly toward the ornate double doors, which would lead him back outside.

He was about to kick them open.

Then somebody rang the doorbell.

Juan froze in his tracks and tried to scowl as he muttered, "What the fuck?"

Then, like a host expecting a guest, he opened the door.

The girl was standing on the porch. Before Juan could recover his composure, he received a well-placed kick in the stomach.

The next thing El Bautista knew, he had landed in a large kitchen and was trying to get back on his feet amid debris.

Lupe stood ready, expecting her enemy's counterattack.

It didn't come.

In those moments, the only noise that could be heard was generated by pieces of the house falling to the floor.

Impatient, seeing no reason for caution, she rushed into that kitchen. Then it was her turn to be taken by surprise as Juan caught her from behind, spinning her around, taking her down onto her back as he sat on top of her, trying to pin her down again. With reflexive and immediate savagery, he began punching the girl in the face again and again and again. He was going for the kill, nothing held back, the house shuddering under the force of that attack.

The strength and rapidity of El Bautista's blows did seem to keep Lupe down. Or maybe she had decided not to resist and just let him exhaust his fury. Either way, he was still doing no real damage. Again and again, his hardened fists hit her directly in the nose…without any blood, bone, or breakage…without her body giving in the slightest under the impacts. However, the floor underneath her head was beginning to shatter under the barrage. If there was some chamber underneath, it had probably been constructed with combat in mind, but it wouldn't hold much longer; they would soon fall through.

Yet something else gave way first.

The armored exoskeleton that had been formed around Juan's hands and fingers was beginning to fracture from the repeated blows. Little streams of that reddish smoke hissed out and swirled in the air and were dispersed by the repeated movements of his arms. He stopped his assault, glared at his damaged hands, and then shrieked his rage right into the face of his unharmed adversary.

She laughed silently in reply.

Then she grabbed El Bautista's head with both of her own hands and pulled…pulled with all of her strength and slammed their faces together with a detonation that truly shook that house on its foundation.

After a moment of stillness, Lupe lifted her opponent's head up as more of his substance escaped into the atmosphere. The face was a caved-in ruin. She maintained her hold as she sat up, forcing him upright as well and wrapping her legs around him, trapping him even more. He tried to resist, but that resistance was feeble. Still keeping her grip, she did the same thing she had done when she had first fought Juan: she began to twist. For just a few seconds, the neck refused to give…until there was a loud, harsh, and severe sound, almost like that of a hammer breaking a stone, as Juan's cranium was turned backward yet again.

A thick fog of those noxious vapors escaped from the fissures and began to envelop both antagonists. Lupe inhaled them, inhaled deeply, and blew them out and away.

Juan no longer moved. He was limp and inert in her grasp.

Lupe released her legs and tossed the body off to the side and got up. The smoke she had blown was beginning to eat away at the paint on the walls. She contemplated that process for a few moments, showing a slight trace of distaste, then she went back outside, leaving that house at her back.

She still had an appointment with the army.

Catrina watched that house intently, never taking her eye from the sight. She thought she heard a sound like distant thunder and she saw the glass cracking in one of the windows.

"Can you tell what's happening?" demanded the general as he fumbled with his binoculars.

"No, sir, but they must still be fighting."

Then came a sharp noise, like that of a dry tree branch being broken.

Silence…except for the wind.

The lieutenant's finger squeezed the trigger ever so slightly, but not enough to fire the round that was ready. Was it only a few seconds later that she saw the door open? Time was passing so slowly. She saw the girl come out alone and walk away from the house.

"I think we have a winner, sir!"

"Shit! What now? Did that other…whatever it was…fuck things up? We still have to get that bitch up to the main house!"

"I think we're okay, sir. She seems to be heading back that way."

And it was true. Lupe was marching back toward the citadel of the Boss.

What was left of Juan El Bautista lay discarded back in that other narco mansion. Lupe had gotten the better of him again. For those few minutes—the same minutes that saw Lupe slowly advance up the hill toward the first and finest home—that body hadn't moved.

Was he dead, dying, or damaged beyond repair?

No, the fingers began to move.

The arms and the legs began to twitch.

Then the torso was rocked and shaken by convulsions.

The head began to expand and splinter. The crumpled face suddenly exploded outward, sending fragments of that hardened skin in several directions. Something like a combination of lava, slime, and mud came gushing out through the exit that had been created, rapidly leaving the shell behind. At first, it was just a shapeless, steaming mess. But it quickly became more solid, taking a form, standing up on newly made legs as it took on a vaguely human form. A sickly red and rubbery thing, devoid of features or orifices of any sort, with only a partially formed head, stood there. Yet it had arms and it had legs. And as soon as it gained mastery of those new legs, it began to run, clumsily but with speed.

It sprinted out of the house through the door Lupe had left open.

Lupe had regained all the ground she'd given up fighting Juan. Once again, she was walking up the driveway, taking her time. I found my mind brushing against her thoughts ever so slightly. She still didn't think that Juan was supposed to be there, at least not as far as the army was concerned. He was playing his own game. And she would rather have played that game. Juan was unnatural…supernatural…just like she was. His presence in that place was more sinister, mysterious, and important than her fight with the army.

Except for the fact that the military was holding La Ciudad hostage with their artillery.

So, she had to keep playing their game instead.

But that left her with the same question. Where was the trap, the one the general had planned? Her hesitation wasn't based on fear. It was curiosity and even a sense of competitiveness. She wanted to figure out what the scheme was before it happened—not because she thought they could hurt her, but for the satisfaction.

Of course, it was inevitable that she reached the front doors. One was slightly open, just an inch or two.

She tore it off its hinges, tossed it aside, then did the same with the other one.

Nothing happened.

She stood on the threshold, yet there was nothing to see…nothing that had the look of danger. There was an indoor courtyard, marble and gold, a dry fountain dominating the center, two big stairways in the back.

Empty and quiet.

Her face showed only annoyance as she peered inside, trying to find the clue that would reveal the trick. Not feeling rushed in that moment, she examined the scene before her intently.

Where was that trap?

The general was watching the girl, gripping his binoculars more tightly than necessary.

"Go in," he muttered. "Go in. You have to go in. If you don't…"

But the girl didn't move.

He was about to order his man on the microphone to tell her to step forward.

Then Lieutenant Ochoa said, "Holy shit!"

And that was when the general saw…something.

What was it that came charging silently toward Lupe?

Once it had been a man named Juan. I'd never known the true name of his family. Maybe it really had been Bautista. In those last minutes, though, did he really need a name? Because what was coming was losing even more of its human form, losing it rapidly. With each stride, it began to stretch and elongate. The arms and legs lost the semblance of their knees and elbows, becoming more like tentacles as the rounded ends seemed to give up on trying to be hands and feet. The torso became more like a cylinder, the head attempted to become a featureless sphere. But it was hard for that unstable reddish mass of living slime, mud, clay, and rubber to hold any set shape as it fell forward and began to lope on all fours, as it closed that last bit of distance, as it prepared to lunge at the girl's back.

That was what the general saw.

Did she sense something, or was it chance that Lupe looked back over her shoulder just in time to see that the creature was almost upon her? She spun to face it with visible disgust. But that was the only reaction she had time to express as the thing that had been Juan El Bautista rammed full into her and took her to the ground in front of that doorway. It tried to shout something…the noises all muffled and garbled because it no longer had a human throat, or even a mouth…as it tried to pin the girl to the ground, tried to wrap a tentacle-arm around her throat.

Then Lupe landed a solid punch to that round, featureless ball of a head. The sphere lost some of its shape as her fist sank into it. At first, it might have been like an ordinary human hitting a waterbed. The strange substance gave but didn't tear, rippling out to the sides and making the bulbous mass expand in back.

It almost seemed possible that the creature would absorb that impact, even though the entire body shuddered from the shock of it. But the head suddenly gave up its resistance and whipped backward, taking the entire organism with it, flipping it to the rear.

Yet it wasn't even stunned. And it was immediately back up to face a Lupe that had also found her feet. She crouched down, prepared for her enemy's immediate counterattack. Instead, that creature awkwardly stood up on its hind limbs as it flailed the other two around wildly…as if it wanted to keep the girl at bay until it decided what to do next.

I tried to reach into her mind, to talk to her. "That thing is Juan, it's Juan El Bautista…something from another world, a sorceress or something…she turned him into this. I don't know what the army's plan is, but he's here to make sure you don't get away from their trap…even though they didn't invite him to the party!"

Did she give a slight nod? It was hard to tell. At one point I had been able to make, I guess, telepathic contact with her. But now…the connection didn't seem good, like there was interference.

Her eyes stayed on Juan, staring at that featureless head, staring at where the face should have been, trying to find a gaze to meet. But, just like before, there was nothing: no eyes, no mouth, no nose.

Yet some kind of voice was trying to emerge, to emanate from that head, incoherent, obviously angry, and unable to actually shape any words.

Still maintaining her low stance, Lupe slowly moved forward toward Juan and away from the doorway. He responded by moving back slightly, keeping the distance between them the same, still lashing his tentacles at the girl, in a creeping retreat down the driveway.

Then, with a swiftly flowing move, the creature whipped one of its arms straight at Lupe's eyes, trying to catch her by surprise. But she was fully on her guard, reflexively shielding her face by raising both hands. With a loud *whap*, the tentacle bounced off as Lupe skidded back a step or two.

Juan seemed to be about to follow up on his strike.

Lupe seemed about to lunge forward into her own attack.

And that was when a bullet tore a direct hit into Juan's round head.

The general was caught between rage and fear. That creature was so weird, so creepy, so…not right. It couldn't be natural. It probably wasn't even from earth.

An alien thing…it had to be an alien thing.

It was something unknown, something that could be just as dangerous as that fucking girl, something he might not want to have as a foe. But it was threatening the plan. Even though it was no friend of the girl's, it was threatening the plan! It was leading her away from the house! And it showed no signs of actually being able to defeat her. So that made that creature just another problem, a problem that was going to ruin what they had been working on for so long.

No, the enemy of the general's enemy was not his friend.

"Shoot it," he said.

Catrina didn't say a word, didn't hesitate. She wanted the chance. She wanted to make history. So, she found the target and immediately took the shot.

Lupe's eyes widened as Juan's head exploded.

At first there was a sudden burst, then a slowing down to an almost frame-by-frame rate of action. What had been a sphere completely lost its shape as its substance was propelled randomly in all directions, the outer membrane struggling to keep it contained. But in the end, none of the ingredients were lost, because just as it reached the point where the splatter should have been set free, the whole process froze, creating something that looked like a deformed flower. Then, just as slowly, the process began to reverse itself. The entire mess began to retract, inch by inch, still fighting against the kinetic energy that wanted to destroy it.

Juan's benefactor wasn't going to let him go down like that, not that easily.

The head was going to restore itself.

Lupe could see what was happening. So, she took that opportunity to strike, rushing at the enemy's torso, easily avoiding the uncoordinated tentacles, to land a series of punches that drove and bounced Juan farther and farther down the driveway, farther away from the mansion, leaving huge craters in the body even as the head continued to reshape itself.

Then the girl kicked the legs out from under her foe and it fell over backward. She jumped on top, taking both hands and seizing the mass that was still trying to become a sphere again, pulling at it, stretching it, trying to tear it apart. And for a few moments, it seemed like she might manage it. Then, one of the wildly moving tentacles found her waist, wrapped around it, and yanked her away, tossing her off to the side. She rolled with the impact when she hit the asphalt and ended upright, only to see Juan back up as well, the head swirling back together.

Once again, they were face-to-…no-face…both ready to keep fighting.

◈

Catrina took a second shot, another perfect shot. She didn't wait for an order; she didn't even think of waiting for an order. All she cared about was that weird beast, all she cared about was finding out what kind of damage she could do to it, finding out if she could kill it, finding out if she could be the first human being in history to kill an alien…or whatever it was.

The girl had proven to be invulnerable, but that beast—she could damage it. Maybe it could be killed with human technology, with human guile and human skill.

Maybe.

◈

I couldn't be certain, but it seemed like the lieutenant had used another kind of bullet for that second shot. This time, there was no explosion. Instead, that .50-caliber projectile penetrated the core of Juan's body just as he was about to charge at Lupe.

He froze in his tracks; his body shuddered, trembled.

Lupe decided to just watch calmly, perhaps still trying to figure out why the army was going after her enemy, perhaps waiting to see if the second shot would do any lasting harm. For a moment she glanced in the direction of the gunfire, but she didn't seem to locate that well-concealed observation post high above her.

Juan went back down on all fours, his body swelling as something…a liquid or a type of energy…circulated wildly inside it. There was a sickly, gurgling sound, there was a convulsion, and then he began to force himself to stand again.

That was when the third bullet struck.

◈

The general remained silent as Catrina shot again. A smile flickered on his lips. He saw the monster fall, saw that it could be harmed. Maybe he was beginning to see the possibility, the hope, that one of those things might be killed by one of his soldiers, that it could die at the hands of man…or woman. Someone under his command and at his orders might actually kill an alien invader, something not born of the earth, something that might be a threat to humanity.

Her aim, as usual, was perfect.

She took another shot.

He kept the binoculars glued to his eyes, watching the monster suffer.

Catrina took another shot—and another and another and another and another, until she emptied her magazine. She promptly reloaded and prepared to find the target in her scope again.

Until something green blocked her view.

Lupe crossed her arms, looking almost impressed as bullet after bullet tore into her enemy. This time she felt no imperative to attack Juan while he was down. Why not let the unknown sniper have a chance. Maybe if El Bautista survived that barrage, he would direct his attention toward the army. The thought brought a smile to her face. If her opponents turned on each other, there was a chance, a slight chance, that they would forget about her.

She plopped down and watched.

The gunfire stopped.

The creature had fully collapsed onto the ground, losing shape as the gooey gel inside it oozed out of the ruptured body, red vapor steaming out along with it. Lupe wrinkled her nose, perhaps smelling something rancid that I couldn't…since I didn't have my nose with me. But other than that, her attitude had become more relaxed, as if she were observing a competition that didn't really concern her, a match whose outcome didn't matter much to her.

She even pretended to yawn.

Juan felt like he was dying. He couldn't be certain, but he knew that he was severely damaged. Unable to move, except feebly, he was losing awareness of anything around him…he wasn't even sure where the girl was, or why she wasn't taking advantage of his vulnerability to finish him off. Maybe she could tell that he was finished, maybe she was just gloating. There was no pain, probably because he no longer had a nervous system. No, there was just a sense that his spirit was weakening, that his life force was dimming…that the flame inside him was being extinguished.

More than desperation, he felt resignation. Instead of following the plan, he'd tried to kill that girl all by himself. He'd wanted to crush the life out of her with his own superhuman power, to see her die, to feel her die by his hand, by his strength, by his will.

But she was the one who had remained invincible, and he was the one who had withered. He was the one who lay defeated, becoming an amorphous mass as more of his substance flowed away.

He was going to die as a puddle.

Fuck.

Some kind of large insect began to fly around Lupe's head. By human habit, she absentmindedly tried to shoo it away with her hand…only causing it to hover in front of her face, just out of reach. It was only then that she realized something wasn't right.

It looked like a beetle, a huge beetle, a huge green beetle, larger than any such bug she had ever seen before. Oh, but there was more wrong than that. The thing had eight legs; shouldn't it have only six? And it had a mouth that no insect should have…something like that of one of those parasitic eel-shaped fish…the mouth of a lamprey. A tongue of thorns flicked in and out of that mouth, as if eager to strike at Lupe's face. But worst of all…the eyes…tiny humanoid eyes that glared at the girl with intelligence and evil intent. Even the humming blur of its rapidly beating wings seemed to conceal a mocking laugh.

"It's her! She's the one that made Juan into—that!" I tried to say. But the drone of those tiny wings seemed to drown my mental voice. Once again, I couldn't be sure that Lupe had heard me.

But she stood up, well aware that she was confronting something else that didn't belong in our world, some new challenge. She tensed up, preparing to attack or be attacked.

Instead, the beetle darted away and landed on top of what had once been Juan's head.

Catrina had promised herself, years ago, that she would never scream. It wasn't something a soldier would do, and she was a soldier.

And for all of those years, she had kept that vow.

Until that day...that moment...when she was so suddenly and unexpectedly attacked by a swarm of monstrous insects. A dense cloud of giant green beetles surrounded her, hiding everything else from her sight. They were trying to land on her, trying to get in her hair, trying to get on her face. Her rifle was useless; she had to let go of it so she could employ her hands to try to keep those things off her.

God...their buzzing, their hideous buzzing, which seemed to hide an undertone of a maniac's laughter!

Most of her body was protected by her uniform, her gloves, her boots. But they were trying to get at her, trying to get at her face, moving so fast even though they were at least the size of her thumb, with those horrible mouths that seemed designed to rip flesh and suck blood.

She batted at them with all the fear and fury she could muster... knocking them away again and again with loud, nasty thuds.

Then one of them managed to tear into her cheek.

That was when she failed to keep her promise.

A moment later was when she lost consciousness.

Juan El Bautista was beginning to feel better.

He had suffered no real pain, not since his resurrection. After that, and after he had rematerialized for battle, nothing the girl had done to him had really hurt anything that wasn't pride. Catrina's bullets had also brought something far less than agony. He'd been severely damaged, there was no doubt about that, but he hadn't suffered, not in the way a human would have suffered.

It was really only discomfort...and he could tell he was beginning to regenerate again. Maybe he would even go kill the person who was shooting at him, probably that sniper bitch he should have murdered already, before he renewed his fight with Lupe.

All he had to do was wait...even relax.

That was when he felt it more than heard it.

The voice of a wrathful goddess.

Suddenly, there was pain. Suddenly there was an agony like he had never known...an anguish that was chewing, boring, digging, devouring its way into his brain...to where his brain had been. He wanted to react, to contort and flop around, to try to escape that unexpected suffering.

He wanted to scream.

Yet his leaking mass of a damaged body was only able to throb slightly.

It had to be that girl. What the fuck was she doing to him? For the first time in his life, either of his lives, he wanted to beg…beg for mercy.

Then somehow that torture, those waves of torment, began to form into words, words spoken in the language of that misery. Each syllable was a drop of acid eating through his mind.

"You are such a disappointment! I've wasted so much energy on you! I thought a being of your skills could do a few simple tasks for me, but it seems I misjudged your competence! I should have just projected myself ahead of myself…and done the job myself! Do you realize how much time you are costing me? The trap is set and I'm going to spring it now!"

That was the moment when Juan lost what was left of his awareness; that was the moment when those words, each one a separate act of cruelty, bit like sharp fangs into what was left of the marrow of his consciousness.

◈

Lupe watched as the sloppy mess that had been Juan El Bautista began to bubble, to boil, to melt even more, releasing a cloud of reddish-brown smoke. There must have been a truly foul stench that emerged along with it because she covered her mouth and nose tightly with her hands as she stood up to back away, with revulsion, not fear, as the smoke began to form into a fog that concealed her enemy. She removed her hand only when, once again, she remembered that breathing was only a habit and not a requirement.

Then something changed. The murky vapors began to turn green, a sickly green, like the sludge that grows on the surface of a polluted pond. And that green began to absorb and dominate the red, refusing to disperse, coagulating thickly around Juan. Lupe chose to continue her cautious retreat back toward the mansion, clearly expecting something to emerge from that cloud, obviously wanting to have enough time to see what it was before she had to fight it. Then she decided that she had gone far enough and stood still, on her guard.

For a moment, the mist seemed to thin out. Was there a figure inside it, standing over Juan's body? Perhaps it was the shadow of a woman with long hair, tresses that twisted in a wind that was no longer blowing.

It was hard to tell, because if it really was there, it was immediately swallowed back up and obscured in the roiling green fog that continued to cling to its small area of ground, not showing any sign of dissipation.

But Lupe had tensed up. She'd seen it too.

Then something seemed to whisper in the mist. Was it really a voice? Was something trying to speak?

If there was any meaning in that sound, I couldn't make it out.

Lupe put a hand to her ear, listening carefully as well. And the whispers did become louder, more sinister, more menacing…a chorus of incoherent threats…before it began to fade. Lupe finally gave up trying to understand and took a moment to look around, making sure that it wasn't all just some diversion from some other threat.

Nothing.

She glanced up the high hill, in the direction the shots had come from. But there was nothing there either, nothing that she could see.

The whispering grew louder again, drawing Lupe's attention back toward their source. Yes, there were definitely several murmuring voices, but still they made no sense. Lupe was becoming visibly annoyed, impatient.

She was ready to fight.

The whispers became more muffled.

Finally, she clenched her fists and marched straight back toward the cloud, trying to keep in mind that she didn't have to inhale any of its noxious stench, confident that she was beyond the power of any poison. And she didn't hesitate; she was going to charge straight into that fog.

But then…the screaming hell broke loose.

Catrina opened her eyes.

It took her some seconds to remember where she was, what had been happening. She'd lost consciousness. But for how long? A few seconds? Minutes? An hour or two? It couldn't have been much time; the sun still seemed to be where she had left it.

She was lying on her back, twisted in an awkward position. Yet the only pain she was aware of came from the wound in her swollen cheek, deep and jagged, bleeding slightly. Damn, it hurt. She touched it, felt how inflamed it was, felt a burning sting. Had that thing, that bug, been venomous?

It was hard to tell, but it didn't seem like her life or vitality was threatened.

And it was so quiet. What had happened to the others?

She straightened herself out, rolled onto her side, and saw them… the few others who had been at that outpost.

They were all dead, even the general.

His uniform was still intact, but the meat that had formed his face looked like it had been chewed up into wads of flesh and stuck back on his skull haphazardly. The eye sockets were empty…except for the stems of the optic nerves, which had been pulled out to extend beyond those vacant pits.

The other bodies were in the same condition.

Only Catrina had been left alive, only Catrina had been allowed to survive.

She was trying to wrap her mind around that, trying to understand why she was still alive, trying to decide what to do next.

Then something snickered.

Reflexively, she turned to reach for her rifle…then stopped cold. The source of that mocking sound had been one of those green beetles, one alone, perched on her weapon.

"Shit."

The thing snickered again, vibrating its wings, the tiny eyes, those horribly humanlike eyes, observing her with contempt as it waited for her reaction.

Catrina understood the message. "I promise I won't shoot anymore," she said softly.

The beetle immediately flew away, leaving the lieutenant to take some deep breaths as she waited to see if it was a trick, a false hope, knowing that the swarm could reappear and finish her off.

But nothing happened.

For some reason, the evil insects had spared her.

So, what about that girl and the creature down below? Despite an aversion to getting close to the body of her commander, she thought it would be safer to take his binoculars than it would have been to try to use her rifle scope. She didn't want that horrid insect to think she might fire her weapon again.

And that was how Catrina Ochoa got to be the only witness wearing flesh and blood to see what happened next.

Even though Lupe was fully expecting the attack, some form of attack, at any moment, she was still caught unprepared for the form and speed of the actual event.

It was something like a serpent, the form of a snake that erupted out of that clump of cloud still clinging to the ground in front of the girl, sailing out on withered and half-formed wings. The flesh of what had been Juan was still red and rubbery but now transparent, revealing a dark-green core. In the center of the eyeless, triangular head, something like an emerald flower bloomed. It did have a mouth, wide open, with huge fangs dripping venom, striking directly at Lupe's neck, carrying her backward with the impact as it tried to penetrate her flesh.

But against Lupe's skin, those twin daggers broke like glass, splattering the useless poison in all directions. Yet still the mouth managed to get a grip on her throat, and its serpentine body was able to wrap itself in tight rings of constriction around her body, crumpling its own wings in the process.

Lupe struggled against those coils but was able to get that weird, elastic flesh to give only so much. She wasn't able to free herself, not immediately…it was going to take some time. For the moment, her enemy had her in its power.

Only then did the creature release its jaws and raise its head. Even with no visible organs of sight, it appeared to survey the scene. Was anything left of El Bautista inside its substance, or had it been completely taken over and possessed by…something else?

The fog was rapidly fading away. It must have served its purpose.

For a moment, that eyeless gaze seemed to regard the heights of the hill. There was still no gunfire. Was that a hint of a smile on the snake-thing's mouth?

And then the head turned toward the mansion, still silently waiting. The snare that was still waiting.

With effort, the creature began to slither and roll, began to drag Lupe toward that house, straining to hold her captive, straining to resist her strength. The coils were loosening a bit more as she tried to break free, to break their grasp. Their time was obviously limited; that infusion of new form and new substance wasn't going to last much longer.

A sense of urgency took control of the serpent as it bounced and lurched and slid toward the open doorway.

Sudden anger, not desperation, was driving Lupe. She began to dig her nails into the translucent epidermis of her opponent. At first the flesh was able to resist, but then it began to surrender, forming holes for her fingers—and then the tissue began to tear.

The snake managed to reach the doorway and stick its head over the threshold. Now puffs of green smoke began to emerge from the wounds Lupe was gouging into its body.

In seconds, she was going to be able to tear out some huge chunks of that flesh.

But...it was too late.

The serpent yanked the rest of its mass, and Lupe, all the way into the mansion, coming to rest at the base of a stairway.

Instantly, the floor fell away beneath them, and Guadalupe Castaneda and the creature both plunged into the abyss underneath.

Lupe's fall was silent. But as the serpent plummeted, the greenish substance billowing out of its body, it let out a long, horrified scream, a male scream, the scream of Juan El Bautista.

I didn't follow them. Instead, my awareness was let go to sail back outside and up and up...and then back down to my home and to my body... and to Flor.

The explosion shook the town. It broke windows, knocked things off shelves, cracked walls, and collapsed quite a few roofs. They felt it even up in El Norte. Probably most people thought it was an earthquake. But it wasn't.

The trap had been sprung.

And I was lying on the couch...my couch...in my house. I was choking. I felt like I was drowning under some strange, liquid surface. I looked up...my eyes looked up...my gaze seeming to swim back up as I gasped for air. A blurry form slowly fused into Flor. Concern was fastened on her features.

"Yes...yes...I'm okay," I mumbled.

"I'm okay," I muttered and sputtered.

"Yes, I'm all right!" I said, my speech finally focused into coherence.

I could tell that her worry was fading, but she was still fussing over me: loosening my collar, wiping sweat off my face.

My breath was slowly catching.

Then I said it: "They buried her! They fucking buried her!"

Those words cast a spell that froze us both for some moments in time and place. I could hear my clock tick-tick-ticking. Then Flor slowly sat down beside me, and we both just sort of stared forward at nothing.

"They fucking buried her!" I repeated after some seconds or minutes or hours had passed. "Buried her!"

That had been the trick to the trap. They'd dug a wide and deep shaft straight down below where the Boss's house had been. I don't know how many hundreds of feet, but I'm sure it was as full down into the rock as they could possibly get it to go. And that house, I'm sure, had been destroyed and replaced with a replica after the digging was done. It had been a fake, just as I had sensed. It had been atomized when the ton of explosives had been detonated, along with much of the rest of that obscene neighborhood, as thousands and thousands and thousands of pounds of stone and earth followed Lupe down that hole.

A double plan: if the sheer power of the blast and the crushing avalanche of debris couldn't destroy her…couldn't damage her…then she would be buried. She would be buried so deep and under so much weight of rock and rubble that she would be crushed down and held immobile forever in her immortality. Bury her deep down in there, repress her like a bad memory, a trauma you wanted to forget. Even if her invulnerability knew no limit, there still had to be a limit to her strength. She could still be contained by the gravity pulling all that shit down and down on her.

That was what they had been doing all that time and with all that equipment, while they played .50-caliber tag with Lupe.

Yeah, dig a shaft as far down as you possibly could, seemingly bottomless, and seed it and surround it with enough explosives that it really would seem like a nuke was going off.

Have the girl step onto what might have been the biggest non-nuclear blast in history.

Girl falls down the hole.

Detonate.

Girl, hit with unlimited force from every direction, won't just be bounced away like all those other times. Would that finally crack her skull?

If not…if she survives that…she'll still be held down under so much weight that she won't be able to do anything about it.

Another goddess forced into the underworld and imprisoned there.

And the army crept out of hiding and formed a perimeter around what had been the citadel of La Ciudad and the remains of its surrounding estates, that barrio of bad dreams, that narco Shangri-La. It would have probably more than amused the general to take out that place…to show the extent of his own resources and power. But the general had no more power and he would never be amused again.

It was now the turn of the soldiers to wait and to watch.

To watch and to wait some more.

What would they have done if Lupe had risen up out of that devastation and strode toward them? Probably scattered in all directions. What else could they have done at that point?

But nothing happened.

And it kept on being their turn to just keep waiting…

…and waiting…

…and waiting.

Then they began to slowly and carefully withdraw. Not turning away, still alert, and still afraid that Lupe would emerge from the destruction, as invincible as ever.

But she didn't. As night fully fell, those newly created ruins remained as still as death.

A Few Days Later:

Flor was shaking me…and getting kind of rough about it, too. "Cervantes! Cervantes! Wake up!"

"I am awake," I finally mumbled.

"We need to get out of here. We both need to get out of here. I can feel it…I can tell. My reprieve is over, and so is yours. We both need to get out of here."

"Can't yet." My body didn't want to move. It seemed inert and inanimate. If it weren't for Flor's insistence, I might have mistaken myself for a corpse.

I knew what Flor meant, though. If the Guadalupe Castaneda war was over, there was nothing to keep the army from turning its full attention back on La Ciudad. And there would be nothing to keep them from knocking on the door of one of the old order's reporters on the take. And there would be nothing to keep them from going after the priestess of a cult who had a tendency to run her own independent operations.

It wasn't that either of us was all that important. But that was the point. Terror was instilled by making the bit players feel like they could be eliminated at any time and for any whim. You always have to be ready and willing to show everybody who's the boss, whether you're a criminal or a general. And there would be a new officer, a new general, taking the reins of the chain of command. He would probably want to eliminate anybody who might be able to tell the tale of what really happened in La Ciudad.

That's how you create the climate of control.

Yeah, we packed up some shit real quick, got in my Beetle, and left town. I was worried that they would already be taking back control of the city, that there would be roadblocks and checkpoints to promptly "restore" order, that the general's weird death would frighten them into quick and drastic action.

But...nothing...no problems. Perhaps that death had confused them into inaction instead. Or maybe they were still looking over their shoulders to see if Lupe was suddenly going to be up on their asses again.

Either way, it would still be a few days before they felt confident enough to take back control of the streets.

And by then we were gone.

A Few Months Later:

We ended up in El Norte.

It's not like I intended to go that way, or any way, when we first fled my house. But where else were we going to go? South and farther into Mexico? If anybody really gave a shit about Flor and me, if they really wanted to find us, that wouldn't have been a good idea, not a good idea at all.

I was afraid that they would be watching the border, that we would actually be stopped by the authority on our side.

But…nothing. There was no problem.

So, we slipped north for a shopping trip; we seemed respectable enough to pull that off.

And we stayed.

Flor had money and she had connections. After all, she ran a network that got people into Gringolandia. What she had done for Lupe's family, and so many others, she did for us.

I decided that it was a chance to improve my English.

We were somewhere in Texas…and we were going to be somewhere in Texas for quite a while. I won't disclose exactly where. It wasn't like we were under deep cover, that we'd gotten plastic surgery, that we were hiding in a bunker on some farm. There was no way I could live a life that paranoid. But there was no way we felt safe going home right away, either.

In many ways, it wasn't a lot different from my life in El Sur. I lived in a little house, I drank my mescal, I smoked my cigars. Instead of taking payment to write up the "news" that "they" wanted, I let Flor pay the bills, and I began to organize my notes and memories of all the interviews, of all the dreams and visions, so that I could begin to write this story. That was what she wanted me to do. It was what I wanted to do.

The thing I didn't know at the time was the degree to which the story I already had in my hands was only a prelude.

As far as the aftermath in La Ciudad, it was pretty much what you would expect. They kept the city on lockdown. They claimed there had been a heavy ordnance battle against the narcos in their own fancy neighborhood outside town, wiping out the whole place. The earth had shook because some drug-crazed godfather had wanted to outdo Tony Montana, blowing up himself and his own house with a few tons of contraband explosives so he could take some of the attacking troops with him. He even managed to assassinate the first general appointed to command the operation.

In English and in Spanish, the media ate it up.

"A military spokesman expressed confidence that the tide had definitely turned against organized crime in La Ciudad, and that very soon control would be handed back to a newly reorganized local civilian law enforcement."

"The president and local politicians praised the army's efforts and discretion in carrying out a successful mission that will be an example and model for any such similar actions required in the future."

"The city of La Ciudad will be safer than ever, and willing and able to welcome back the tourist trade. A major public relations firm has already been hired to come up with advertisements and promotions to entice visitors to return once martial law has officially been revoked."

Etc. Etc. Etc.

What they should have said:

"Military takes over town, gets rid of troublemakers—the crazies who live the nightmare and don't want to pay the bills. Same Boss still in charge. Drug traffic smoothly reformed. The folks who need to get their cut will get their cut. Business to continue with a lower profile, more professional, more dignified. And don't talk about that girl: just an over-the-top urban legend."

◆

Flor and I liked to go out to Mexican restaurants. It amused us. We would sit, eat, and talk, just like we did in La Ciudad. But for some reason, up in Gringolandia, I found myself wanting to cut back on mescal, so I usually opted for a bottle or so of red wine.

One day, after some adequate enchiladas and three or four glasses of that wine, I asked Flor, "Is my life over?"

She looked at me intently, silently, inviting me to continue...or not.

"I'm getting old...actually, I've been old for a long time...so I'm getting older. I'm fat, I drink too much, and I smoke. And I don't really want to change any of those things. I'm still in love with a woman who's either dead...or at least sure the fuck is gone and stopped giving a shit about me a long time ago. And my career has been nothing but a fraud.

"In short, my dear, I am not a man of great accomplishment."

I paused, wanting to give her a chance to respond. She just kept my gaze, showing no sign of agreement, argument, or sympathy. But perhaps there was a trace of acceptance. So, I continued.

"And yet, strangely, my life has been fulfilled. I know it now. I've seen it! There is…there really is something in the world that cannot be explained. There really is a mystery that transcends everything that humans claim to know. Yeah, I saw it with my own eyes and even with my own spirit. I've seen *her*. And that means nothing…nothing…nothing can ever be the same for me again. All those stories I pursued years ago…all that seeking…all that hope. That's all been fulfilled, even if my life has been a failure in every other way. Because now I know for sure that there is something hidden behind the veil that's more real than real.

"I could seek answers to other mysteries. But it doesn't really matter if I find those answers or if I don't. One has already been revealed to me as absolutely true. Nothing can take that away from me."

"Absolutely true," Flor said, finally breaking her silence. "I like that."

I'd been leaning forward, intent on my own words. Realizing that, I settled back and took a breath. Then I poured us both another glass of wine. "I may be the world's most successful failure!"

"I wouldn't phrase it that way, Cervantes. That could be taken to mean that nobody has ever failed better than you!"

We laughed.

I raised my glass. "Then perhaps a failure who has been redeemed by knowledge? To the gnosis of the girl who cannot die!"

"Perhaps. But what about Lupe? I haven't asked you in a while. Do you still feel your link with her? Do you know what happened or is happening with her?"

I breathed in deeply, exhaled. "I think…I think I still sometimes dream with her. But it seems so…I guess I would call it distant and remote. That first time, when I had that vision of her life and of her death, I was with her, I was in her soul. Later, just before they buried her, I could see her only from the outside. Her spirit was closed to me. And now…now I get only these little dreams…faint things…like a voice you can barely hear on the phone."

"But there is something?"

"Yeah, something."

And then Flor waited again, patient again…letting me figure it out.

Another swallow of wine for me. And another.

"She's still down there. I think Juan was destroyed, but she's not hurt at all. Yet she's not moving, not moving a muscle."

"Is she trapped, then?"

"I'm not sure, not totally sure. It feels like she doesn't want to move."

Flor didn't seem surprised.

I shrugged. "Maybe she wants to rest. I think maybe that's it. She can't find her killer, and the battle with the army was getting monotonous. And they were ready to wipe out the town if they had to. So even if she could dig her way out, then what? They'd just find other ways to hold all those residents hostage. So why not just accept it? Why not just stay down there? Why not just rest and think and plan? Let them think she's not coming back from that. Let them think they've won."

Flor smiled. "Let them think that they have won."

"I mostly dream it like that, Flor. It's all pieces and bits and scraps. But that's how it all comes together when I think about it. She wants a break."

"How long?"

"I couldn't tell you. Years if she wants…decades. She doesn't need food, water, or air. I doubt she even ages anymore."

There were also times when we talked, when we speculated, about the green woman who had manipulated Juan from behind the curtain that concealed unknown spaces and places. We also wondered about those other beings that could be coming, the ones who were closer to our world than that green one. But what could we really know about them? How could we even know if they were real?

Nothing to do but wait, wait and see if any of them ever showed up.

And sometime later, in the deepest part of the night, in the most secret districts of my dreams, I went down and down into the hole with Guadalupe Castaneda.

Just a spirit, only a phantom, yet down in that blackest black I could still sense that weight of those thousands and thousands of tons of rock and rubble that pressed and crushed down on her and rendered her immobile.

And I could also feel another weight…the weight of her soul's fatigue…the weight of her failure to find her true revenge. The psychopathic son of the Boss had vanished. Nobody had seen him or his brutal van driving henchman since the army had invaded La Ciudad.

If that quest for a true revenge was on hold, then what was left to do? There would have been nothing but the constant struggle with an amorphous enemy that would only think of more and more ways to torment her. An enemy that could never destroy her, but that could destroy everything around her.

Yeah, better just to rest and wait.

Just like I'd told Flor.

Better just to rest and wait.

And wait.

And wait.

To gather her will so that she could reap the harvest another day.

◈

But nevertheless…just a little test.

I felt Lupe's hand move.

◈

A Few Years Later:

The sun had been beating down like murder on the unhappy city.

A battered brown van kicked up the dust on a ruined road. Which was in better shape, the road or the van? Probably the vehicle, since the engine still worked and the wheels were able to negotiate the ridges and valleys of what had once, not so long ago, been a smoother surface. It had been an avenue promised by some politician to some people during one of those times when votes had been needed. Surprisingly, that promise had been kept. Unsurprisingly, the road had not been maintained.

The surrounding area was desert and deserted, with the remnants of a shantytown once full of migrant workers. But it turned out that, before those people had lived there, some local factories had been dumping chemical waste there, burying it, but not deep enough to conceal it for long. And so, the migrants migrated again. It was reported to be so toxic there that hardly anyone passed through anymore, not even to dump anything else. Still, many thought of it with reverence, as a special place, as the place where the girl who is Death had once fought Samurai Sanchez.

So, the person who drove that van had to be a little bit daring… or maybe a little bit stupid to be driving in that zone. Or maybe he just didn't give a shit. Or maybe he had that wish for death that you always hear about.

I'll tell you his secret now. He did have a wish for death. But it was a wish to deliver, not to receive.

That driver was monstrous: a huge mass of muscle, long and wild hair with a beard to match, his face covered with a network of scars, eyes of rage. He could have been a warrior from another place or time, perhaps a Viking berserker, except for the brown skin and obvious Latino origins. If he'd had friends the way other people had friends, they might have said that he looked like a Mexican, only four times bigger.

Hunched up and constricted, he barely fit in that van. His eyes were fixed on nothing more than the end of his journey.

Darkness was coming, a twilight that began to nibble and then bite the sky.

And that was when the driver saw her: a young woman slowly walking along the side of the road. Her jeans were torn and dirty, same for her plaid shirt. Her hair was long, tangled, disheveled. Her body thin, almost anorexic. She ignored the van that slowed down beside her, like she was in a trance, sleepwalking.

A smile of pure corruption took possession of the big man's expression as he slowed the van and shouted.

"Hey, babe, need a ride? It ain't safe to be out here…ain't safe at all!"

The young woman didn't stop, didn't look, didn't acknowledge him in any way. She just kept on walking slowly…slowly.

That smile instantly vanished as anger blossomed across that pattern of scars. He stopped the vehicle, put it in park, left the engine running… and got out.

And the young woman just kept walking slowly…slowly.

With half a growl and half a sigh, he lunged up behind her, grabbed her by the hair, and easily yanked her back toward the van. She instantly went limp, not resisting, as her sudden captor opened the sliding door to the back of his vehicle and dragged her in behind himself.

"Told you," he said with a smirk. "Ain't safe at all." He pulled handcuffs out of his pocket.

Not a word or any fight from her as he locked her hands behind her back. She just looked down at the filthy carpeting that covered the floor, letting her chaotic mane of hair cover her face.

"You're easy," he said with a chuckle. She didn't even struggle against the duct tape he put over her mouth.

"Maybe not even worth it," he commented as he pulled her arms back again so he could lock the cuffs to a chain connected to the wall.

Then he waited for a few minutes, just watching her.

There was no whimpering.

No stifled screaming.

No muffled begging.

Motionless, passive, and resigned.

With a disappointed shrug, he once again mounted the driver's seat, muttering, "I can promise that there'll be some noise when you get to where you're going."

Other than the addition of the young woman held prisoner in the back of the vehicle, there was really nothing more to say about the driver's journey. The neighborhoods got a little nicer. But not too upscale, more of a lower-middle-class kind of setting, a place where they had lawns but they weren't always well cared for, a place where the houses weren't falling apart but maybe they needed paint, a place where that old, beat-up van wouldn't draw much attention.

The driveway that the man chose to pull into belonged to one of the nondescript houses. He touched a button under the dashboard and the garage door rattled open. Maybe not everyone around would have that technology, but it wasn't unusual enough to draw any extra attention. And it was better than having to get out and leave a captive inside, unguarded, for even a few seconds, even if she seemed secured. Chances shouldn't be taken, especially so close to the end of the process.

Once the mechanical door had descended, the man got out and opened up the back of the van. He climbed in, disconnected the prisoner, but left her cuffed. Since she was so passive, so slight of build, he simply tucked her under one of his arms and hopped back out onto the concrete floor.

At that moment, another door opened, leading into the house itself, and another man appeared. Unlike the giant, this man was as nondescript as the house. He might have been around forty, average height and average build. Some gray, some baldness, some extra weight in the wrong places, lighter skin tone than the driver's. A person most people probably wouldn't take note of. Yet in that moment he became more than ordinary, because in that moment, when his eyes found the woman limp under the big man's arm, those eyes sparkled with an intensity of delight and lust and savagery.

"Thank you, mi amigo," he whispered…almost moaned. "Take her down and get her ready for me. Yes, it's been too long. Please get her ready for me."

The giant nodded as he squeezed and ducked his way into the kitchen, where he kicked away a rug and pulled open the trapdoor underneath. There was a ladder, but he just jumped down into the chamber below. A steel door awaited him once he landed. He punched some numbers onto an electronic keypad installed in the wall and the vault opened. For a second or two, he looked down at the young woman who hung at his side, then a look of disgust passed over his marred visage as he crossed the threshold.

The room was small and sparse and nearly empty. A tiled floor, with a drain built in, a hose, a thick chain hanging from the ceiling… and a metal surgical table equipped with scalpels, needles, a whip, some butcher knives, and a meat cleaver. Everything was immaculate and perfectly aligned, waiting to be used.

The big man hooked the girl to the chain by locking the end of it to the cuffs with his free hand. Then he let her drop. The end of the chain was just a little too high, forcing the young woman to choose between hanging painfully and standing awkwardly on her tiptoes. Oddly, she made the choice to just hang there with her legs lifted up, silently swinging slightly forth and back, head down, hair still hiding her face. He was tempted to see how long she could hold herself in that position, but then he shook his head and left the room.

He climbed up the ladder. As soon as he was out of the way, the ordinary man began his descent with a smile and a nod of thanks. The giant got himself a glass of water and sat down in the kitchen, took a swallow, stared into space, and listened. The ordinary man was standing at the threshold of the torture chamber, talking to the young woman.

"You think that if you're passive, that if you ignore me, that what's going to happen won't happen? Well, if that's the case, you're wrong in so many ways…and you won't be able to ignore me for long. I guarantee you!" He stopped talking, seemed to be waiting for a response or acknowledgment. But there wasn't any, so he continued. "I've been waitin' a long time for this…very long…very agonizing. You see, a while back, there were some…troubles. Maybe you were here, maybe you remember. I'd been doing this…these things…to you trash bitches…for quite a while. My papa, he knew…and he'd known it for a long time. But he looked the other way. Back then, this city was crazy as fuck, and nobody cared enough to do anything about me or any of the rest of what was going on…at least nobody who could do anything. But then there came those troubles and my fucking dad knew that I couldn't stop doing this to you whores…that I couldn't control myself. So, he fucking had me locked up in a piece-of-shit psych ward hospital…way down south. He's got the connections and he's got the cash, so it was no problem for him. No court orders. No evaluations. No red tape…not for my daddy! I guess it was for my own good…things did get really weird and really bad, and I could have gotten myself killed if he'd let me stay around here and do the things I like to do to you filthy sluts, who pretend to be such goody-good girls. But, Jesus, it was like slow-motion death to be locked up in that place…being kept away from you…from all the girls like you. Papa made me stay there way too long. The trouble was over way back. And I can tell ya now…I am so, so, so, so, so, so, oh so pent up! I've been doing a lot of catching up, that I can tell you! And you're going to be screaming in ways that I don't think any of the others back in the day ever, ever, ever, ever screamed…'cause I've been waiting ever so, so, so, so long to be back and doing the things that I do!"

And then the armored steel door shut.

The big man finished his water, put the glass in the dishwasher, and decided he would be more comfortable sitting on the floor, dangling his legs in the open trapdoor. He'd waited a long time too, waited for his boss to come back, waited to have a purpose again. He planned to be sitting there for maybe hours, because the ordinary man would probably be taking an extra long time with his indulgences. And he planned to sit in silence all that time, because once that door down there was shut, that chamber of hellish delight was totally soundproof. But that was all right. He liked sitting there. He found it strangely comforting.

Yes, it was good that things were finally back to normal.

So, he just kept sitting there, letting his legs swing idly back and forth. Patient, patient…waiting to be called to help with the cleaning up and then the disposal. That was how it had always been the years before, when he had done the same work in the same place. In fact, it had been the big man himself who had kept the house in order, knowing that sooner or later his master would return. He'd had to hide during those times of trouble too, but he had returned promptly once they'd seemed to be over. His exile had been self-imposed.

Sitting, sitting…expecting to be waiting for quite a long time. But for special events like this one, there had to be a sentry. There had to be a loyal guardian.

Then, suddenly, an intense metallic thud. Something hit the steel door. Something made the whole house shake.

The big man dropped down to the bottom of the ladder, fully alert. But nothing else happened. Maybe his boss was just getting really, really carried away…far away…by his unbridled passions.

It kept being quiet. Minutes passed. The giant began to relax again. He climbed back up top and took the same position as before, legs dangling, gazing into space again, waiting.

Then he heard the steel door open.

How strange.

Perhaps the ordinary man had gotten too…passionate…and had already finished?

Then he heard muffled screams.

Maybe his master had just neglected to seal that door and it had opened on its own?

Then he realized that those stifled sounds of fear didn't belong to a woman.

With animal speed, he leaped down again and bounded to the door. Without hesitation, he grabbed that door and pulled it open all the way so that he could see what was going on inside the chamber.

For a second, he was frozen in place by what was revealed. The ordinary man was hanging upside down from the chain…by one leg. Tape was now over his mouth. He was trying to yell and yell, probably for the giant to come and help him.

The young woman was now the one standing, looking at her captive, with a delighted smile on her face. And her hands were free, no trace of the cuffs.

When the two of them became aware that they were being watched, they both turned to look at the big man almost in unison.

The ordinary man fell silent, desperation in his inverted eyes.

The young woman raised her fists and moved them around. The motion seemed almost like a parody, like a boxer from the 1890s preparing for fisticuffs or a cartoon character putting up his dukes.

With his unbelievable rapidity and strength, the giant charged at her. Before she could even begin to react, one massive hand had her throat in a crushing grip and was driving her into a wall. Her neck should have been broken right then and right there; the back of her skull should have been caved in. She should have died in a burst of brain and blood. Instead, still smiling, she looked her attacker straight in the eye, all her bones still intact.

Baffled, he began slamming her into that wall again and again and again…and again…until fatigue made him stop. Even the big man had his limits. The young woman was still unharmed and still smiling, still staring straight and directly into his eyes. And a strange blackness began to shine in hers.

"It's you. It's you," muttered the giant, all at once filled with recognition and fear.

The tension of aggression began to leave his body. He was going to let her go. But before he could, the young woman grabbed the wrist of that hand that was holding her. She twisted. There was a loud snap. Then the giant did release her, staggering back, holding his injured limb with his good arm. Once she was on the floor, she immediately slammed her hand down and flat onto his left foot with such force that his boot was ruptured in a spurt of blood and bone, while she was bounced back up in the air. He fell to one knee with a moan. She landed off balance and easily got back up. Bracing a foot against the wall, she gave the big man a one-handed shove that caused him to end up flat on his back. Then, almost as an afterthought, she stepped onto his right ankle and ground down, causing another loud crack. His will and strength were so great that he continued to flop around, trying to get up. But with three out of four limbs out of operation, that wasn't possible. Then she put her foot down on his right forearm.

Another snap.

After that, he just lay on the floor. There was really nothing else he could do except be on his back, looking up at the young woman, less than a third his size, who had laid him to waste. He knew that he was a dead man, knew there was nothing he could do. So, he waited for the killing blow. But the young woman didn't move; she just kept watching him. The shock of his injuries became too much.

He passed out.

Dimly surprised to be alive, the big man woke up again. It was all a haze of pink and crimson pulsing and throbbing dull pain. He was lying where she had left him. She was still standing nearby, but he was no longer the object of her attention. Instead, the young woman was carefully and intently examining all the surgical instruments that the giant himself had prepared and laid out on the little table. Finally, she selected a scalpel and turned toward the ordinary man, who was still hanging by one leg, his eyes as wide as moons.

Slowly, almost gently, she used the tool to cut off his shirt and pants, pulling them away, leaving him suspended in his shoes, socks, and underwear. Then she took him by the hand. He tried to pull away, but her strength was unfathomable.

She forced his little finger to extend, and then with the scalpel she began to peel it, to skin it. The big man could do nothing but watch as his master screamed, jerked, and spasmed. Then the giant lost consciousness again.

When he came back to himself the second time, his master was no longer there. The only thing hanging down from the chain was a ragged mess, the remnants of a human body, something that had suffered a severe, merciless, and drawn-out death. There were little bits of raw meat and skin all over the place.

Then he became aware that the girl was still there, standing over him and looking down at him again. Things were getting fuzzy…getting blurry. He tried to stay lucid, tried to face his fate. He even wanted to say something defiant…but he couldn't get his mouth to work.

The young woman laughed silently and saluted him. Then she strode to the door, went out, and shut it behind her. There was a loud, horrible sound of metal being forced to do something against its will.

The giant realized that she had destroyed the lock, the mechanism that allowed that steel door to be opened. The young woman had left him sealed inside the torture chamber.

Tears welled up in his eyes. His death would be slow. It would take its time.